Dream

A Call to the kNight

LRPILLIPSBOOKS.COM
prosper@pris.ca

By: LR Phillips

Suite 300 - 990 Fort St
Victoria, BC, Canada, V8V 3K2
www.friesenpress.com

Copyright © 2015 by LR Phillips
First Edition — 2015
Written - 2010

Cover illustration by Tomas Krejcar.

All rights reserved.

No part of this publication may be reproduced in any form, or by any means, electronic or mechanical, including photocopying, recording, or any information browsing, storage, or retrieval system, without permission in writing from the publisher.

ISBN
978-1-4602-6278-8 (Hardcover)
978-1-4602-6279-5 (Paperback)
978-1-4602-6280-1 (eBook)

1. Fiction, Fantasy, Historical

Distributed to the trade by The Ingram Book Company

*I would like to dedicate this book to my loving husband,
David, who believes in me.*

*Also, to Chrisanne, the truest of all friends.
Without her encouragement this book would not have been published.*

And finally to Michael, who dreamed of a Dragon in a fortress.

he ancients speak
of another time, another place,
where the unseen met the seen.
Where Dragon's rage and knight's battle-cry,
a call for Deliverer to come.
The Great Creator looked through the mist,
to the land of His heart's desire.
No knight braver than a Prince
to vanquish the ugly beast
strip it of its power.
So the Creator sent His own Son
in battle wage the war.
Woe I say, the people believed the foe,
and not the Deliverer.
So they turned to stone for help
a fortress with high walls built
to keep the beast out.
The Dragon's lies that dripped a slime
became the mortar for the stone.
Never once did they think
that they had built
the very place for it to dwell.
For fear of it who has no power
and lack of trust in Him who saved,
Will build a fortress every time
and make a dwelling for the beast.

The Ancients say… "He led captivity captive and gave gifts unto men."

Proem

Treasa ~ strong
Shylah ~ loyal and strong
Cathaoir ~ warrior

In the time of the ancients...

The battle raged on for three days in a land that was unseen to the bewildered and frightened pilgrims. Finally, the Dragon lay at the Prince's feet, its head wounded. The Prince raised His sword high, throwing His head back as He laughed. In the dark, desolate place, a bolt of lightning from high alighted His face. The brilliance of the impact lit the entire land and in the light could be seen many people, lost and wandering in the gloom. As they looked upon the face of the Prince and saw the fallen Dragon, their shout could be heard to the far reaches of the land. For some, it was the shout of triumph ~ for others, it was the shout of fear. The Dragon writhed in pain, holding its head, trying to stop the flow of life that was leaving it powerless. The Prince slowly began to ascend into the lightning bolt. Then those who rejoiced in the Prince's victory rose one by one with Him, disappearing from the sight of the wounded Dragon and those who had cowered in fear.

~

Years later...

As far as the eye could see, the spray from the artesian well flew high into the air like a million diamonds glittering in the sun. The well had hardly flowed for years, but in the twinkling of an eye it had begun to rumble and gush forth its bountiful supply of cool, clear water. The water shot up to the sky, as if the earth itself was squeezing with all its might to issue forth the last drop. The spectacle was magnificent. Thousands of raindrops of water showered down upon the dry earth, forming a raging river where once a small trickling stream had meandered down the mountainside.

Appearing like a mist in the shower of water was the form of a huge, princely warrior. His face was intent upon the valley below and a lone tear lay upon His cheek. Reaching up His hand, He wiped the tear and, catching some of the gushing water with it, He flung it over the valley below. A smile broke forth on His regal face as His laughter filled the air and joined the sound of the gushing water. Tipping His head back, His voice boomed and echoed off the ragged crags of the mountain above. He cried, "I have heard and I have come!"

~

At this time...

Down in the valley, in an old neglected fortress, people were milling about, doing their daily duties. In the middle of the fortress was a large pool, and the green illumined water began to churn and bubble. Oblivious to the churning water, the people just continued to work at trying to repair the worn-out building. In the depths of the pool, a large unseen Dragon was grabbing its head, reeling in pain from an ancient blow. The Dragon was a hideous creature to be sure, with a large, flat head like a cobra and wide-set yellow eyes that gleamed with a dim flickering light. The long neck twisted down to a large body with gigantic wings that it used like fins to swim in the depths of the pool. Its short front legs had feet with reptilian-like claws that were scratching at what looked to be a scar that spanned the Dragon's forehead and ran down the side of its face through the left eye. The long, muscular back legs and massive tail were swirling the water at an ever-increasing rate.

Finding no relief in the water, the Dragon pulled itself from the pool, snarling at the people. Grabbing its head, as the remembered pain shot like a hot dagger through its skull. The people seemed to sense its presence, but had learned to carry on, for they could not see the Dragon. Suddenly, the beast stopped thrashing and looked through the walls of the fortress to the countryside. As its vision pierced the stone walls, and saw the mist falling over the country-side like a spring rain. The unseen Lord was on the move!

Lunging away from the pool, the Dragon knocked down a young man who, to all the others, seemed to have fallen for no reason. Then, sweeping its hulking frame away from the fortress, the Dragon flew out across the land. Cursed be those mediators! The Dragon knew they had called for the unseen Lord of the land.

~

Close to the mountains...

Treasa and Shylah were down on their knees again, petitioning the unseen Lord. Shylah's long blonde hair was swept up from her neck in a neat bun, her lovely light complexion flushed with renewed hope and anticipation. Her long lashes lay delicately on her fair face as she breathed out her petitions to her precious unseen Lord.

They did not want to give up. The days had dragged into months, and the oppression persisted with no relief. Sometimes others would join them for a time, but then they would leave, tired of trying to mediate between the unseen Lord and the slumbering people who lived in the land. Rising to her feet, Treasa felt a sudden refreshing breeze caress her face as she walked by the open window. Looking out, she tucked a stray strand of her auburn hair back into her braid and smiled. A fine rain was falling on the land below their small farm.

Their farm was nestled at the foot of the mountains, close to the Source of the stream that had once been a mighty river. That, too, they had been petitioning the unseen Lord about ~ to return the water to its former glory. Shylah rose slowly, gave Treasa a hug, and quietly left to go home to the neighbouring farm. Treasa walked over to the cupboard and began to make supper preparations for her husband Cathaoir ~ who would be home soon from the fields. The drought had been long and hard, but the unseen Lord had prompted Cathaoir to plant the crops. A smile illuminated Treasa's aging, pleasant face as she looked out at the fine rain that was falling on the land.

You are so precious to me, my Lord. So very good to all of us.

- 3 -

As she peeled the potatoes she remembered the stories she had heard of former generations of mediators and their cries for the river to return. However, Shylah and Treasa's petitions went beyond matters of water and crops. They called for the unseen Lord to talk to His people again. She knew in her heart that He had always talked to those who desired His company. She had also heard Him speak to her frequently. She could not deny that she wanted more ~ she wanted all those who followed His teaching to hear Him as well. She remembered back to the days in her youth when she had wanted to live in the fortress and just mediate all the time, but she was never allowed because of the farm. Then, suddenly, it had happened and her family even stopped visiting the fortress. Treasa bowed her head in silent thanksgiving; how glad she was that they had left. As the peelings fell into her pan, she remembered how the unseen Lord had said He would raise up a generation that would make it their quest to know Him.

At one time, there had been a people of the unseen Lord who had known Him intimately. The ancients told of this time, which had been before the construction of the fortresses. They told of when the pilgrims of the unseen Lord had lived among the people of the land and walked faithfully with Him, and of how the mediators of that time could walk among their neighbours with an anticipation of bringing someone who did not know the unseen Lord to the peace of knowing Him. The people lived in harmony and joy with one another, sharing and visiting, mediating together. Then, the fortresses came...

Treasa straightened and stretched her shoulders, putting the potatoes into the large pot that was on the fire. As she lifted the lid, the aroma of the boiling soup bones filled the small cottage. Going to the cupboard, she began to peel and dice the onions.

Soup for my Cathaoir tonight.

She shook off the feelings of regret that filled her heart as she remembered what the ancients had said about the construction of the fortresses. A long time ago, the pilgrims had begun to scatter, and some of them were saying they had heard from the unseen Lord when they had not. The Dragon was no longer afraid of them and began to manipulate the people, bringing many of them into its fold. No one seemed to care if the people of the land even knew of the unseen Lord, and mediating had become almost unheard of. To mediate was just to have a loving heart and be willing to talk to the unseen Lord on behalf of those who could not, or did not. Unfortunately, the people were more concerned about their own lives to care for those around them. Treasa smiled sadly and then thought, *Or those who would not mediate for themselves even.* The elder pilgrims during that time had thought that if they put someone in charge of the pilgrims. To build a fortress to contain them, then they would be able to keep out the lies of the Dragon, and its attacks.

A tear trickled down Treasa's face, for although she could understand their human reasoning, no one had consulted the unseen Lord about the scheme. The fortress builders, with one accord, threw their backs into the work, ignoring the words of warning from the few mediators that were left. The construction of the fortress took so much time and cost them all so much that at times it could hardly have seemed worth it. However, they had one purpose then, and it drew them together. So they built, not out of faith, but out of fear, and they trained guards to protect them from the beast and to seek the unseen Lord on their behalf. Only after the high walls rose around them did they realize that they had built far away from the Unchanging River ~ the very water that the unseen Lord had given them for strength. So they constructed aqueducts to bring the water to them.

The ones who did not join the fortress builders travelled to the Source of the river, high in the mountains, and made a settlement there. These Source pilgrims were an isolated people, but they traded with the people of the land, and Treasa liked any of them she met. It was just the fortress dwellers who were suspicious of them and would warn people to stay away from the Source people.

Everything had seemed so beautiful and full to these fortress dwellers, with their lovely fortress and secure homes within its walls. Some of the people of the land would go to visit them, and some even stayed. However, as the years went by, it seemed that many fortress dwellers forgot that their purpose was to be the unseen Lord's pilgrims and servants. So gradually it was barely noticed, they had exchanged this great honour to become the servants of the guards and the fortress. The mediators, who had been uneasy about the fortress from the start, were the only ones who seemed to recognize what was happening.

Over the generations, many mediators had risen up to ask bold questions regarding the purpose of the fortresses. Nevertheless, most were silenced or else they would leave and build their own fortresses because that was all they knew. Some, however, would go and join the Source pilgrims.

She cringed as she remembered her first encounter with the Dragon within the very fortress walls that were supposed to keep it out. She had not believed it to be true, though her heart at the time told her otherwise.

Putting the onions into the pot, she stirred the broth and scooped out the soup bones for her faithful old dog. Then, picking up her knitting, she sat down by the table and spoke to the unseen Lord. "I am so thankful that it happened, Lord. Although, it was a shock to me ~ and to the others, as well, who were mediating during that time."

"I know, my precious daughter. Are you not glad that it did?" He spoke gently to her as He sat down beside her and watched her knit.

"Yes, I am...But sometimes it is hard, when they who are still in the fortress think evil of me. Forgive me, Lord, for I know that it happens to You all the time. But I do need Your strength at those times." Treasa dropped her eyes as she confessed her weakness. Laying her knitting upon her lap, she sat there in silence as she felt His presence surround her and comfort her heart. That was all she needed ~ His presence ~ and she could go on. The unseen Lord held her for a long time and then left her. She sat there in silence and peace, waiting for her husband to return from the field.

As she knit, she remembered the story of one young man, whom the unseen Lord had used to change her heart and the hearts of many. He had been called to be a Knight and battle the Dragon from a young age. She knew that the Dragon had tried everything to win him to its dark side...

The Ancients say... "He is a Father of the fatherless, and a judge of the widows..."

Chapter 1

Caedmon ~ wise warrior
Wynne ~ one who is light complexioned
Vaughan ~ little, small one
Carden ~ to clean the wool

As the unseen Lord entered the room, He only had eyes for the young couple. His heart swelled with joy at their happiness. A beautiful young woman was lying on the cot with her arms around a small babe, and, beaming down at them, was her young husband. A deep sadness settled over the unseen Lord's countenance. He knew the decisions they were going to make, and how they would change His heart's first plan for them. He gently laid his hand on the sleeping babe, and His smile warmed the room with peace. The parents looked at one another and exchanged looks of contentment.

They struggled with weakness of character, selfishness ruled their hearts, and the teachings of the fortress dwellers confirmed their preferred lifestyle. They wanted their child to serve the unseen Lord in spite of their own lukewarm relationship with Him. Looking adoringly at her husband, the young mother said, "Let us call him Caedmon, after the great messenger who came to announce the coming of the unseen Lord."

The Lord, turning to leave, looked back at the happy scene. He knew that they had felt Him, but they had not recognized Him. They were caught up in the happiness of the moment. He would meet with them again in the future, that was for certain.

∼

Wynne, stroking the soft down on her baby's head, watched him suckle at her breast, a dreamy look on her face. Her life was full. All she had ever wanted was this ~ a loving husband and a child to call her own. She tenderly wrapped her baby in his blanket, for he had fallen asleep on her breast. Laying him in the cradle that his father had made, she quickly went about the supper preparations. This morning she had put on a stew with the supply of goods her husband had brought home the day before. She decided to make some pan bread to go with it, and just as she was up to her elbows in flour kneading the dough, she heard the baby fussing. Trying to ignore the wee babe, she finished putting the dough to rise in the warmth of the hearth and stirred the stew that was simmering in a large copper pot on the back of the fire. The baby began to scream. Exasperated, Wynne went over to rock the cradle. She tried humming to the baby, but to no avail. He would not settle.

"What is the matter, Caedmon? Oh, let me see. You fell asleep before you were finished eating, I'm thinking. How will you grow big and strong if you don't stay awake to eat?"

Lifting the squirming baby out of the cradle, she laid down on the bed and snuggled him close to let him suckle again. However, when he settled in to feed, she smelled the stew burning on the fire. Laying the baby back down, she quickly went to the pot and stirred the stew, moving it further back on the fire, where it wasn't so hot. Caedmon began to scream, flaying his tiny fists in the air. Wynne quickly put the pan of bread onto the coals and returned to feed the baby. His tiny form settled down and began to drink hungrily at her breast.

Tears of frustration flowed down Wynne's face. How she wished her mother lived closer! Her mother-in-law lived close by, but she was critical of Wynne and was very addicted to ale. Wynne had sometimes asked her to come over, but found the woman had only one answer for every problem.

"Just a little sip of ale would help you handle the difficult situations."

Wynne remembered what the ale had done to her stepfather, and she had no desire to try it. It had destroyed so much of her childhood and her mother's life. She had married young to get away from that. Her father saw no wrong in his actions, as he was a fortress dweller, a man who said he served the unseen Lord of the land. She could not understand how he could say that in one breath and act so unloving to his own family in the next.

Caedmon again fell asleep on her breast, but this time she tickled his chin until he began to suckle again.

"You little sleepy head, Mama needs to get supper on for Papa. Let's finish eating, please."

Vaughan arrived home from his long day at the mill and found his wife fast asleep with their tiny Caedmon in her arms. He could smell the stew on the stove and the pan bread burning. His frustration surfaced as he quickly went and took the bread off the coals, slamming it onto the hearth. Stirring the stew, he yelled in exasperation, "Wynne! Wake up!"

Wynne jerked awake, tears filling her voice, "Oh Vaughan, I am sorry. Caedmon has been very fussy these last few days, and I have had so little sleep. Here take him ~ I need to get the bread off the coals."

Angrily, Vaughan responded, "I already took the *burnt* bread off the coals! Wynne, all I have asked is that you have a meal ready for me when I get home. Is that too much for you? You have all day to look after my son. Do you need my mother to come?"

"No, I need my mother to come," Wynne retorted angrily. She had expected to have everything perfect tonight. *Why did I have to fall asleep?*

~

Wynne worked hard to please her husband, because his pleasure made her life more endurable. If she ever would have sat down and thought about her reason for serving him, she might have been surprised, for she was pleasing him only because it gave her pleasure ~ not because it made her husband's life better. The Dragon had been careful to come and visit her occasionally, letting her know that she had it hard and that her husband was the one in the wrong.

Caedmon was developing quickly. He was a lively baby who kept his mother on her toes. Vaughan would come home from work, tired, and take Caedmon. They would lie by the fireplace on the mat, Vaughan falling asleep while the baby played with his beard or the buttons on his shirt. Wynne would get supper on the table and then look at her family with a far away look, wondering where the joy had gone. Vaughan only touched her now when he wanted to fulfill his own desires. He never talked to her. Wynne knew that he was tired, but her lonely heart did not find comfort in any of these excuses.

Wynne's loneliness at last had driven her to turn to Vaughan's mother for friendship. She visited often now, and had talked Wynne into taking a little sip of the ale for her emotional trouble. Wynne found it really worked, and now she looked forward to spending time with her mother-in-law. Her frequent visits made Wynne even more dissatisfied with Vaughan, though. She could not drink the ale around him, and she found that the more she consumed ale to take off the pressure of her life, the more she did not like life without it. She soon bought her own bottle of ale and kept it hidden under the cupboard by the fire. Wynne was careful to take only a little sip, and only when things had become unbearable. As she looked around their dingy home with its bare furnishings and her worn-out clothes, her heart would yearn for the wealth that she and Vaughan had dreamed about. How could she imagine the future that Vaughan was saving for, when she was locked in this dull present all day and night? Her heart became a little harder with each passing day.

One day, smelling the ale on her breath, Vaughan broke their silence to ask, "Do you think Mother's visits are good for you?"

"Now, Vaughan, you had wanted her to come, and now she is a dear friend to me," Wynne said without any emotion. "Besides, it is what you had suggested in the beginning. She sometimes helps me with Caedmon, but mostly she just gives me someone to talk to."

Vaughan felt his conscious pricked knowing that he should talk with her more, but true to his nature, he looked to the future ~ blinding him to the present. The Dragon had not been idle regarding Vaughan, either. He had carefully planted lofty dreams of the future into Vaughan's head. He knew that these thoughts would make Vaughan incapable of being a good husband and father for the now.

Caedmon, who was a very energetic toddler, was not content to lie on his father's chest while Vaughan slept after work. He would lay there until the snoring started and, taking that as a cue to leave, would crawl over to his mother and pull himself up on her leg. He was almost walking, and constantly talking in his baby language, laughing and cooing.

Wynne looked down protectively at her son. She was planning to leave Vaughan. She was going home to her mother. She knew that, when Vaughan saw how terrible his life was without her, he would come to her, to apologize to her. He would swoop her off her feet again. His love would be rekindled, knowing that he could not survive without her.

She remembered how they had once loved one another. They had met in the large fortress, called Evergreen, where her parents occasionally lived. Vaughan had seduced her with his charm and attention, and even though they had not waited to sleep together until marriage she had not cared, for she had gotten what she wanted. Like a prince, Vaughan had come to rescue her, taking her to his homeland and offering her lofty dreams of their future life together. It was shortly after they were settled in his village that the reality of living hit them both. Wynne delivered Caedmon just a few months later and Vaughan had to work to provide for them. He was hired at a wood mill and he took great pride in his work. He soon felt so fulfilled by his job that he forgot that his family was waiting for him at home, needing him.

Wynne, feeling bitterness raising its ugly head inside of her, walked over to the cupboard and took a small sip of the ale. She would need courage to do what she had to do, Vaughan needed to learn a lesson. She knew how to make him regret his neglect of his family. She would have been shocked to see the ugly head of the Dragon looking in through the window, its lip dripping with drool. She was becoming more the beast's plaything everyday, and she did not even know it. Taking another sip, she put the bottle back under the cupboard. She did not want Vaughan to smell it on her breath again.

Vaughan awoke, stretching his small frame and sighing; he rose sleepily from the bed. Approaching Wynne, he gave her a light kiss on the cheek. He knew he should be giving her more attention, but there were not enough hours in the day. Besides, when he had the money saved to own their own place, he would have plenty of time for both Wynne and Caedmon. She just needed to practise some patience. Wynne clung to him, hoping that he wanted to hold her tight like he had before, but he gently pushed her back and sat down at the table.

She looked down on the top of his head, feeling vile hatred rising inside her. *Oh, how I hate you.* She wanted to scream or do something to let loose the bitterness that was building in her heart. Straightening her shoulders she walked stiffly over to the fire and drew out the pot she had simmering. She stacked the fried meat on his plate, then covered it in steamed onions. Slicing thick slabs of the fresh bread, she set it on his plate. She put the plate down in front of Vaughan and, without a word, walked away from the table.

"You're not eating, Wynne?" Vaughan asked indifferently, as he shovelled the hearty meal into his mouth.

"No, I ate while you were sleeping," she lied as she nervously tucked a stray strand of hair behind her ear. She was too excited about her plan of leaving to even think about eating. Wynne put Caedmon on a chair and began to feed him some bread soaked in milk. She had their few belongings sorted and put in a crate under their cot. Vaughan would not consider this cache to be out of the ordinary, for Wynne was always sorting through things, finding it hard to arrange their meagre house the way she wanted it.

The unseen Lord stood in their midst and looked from one to the other. His look stern but compassionate.

"Carden, did the Dragon leave?"

"Yes, my Lord, the minute he saw me standing sentinel. This couple has refused to be shepherded. Is there not anything that can be done to dissuade her from her plan?" The large man with shepherd's garb asked.

- 12 -

"I am afraid not. I have tried to talk to each one of them, but they do not hear My voice any longer. I am afraid that Vaughan is so blind to the present by his pursuit of the future, and Wynne is so blind to the future for her pursuit of the present, that they can only see the fault of the other and not their own. I do have a plan to restore them to Me however, they will still have to chose then the path they want."

Walking behind the little boy, He gently laid His hand upon the child's head and then disappeared from sight. When the Dragon saw the light dim within the flat it returned to watch in through the window, smiling sardonically to itself.

The next day when Vaughan was gone to the mill, Wynne packed her small boy and the crate of belongings out the door. She took one last look at the flat where she had thought her dreams would come true, and a tear coursed down her cheek. Nevertheless, instead of remorse, Wynne felt anger build inside. *This is not my fault*, she told herself. Stiffening her spine she went down the stairs and did not look back again.

The Dragon spread its wings and flew silently off toward the fortress where Wynne's mother and stepfather lived. Fatherlessness ~ that was its goal and it had just accomplished it again. This longing for a true father would keep Caedmon and Wynne prisoners forever. They would never recognize the loving fatherhood of the unseen Lord now.

It had been two months since Wynne had left with Caedmon. At first, Vaughan thought he would die from the grief. Coming home and no supper made, no little squeal of delight from his son, Vaughan would just sit and stare. He then reverted to raging over Wynne's selfishness ~ he would show her how wrong she had been for being impatient. When he had saved enough for a home and went to get her, she would come back full of regret for leaving him. However as the days went by Vaughan began to notice the young daughter of his landlord, and she noticed him. She was a happy, loving girl, and she did not mind that he had been married before...

~

Edan ~ flame, fiery

The little boy, with jaw set and feet planted apart, raised his stick, making ready to decapitate the foe. He could see his imaginary enemy towering above him. The large, slithering dragon had fire coming out of its nostrils and large green scales covering it's huge frame. The boy, raising his sword high into the air, ran ahead with the cry of a warrior, burying his stick deep into the belly of the beast. Jumping back, out of the way of the falling enemy, he wiped his brow. He had got out of the road just in time, or else he would have been squashed.

"Who you fighting now, Caedmon?" Caedmon's friend Edan asked as he walked up to the small boy playing on the street.

In a high-pitched tone filled with authority, Caedmon proclaimed his victory. "It is a terrible dragon that breathes fire out of it's nostrils. But I killed him. There the beast lies."

Caedmon pointed with his stick to a pile of litter in the village street.

"Oh, it is a ghastly creature, that is for sure. Can I cut off its tail and keep it for a trophy of your great victory?"

Caedmon handed his trusty sword to his best friend. He did not part with this stick lightly as it had won him many battles of late. Edan took the stick and began to saw through the imaginary tail, but Caedmon stopped him.

"Young man, are you blind? That is its toe! Over there lies the foe's tail."

Shrugging sheepishly, Edan went over to the imaginary tail and brought down the stick with a strong whack. The sound of splintering wood sent a chill down Edan's spine. He looked with shock at the one piece of wood he was still holding, while the other end lay at his feet.

"I am so sorry, Caed! I am afraid the tail of the beast cut much easier than I thought it would!"

Caedmon, with red face, strode over and yanked the broken sword from Edan's hand. He wanted to strike his friend, but he knew that Edan was stronger and that might not be wise. He picked up the other end of his sword off the ground. Cradling his beloved sword like a baby he walked out to the countryside.

"Where are you going, Caedmon? Are you going to get another sword? Can I help, pleeease?" chimed Edan, giggling as he caught up to him.

Caedmon turned sombre eyes to his friend. How could he make him understand this was no laughing matter? Without replying, Caedmon took the road out of the village. Upon coming to the countryside, he turned off the main road and onto a well-worn path that led to the great fortress. The path, packed hard by all who came that way, was lined with huge old trees. Caedmon suddenly turned off the path and headed into the trees to a place where the soil was soft. Using one piece of the stick, he dug a small trench and laid his broken sword into it. With his hands he gently covered the sword with the loose soil and lovingly patted the mound. How he would miss this trusty sword. It had been given to him by his imaginary King. The King had knighted him "Sir Caedmon, Keeper of the King's Village."

Looking up at Edan, he smiled. *How can I expect this light-hearted friend of mine to understand?* Edan had loving parents, and a brother and a sister whom he could play with. Caedmon was eight years old now, and his greatest desire was to have a father and maybe two or three brothers and sisters.

"Come on, Edan. Let's go get two new swords. There are some good sticks in the field beside the sheep farm over across the aqueduct. Last one there is a girl!" Caedmon shouted over his shoulder as he took off at a fast run.

Not only did they find new swords, but they let their imaginations run wild. They met three more dragons that had to be killed to save the village. On the way back, they captured an imaginary strange-looking creature and tied it to a large tree, vowing to return the next day to see if it was still alive. The sun began to slip behind the mountains that surrounded their valley, and the sky was becoming red and orange, like a huge fire behind the towering sentinels. The boys had played hard all afternoon, and knew it was late and time to go home.

As they walked along kicking the stones off the path in front of them, Edan asked Caedmon, "Do you believe in the Dragon they talk about? You know, the one that is mentioned at the fortresses and by the people who live in them."

Caedmon stopped and looked at his friend, the hair standing up on his neck. "No! Well, I mean, I hope there is not a real Dragon. It would be awful to think of one sneaking around watching us. Grandma and Grandpa told me that I needed to call out to the unseen Lord so that the Dragon wouldn't get me. Mom told me not to be scared, because I was a good boy, and that no old Dragon was going to get at me. She wouldn't let it."

"Well, you know," Edan said with an eerie tone entering his voice, "I have heard stories about it ~ that it has got people and eaten them right up. I heard my parents talking about someone they knew who had been led out of the fortress by the Dragon and was never seen again."

"Oh, stop it Edan! That stuff gives me the creeps," Caedmon said as he picked up speed to get back to the village while it was still daylight.

Keeping a few steps ahead of them, the unseen Dragon listened with growing interest to the boys. How it loved to hear them talking so fearfully. Drool dripped and flowed across the path where they were walking, causing the boys to become frightened that someone was with them on the path. Both boys ran all the way to the village gate.

"Caed, do you want to come to my place tonight? Mom is making some mutton stew. I could smell it this morning simmering away in the big pot on the fire," Edan said, panting for air and not wanting the day to end.

Caedmon looked longingly at his friend, but he knew it was out of the question. His second father had just left them. He couldn't even remember his first father, but he wished he could. All his mother had told him was that his real father's name was Vaughan

- 16 -

and that he did not want them. *Why can't I have a father of my own, one who would love me and care for me?* Slowly, he shook his head. His mother would be wanting him home. He let Edan know that he would ask for another day, perhaps. Caedmon made his way home slowly, bracing himself for whatever he would find when he arrived there. Climbing the back steps slowly, he opened the door and looked around.

"Mom, where are you?" Caedmon could smell supper cooking, but his mother was nowhere to be found. He peeked in the pot and smelled the sweet aroma of cabbage stew. They had eaten plenty of cabbage stew lately. He knew enough not to complain as it was all they could afford. His second father had been a drunkard and had encouraged his mother to drink as well. Caedmon thought that now that his stepfather was gone, maybe things would improve. His mother had gotten employment at the inn as a cook. That news made Caedmon smile. She was to start in two days. Only two more days of cabbage stew.

They lived in an upstairs flat in a rundown rooming house. It was modestly furnished and they had to haul their water from the cistern in the back lane. Caedmon, tummy rumbling, looked out the window onto the street. Where was his mother? He rubbed his hand against the window pane to clear the smoke, from the lamps, that had settled on the glass.

In the alley below, he was surprised to see his mother talking to his stepfather. Her hands were moving in an agitated manner. Wynne kept shaking her fist at his face, but he would brush it away, laughingly trying to pull her to him. She shoved him back and Caedmon could tell she was angry. She kept putting her hand out like she wanted something and he would push it away. He grabbed her again and kissed her on the mouth. She pushed him back, spitting in his face. His stepfather raised his hand, and Caedmon thought he was going to strike her, but instead he laughed, turned, and left. Wynne whirled and charged towards their flat.

Caedmon went to the corner of the room where his little cot was. He settled onto the bed and pulled the small threadbare coverlet up to his face. He wished that he was a real knight who could save his mother. He never really loved that man; he had so wanted him to treat him like a father should and love him, but the man only tried to give him some ale. The little boy on the cot did not understand why. All he knew was that he hurt right down in the pit of his stomach, and that he was scared.

Wynne came into the room and saw him cowering on the cot. Anguish filled her heart. Walking over, she sat down and pulled him onto her knee. She held him close for a long time, crying with him, trying to soothe him. Wynne wanted to tell him that she was sorry, but she found the words stuck in her throat. She was trapped into blaming others for what was happening to her family.

"I spoke to your father. He has no money to help us," Wynne said, taking a deep breath before going on. "I know this must be hard for you, but we don't need him anyway. Men ~ they are all alike you know. Anyway, when I start work, I will make sure that you have some new things. Would you like that?"

"Oh yes, Mama, I would like that, but...." He hesitated for a moment, trying to put his thoughts into words, "Was my real father like that too? Did he make you work and drink ale?" Seeing the pained look that his question brought to her face, Caedmon reached up and tried to wipe the tears from her face with his dirty hand. Wynne looked with horror at the grubby little fingers that were wiping her face, but more than that, she did not know how to answer him. Instead, she scolded him in good nature to change the subject.

"Young man, you get over to the basin and wash those hands, and I will dish up supper. Guess what we are having? You're right! Cabbage stew, again ~ but not for long. You just wait and see."

Wynne did not like the need for a drink that kept coming to her. She had never had this feeling before, but it was getting stronger every day that she went without. That was why she had wanted the money, to buy a little ale, but her good-for-nothing husband had already drunk his pay away. She could not understand why she had married him, but he had seemed different in the beginning, she reasoned. He had only drunk a small amount of ale, just like her. When did it all change? Her head hurt. She did not want to think about

- 18 -

it. She needed a drink. She did not like the fact that Caedmon had brought up Vaughn again. She thought she had convinced him that it was his father's fault for them leaving. The Dragon drummed its claw like fingers against her temple, allowing drool to drip down and fog her mind with lies and denial.

Wynne did start her job at the inn, and when she met another man who promised her the world, he moved in with them. He was just like her first two husbands as he did not try to understand her or care for them either. He, too, failed to take an interest in the little boy who needed a father so badly. The ale drinking started again, and things went downhill quickly. Time went by and he, too, left them. This negative cycle was spinning out of control. Wynne would find someone and live with that man or even marry him, and Caedmon would be excited to have another chance at a father, only to find out that a son was not part of the arrangement. His mother was losing sight of the one thing that was really important to her ~ her son. She continued to go from man to man, and none of them was of the kind who could change her life to the better. This whole time, the unseen Lord would come to Caedmon and try to comfort him, but the growing boy was oblivious to His presence. The unseen Lord would in turn go to Wynne, and try to inspire a change in her lifestyle, but she would block out His counsel. Her heart had grown hard and unresponsive to sound reason.

Caedmon tried his best to be a good son, but he so wished that his mother would change. He missed his kind, loving mother, even though this version of her provided material things for him. Their life became one of moving from place to place. Sometimes his grandma would come and live with them. Caedmon loved that. She would spend time and talk to him, encouraging him to not lose hope. She tried to share about the unseen Lord with her grandson, but it made him uncomfortable and he would change the subject. Unbeknownst to him, the Dragon was ever-present, making him question the truth. Caedmon formed some new friendships, but some of the street urchins he played with were not the best company. They taught him how to steal and do other mischief. His mother

- 19 -

was too involved in her own life to even take the time to know what he was up to.

Caedmon stared out the window at his latest father's sudden departure. The fight had lasted for four days and now the man packed his things and was leaving. Disgust raised its ugly head again in his heart and mind. Why did she always make him call them father? She did not really care for him anymore than the man staggering down the street. He had lost count of the men that had came through their life. *Will it never end?*

~

"Hey, Caedmon, wait up," yelled Edan. "Where are you going in such a hurry?"

"I don't want to talk right now, Edan ~ Please leave me alone!" Caedmon cried out.

Edan stopped and watched his friend run down the littered street. The high walls of the dingy buildings blocked out the evening sunlight. Edan slowly turned and started to walk home. He had not heard from Caedmon in a long time, and he missed his friend. When they had turned twelve years of age, he had noticed that Caedmon preferred the new friends he had made. It had hurt, but he knew that it was because of Caedmon's mother. Edan was thankful that he had both his parents. Even though they did fight terribly, at least there was no drinking of the ale in his home.

I decided long ago that if Caedmon wants to be my friend, he will have to come to me! These thoughts did not comfort his heart.

"Why should I wait for him?" Edan spoke out loud as he watched his upset friend run down the street. "I don't care if he doesn't want to talk to me, I am going to follow him anyway. I am his friend whether he likes it or not."

Caedmon knew in his heart that he had been too harsh with Edan, but he just wanted to be alone. His mother and her latest boyfriend were fighting again, and he hated it. He did not like that his heart was turning cold towards his mother, and yet he could not live with her constant upswings and down crashes. The pain was

- 20 -

unbearable. His rebellion towards his mother was now very evident to both her and his grandma, though he did not care.

Even though it was hard, he was becoming used to change. Depending on who his mother was with, they would live in horrible places or very grand places. His mother had wanted him to look for work so they could have more income, but everything within him wanted to refuse, knowing his earnings would be wasted on ale.

He darted down one of the back lanes to meet his friends at their secret place just outside the village. It was in the shadow of the large fortress, Evergreen, where his grandparents lived. No one would ever expect them to go so close to the fortress. Caedmon came to the edge of the village and headed out to the countryside, leaving the dinginess of the cramped buildings for the lovely evening light. The sky was streaked with golden rays of light, like hands reaching out to gently stroke his anxiety away. He slowed his pace and let the peace of the countryside soothe his angry heart.

The gentle breeze had the lovely sweet scent of fresh-cut hay. He was used to the smell of lamp smoke and the filth of the village. Caedmon breathed the refreshing fragrance deep into his lungs.

Hearing his name being called like a whisper on the wind, he hesitated.

Coming to an abrupt stop, he looked nervously around. All that he saw were the rolling hills with huge towering evergreen trees casting their shadows over the road. Behind him the village was bustling with activity, but no one was in sight on this road. Walking slowly out onto the road, he heard it again.

"Caedmon... Caedmon ~ I am calling you. Do you hear Me?" the soft voice spoke again.

Caedmon stopped, he was sure that he was being followed by someone with ill purposes. Looking around, he considered his options. He was an expert tree climber and he wondered if he could get to the closest tree in time.

"Caedmon... Caedmon... I am the unseen Lord of the land. Do you want to hear me?"

Caedmon ran to the side of the road, trying to get a grip on the base of a huge old tree. With a glance back, he began to shimmy up the trunk. He hid himself as well as he could, deep within the dense branches, peering out through the leaves to see if he could spot anyone.

Immediately, behind him he heard, "Caedmon, you cannot hide from me." Caedmon gasped in fear.

"I hear you, Lord. What do you want with me?" he replied tremulously.

"Caedmon, I have called you before, but you were young and you refused to hear me. Are you ready now?" The unseen Lord sat cross legged on a branch behind Caedmon.

Caedmon slowly climbed down out of the tree, remembering when his grandfather had first heard from the unseen Lord. Grandpa had told him all about the incident. He had been only six at the time. He had been glad that it had made his grandpa happy. His child heart at the time had never considered it as an actual happening that he could possibly have. He had told himself that it was just like his play fighting with the imaginary dragon and other foes ~ that it was only pretend. Though Caedmon knew honestly that he had not *wanted* to hear because perhaps he would have had to stop his play fighting. *Everyone knew the unseen Lord didn't fight dragons.* In fact, he did not think anyone even believed in a real dragon anymore, let alone a *real* unseen Lord of the land.

Caedmon dropped his head and tried to consider what talking to the unseen Lord would mean. He knew of others that had said they heard Him, but he had never expected it to happen to him ~ his own opinion of himself was too small. How could he be of any service to this majestic Lord whom he had heard of from his grandparents? He began to weep as he thought of his life and the way he had been acting. *Will this Lord want me to answer if He knew how hard and resentful my heart is towards Mother?*

With great compassion the Lord looked at Caedmon. Oh, how He loved this boy. Now was the time, the Lord knew, or else it would be too late for him to hear, for He knew that the boy's heart was hardening more every day. Reaching out His hand, the Lord lightly touched Caedmon on the cheek. Not feeling the touch physically, however Caedmon suddenly felt reassured in his heart.

"Caedmon, I do know what is in your heart. I know of your life, how hard it is, and I have come to strengthen you. I love you and I see in you a strength that you do not see. You need to understand, Caedmon, I created you and I know who you will become if you entrust yourself to Me. However, what you become does not alter the love I have for you now. No matter what you choose My love will never change. I will heal your fatherless heart." The Lord answered the unasked questions in Caedmon's soul.

Dropping to his knees, Caedmon cried out to the unseen Lord, "Oh Lord, forgive me for my bitterness to others and the cold feeling I have had for You. I am so young and weak. How could You ever love me? I will serve You no matter what the cost. I am Yours. Take me ~ I am Yours."

Relief flooded Caedmon's entire being as the anger and pent-up frustration eased out of his heart. The unseen Lord of the land knelt down beside Caedmon. He gently put His arms around the lad's shoulders, holding him close to His heart, and then laid Caedmon down onto the grass. Caedmon felt overcome with feelings of acceptance he had never before experienced. Peace and love flooded his soul as he felt himself float down onto the grass. He did not know how long he was lying on the grass. After a time, he heard someone approaching. Rolling over onto his back, unashamed of the tears running down his cheeks, he looked up into the sky.

"Caedmon, what is the matter with you? You're acting like a girl," Edan teased, but then he looked closer at Caedmon. "You look so different. What has happened?"

Edan slowly knelt down on the grass beside Caedmon, waiting patiently for his friend's response. Caedmon looked off into the sky, not moving or responding. He did not want this feeling to leave him ~ the feeling that was so new and precious to him. He had never felt so protected, so loved, and so cherished in his life and now here was Edan to steal the moment.

Rolling onto his side he looked up at Edan. Edan had always been there for him, in spite of his hasty words at times. Hopefully he would understand. Taking a deep breath, he began to tell Edan what had happened.

Edan listened, his heart stirring deep within. Was not this the same unseen Lord he had heard of all his life? He was concerned immediately for Caedmon. "Whoa, Caed, I have heard about Him all my life from my family, in the fortress where we dwell," said Edan. "That is not the way you hear Him. Not this way, with Him just talking to you like I would."

A shiver ran up Edan's spine, "You know what?...You sound like one of those mediators. You'd better stop now before there is no hope for you. The guards were put in place to hear from the unseen Lord for us ordinary pilgrims. The mediators think they can hear from Him without a guard. Its wrong I tell you! Beware!"

Caedmon stopped, fear gripping his heart. He did not want to fall into something that was wrong. Though, as he slowly got up, his heart could not deny what had happened. He longed to hear the unseen Lord again. He knew that it had to become his quest ~ a quest wholly unlike his imaginary ones when he was a child, but a true quest, one given to him from the greatest of all Lords.

He smiled at Edan and grasped his hand to get up. He knew that their paths would separate again for a time, and he felt a sadness with the realization that his life would never be the same again. Even though Edan and him had not been spending any time together, he had always known that he was there for him. Caedmon's heart trembled with trepidation. He had a strange feeling that he might be lonely in the days to come, and his new friends were such a large portion of his life.

Edan smiled at Caedmon, slapping him on the back. The boys continued on toward the fortress. The night was almost upon them, and it was getting hard to see. When they reached the fortress gate, Caedmon told Edan that he needed to talk to his grandmother and grandfather in the fortress. Edan shrugged and left, worried for his friend, but knowing he had to get home for supper or his mother would be very upset.

Caedmon peered up at the fortress, the large door looming in front of him. He had come before to see his grandparents, but this time he was aware that he was entering the unseen Lord's house. He felt small as he rapped the knocker on the great wooden door.

Caedmon heard the knock echoing throughout the fortress, and a feeling of awe swept over him.

One of the greeters opened the door, smiling as she recognized him. Welcoming him in, she asked him to wait in the large atrium as she disappeared up the long staircase. Caedmon looked around the vast atrium as he waited for his grandmother to come to him. It was very grand and ancient. He wondered who had built it and what the purpose of it was. None of this had interested him before, he suddenly realized that something had changed within himself.

In the centre of the room was a large pool. An iridescent green light was emanating from it. Caedmon slowly walked over to the pool, which looked inviting. Reaching down, he touched the water, but as he heard his grandma approaching behind him, he quickly straightened and turned towards her.

Down in the depths of the pool, the wide yellow eyes of the Dragon looked in shock at who was gazing into the pool. *How has he gotten into the fortress, and why is he here?* The Dragon had the uncomfortable feeling that this young man had changed. Dragging itself out of the pool, it listened.

His grandmother, seeing Caedmon, felt anxiety rise within her. Hugging him affectionately, "You have come so late to see us." She nervously asked, "Is it your mother again?"

"No, Grandma, it is not my mother. I just had some questions to ask you and Grandfather. I also need to share something that has just happened to me."

His grandmother led him to their humble quarters. When he entered, he was greeted by his grandfather's weak but genuine smile. His grandfather, by marriage, had struggled through his life. Sometimes, he would take them out of the fortress and turn to ale and live his life by his own desires, but then, when things got hard, he would turn again to the fortress for help. They were not very respected at the fortress, for his grandfather's behaviour was not acceptable and it kept them from taking an active part in its daily routines.

"Well, Caedmon, you have come to see your old grandpa, have you? Come closer and let me see you."

Caedmon walked over to his grandfather, who was sitting on the edge of his bed. He was old, but the drink of ale and hard life had aged him far more than his years. Caedmon sat down on the bed beside him as his grandmother pulled up their only chair in front of them and sat down.

"Grandpa, Grandma ~ I heard the unseen Lord of the land this evening. He spoke to me and called me to follow Him," Caedmon quietly shared with them his precious story.

Tears of joy flowed down his grandparents' faces as they listened to the whole story, their old hearts filling with happiness. His grandfather too had heard the Lord years before, but the pull of the ale had been so great that he had walked away from Him. When he had searched for Him again, he had somehow had got lost in between the fortress and the land. His grandfather truly did love the unseen Lord even if his nature had been too weak to serve Him consistently. He reached out and took his grandson's hand. How he loved this boy!

Caedmon looked long into his grandpa's eyes and knew that what he had heard was real. He also knew that he would have to be careful or else he, too, might get lost in his search for the unseen Lord.

He hugged his grandpa tightly to himself. Caedmon was going to do better. He would try to make them happy because he knew that his mother's life had broken their hearts. Taking his leave he walked quietly home, gazing up into the night sky at the twinkling stars. The Dragon lost sight of him the minute he left the fortress as the light of the unseen Lord blinded it from seeing Caedmon. The Dragon, hissing out its anger, swept back into the pool to plan its attack on this young man. The moonlit path wound in front of Caedmon as he strolled along, again feeling the same wonderful peace flood his soul. He would look for work, he determined, and try to be a good son ~ then maybe his mother would come to know the unseen Lord of the land through him.

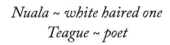

Nuala ~ white haired one

Teague ~ poet

Treasa shook herself from her recollections of the story of the young boy knight. She put down her knitting and finished her preparations for her husband's supper.

Later that evening, with the supper mess cleaned away, Treasa gathered her knitting and went to the other end of the large room to sit with her husband in front of the fireplace. Cathaoir's chin was resting on his chest as he sat slumped in his chair, sound asleep. She did not disturb him, knowing that he was exhausted from his long day in the fields. Examining the sock she was knitting, she began to work, the needles clicking in a steady rhythm.

She remembered back to when she had first met Caedmon at Evergreen. She had been shocked at his single devotion for the unseen Lord. It was in those early years when Treasa had become acquainted with Caedmon and his grandma, Nuala. He had become a good friend of Teague, their son. Then Edan had joined them. Those had been good years ~ a time of building bonds that still ran deep. Those few short years had been packed with a lot of living...

The Ancients say… "The fear of man bringeth a snare: but whoso putteth his trust in the Lord shall be safe."

Chapter 2

Carew ~ from the fortress
Keelin ~ slender and fair

Caedmon stretched out his small frame, so like his natural father's, on the cot. The sun was just rising on the eastern horizon, it was so early, but he had to get up. He worked in the village for a wealthy baker who owned shops in all the villages of the valley. His boss would deliver the fresh bread to the door of anyone who could afford it. Caedmon was the storefront sweep, and he would deliver bread when they had more orders than the regular delivery man could handle. He took his job very seriously as it was sometimes their only means of income. Wynne was working less and holding down the jobs she did get was becoming hard with her growing addiction to ale.

She had just broken off her relationship with another man and was considering moving into one of the fortresses. Caedmon hoped they would. She would be happy there, he knew it. She was fun and lovely when she was sober. Maybe she would find a good man in the fortress ~ one who would not abuse her, and possibly may even love him like a son.

Caedmon had spent every free moment at the fortress these last months. He was liked by all, especially Carew, the guard's son, who treated him like someone special. It filled that empty feeling that he'd fought against for so much of his life ~ to have an authority figure who loved him, like a father might. Later in the day, as Caedmon was sweeping the store and the smell of fresh-baked bread filled the air, life was good. He heard the front door open and, looking up, saw his old friend Edan come in. Edan smiled at Caedmon and walked over to him.

Edan, his eyes alive with merriment, asked, "Can you take a break from your work, Caed?"

Caedmon went to the back of the bakery and asked the owner, who gladly gave him a break. Caedmon had proven to be one of his most faithful workers and he could trust him, for not once had he tried to get out of work or complain. After Caedmon returned to the front and grabbed his coat from the rack, the lads headed for the open square in the middle of the village. The cries of vendors selling their wares out of wagons, the smell of the livestock and the laughing of children who were playing in the open square, filled the air. They found a spot by the large cistern in the middle of the square and sat on the trough's stone edge.

"So, Edan ~ your eyes are full of joy. What is it?" Caedmon asked with a quizzical look.

"Caedmon, I have been listening to everything that you told me and, well, I got jealous. I wondered why I hadn't heard from the unseen Lord as well," Edan explained honestly. "I tried to copy you and be good, but before I knew it I would lose my temper at Gallagher. You know that brother of mine, he always knows how to make me angry. I became so discouraged and then, last night, I couldn't sleep so I went for a walk out in the countryside."

Caedmon inched closer to Edan, his curiosity aroused. He tipped his head as he whispered in excitement, "Go on. What happened?"

"Well, I was walking really fast, trying to out-walk my thoughts you know? And then I heard Him, right beside me. He said, 'Edan, do you want to believe in Me?' I just stopped dead in my tracks. The hair stood up on my neck! I tell you. So I looked around and then I started to walk again, this time really slowly. You know, it was quite dark last night, but I could make things out by their shadows. Even so, as far as I could see, I was the only one on the road."

Edan stopped talking and kicked at a clod of dirt at his feet. Then, with eyes shining, he looked back at his friend. "He began to talk to me and tell me that He was the unseen Lord and how much He loved me, and I guess the next thing I knew I was crying and... Then it was as if He was holding me in His arms, and I cried and cried. I will never doubt again. He is not only real, but He wants to talk to us!"

Caedmon slapped his friend on the back, laughing with a joy that comes from genuine, heartfelt relief. He had been concerned because of his friend's indifference to the unseen Lord and that was all wiped away in one encounter.

They talked non stop on their way back to the shop. They were so excited that they could now share this precious relationship with the unseen Lord with one another.

Edan was so different since he too had heard the unseen Lord call him. Edan started coming to Evergreen with Caedmon. His parents at first did not understand why he had to leave their small fortress, but he showed them by his life that he really had changed. So, they let Edan go with their blessing. The fortress dwellers in Evergreen were hoping that one day the lads would be able to live in the fortress with them.

They were exceptionally kind to the them and encouraged the boys to follow the unseen Lord of the land. Edan and Caedmon would meet every week and walk to the fortress together. Caedmon told Edan what he had learned from the older fortress dwellers about the pool ~ that the pilgrims had been told long ago that this water was from the Unchanging River that the great Father of the unseen Lord had made for them, and that it had life in it to restore them.

Caedmon also informed his friend ~ that the first builders of the fortress had laboriously constructed a special aqueduct to bring the water from the Unchanging River. Back then it had been a mighty river, and they diverted its waters into the fortress pool. The pool was very deep, and the water was used to refresh the people who lived in or visited the fortress. The access to the river through the aqueduct had been closed up years before and now the water was painstakingly brought in by hand. Visiting guards would carry the water to them ~ sometimes their own guard, when the supply was low, would arrange a large task-force of fortress dwellers specially commissioned by their guard to bring in the water.

Caedmon had asked them why they went to the effort of carrying the water in and he was told that the water in the aqueducts had become defiled because it travelled through the land. When he asked why the fortress had been built so far from the river, they had responded they were not sure. They knew that it was necessary to bring the water to them, moreover, they had added that it was not for them to go to the water. They had been glad they had, as the river had changed over the years into a meandering stream, but they hoped one day it would flow like a river again.

Teague, Treasa and Cathaoir's son, became a very close friend of Edan and Caedmon. Treasa began to spend time with the boys when Teague brought them to the farm. The young men would spend every free moment together, making music. The lads loved to sing and play the lyre. Edan would thump away on anything that made a sound like a drum. Carew, the guard's son, loved to make music as well, and he too became a close comrade of theirs. As a mediator, Treasa had been encouraged by the fact that men so young had a desire to hear from the unseen Lord, and that they wanted to share this knowledge with the people of the land. They were already beginning to mediate through their music.

The Dragon was not impressed that these young men had infiltrated its place, and it tried to discourage them continually. One day, as it was swimming around and around in the depths of the pool, it became aware that someone was staring at it. The Dragon looked up from the depths, gliding to a stop and staying absolutely still. Whoever was there was leaning over the edge and looking down through the water directly at it.

Cursed be those young would-be mediators! The Dragon thought. *Which one of the lads was it?* It had to find out. So swimming slowly up to the surface, it looked right into the face of Caedmon. The boy did not flinch, but continued to stare.

"Hey, Treasa, come over here. Would you please?" Caedmon called over his shoulder to Treasa, who was walking by in the large atrium. "Look into the pool. Do you see something swimming in the water?"

Treasa knelt down beside Caedmon and looked into the green water. It appeared clear, but the strange green light that emanated from it made it hard to see. Looking carefully, she could barely make out the form of a shadow that seemed to be floating in the water about six inches below the surface.

"I think it might be a shadow," Treasa responded. "Possibly it is caused from the strange light in the pool. Here, let me stick my hand in and see if I feel anything."

Caedmon gasped, he knew now that one should never touch the pool without permission.

"Wait," Caedmon cried. "Don't do it. Let's go get the Guard, it is not up to us to touch the water."

"Don't be ridiculous, Caedmon. This is the same water that is in the Unchanging River, which runs through our farm. The unseen Lord did not say we could not touch it. Don't you know that the Ancients spoke of a time when pilgrims everywhere would come and drink freely from the river? Don't look so horrified!" Reaching over, Treasa stuck her hand suddenly into the pool and struck the Dragon right in the eye. She did not feel anything with her hand, but a strange vibration ran up her arm and down her spine. The Dragon dove to the bottom of the pool, holding its eye in pain. It felt like she had stuck a hot iron into its eye. The Dragon screamed and cursed at the woman. It would get her. After all, she was a mediator, and it hated mediators!

"Did you see that?" Caedmon's voice shook with excitement.

"No, I did not see anything, but I did notice that the shadow disappeared and a horrible crawling feeling went up my arm and down my spine. Also, when I brought my hand out of the water, it felt like I was holding a sword. I must have an active imagination today," Treasa laughed, unconvincingly. She sighed as she looked at her wet hand. Oh, how she had hoped that the sword she'd felt was real. She had heard of the wonderful armour the early pilgrims had had.

- 32 -

"Wow ~ Not only did I see the shadow go down to the depths of the pool, but I am sure that it was looking right at you!" Caedmon could not keep the excitement from his voice. "Let's go get the guard and tell him about it."

Treasa and Caedmon went to find the guard, who was busy with someone else and told them to come back later. As they strolled back to the atrium, Treasa said to Caedmon, "I need to get home. Maybe we should keep this to ourselves until we can check it out further."

"Yes, we don't want to sound crazy. We're not are we?" Caedmon asked with a mischievous smile as he hugged Treasa farewell.

Caedmon did not keep the experience to himself, though ~ it was too exciting for the young man. He shared it with Carew. Carew looked at him.

"Come let's go see my father. He will know if it is anything."

The guard rose slowly from his chair in front of his ornate fireplace. Walking over to Caedmon, he tried to find the words to warn this boy of the dangers of looking into the pool and to caution him against listening to the mediators.

"You know son... Do you mind I call you son?"

Caedmon shook his head, as the Guard put his arm around Caedmon's shoulder and guided him to a chair in front of the fireplace.

"Sit down. Let me explain a few things to you." He took a deep breath.

"The reason the guardship was established was because the pilgrims were unable to fight the Dragon and keep its lies off of themselves. However, since the beginning of the fortress there have been those ~ specifically the mediators ~ who think they can continue to live the old way, the way the Ancients wrote that pilgrims lived before the fortresses came. But we cannot continue to live that way. Things are different now. What Treasa did was wrong and against the unseen Lord. She has had no training to deal with the water in the pool, or even to touch it without the proper authorization. I know that she is a good woman, and her family does a good job here. They supply much food from their farm for the fortress dwellers, and they have opened their home for pilgrims to stay. As far

- 33 -

as what she told you about using the water from the Unchanging River for refreshing yourself, that is simply not true. The people of the land might try to do something like that, but the water out there is entirely different from the water in the pool."

Caedmon interrupted the long speech. "I thought the water in the pool is water from the Unchanging River."

The guard sighed in exasperation. Sometimes these pilgrims were so difficult! "Yes, and no. Let me explain. The water now has to be touched by a guard or someone commissioned by a guard. It then has to be put into a pool in a fortress to realize life-giving qualities. Do you understand that? The unseen Lord has changed the whole scheme of things because of the ignorance of the pilgrims."

Caedmon could not help but be in awe that the guard was taking the time to explain to him about the water. His lonely fatherless heart decided right there and then to believe this man. He would warn Treasa that she was in error. Still, something deeper down inside of him felt troubled, though he did not give in to it.

"Why don't you stay and have supper with Carew and me! Would you like that?" the guard asked him in a gentle tone.

"Oh yes, that would be wonderful!" Caedmon could not believe his ears. He must truly be loved by this man. His young heart felt a joy it had never felt before, and oh, how he liked it.

Caedmon and Edan began to spend much time with Carew and his father, and both of them revelled in the fact they had been singled out for such an honour. Caedmon and Edan were warned by the senior guard to not spend too much time with the mediators. Even though they were a very good-living, conscientious lot, they were very extreme in their desire to hear the unseen Lord and they did not submit to the proper, unseen Lord-given authorities.

Teague felt the other young men pull away from him. He knew it was because his mother was a mediator. Teague's music took on a sorrowful plea to the unseen Lord. The music began to move the hearts of those who lived in the fortress, and soon they wanted Teague to come and play for them all the time. Teague's younger sister, Keelin, became his confidant and friend, even though many years separated them in age. Keelin's petite fingers played the flute and would try to flow with Teague's ever-changing, spontaneous music. They found that when they played their music, it was as if the unseen Lord walked with them and talked to them ~ and even talked *through* them in the words of their songs. The guard finally warned them that they had better not come any more to bring their music to Evergreen.

~

"Lord, You who are unseen. I truly would like to go to the Source of the Unchanging River one day," Caedmon quietly spoke as he gazed into the shimmering depths of the pool. Treasa had told him that at the Source of the river was a wonderful artesian well. A strange longing often came to him to go there. He felt that he might somehow feel closer to the unseen Lord there. Caedmon was surprised by how difficult it was to hear the unseen Lord when he was in the fortress.

Shrugging his shoulders at the silence, he continued to gaze into the pool, realizing just how much he loved it. He so wished he had been there when it had been made. Suddenly, Caedmon, thought he saw a shadow down in the depths of the water, but rationalized that it was probably just an illusion caused by the strange light that seemed to emanate from it.

Out of depths a pair of eyes watched him warily. Why did this lad continually look into the pool?

Caedmon and Edan became obsessed with the pool that was in the fortress. The water in it was so refreshing! Carew, who was in his final year of guard training, had earned the privilege of giving them some, when he did, they would take it carefully, sipping it slowly. Carew planned for his young friends to experience as much enjoyment as they could in the fortress, so they would want to come back or even live there with the fortress dwellers forever. He also felt important as he tried to teach them the ways of the unseen Lord by teaching them, everything he had learned from the guards before him. He had been trained to use his outgoing personality to draw the young of the land, and many came every week to visit the fortress. The only thing that saddened him was that Teague did not come anymore. Teague wanted to be a mediator, evidently misled by his parents.

Caedmon found that his favourite person in Evergreen was the guard, Carew's father. He was a kind man, and truly interested in Caedmon's life. Whenever he was allowed to, Caedmon would spend hours in the guard's private room just listening to his wisdom. The older man seemed to fill part of the deep longing for a father. This feeling would rise to the surface at times, but Caedmon would be careful to push it down, deep within his heart.

Sometimes he would join his grandmother and go to the grand assembly, listening to the special music and the guard's speech on how they were to live. After these assemblies, Caedmon, trying even harder to live properly, would separate himself from the people of the land. He did not want to be contaminated by their loose living. However, concerning his mother he found this very difficult. He could not comprehend how she was able to talk of the unseen Lord of the land even though she was under the influence of the ale.

She would cry and wail, "I love Him so much, Caedmon. You just don't understand how hard I have it! If He knew how hard it was, He would not ask me to change! I loved Him once and tried to serve Him, but your father stole any love I had."

Then she would cry and mumble out her hatred of the fortress dwellers, telling him that if they cared for her they would do something for her. He would plead with her and tell her that her parents were fortress dwellers, but she would only include them in her angry tirade. They had let her marry *that man,* she would complain.

- 36 -

*The Ancients say… "He satifieth the longing soul,
and filleth the hungry soul with goodness."*

Chapter 3

*Scully ~ town crier
Gilroy ~ servant of the King*

Treasa's heart longed for the unseen Lord to bring Caedmon and Edan back into Teague's life. However, as the years went by it looked as if He had other plans for these young men. Cathaoir and her had stopped going to Evergreen when the assault against the mediators became openly spoken of. Her heart never stopped hurting for the pilgrims there and their blindness to the truth. Her mediations rose to the unseen Lord daily on their behalf.

Setting aside her knitting she stood and blew out the candle. It had grown very late with her reverie and her tired body ached for bed. As she headed for their bed chamber, she pondered. *It is time to lay the past aside and enjoy each new day the unseen Lord gives us.*

Life had been a difficult journey for the last few years. Caedmon was leaving childhood forever and was now a young man. For a short while his mother had moved into Evergreen. Everything had started to improve, but then another man had come into her life and the cycle started again. Nevertheless, Caedmon had determined that he was not going to lose hope for her.

Tonight after work, if things were good at home, he hoped to join the young for the evening in the fortress. They were having in a special guard to speak to them, and jugglers to entertain. Caedmon had heard that this guard was bringing some fresh water directly from the Unchanging River, so he could hardly wait for his work to be done.

When Caed arrived home, the whole flat was in an uproar. His grandmother was there, and he could hear arguing. Grandma was trying to talk Wynne out of something. Wynne was yelling back and throwing stuff around. Caed peeked around the door and saw his mother throwing her belongings into a crate. Looking up and seeing Caedmon, she stopped. Straightening her shoulders, she took on a voice of authority.

"Caedmon, pack your things. We are moving! We are getting out of this hole in the ground. We are going to the other side of the mountains, to another valley. A new valley, a new village, and a new start!"

"Mom, why? I have a good life here," Caedmon said pleadingly to his mother.

She shot him a fearsome look, and walked towards him like she was going to strike him. Caedmon cowered waiting for the blow. Changing her mind, she tried smiling instead.

"Listen, Caedmon, you don't have that good of a life here, either. You only have those few friends in the fortress, and you have no special girl. Look, we can start over. You are young and strong, and I am very capable. We will do fine, trust me, I ~ "

"Why are you always so bull headed, Wynne?" Caedmon's grandma cut in. "You know very well that you are just running away and dragging your son with you. Let him stay here with us."

Wynne's agitated voice was shrill with emotion. "Don't be ridiculous, mother. You are always talking about trusting the unseen Lord. Well, trust Him now. I feel I am to go where no one knows me and it will give Caedmon a new start as well. There is much work there and I know that both Caedmon and I will be able to have a good life!"

Caedmon's heart stopped. Oh, he was still breathing, but his mind was not functioning as he went through the motion of packing his meagre belongings. How would they travel? On foot? His mother didn't even like to walk across the village let alone out of the valley. He was snapped back to reality when his mother shouted at him from across the dingy room.

"Caedmon!"

Wynne walked over and grabbed Caedmon's arm roughly. He could smell the strong odour of ale on her breath. He looked pleadingly at his grandmother but she had already turned and was stomping out of the flat. Wynne staggered and released her grip, trying to steady herself with a hand against the wall. She straightened and looked angrily at him.

"Caed would you hurry up? We are getting a ride with the bread wagon. I was in to see your boss today and he said we could get a ride to the last village in the valley tonight. Quit looking at me like that! And ~ for goodness sakes, hurry up. I do know what is best for us," the words slurred out of her mouth.

Well, that answered Caedmon's question about how they were getting there ~ or at least how they were getting part of the way. He carried their crates of belongings down to the street, tears coursing down his cheeks as he realized that he would be cut off from the fortress, Evergreen. How would the unseen Lord ever find him in a strange land? He didn't even know if the next valley believed in the unseen Lord of the land, or if there were any fortresses there. How would he stay true to his quest if he was living out in the Dragon's land without the protection of the fortress and its guard?

His mother joined him in the street. His grandma, who had been huffily waiting about in front of the doorway, hugged him goodbye, clinging to him for a long time. "I will talk to the Lord for you, Caedmon. Remember that."

"Yes, Grandma. Say goodbye to Grandpa for me, and to the people in Evergreen as well, would you?"

Grandma nodded her head and started the long walk home, her head hanging low, sadness gripping her heart. What would it take to bring her daughter back? She pondered these things as she made her way back home to their dusty old flat in the centre of the village. They too had left the fortress again because her husband started to drink ale again. She so wished that things were different, but she could not figure out what had gone wrong. She had done everything that the fortress dwellers had told her to do, but she still couldn't find the peace that she'd had in the beginning of her relationship with the unseen Lord of the land.

∼

Treasa gathered the mediators when they heard that Caedmon had been taken away. In her heart she knew he was called to be a mediator. What would happen now? Carew, blinded by the arrogance of youth and by his guardship training, had been careful not to let the young spend too much time with the mediators. It was sad. If only Carew had known that he too was called to be a mediator.

An old man in a covered wagon pulled into the yard during the mediators' cry to the unseen Lord. He was a large man, even though Treasa could tell that he had lived many years upon the land. His golden beard was frosted with white, and the wrinkles around his eyes were creased from good humor. He was a very handsome man with a gentle, kind countenance. He told them he was on his way to the next valley, but he felt the unseen Lord had told him to stop at their farm.

Treasa and Cathaoir welcomed him in to their humble farm cottage and found that he was from the River's Source.

"My name is Gilroy," he told them, and then added, "The unseen Lord has asked me to let you know that He is with you and not to lose heart. He says that you will need to be strong, for He will bring distraught pilgrims to your farm to be refreshed and cleansed from the Dragon's lies."

Gilroy stayed the night and soon they felt as if they had known him for a long time. Treasa's heart stirred deep within her as she heard of his family and his life at the Source. She hoped that someday she would go to the River's Source and see it for herself.

The wagon rumbled on into the night. Caedmon and his mother had made themselves a little bed in the back between the sacks of bread. Caedmon had not seen his mother come into the shop that day. He must have been on an errand of some sort, maybe making a delivery ∼ it had been such a busy day. He wondered what fun his friends were having in the fortress tonight without him. Caedmon

hadn't even time to tell Carew and his father, the guard, to petition the unseen Lord for him. He would miss his childhood friend,
Edan, and he hoped that Edan would stay safe in the fortress.

He pondered what he had been taught about the Dragon, how
it devoured those who would leave the fortress. He could see the
Dragon's effects on his mother's life, how its lies stole any hope of
normalcy for her at the time. How Caedmon had wished she would
move into the fortress for protection from the Dragon.

The Dragon slithered behind the trees watching the wagon leave.
It was glad that Wynne had listened to its whispering, slimy lies.
It could see the green slime still dripping from her ears. However,
the Dragon did not like the attitude of this young man, Caedmon,
who appeared to have no fear of it. Though the Dragon had tried
diligently to instil fear in him, Caedmon's constant, unflinching
stare into the pool unnerved the beast. If he was allowed to understand that he was a mediator, he would become powerful ~ of that,
the Dragon had no doubt. It had to separate Caedmon from any
possibility of getting together with other mediators and learning
the truth.

It would not do for Wynne to change her mind, so the Dragon
sent a spy to counsel her that she was doing the right thing. Wynne
slipped from beside Caedmon and moved forward to the driver's
seat, "May I sit up here for a while?"

The driver, Scully, smiled with pleasure for he loved the nightly
adventure he was on. He seldom had someone riding with him to
pass the time by sharing gossip, his favourite pastime as he travelled
through the valleys delivering bread. He knew how to milk every
motive and thought out of a person. He then would either twist it
just a little to make it more tantalizing or just leave it alone for it
was good enough. He had no idea that the Dragon used him end-
lessly to destroy people's lives with gossip and insinuations.

"Yes, ma'am. By the way, I think you are doing a brave thing,
starting a new life with your son." The old man spoke with conviction. "I have lived many years and I have met only a few who have
done this very thing that you are doing ~ leaving family and friends
and starting again."

- 41 -

"Well, I won't say that it is easy, but I know that I have to do something. Caedmon is such a good son and I want what is best for him. Besides, no one forgets or lets you forget, either. They will bring up all your mistakes every time something goes wrong. My mother is one of the best at this."

The old man loved this new gossip because he already knew all about this woman and her son. He relished the fact that he was gaining new information to add to the already awful tales of this struggling family back home. He felt himself get excited over giving his own advice.

"Maybe you should go to the first inn in the village when we arrive there. They have all sorts who come through there from the other valleys. That inn is the stop over for travellers when they first come into our valley."

Scully also knew the proprietor, and he looked forward to being able to tell him this latest bit of information tonight while it was still fresh. This innkeeper would, in return, keep him informed if he heard anything about this pair in the weeks ahead.

"Why, that's a good idea. Thank you so much, you have made me all the more determined to do this thing. You are too kind," Wynne replied with great relief. "Now, I better get back to my son."

The Dragon had heard enough and slithered back into the darkness, turning to go back to the fortress to spread its vileness there as well. Suddenly, it felt its old wound begin to throb. Turning, it looked at the wagon. Caedmon had awakened when his mother returned to their bed and he breathed a silent plea, "Lord...help me."

Invisible to the human eye, a bright light enveloped the wagon, causing the Dragon to recoil. The unseen Lord was present. Wheeling around in a rage, it headed for the fortress. The Lord would pay for interfering with its plans for the boy ~ the Dragon would make sure of that. It would ensure that the boy and his mother were never welcome at the fortress again by inciting a deep dislike for them amongst the fortress dwellers. Then, who would they have if they came back seeking comfort? No one! The Dragon would be free of the possibility of the boy awakening his dormant power.

The Lord looked at the Dragon as it slunk away into the darkness. Caedmon felt the presence of the Lord all around him and he smiled. He was not alone. The unseen Lord was there with him. He knew it ~ he could feel the peace.

The next day, after spending the night at the inn Scully had recommended, they caught a ride with a very kind merchant, whom Caedmon found out also knew the unseen Lord of the land. The Lord had told him he would be picking up a young lad and his mother and he was to take them to the first village in the next valley. The unseen Lord wanted him to minister life to them and to give them a drink of the water from the Unchanging River, but only when they asked for a drink.

The merchant told Caedmon of the place where he lived in the mountains, and of the beautiful river that gave the people there life and joy. He shared his heart with the lad. Anything Caedmon wanted to know, he shared with him. As the afternoon wore on Caedmon's thirst became unbearable, but he was too shy to ask for a drink. He finally could not stand it any longer, for his mother was whispering her complaints of thirst into Caedmon's ear over the miles.

"Sir, we are thirsty. Could we stop and drink from one of the aqueducts?"

"You don't want that water, Caedmon. It is corrupt. Here, have a drink from my supply. This water is from the river where I live ~ the river that the Lord gave us to drink from so we would live."

Caedmon's mother briskly reached over his shoulder, grabbing the canteen. She began to drink hungrily, but then stopped, looking shocked. Her thirst had been quenched with the first gulp. She handed the canteen back to Caedmon feeling ashamed of herself for her greed. She could not describe it, but she suddenly felt strange.

Wynne remembered back to when she was a little girl and had believed in the Lord of the land, and to when she had heard Him call her name. Regret filled her heart, but she did not like the feeling so she lay down upon the back seat of the wagon and tried to go to sleep. She wanted to escape the uncomfortable feelings that were rising in her heart, so she slipped her flask out of her satchel and took a sip. She hoped that the ale would chase away her regret as it usually did.

Caedmon held the canteen carefully and took a long sip of the water. He had expected stale warm water from the small earthen jug, but instead, cool refreshing water coursed down his parched throat. He felt his whole body fill with energy, and his mind became free from all doubt and fear. He looked at the driver, who was smiling as he watched him. Caedmon then took another, longer drink and felt life flow down through his system to his very toes. Caedmon suddenly wanted to get down from the wagon and outrun the horses that were pulling it. He looked again at the driver in amazement.

"Where did you get this water?" Caedmon asked incredulously.

"This is what we drink. It is from the Unchanging River. It is the Lord's river of life for all who believe, and even for those who do not."

"We get water from the same river in our village back home, but it is nothing like this! Our water is stale and lifeless compared to this water," Caedmon said.

The driver took a long time to respond and Caedmon wondered if he had heard him or not. Finally he looked at Caedmon, his eyes misty with emotion.

"The people of the land thought they knew better than the natural course that the river took, so they constructed their own aqueducts to channel the water to them, instead of traveling themselves to the water. When you dictate to this water instead of letting it lead you, it will lose its life-giving support and become just like ordinary water. There are still some who know of its value and cherish it. There are traveling knights who will carry it for miles to quench the thirst of those in the fortresses, but more often than not, the guard of the fortress will have them empty it into their fortress pools instead of giving it directly to the people. The individual guards regulate who drinks the water and when, for they feel that only they are qualified to give a drink to the people of their particular fortress. If only they knew that the minute they pour the water into the pools it becomes ordinary water," the driver lamented sadly. "However, there are still some who get a drink and are refreshed for a season. The unseen Lord makes sure of that."

Caedmon wondered at all he was hearing. It was all so foreign to him, and he knew in his heart that this information would not be received back at his fortress. Despite that, he knew that what this man was saying about the water was true. Treasa had told him he could drink from the water in the river if he wanted to go there, but the Guard just laughed when Caedmon had shared that with him. He wondered, *why?*

Caedmon's mother had fallen into a deep sleep on the back seat of the wagon, looking more at peace than she had in years. Caedmon's heart ached for her, but he knew that he could not force her to believe. He turned his attention back to the driver.

"Sir, what is your name?" Caedmon respectfully asked.

"Gilroy," he replied quietly. "The unseen Lord gave me that name many years ago. You were named after one of his generals of the unseen army. Caedmon, the great warrior! The unseen Lord told me to come to you and to care for your needs until you get to your destination. Would you like some bread? My wife baked it for me. She bakes it with figs inside and it is very good."

"Yes, please. I am hungry." Caedmon was famished, for they had not been able to afford much to eat at the inn's kitchen the night before. "Do you mind if I save some for my mother?" he asked hesitantly.

"No, do not save any of yours for her, eat it all. I have more for her as well," Gilroy spoke to Caedmon reassuringly.

Caedmon leaned back against the wagon seat and enjoyed every bite. The bread was unlike anything he had ever eaten. He knew that it had been baked with much love and devotion. When he had finished the last crumb and had another drink from the flask, he leaned over on to the driver's shoulder and fell fast asleep.

Gilroy looked down on the lad asleep on his shoulder and felt ~ his heart stirring within him...

"Lord, I have done what you have asked. Please bring him to the mountain someday for he has the sensitive spirit that you desire."

The unseen Lord spoke encouragingly, "Yes, you are right, my servant. He was chosen before the foundation of this land to be one of My knights, just as you were. He will need your help again, Gilroy. He will not let go of the fortress easily. It has been the only sense of protection he has had in his short life. He will come to the mountain soon. What he does with the knowledge that he will glean there will be up to him, but we will make everything available for his choices."

"What of his mother, Lord? Is there hope?" Gilroy dejectedly asked. "She could only take one gulp from the flask."

"There is always hope, Gilroy. The path she has chosen is a hard one, but I won't leave her."

~

Treasa sat brushing her hair out before bed time, asking the unseen Lord to be with Caedmon. He had been gone for months now. Cathaoir came quietly up behind her, and placed a kiss on the back of her neck. Whirling around, Treasa looked wide-eyed at her husband. "You scared me half to death ~ Shame on you!" She added with a smile teasing at the corners of her mouth. "I think your mind is hundreds of furlongs from here. Come, let me brush your hair for you," Cathaoir said as he began to brush her greying, auburn hair down her back. Cathaoir and Treasa chatted about the rain and the rising of the mighty river. They had hope in their hearts that things would change for the better in the land for the slumbering people.

Handing the brush back to Treasa, Cathaoir went to bed, leaving his wife to put a braid in her hair. Letting the silence wrap its comforting arms around her, she thanked the unseen Lord for the rain. She talked to Him about the condition of the people's hearts and the great divide that was growing between them and the fortress dwellers. The unseen Lord comforted her heart, reminding her that sometimes things appear to be getting worse when really the great breakthrough is preparing to come.

"Don't be afraid. I have led you thus far and I will lead you on," the unseen Lord spoke lovingly to her. She wondered what the morrow would hold.

The Ancients say… "mischief also and sorrow are in the midst of it."

Chapter 4

eague ran all the way home to the farm. Out of breath he yelled, "Mom, where are you?" Treasa, wiping her hands on her apron, left the full dishpan to answer her son's frantic calls.

"What is the matter, Teague? Here, sit down and catch your breath. What has happened?" Treasa asked with apprehension rising in her.

Teague leaned forward, trying to steady his breathing and quiet his racing heart. His mother went quickly to call to Keelin, who was in the garden, sending her to get Cathaoir from the field. Shylah arrived to mediate with Treasa, Teague told her she would want to hear what he had to share. Soon they were all waiting anxiously for Teague to speak.

"This morning I decided I would stop by the fortress to see Carew and Edan. I wasn't sure if I should since they had made it clear that me and my music wasn't wanted. However, Carew and Edan seemed somewhat glad to see me. I think they have been bored since Caedmon left, even though the people there have been saying such bad things about him and his mother. Anyway, we were sitting in the atrium, talking and looking toward the pool. Unannounced this stranger walked in. He was tall and young. He walked over to us and introduced himself as Arthmael. Then he shared how he felt that the unseen Lord had spoken to him to come and let those in Evergreen know that there was armour to fight the Dragon with. He told us that it was time for pilgrims everywhere to begin to fight the Dragon. Well, Carew began to rise from his seat but before he could get right up, Arthmael continued. He said that the Dragon lived right in the fortress pool!"

Teague stopped and took a breath. They all exchanged nervous looks, and Treasa remembered her and Caedmon's experience at the pool.

"Anyway, he asked if he could stay at the fortress for a while and Carew said that they should go to the guard, his father, and ask about it. You know when I was going there I would feel this kind of eerie sensation around the pool. So Edan and Carew took Arthmael to see the guard."

"Where do you think he came from?" Treasa asked.

"I believe the Source of the Unchanging River," Teague answered. "Because he said that at the Source the pilgrims there know all about their armour. He was so friendly and kind, but I could tell that he was alarming Carew. You know how Carew has been taught not to look for solutions outside the fortress."

As they listened to Teague tell them about the incident, they began to mediate, each one talking to the unseen Lord in their own way. Eventually, Keelin went back to the garden, and Cathaoir to the field. Teague went to his loft, and soon the women could hear the lyre and his song filling the air.

"Oh Lord, what does this all mean?" Treasa asked aloud. "Did you send Arthmael to the fortress for a purpose?" The unseen Lord came and made His presence felt to the women.

"Yes, but not with words. I gave him a heart of compassion and it causes him to want to give the truth to all people. Have you noticed that the rains have stopped again? This is because the mediators are few now. The ones who are left are so concerned about their fortresses they have lost completely their heart for the people of the land. They are so removed from what is going on around them living in those places. So a time of unsettling must come to make people re-evaluate their choices. They may seek guidance from you ~ prepare yourselves. Some will come to you and you will need to deal with the bitterness that still lies within your hearts," the unseen Lord spoke soberly to them and then squeezing their shoulders with His hands, He left to go to the others and encourage them.

Days passed and rumours of Arthmael trickled around through the pilgrims, from those who dwelt in the fortress to those who did not. At first the guard tolerated him, but then he asked him to leave for he was troubling the people of the fortress, especially the children. The mysterious stranger continued to warn the people that the Dragon was in the pool, and that he had seen it. The reality was that the young seemed to love Arthmael and followed him around continually.

One day soon after, Gilroy, the merchant, had come to Cathaoir's farm, with a heavy heart. He told his new friends that Arthmael was his son, and shared how he was concerned for the young man. Gilroy told them that Arthmael had come home from giving his message at Evergreen, and his heart was pining to help the people who evidently did not want to hear his message.

Treasa and Cathaoir, exchanged worried looks. *Where is it all going to end?*

Shortly after this visit, Edan came to the farm. He asked to speak to Teague, but Teague was out in the field helping his father plough.

"Come on in, Edan. It has been a long time since we saw you last," Treasa said encouragingly seeing his discomfort. "The men will be in soon for the noon meal. Come into the kitchen and sit while I finish the cooking. For goodness sake, Edan, I am not going to bite you." Edan laughed nervously and followed her into the kitchen.

"Well, it is just that I have heard so many things about you mediators, so I feel a little nervous." Edan tried to sound honest, but his heart smote him. He knew very well that he too was being called to mediate. However, he liked the approval of the fortress dwellers, and he wasn't sure he could follow his own heart.

"How are things back at home, Edan? You live in Evergreen now, I heard," Treasa asked gently.

"Actually, Treasa, I have let the opinion of others outweigh my desire to follow the unseen Lord. And ~ well, it is getting really bad back at the fortress. Lies are flowing. Not outright lies, nevertheless the truth is construed in such a way to make people think that only their way is the truth. I came here today to hear Teague's side of things, but deep down I know that you people won't say anything."

"You are right about that. I am sorry that your own heart has been caught up in this mess. I don't even know how it happened, but I just knew personally that I had to stop visiting the fortress. Something was wrong there. So I stayed here at the farm, then Cathaoir stopped going there as well. Teague, as you know, goes occasionally and Keelin is still going randomly, as well," Treasa said with her voice taking on a reflecting tone as she continued. "We do not promote people to leave the fortress. That is, until now. Teague has told us about Arthmael. You know, Edan, you should meet Arthmael's father, Gilroy. He is the most incredible pilgrim you will ever meet. He is so close to the unseen Lord. They live at the river's Source. I am going to go there someday."

Treasa's intentions had all the appearance of purity and Edan hung his head, shame covering his soul. His thoughts began to wander haphazardly. Only that morning he had overheard the guard and Carew talking, about the condition of the fortress. It was because of the condition of the building that the Dragon was on the loose inside it. They had discussed about raising the funds to fix it. They went on to say, if the mediators, who had left, took their responsibility to the rest seriously they would be there to help. Instead, they thought petitioning the unseen Lord was the most critical thing to do at this time. Edan had been shocked. Did they really think that the building was more important than their relationship to the unseen Lord? Was that truly the reason the Dragon was inhabiting the fortress? They said one thing to each other, but to the rest of the fortress dwellers, they kept telling them that hearing from the unseen Lord for them was their highest calling. Edan knew then he had to come see Teague to talk over these confusing thoughts. He had seen how Teague had been troubled by Arthmael's speech to them when he had first arrived.

Teague came in from the ploughing, covered in sweat and dust from walking behind the mules. Seeing Edan, a smile broke out over his grimy face. "Just let me wash and then I will greet you proper-like."

Teague quickly went back out to the well and washed in the large trough beside it. Grabbing a rag on the way through the door, he dried himself. Striding over to his friend, he hugged him like a bear.

"What a pleasant surprise on a hot dusty day!" Teague exclaimed as he pushed Edan back to arm's length and smiled at him broadly.

Edan dropped his head in shame. Sitting back down in his chair, he burrowed his face into his hands. His heart was overwhelmed by his friend's love and acceptance, even though he had done nothing to cultivate the friendship lately. The men quietly sat down at the table. Keelin joined them. She had been out in the barn, feeding the cows and pigs. She looked at Edan, who still had his face covered in his hands, bending over his knees.

They all waited until Edan was calmed. Then Treasa dished up the stew on to each of their plates as Cathaoir spoke, "My Lord, my Friend, I welcome you here in our midst. I want to thank you for this bountiful supply. Thank you for my Treasa and her faithful cooking ~ and for this returning young friend. Lord, could you somehow comfort his heart today?"

The unseen Lord quickly came into the room of bowed heads and gave Edan's shoulder a firm grasp. Edan immediately felt better, as if an extreme energy was surging through his veins. He looked up, astonished by the feeling. Letting out a gasp as he looked at the rest around the table. Each of the others had a sword drawn, raised skyward, their faces shining with a glorious radiance. Before Edan could say a word the swords disappeared from his sight. He stared at the faces around him as they began to eat as if all was normal. Teague was the first one to look up from his bowl, he could tell by the shocked look on Edan's face that he had seen the swords.

"You have one too. Did you know that?" Teague asked.

Edan answered him sceptically. "Sure Teague, and what have you been drinking?"

"No, seriously." Cathaoir answered. "We all have armour, and you do too. However for years we relied on someone else to battle for us, and the armour disappeared from our sight. Since we have been relying on the unseen Lord and not the fortress to protect us, He has shown each one of us our armour again." Seeing Edan's mystified look, he continued. "There is more than just swords, you know. He has equipped us with enough armour to vanquish the Dragon every time. Now stop looking so puzzled and eat! We have to go back to the field, for tomorrow the unseen Lord will send us a little rain."

Edan began to eat. He felt his heart burning within him. He began to desire to see his own armour and then he realized that something had altered within himself. He believed his friends wholeheartedly, and with that belief came a renewed courage to embrace the call of the unseen Lord. He determined that he would join them in the fields. He would stay if they let him, to learn more from them.

Keelin was the first to rise from the table. She started gathering the bowls and spoons to help her mother with the dishes. Treasa, rising, took the water off the fire that was boiling in the large black pot. Cathaoir, Teague and Edan took one last drink of water as they left for the field. Edan pondered that Cathaoir had said it was going to rain, even though it had been dry for so long. He wanted to be here when it did.

~

Back at the fortress, unrest was growing among the pilgrims. The Dragon was spewing its lies and causing dissension everywhere. The guard found his days full of settling one dispute after another. If only he could get these pilgrims to understand how important it was to fix this dilapidated fortress! He would try to come up with another plan. Maybe his son could help him. Showing some devotion to the fortress wouldn't hurt him, that was for sure. His son it seemed to like the easy ride he had and took little responsibility for the pilgrims. If Carew was going to be a guard of a fortress someday, it was high time he made him get serious about his role in the fortress.

Getting up from his leather chair with a huff, the guard made his first resolution ~ Carew was going to stop all contact those mediators who had left Evergreen, for they were distracting him from his work at the fortress.

- 53 -

The Ancients say… "My heart is sore pained within me: and the terrors of death are fallen upon me."

Chapter 5

Gallagher ~ eager aide

Edan's brother, Gallagher, came to visit him at the farm. He was very sceptical of the things he'd heard about the pilgrim way. In fact, he himself had left the fortress as a young lad, when his parents did. Gallagher had not wanted anything to do with the unseen Lord or His kind. He loved living a wanton life, carefree and reckless. His parents had moved to the fortress of Evergreen just recently. The last few weeks had found him thinking of going back to fortress living just like his parents had. His life was costing too much ~ he could not make enough to carry on. He wanted more from life than the constant rush of his friends, drinking ale, and running with hard, wild women. Gallagher spent a couple of days at the farm and then carried on to the fortress. To the joy of his parents, their wayward son was home.

Arthmael also came back to the fortress, trying to keep his opinions to himself. He so loved the fortress dwellers, even though they often treated him with suspicion. He tried to help where he could, always finding some repair work to do on the old fortress.

One day he sat in the atrium, the only room in the whole fortress, except for the guard's quarters, that did not need any repair. The mortar in the walls of the atrium always seemed fresh and free of cracks. As Arthmael pondered these puzzling things he felt agitated, he heard the water beginning to boil and churn in the pool.

Running to the edge of the pool, he saw the Dragon pull its heavy body from the water and ascend the large staircase at the far end of the atrium. Arthmael followed slowly behind it, watching the beast turn and go through the wall into the guard's chambers. The guard emerged shortly after, slime dripping from his head, but he seemed not to care or was not even aware of it. He was dressed in a full suit of armour. He had received it when he had been trained for the guardship. The guard walked unsteadily, as the armour was heavy and he had not felt the need to wear it for a long time. He looked at Arthmael standing there and went by him quickly. Reaching out Arthmael grabbed his arm.

"Stop! The Dragon's drool is dripping off your head."

Yanking his arm back, the guard stared in disbelief at Arthmael.

"You are crazy! Do you think I care about your opinions. What utter foolishness! Dragon's drool ~ " the guard spat out.

"I'm not crazy," Arthmael's tone became calm. "I know very well that you have thought your mission is to glorify the fortress."

The guard's eyes narrowed and turned to hard steel as he said, "I have finally figured out how to get the people to give! I have been given the most incredible knowledge. I know that I can persuade them to help repair the walls. Now young man, stop your raving and let me get about my job!"

Arthmael stared after the guard. His heart felt like a heavy stone in his chest. The unseen Lord, laid his hand upon Arthmael's shoulder.

"Come my son. It is time to go. They do not believe that the Dragon dwells here. Come."

Arthmael turned to go, his heart breaking over the ignorance of the people.

"Oh, Lord, let me try one more time." The unseen Lord looked long and hard at this young man. He knew what the outcome would be if Arthmael stayed.

"If you stay, they will not believe you. They will do you harm. Are you ready for that? However," the Lord paused and then finished, "there will be some who will see the truth because of you."

Arthmael could feel the seriousness of the situation. The unseen Lord clasped him close, empowering him with the strength that only He could give. Arthmael felt the strength flowing into his heart from the presence of the One he could not see, and he nodded in answer. He drew his sword and walked cautiously down the stairs to the atrium below.

- 55 -

Arthmael could hear the guard encouraging the people to give as he descended the staircase. There was a stillness in the air as he made his way to the assembly hall. As Arthmael looked into the room, he was shocked to see the people taking handfuls of coins and laying them down at the guard's feet. The guard's lofty words were telling them about the need to unite and fix the walls together. He expounded on the reasoning that if the walls were repaired, the Dragon would not be able to gain entrance. Lifting his hand high, he told the people to not listen any longer to those from the outside who told them that the Dragon dwelt in their fortress. He let them know that the Dragon could not and would not enter their refuge ~ the unseen Lord would not allow it. The guard paused, and taking a deep breath, he went on with a magnificent tale of the great victory they would win by the sacrifice they were making.

Arthmael felt the power of the guard's words causing him to doubt that he had seen the Dragon. As the lecture went on Arthmael could feel the strength leaving him and self-doubt began to torment his soul. He was so absorbed in what he was listening to that he did not notice the Dragon come into the room from the back wall. It saw Arthmael in the door way with his sword drawn though it hung limp at his side. It snarled at him, jolting him out of his reverie, then it roared thunderously over the heads of the pilgrims. Sudden panic and fear gripped their hearts as they fled from its presence, fearing that a natural disaster was striking their beloved fortress. Though none saw the beast, its presence was all darkness and evil, and the fear of doom caused them not hear the pleas of the guard for them to remain calm.

The guard's armour was covered in slime as the Dragon spewed its drool on him. The guard became angry at the fleeing pilgrims, and his mind filled with disgust because they were such a weak-hearted lot. He felt a certainty that his Evergreen could withstand any natural disaster. Turning from them, he began to gather the money into a basket.

He heard the thudding of the Dragon as it walked up to the raised platform that he stood upon. Opening his mouth to scream, his eyes beheld the massive beast for the very first time. The monstrous creature was drooling and its slime pooled around the frightened guard and dripped off his head into his gaping mouth. Everything went into slow motion for Arthmael as he watched the guard fling the money at the beast. The golden coins slowly fell, one at a time, at the Dragon's feet. Beginning to suffocate in the slime, the guard dropped to his knees in front of the beast, and then fell headlong off the platform onto the floor. Arthmael ran from the room hearing the guard gurgling out his final breaths as the beast laughed, mocking the fallen man.

Panic spread throughout the fortress, as the pilgrims did not know what was happening ~ maybe an earthquake. They fled from the building. Arthmael saw the Dragon chasing after the fleeing pilgrims out the front doors. He lifted his sword and began to go after the Dragon when he heard the whimpering of children. In the alcove of the atrium there were some small children cowering. Compassion overruled Arthmael, stopping he spoke softly to them and took their hands leading them up the stairs away from all the terror. Tucking them into their little beds, he shushed them with a finger to his lips, kneeling down he waited. He knew that the Dragon could not see the unafraid. Arthmael reasoned that if the children were asleep, trusting in Arthmael, the beast would not see them.

The time went by slowly as Arthmael heard others screaming and fleeing from the beast. Evidently the Dragon had re-entered the fortress to find more prey to terrorize. Mass confusion was rampant, no one knew if it was an earthquake or what was happening ~ all they felt was terror and a need to find safety. The Dragon was glorying in its moment of full advantage, but it knew that Arthmael, one of those cursed mediators was about with the true sword of the unseen Lord. It could feel its old wound throbbing in pain as it neared the room where Arthmael was. Looking into the room, the Dragon could not see the children sleeping in their beds. Arthmael saw the Dragon look right through him and around the room. It withdrew its head and resumed the rampage throughout the fortress.

Arthmael, got up and left the room, taking one last look at his little friends asleep in their beds. How precious these children were.

It was worth it, he realized, even if one of these little ones remembered and saw the truth.

After some time, the people thought that the danger had left the fortress, but Arthmael saw that the Dragon was still there. The beast was going around, spitting its drool upon their unknowing heads, spreading its invisible lies like gangrene. The people began to assemble in the meadow outside, checking for casualties. The only one missing was the guard. Two men went in search of him and found his body in the grand assembly hall. They began to reason that it had simply been his time to go beyond the veil to the land of the unseen Lord, and that, it was because he was so faithful that he had been taken early. Carew held his mother and they both wept together, wondering how they would ever go on without their blessed husband and father.

Arthmael stood his heart breaking for them, but they turned a cold shoulder to him, poisoned by the Dragon's slimy lies about him. Dejected, he wandered back into the atrium where he could see the Dragon watching from the pool, a look of pure hatred and malice in its eyes. He knew that the people believed its lies, and his time was short. The people, in one accord, followed Arthmael into the atrium.

"Why are you here? Go away! This happened because of you! Nothing like this has ever happened before until you brought your lies here! We were never in danger until you came! We should have listened to the guard and kept you out. He did not trust you!"

Their shouted accusations drowned out Arthmael's pleas for them to listen. Gallagher stood in shock at the top of the stairs, watching as the crowd pushed Arthmael out the large front doors of the fortress. Carew was now leading the mob. Gallagher ran after them as they shoved and pushed Arthmael to the edge of the precipice by the side of the fortress.

Arthmael pleaded for them to stop, but they closed their ears to him and screamed, "You will die, and your lies about the Dragon residing with us will leave with you! You are its servant, not the servant of the unseen Lord."

With a final shove, Arthmael fell over the edge, calling out, "Forgive them, Lord!" ~ as he plunged to his death on the rocks below.

Gallagher ran to the edge of the precipice, and, seeing the mangled body of the young man below, he turned his wild eyes upon the crowd. Looking at him blankly, they turned to go back into the fortress. A great relief flooded their hearts now that they had finally dealt with the Dragon. Carew, sick in his heart, looked at his hands. He knew they were covered in innocent blood. Dropping his head, he pushed through the crowd, heading for his own chambers. Gallagher ran to the farm to get his brother Edan and Teague so they could retrieve Arthmael's body. In that instant, Gallagher knew that Arthmael had been right and that the Dragon truly did live in the fortress.

Arthmael had felt himself falling and, wondered why it was all happening. He didn't feel the impact of his body on the rocks. One moment he was falling, the next he was standing in grass that was knee deep. It was soft, and green ~ the grassland spread out before him in every direction. The waving of the grass looked like the waves on the ocean, and the sky was as blue as sapphires, and he could see two swans flying high overhead. He wondered where he was and what had happened. As he was pondering these things, he saw Him. In front of Arthmael, coming in long strides was the most magnificent warrior he had ever seen. The man was much taller than Arthmael and His armour glistened in the light. His face shone with regal brilliance. His close-cropped beard and the hair upon His head were as white as snow. Smiling broadly, He came close and Arthmael knew Him instantly, even though he had never seen Him before ~ it was the unseen Lord. The men embraced one another, and turning they disappeared.

A small band of pilgrims gathered in Cathaoir's cottage. The young men had returned with Arthmael's body on the wagon. Edan and Gallagher would take it to the river's Source, to Gilroy and his wife. Tears flowed as each one went over to the body and touched the young man they'd barely known in a heartfelt farewell gesture. Then, with swords raised and heads bowed, they knelt until the wagon was out of sight, knowing their days of visiting the fortress were over forever.

The Ancients say... "The words of his mouth were smoother than butter, but war was in his heart..."

Chapter 6

Caedmon had finished working at the stable for the day, and ran all the way home. He and his mother lived a short way out in the country in a very small fortress. Caedmon's boss liked him and gave him many chores because he had shown himself trustworthy to finish a job he had started. His boss was planning to train him to be a blacksmith.

The people of the fortress had been kind and took them in right away. It had been two years since he'd left the old place, but he still terribly missed Edan, and Carew, and his grandparents. Wynne had been changing for the better daily, even though she still did not understand the importance of seeking the unseen Lord's company on her own. Caedmon, on the other hand, used every spare minute to listen to the unseen Lord and find out what His desire was for him. He was maturing and growing in his devotion to the unseen Lord by the day. His quest to hear the unseen Lord seemed to be fulfilled.

Arriving at the fortress, Caedmon quickly ran to their rooms. Passing by his friends on the way, he did not stop to talk, but just waved a friendly greeting. When he got to their rooms on the second floor, the door was ajar. That was strange; his mother should have been at work at the mill. Cautiously approaching the door, he listened to see if anyone was inside.

The Dragon was watching from down the hall, its huge frame filling the space, but invisible to Caedmon. The beast's drool was dripping down on to the floor and running into the room like a stinking, green, wet blanket.

Caedmon heard voices coming from the inner room of their apartment.

"I thought you said the lad would not be a problem," a sinister voice muttered.

"Master, you know that I have done all I can to caution him to stop his communication with the unseen Lord," a whining voice replied. "Besides, he is very weak and small, insignificant really. No one would ever take him seriously."

"Shut your mouth! You are speaking foolishness. You don't know what you are talking about. It is his kind that causes the most trouble in the fortresses. Have you not heard of all the trouble the fortresses have had lately with the mediators on the rise again? Only this time, they are leaving their old fortresses and not building any new ones. In the other valley, one of the larger fortresses, called Evergreen, under our care has had several unexplained incidents. I believe it is directly linked to all this mediator interference. Did you find any evidence here of the lad being involved in something we could accuse him of? Does he have a vice of some sort?"

Caedmon sucked in his breath, *Evergreen* ~ his heart began to pound loudly.

"No, my master. He has a few manuscripts of the Ancients marked up, a few drawings, and very few clothes. On the other hand, his mother has a bottle of ale hidden under her cot over there by the window."

The other man sneered. "Well, we can expect that, can't we?"

Caedmon ran to the end of the hall and hid around the corner, his heart pounding. He peeked around the corner and saw the two men leaving the room. One of them was the guard, the other was a tall, distinguished-looking man. They walked down the long corridor. The Dragon smiled viciously at Caedmon, then turned and left with the men. Caedmon, squinting his eyes, was sure he saw a shadow following them.

He ran into his room, wondering why those men wanted him to stop talking with the unseen Lord. He'd had so many close times with the unseen Lord lately. It seemed that whenever Caedmon was out walking, he would feel His presence with him and they would talk. Though it was hard for him to hear the unseen Lord here in the fortress, Caedmon trusted that the guard was hearing for him.

- 62 -

The guard had encouraged him to hear for himself, but cautioned him to tell him everything the Lord had told him. It had made Caedmon feel so special when he'd heard the guard telling the people something that the unseen Lord Himself had shared with Caedmon. Caedmon never questioned the fact that his name was never mentioned. He knew that it must have been a very good thought, for the guard, in turn, to share it with everyone.

Who had the guard been talking to? He had to find out, but first, he would check his mother's cot. Could it be true? He had not smelled ale on his mother's breath in a very long time.

Caedmon's heart sank when he saw the flask under the corner of the cot. It was full, so she had not been taking any, but the fact that she had it there troubled him deeply. Putting it back, he left and headed for the main meeting hall to see if anyone was about. Entering into the grand assembly hall, he saw the guard talking to the man near the raised platform at the front of the room. Looking up and seeing him, the guard smiled and beckoned him to join them. Caedmon headed toward them hesitantly.

The guard smiled uncomfortably and greeted Caedmon, "Hello Caedmon."

The tall man smiled a strained smile. "So this is the young man you were telling me about."

"Yes, it is. Caedmon, this is the head guard of our fellowship of fortresses. He is very sensitive to the unseen Lord of the land."

"Pleased to meet you, sir," Caedmon tried to sound pleasant, but his heart was beating in his ears.

"So you think you hear from the unseen Lord of the land, do you? What kind of training have you had?" asked the man with a very stern look.

"I didn't know you needed training, sir. The unseen Lord never told me that," Caedmon answered.

"You have to be very careful, young man. You know, the Dragon has been known to whisper lies to our people, leading many astray. Without the protection of these walls, you could end up just like one of those so-called mediators. We know that most have them have left the fortresses completely and are out in the Dragon's lair.

My suggestion is this ~ that if you hear this voice calling you again, you are to come immediately to your guard. He will listen with you and let you know who is speaking to you." The man spoke in a condescending manner.

"But sir, it usually is when I am out walking in the evening and sometimes on my way home from my work. Very seldom does He speak to me here. Though it has happened a few times, when the Lord wanted me to be kind or help someone." Caedmon could feel the man's anger building and decided to appease him. He had learned to do that with his mother when she was in one of her dark moods.

"You are right though, and I will come to my guard immediately. I will ask the unseen Lord, when He goes to speak to me, if He could wait to talk to me until I get to the guard," Caedmon answered humbly.

"You are a smart young man," the tall stranger replied, "and I think you should consider taking training for the guard-ship. You have many qualities that would make you a good guard."

The man smiled at Caedmon, thinking to himself that this young man was very gullible, which would make him less of a threat than he had thought. Caedmon, on the other hand, felt like someone had stabbed him in the heart. *How can my talks with the unseen Lord have been wrong?* Those talks had helped him carry on when things were bad, and those talks had helped others many times. He decided that he would remain quiet for a while. How could he stop the Lord from coming to him? As he pondered this, he realized that he could not stop the unseen Lord ~ and that he did not want Him to stop, either.

Caedmon bade them farewell and walked slowly back to his own rooms, feeling sad and confused. The Dragon breathed out and its lies followed Caedmon, telling him he was no good. It began stirring the thoughts in his mind with one of its long talons, laughing cruelly.

Caedmon shook his head. He felt so confused. He wished with all his heart that he could go back to Evergreen. They understood him better. He knew that Carew's father, would never speak to

- 64 -

him like these men had. That night Caedmon lay in his bed for a long time, looking up at the ceiling, his heart longing for comfort and direction.

"Caedmon... I am sorry you had to find this out," the unseen Lord spoke gently to him, sitting on the edge of his bed and gently stroking his hair from his eyes.

"I know, Lord. Blindness to the truth is not protection ~ You have taught me that. What is the truth? Why do You allow these men to dictate who can hear from You?" Caedmon asked in exasperation.

"I do not, Caedmon. My people do! I still speak to whomever is brave of heart. And you, My son, have a brave heart."

"They think I am a fool. I could tell by their condescending smiles and the way they talked to me."

"Being innocent of evil, Caedmon, is many times thought to be foolishness or as some say, gullibility. You must learn not to put so much thought into what others think of you. They do not know you for who you are. Only the Great Creator, My Father and I really know you."

Just then, Wynne came quietly into the room. Caedmon wondered why she had to work so late at the mill again. She lit a small candle and began to slowly pull her things out from the cupboard and place them in a crate. She then reached under the bed and retrieved the flask, which she also put into the box. Caedmon watched as she packed all her belongings. Then, she walked over to his side of the room and began to pack his belongings into another crate. She was trying not to disturb him as she worked quietly and quickly.

"Mother, what are you doing?" Caedmon spoke loudly.

Letting out a scream of surprise she whirled around and, with eyes wide looked at him on his cot.

"Caedmon, don't you ever do that again! What does it look like? We are leaving tonight. I have met the most wonderful man from the neighbouring fortress. We have been seeing each other for a few weeks now. I didn't want to tell you until I knew for sure he was the one. I know that you have been so disappointed before, but he is a truly good man. And ~ he will be an excellent father for you."

- 65 -

Caedmon, who had heard this so many times before, felt the numbness of his heart. Still he tried to encourage her, for he had learned not to argue with his mother.

"Whatever you say mother. I trust you. However, why must we leave again? Are we moving to his fortress?"

"Well, no. We are moving to his home valley. It is far from here. Maybe you would want to go back home to our old village? To see your grandmother and your old friends? Just for a small while. Just until we find a place for us all to live."

It was exactly what Caedmon wanted to do. But what would happen to his mother? She was so weak and she depended on him so greatly. Then again, maybe this man really was a good man, and they would be fine without him. It would give them time to know one another and not have to worry about his welfare.

"I think that would be good, Mother, but how would we ever be able to afford for me to travel back to our old village?"

"Do you remember that old driver, Gilroy, the merchant?"

"Yes, I remember him. He was very kind to us."

"Well, I met him yesterday outside the mill and he was asking how you were doing. When I told him I was planning to be married, and that we would like some time to set up before we sent for you, he said he could give you a ride. He would make sure you would arrive home safely, or even stay with him and his wife in the mountains for a while if you wanted. He said that there is much work there for a strong, young man."

"It might be a good change," Caedmon admitted, reflecting back on the day he'd just had. "When do we leave? Not tonight, surely?"

"Yes, Caedmon, we have to leave tonight. I need to go, and Gilroy is leaving tonight for home. He said that he will make sure that you make it to Grandma's from his home."

The Dragon panicked when Caedmon disappeared. It had seen them leave, and before it could wake the Guard, they were gone out the back door. Caedmon had gone with one of those cursed mountain dwellers, a mediator. The moment he had gotten into the man's wagon he had disappeared from the Dragon's sight. The mother, on the other hand, had left with one of the Dragon's servants. The

- 66 -

Dragon laughed, knowing that the man would not be able to control his temper for long and that someone would be hurt.

Whirling and lifting its hulking frame, the beast flew out of the valley, back to Caedmon's homeland, hoping that this was where the young man was going. As it flew, it let drool spill over the land in a hideous canopy of green slime. In every home that the slime touched, people had nightmares and little children screamed in fright of the dark. Its dark army that had been posted throughout the land, raised howls of delight seeing their commander fly unhindered over their heads.

The Ancients say… "Awake, O north wind; and come, though south; blow upon my garden, that the spices thereof may flow out. Let my beloved come into his garden, and eat his pleasant fruits."

Chapter 7

Treva ~ prudent one

he night was long. Caedmon had fallen asleep on the small bed in the wagon. The rolling of the wheels on the road and the rocking motion had put him to sleep very quickly. It was a welcome relief from his stress, which had been so great with everything that happened that day. His sleep was fitful and he felt ill. Rolling over, he woke up, trying to grasp all that was happening. His life had been turned upside down suddenly, just when he thought things were going so well. He tried to go back to sleep, but his head would not stop thinking over the day he had just lived.

He could hear Gilroy quietly singing a song of thanksgiving to the unseen Lord. In his sleepy state, he thought that he heard the unseen Lord singing in return. A deep comfort came over his soul. He was safe for now. The harsh counsel of the head guard faded from his mind, and the sweet presence of the unseen Lord stilled his soul.

The sun was breaking over the mountains when Caedmon fully awakened. He was surprised that they were stopped. Pulling himself up, he looked out the back of the covered wagon. The sun was sending warm morning rays upon his face. Smelling the wood smoke of a campfire and fish frying, his stomach rumbled and he realized he was starving. The fish smelled so good!

Crawling out of the wagon, Caedmon stretched and walked over to Gilroy who was busy watching his fish cook and keeping the fire going.

"That smells good," Caedmon said in greeting as he looked at the surroundings. That was when he realized they were high in the mountains, he could see the winding road they had come up and the valley far below. The view was breathtaking, he had never been in the mountains before and he felt like he wanted to run and do a flip or maybe even walk on his hands. He laughed to himself. He hadn't thought or felt that way since he was a child winning one of his imaginary battles with a dragon.

"You are in a fine mood this morning Caedmon. You slept well?" Gilroy asked.

"Yes, I finally fell into a deep sleep and didn't even feel the wagon stop."

Caedmon took a seat on a rock beside Gilroy, telling him everything that had happened since they had last met. Gilroy was silent as he listened to every detail. His heart hurt as Caedmon shared the incident about the head guard and their conversation. He was so young to have made this discovery. Gilroy kept silent and nodded slowly, knowing that it must be in the unseen Lord's plan for this special young man.

Caedmon tried to be gracious and even made excuses first for his mother and then for the guards. He just couldn't bring himself to lay the blame on others; he was used to taking it himself. This, though, was difficult because he really did not know what he had done wrong.

The morning passed and Caedmon noticed that Gilroy did not seem to be in a hurry to get on his way. He was probably very tired from the long night's drive. Caedmon, relaxing when he saw that there was no rush, began hesitantly to tell Gilroy of his life. When he saw that Gilroy was thoughtful and no look of harsh judgment had come over his face, he told him everything. He felt a burden that was like a heavy stone on his back slowly roll off. He cried when he shared how his heart felt numb towards his mother. Gilroy gently patted his back. Then, looking at Caedmon tenderly, nodded. His own heart was hurting too much to trust himself to speak.

"You know, Gilroy, you are the only one I have ever told about my mother. I guess it's because I know that you are talking to the unseen Lord all the time. He would not let you think evil of her."

"Oh, Caedmon. The unseen Lord does not stop me from thinking evil. I can really do and think what I want you know, my relationship with the unseen Lord is not based on my being good all the time. But because I love Him and want His purposes for my life, I try to keep my heart clean before Him. Do you understand that?"

Caedmon pondered this truth for a long time as they cleaned up from their breakfast and packed their things in the wagon. Gilroy went to get the horses that were tied in the tall grass. Leading them to the river to drink, Caedmon followed and wondered why the Lord couldn't ~ or wouldn't ~ make people be good; it would be so much easier if He did.

Caedmon loved Gilroy already and felt a oneness with him, like he had felt with no other person before, except maybe his grandfather at times.

The river tumbled down the mountain side. It was much wider than the Unchanging River, but it looked pure and good to drink. Caedmon leaned down and cupped the water into his hand to drink. It tasted refreshing, though not like the water from the Unchanging River. He looked at Gilroy, who was gently stroking one of his horses while it drank. He was smiling at the animal.

They are fine looking beasts, that is for certain, Caedmon thought. Their black coats shimmered in the morning sun. He had never seen as fine a team the whole time he worked at the stables. Returning to the wagon, they hitched up the team and started on their journey again. Gilroy had informed Caedmon that they were just about home and would be there by early afternoon.

Caedmon felt a nervous tremor run through him. He knew that if anyone from the fortress found out he had gone to the village at the river's Source, he would be ridiculed and censored even more. Shaking off the unwanted feeling, which he was used to doing, he began to look forward to meeting more people like Gilroy.

"Will your wife and children mind me coming home with you?" Caedmon asked hesitantly.

"Well, Caedmon, my wife is always prepared for company; it is what we do as servants of the unseen Lord. We never had any children of our own. Years ago we finally knew that the day of our having our own children was over." Gilroy became sombre and continued, "But, the Lord has been faithful to bring us many like yourself who needed us to look after them for a season, and they have become like our own. So don't be surprised if my darling, Treva, smothers you a little with her mothering."

"I don't think I would mind a bit," said a very happy Caedmon. "I will try to be a good help so she isn't burdened with the extra work I will cause."

"Well, I don't think you'll be any burden whatsoever, but Treva will enjoy your help. She likes work. However, she likes help even more," Gilroy chuckled, as he could just imagine his wife with her hand on her hip, scolding him for not hanging his coat on the hook.

The wagon came out through the trees and they saw a new valley stretch out in front of them as they reached the summit. Caedmon could see the beautiful Unchanging River off to his right, coming down through the mountain pass. Far below, it wound its way through the valley's farmland. What a different perspective looking from above gave him!

Instead of the villages being built on the river, they were far back from it. Even from here he could see the man made aqueducts, like silver threads going from the river to the villages. He remembered what Gilroy had told him about the water and pondered why the people had done it. Caedmon squinted his eyes and saw his village in the distance. He was almost home, and his heart lifted in thanksgiving to the unseen Lord.

The road wound along the top of the high ridge. The trees were sparse on the one side but dense and tall on the other. The wind blowing through the tall firs sounded like a sad song being played upon a lyre, and intertwined with this background wailing was the chirping of birds as their melodious happy songs blended beautifully. Caedmon thought about how life was like that ~ joy and sorrow ~ harmonizing together to make one song. He loved the joyous times, but even for one so young, he knew that it had been in the times of sorrow that he had come closer to the unseen Lord.

Soon Caedmon smelled wood smoke and knew they must be coming close to the village. He was not prepared for what he saw next. The small cottages were nestled in a grove, and tall trees were scattered throughout the whole village. Small barns and outbuildings were nestled beside each cottage. Beautiful mountain flowers were planted along the paths leading to the front doors of the homes, and small white pebbles had been placed on them, making the paths look like ribbons. Lovely gardens were growing in the yards, which were fenced in with sticks to keep the deer from eating the vegetables.

"We're home," Gilroy said. "These are the dwellings of the mediators."

Caedmon stared all around himself as they drove down the main lane into the heart of the settlement. People out in the gardens or walking along the road stopped and waved, calling greetings to Gilroy. Entering the centre of the settlement, Caedmon was spellbound. Out of the ground bubbled a fountain of water. The water wound its way through the other side of the village in a stream. As they came closer, he could hear the water gurgling and splashing up out of the ground. Gilroy stopped the wagon.

"Yes, it is the Source of the Unchanging River. Breathtaking isn't it?" Gilroy asked quietly.

"I don't know what to say; it is beautiful."

Caedmon spoke at last, "look at all the colours hovering over it, like a million rainbows all around the water spray. And the flowers ~ oh, they are beautiful. I have never seen so many colours."

"Oh, look..." Caedmon pointed to the far end of the fountain. "There is a deer, drinking with her fawn, right here in the village."

"Yes, the wildlife love this river. They know their Creator made it for them as well," Gilroy told him. "Years ago this was a mighty artesian well, and the water roared into a large river. However, now it is only small. We are asking the unseen Lord to return it to its former glory."

Gilroy clucked to his horses, drove past the Source, and turned down a side lane. They stopped in front of a small cottage made of logs with a thatch roof. Smoke was coming from the chimney in the centre of the home. One of the horses tossed his head impatiently, stomping his foot. He did not want to stop, but go straight to the barn. He knew he was nearly home. Gilroy let Caedmon get down from the wagon. He handed down his crate of belongings and told him he would meet him in the cottage. Then he drove the team further down the lane to the barn. The horses, picking up speed, thinking of their well-deserved rest and feed waiting for them.

Caedmon knocked nervously on the front door. He noticed an inviting bench along the outside wall under the covered porch area. A straw broom was leaning beside the door, and a large black cat was curled up on a rug beside it. The cat lifted his head sleepily to look at Caedmon and then put it back down to resume his nap. Caedmon was waiting patiently at the door when he heard footsteps coming up behind him. Turning around, he saw a petite woman with a broad smile on her face.

She came up to him and offered her hand. "Hello there, my name is Treva. May I help you?"

Caedmon shook her hand and then nervously stammered out. "My name is Caedmon. Gilroy brought me home with him."

"Well, bless my heart. Yes, yes. He's told me of you!" Treva swept by him and opened the door. "Come on in, I have everything ready for you."

"You knew I was coming? How?" Caedmon asked incredulously.

Treva showed him into the small but cozy sitting room.

"Here, let me take your things and put them in your room. Gilroy will be in shortly. I have to finish the meal preparations," Treva told him.

Halfway through the door, she turned back to face him. "Oh, you asked how we knew. The unseen Lord told us that you would be coming to us, and that we were to prepare for you."

With that, Treva left the room. Caedmon could hear her bustling about the kitchen. He sat on the edge of a handmade wooden chair, near the huge stone fireplace. Feelings of peace washed over his soul. He was safe. He was home.

The Ancients say... "Greater love hath no man than this, that a man lay down his life for his friends."

Chapter 8

Many days passed and Caedmon soon fell into the routine of his new home. Their day started very early, before the sun had even peaked above the horizon. Each had their chores to do before breakfast. Caedmon was given the job of cleaning out the barn, and then bringing in the wood that Gilroy had split for Treva's cooking fire. Treva busied herself preparing the dough for bread and cooking the ham for breakfast. Caedmon loved to hear Treva singing while she worked around their cozy cottage.

Caedmon grew strong and healthy in the mountain air. Drinking daily of the water from the Source, he felt himself being restored. What a joy it was to hear from the unseen Lord daily and to hear of what He had spoken to others in the village. Everyone here seemed to hear for themselves, and couldn't wait to share what they had heard with others. Neighbours visited every day with each other over a meal, or as they worked together. Several times now the other young men had come over, helping Caedmon with his chores. They had even invited him to go fishing and hunting with them. Caedmon had gone, but he did not like to leave Gilroy and Treva for too long a time. He just couldn't get enough of their home life.

One morning after breakfast was done, Gilroy, who had been quiet and withdrawn, got up and walked into the sitting room. Caedmon did not know what to do. He looked imploringly at Treva, who was wiping an unbidden tear from her eye. She nodded her head to Caedmon and gestured with her hand for him to follow Gilroy. Coming into the sitting room, Caedmon stopped. Gilroy was sitting, and across his lap lay a beautiful walking stick. He was gently stroking it. His eyes were wet with tears, and his lips were moving silently.

"Are you all right, Gilroy?" Caedmon asked tenderly.

Gilroy patted the chair next to his own, inviting Caedmon to sit with him. He again gently stroked the walking stick. He was staring across the room, but his eyes were looking somewhere far away. Caedmon sat down on the seat next to him and waited, wondering about the walking stick. Gilroy gently laid the stick into Caedmon's hands. Caedmon examined the beautiful carved handle, a magnificent lion's head, the wood had been rubbed until it shone. The gnarled and irregular shape gave it even more beauty.

"Arthmael made this for me. He hand carved it himself. He was in training to be a carver. We have many carvers here; you have met some. That is why I travel so much ~ I am their merchant. I take their wares to the villages in the valleys and in return, I either get money or goods for them."

"Arthmael?" Caedmon asked, wondering who he was.

"We have not spoken of him to you yet, for our hearts are still not entirely whole concerning him. He lived with us like a son from the time he was a toddler until a year ago. He was a good boy, and he brought much joy into our home. He could hear the unseen Lord plainly," Gilroy paused.

Then he called, "Treva! Could you come in here, please? I think the Lord wants us to tell, Caedmon, Arthmael's story."

Treva came into the room, wiping her hands on the dish towel she was carrying. She had known that this day would come. She had wanted it to come quickly, but on the other hand she did not want it to come at all. There would be fresh pain in the telling. She knew that Caedmon needed to hear it, as he, like Arthmael, needed to learn to trust what others were hearing from the unseen Lord. Taking a seat across from the men, she waited for Gilroy to start.

The morning hours passed as they recounted story after story of their little Arthmael. He had come to them as a toddler, an abandoned child. His mother and father had had their wagon axle break on the road past the settlement, and had come to them for help. They were poor and were trying to get to the next valley to find work, they said. Gilroy and some of the other men had helped them fix the wagon and stocked them with provisions for their journey ahead. They had stayed with them for several days. Treva had looked after Arthmael while his mother rested; she seemed worn out for one so young.

One morning when they got up, the couple was gone but Arthmael was still in his little bed. There was a note in poor handwriting that said they could not look after the child like Gilroy and his wife could, so they were leaving him with them to raise. They never heard from Arthmael's birth parents again, even though Gilroy had looked for them on his merchant trips and asked about them in every village he passed. With time, Arthmael became so much like their own child that even the neighbours forgot where he had come from.

When Arthmael became a young man, not much older than Caedmon, he started to ask questions about other people that knew of the unseen Lord. Gilroy and his wife shared freely with him of the fortress dwellers in the valleys and about how those people believed deeply in the unseen Lord, but did not pursue Him on their own. They told him about how these people waited for the guards of their fortresses to do that for them. This broke Arthmael's heart because he could not believe that anyone would not want to pursue the Lord on their own. He became increasingly intrigued by the fortress dwellers. That was when they started to realize that he was considering moving to one of the fortresses.

Arthmael eventually did just that. He had such a desire to share the relationship he had with the unseen Lord. Treva and Gilroy had warned him of the Dragon, and of how it lived in the fortresses. At this point in the story, Caedmon gasped. Surely, this could not be true.

"Yes, Caedmon, it is true, and if you were honest with yourself, you would see its effects on the people there," Gilroy said, his voice filled with sadness.

Caedmon tried to be honest with himself, but found it too difficult at the moment. *The Dragon in the fortress, lying to people, devouring them with its evil? Impossible!* Nonetheless, he was also aware of the same problem that Arthmael had seen ~ the people who lived in the fortresses were content with the guard hearing from the unseen Lord for them.

"Some of what you say is true, but I find it difficult to believe that the Dragon has access to the fortresses. That was what they were built for, wasn't it? To keep the Dragon out?"

"Well, not exactly," Treva replied. "The fortresses were built so that the people would not go astray on their own, but stay subject to one another. They were afraid that if they let the people stay on their own, they would fall into deception. So they built the fortresses to keep the people inside. They took them off of the land, the very land the unseen Lord is lord of. In reality, their fear of deception and of being led astray opened the door for the Dragon to dwell with them, for it thrives on fear and lies."

This was too much for Caedmon to swallow all in one sitting, but his curiosity over their adopted son won out over his own contrary thoughts.

"Please go on. What happened to your son?"

They went on to tell Caedmon of how Arthmael would visit the large fortress in the valley, stay awhile and then come home for a time of refreshing. Arthmael really felt he had something to offer them ~ a gift to share with them.

Caedmon interrupted. "His carving, you mean?"

"Oh, no. His gift that he'd received from the unseen Lord ~ his ability to see the Dragon," said Treva.

"Not always, mind you," Gilroy added. "Only when the unseen Lord saw that it was necessary for him to see it, to protect himself and others. He was very careful with this gift. Discreet would be the right word. Wouldn't it be, Treva?" Gilroy asked.

"Yes, he was discreet about it. No one really knew about it outside of our small village, but the unseen Lord had used him many times to rescue those in the valley from the Dragon's lies. He was a great mediator for the people, though many never knew it."

They picked up the tale again, telling of how their son felt drawn to the large pool in one of the fortresses named Evergreen. Caedmon jerked inwardly but kept his composure as he continued to listen to the story. Gilroy told that this was where his problems

- 78 -

began, he had seen the Dragon in the pool, so he watched it to see what it was doing there in the fortress. Arthmael would hide in the large atrium where the pool was and watch the beast slither out of the water, spewing its green slimy lies onto the people. The Dragon whispered to them that their building needed much repair, and if it was not fixed, they would not persuade anyone to join them. That the people of the outside would only want to come to a place that was extraordinarily beautiful. They had no idea it was the Dragon twisting their thoughts. It would tell the guard that if he raised enough money to fix the fortress, they would be able to keep the Dragon's influence out.

The guard, who everybody thought to be a gentle, good man, tried everything to persuade the people to give and give. However, the Dragon whispered to him that it was never enough. The people became tired of it and the old guard was becoming increasingly frustrated with the people's excuses.

Arthmael tried to warn this guard. He told the people that he saw the Dragon come out of the pool. No one believed him. They told him he was being a lunatic and to go back where he had come from. That was the last time his parents had seen Arthmael. He stayed home with them for a few weeks, and then six months ago, he had gone back to the fortress.

Caedmon watched as they struggled to go on. He gently laid his hand over Gilroy's. His own heart was breaking, for he knew that it was his beloved fortress they were talking about. Shuddering, he remembered the shadow he himself had seen in the murky green depths of the pool.

Gilroy began to speak again, bringing Caedmon out of his own memories.

"Two weeks after he left, we heard about our son from Edan, a young friend of mine in that village."

"You know Edan? He was my truest friend! This is amazing. Does he come here?" Caedmon interrupted with joy.

"Yes, him and his brother, they come often," Gilroy answered. "They started coming after..." Gilroy trailed off, unable to finish.

Treva picked up the story. She told Caedmon of how the guard had become so covered in slime from the Dragon, it easily drowned him. Then the Dragon had chased the people with wild fears of disaster. The whole fortress fell into an uproar as they fled outside. They knew something awful was going to happen to their fortress. Arthmael had saved some children from the lies of the Dragon as it roamed at will throughout the fortress, spitting lies on whoever was in its way. Several times the beast tried to get Arthmael, but the unseen Lord blinded it from seeing him.

Arthmael had the children crawl into their little beds and pretend they were sleeping, then he knelt down to talk to the unseen Lord. The Dragon stuck its head through the door, but it was as if it couldn't see him. The beast went on its way causing fear and lies to spread like a disease throughout the fortress. The Dragon whispered to the people the need for someone to be sacrificed ~ to be ridden of. If they cleansed their midst of someone who had an evil presence then it would leave them alone. Its lies convinced them, that it was better for one to be disposed of than for them all to die. It infested them with its slime concerning Arthmael.

Caedmon leaned ahead on his seat, listening attentively as Treva continued on with their sad story.

"They would not listen to Arthmael's pleas for they hardened their hearts to the truth. 'You should have listened to the guard and left our fortress,' they shouted at him, along with many other unfounded accusations," Treva took a shaky breath. "Then they pushed him over the precipice to his death."

She lowered her head. Silent tears ran down her cheeks, and she felt exhausted. Looking up at Caedmon she whispered, "Gallagher was there. He witnessed it all and said the last thing he heard Arthmael cry was 'Forgive them, Lord'."

Caedmon rose from his chair and, walking over to Treva, he knelt down and held her tight. She sobbed onto his shoulder, clinging to him.

Gilroy spoke gently to Caedmon. "Edan and Gallagher have left the fortress, along with several other families. They had not believed the Dragon, but had believed Arthmael. We meet with them whenever we can, to encourage them to continue on with their walk with the unseen Lord and not be bitter. The mediators were told specifically that they were to desist from hearing from the unseen Lord, and to report everything to the new guard. So they have left the fortress, and now they gather and mediate in their homes and encourage one another."

Caedmon rose. Walking over to Gilroy, he decided that he needed to be honest. "I, too, saw a shadow in the pool. However, I thought it was just an illusion from the light in the water."

Reaching out his hand, Gilroy grasped Caedmon's hand and pulled himself up. He put his strong hands, on Caedmon's shoulders. Looking Caedmon straight in the eye, he spoke sternly to him.

"Arthmael had been warned not to go back. Several had told him that it was of no use. They had heard it from the unseen Lord Himself. However, he would not believe them. His own heart was so caught up in his compassion for them. He believed that his compassion could break down any barrier. Caedmon, I am now telling you too, be careful, for it seems that you have the same gift as Arthmael. Don't go unless you know for sure that it is the unseen Lord, and not your own heart's desire leading you. Promise me this?"

Caedmon looked long into Gilroy's eyes. The intensity he saw there scared him. This was real. The Dragon was real; he knew it to be true but hadn't known it at the same time.

Swallowing the lump that had formed in his throat, he spoke with firmness, "I promise you."

~

Shylah ran into Treasa's home, completely out of breath. Treasa looked up from the tunic of Cathaoir's that she was mending. Startled speechless by Shylah's wild look and breathlessness, she waited for her to speak.

"I have heard the most incredible news! Caedmon is at the Source. He has come back! Edan was up there and saw him. Not only is he living with Gilroy and Treva, he is growing in his gift. He doesn't even realize that he is one of the answers to our mediating."

Both women began to cry, then laugh, hugging each other. They knew that all their mediating had been worth it.

The Ancients say… "Let me see thy countenance, let me hear thy voice; for sweet is thy voice, and thy countenance comely."

 Chapter 9

Seanna ~ God's grace

Keelin strolled along the road from the village with Seanna, her best friend, beside her. Keelin had not seen her since she'd left the fortress. However, they had run into each other that very day in the market, where Keelin had taken some of their butter and eggs to peddle. Seanna had been overjoyed to see her. After Arthmael's death, she too had left the fortress, but Keelin had not known it. Seanna asked if she could come to the farm and stay for a few days, as her mother and father were busy moving into a new flat in the village. Keelin was thrilled. She had been so lonely for friends, specifically girls. All she had lately for company were Teague's friends and it was not the same.

"Is your brother still at home, Keelin?" Seanna asked nonchalantly.

"Yes, he is, and so is his good friend Edan and his brother, Gallagher. Though I must say, those two do a lot of fighting. Mom and Da are always having to break them up, but they are gradually learning to be at peace," Keelin added with a giggle.

"Do you like them?" Seanna teased.

"Not on your life! Well, not that way, anyway. They're all right as friends, but I must say they are a little too energetic for me!" Keelin giggled again as she spoke.

She then stopped on the road and looked at her friend, "Are you interested in one of them?"

"Oh no! I knew them in the fortress, remember? No, just curious, that is all. Has Teague made any other friends?" Seanna asked, trying to sound conversational.

"Oh yes, he has girl friends all over the valley. He brings home at least two a week to introduce to the family." Keelin watched out of the corner of her eye for Seanna's reaction. Seanna stopped in shock, her mouth dropping open, trying to sputter out a response.

Keelin began to laugh until the tears flowed. "I am just teasing, Seanna. Teague hasn't been looking at anyone, and he has made no special attachments. Relax, he might still think you are pretty. He told me that once!"

Seanna stormed ahead down the road, her pride injured. She thought she had not shown any partiality, and to be so easily read was horrible. Keelin caught up and matched her fast pace down the road.

"Boy, we sure will be home quick at this pace. We might even beat the men in from the field. That should leave us plenty of time to pretty up for them..." Keelin spoke with a tone of seriousness and then, broke out in hilarious laughter again.

"Keelin! Stop it! All right, I was interested in Teague, but that was a long time ago and he probably thinks of me as only a child. As the friend of his sister...though I must say that is questionable at the moment." She gave a sideways smile. "Besides, since the fortress incident, everyone has changed," Seanna slowed her pace as she spoke.

"Yes, it was awful, all the accusations and everything. No one wanting to take responsibility for the *incident*. Arthmael was so kind. He would sit and talk to the children. He had no airs at all. He seemed to love everyone the same," Keelin said quietly. "And his father is so kind, too. He has come by the farm many times, but we haven't seen him for a while now. Did you know that Edan has been to the Source, and he saw Caedmon there? Do you remember him?"

"Yes, I do. We were good friends once. Well, isn't that wonderful? I wonder if he is moving back to the village. He was a good friend of Teague's once, wasn't he?" Seanna caught a grin spreading onto her friend's face at another mention of Teague. "Get that look off your face, Keelin," Seanna said as she chased the fast-footed, squealing Keelin up the road to the farm.

- 84 -

The girls arrived just in time to help Treasa get the evening meal on the table. Treasa hugged Seanna. She was so glad that Keelin had her friend back. She knew how lonely she had been lately.

Seanna had grown into a beautiful young woman. Her long, light brown hair hung loose down her back in waves. Her peaches-and-cream complexion glowed with anticipation. Even Treasa could see the girlish blush on her face whenever Teague was mentioned. Seanna's blue eyes sparkled with mirth over Keelin's non-stop teasing. Keelin did promise she would not do it when the men came in the cottage.

Heavy footsteps were heard on the threshold and the women quickly dished up the boiled potatoes and forked the pan-fried meat into earthen bowls. The large pot of greens was drained and put onto the table. Thick slices of fresh bread were stacked on the table. Seanna had not seen such a bountiful meal in a long time. They did not cook as much in the village as for those who worked hard in the fields.

Cathaoir was first in, coming over and kissing Treasa and then sitting down at the table, his face scrubbed red from a fresh wash in the cold well water. Then Edan and Teague came in, and they too red from their wash. Gallagher had gone to the Source. Everyone knew that he was interested in someone up there, but he would only blush when questioned about his frequent visits.

The men all sat down at the table and bowed their heads, preparing for the mealtime prayer. The women folk joined them, and, that was when Cathaoir noticed Seanna, who sat down beside him.

"Oh my dear, Seanna! It is so good to see you! How are your father and mother doing?" he asked.

Teague's bowed head jerked up in surprise and there she sat ~ one of the most beautiful young girls he had ever seen. The Seanna he used to see playing with his sister had grown into a beautiful young woman.

"It is good to see you too, sir. My father and mother are doing well. Father has been very busy with his carpentry, and mother has been looking after my nephew alot for my brother and his wife," Seanna said before she took a small glance in Teague's direction. He

- 85 -

was staring at her with his mouth slightly open. She quickly lowered her gaze, her face turning crimson. Teague stared on until his father coughed loudly, looking pointedly at his son. Teague, embarrassed, dropped his head, but not before he had heard Keelin giggle. He kicked her under the table but misjudged, and kicked Edan.

"What are you kicking me for? I was not the one staring!" Edan said with a laugh. At that, both Edan and Keelin began to laugh until Treasa gave them a withering look.

Cathaoir, after they had hushed, began to offer thanks for the bountiful meal to the unseen Lord, and to also thank Him for their guest. Seanna breathed a sigh of relief as the meal went on without a further incident, though she found her appetite had fled. Teague, on the other hand had become ravenous and kept eating. Edan and Keelin were enjoying it all too much, and Treasa asked them to clear the table for her and start the dishes. Seanna said she would help, but Treasa insisted that she need not, as the other two seemed to have energy to waste.

Teague got up from the table and darted out the back door, his mind in a whirl. *I'm a fool*, he thought. He wondered why he hadn't said something to her. She had always been a nice girl. Why did his heart have to race so? Seanna followed Treasa into the small sitting room and sat in front of the fire. All the while she could hear Keelin and Edan laughing over nothing.

"So Seanna, do you still attend the fortress?" Treasa asked.

"No. Not since Arthmael died. Mother left too, and you know that father is not a pilgrim," Seanna said sadly.

"Well, not yet, anyway. It must have been hard for that last while at the fortress, with the accusations flying. I had already left before all that. I went very seldom after I saw the shadow of the Dragon in the pool at the fortress. Shylah and I have enjoyed talking and mediating together, but we both get lonely for more pilgrims at times," Treasa responded with a dreamy look upon her face.

"It was hard," Seanna agreed. "I felt so torn. I love the people in the fortress, and at the time I had thought it was the way things should be. That has all changed now. I wish it could be like when the Ancients walked the earth, right after the unseen Lord had come back from the dead," Seanna said wistfully.

"Well, I honestly believe that what you've just described is the unseen Lord's plan and that He is working on it now. He has to get that *fortress mentality* out of our minds," Treasa said emphatically.

"Oh, wouldn't that be lovely? I so hope that you are right. I have started to hear from Him myself again. He actually told me that I would come here with Keelin," Seanna added wistfully.

The evening waned on, and finally Teague reappeared to say a brief goodnight before heading towards the loft. Seanna and Keelin stole away to Keelin's room to talk.

The Dragon lurked outside the cottage, wondering how it had lost so many in such a short time. It would have to be more subtle in its attack on these mediating pilgrims. The beast left the farm, flying low over the land, knowing that it had to make its circuit to the many fortresses that night. The fortress dwellers everywhere were getting restless and becoming more aware that something was amiss in their midst.

What they need is something new to unite them, the Dragon thought. *It has to be something that they all fear.* Fear of something has the power to draw people together to fight whatever they fear. The beast would get them back on its side.

The Ancients say... "Take unto you the whole armour of the Lord, that ye may be able to withstand in the evil day, and having done all, to stand."

Chapter 10

Driscoll ~ interpreter

Caedmon, wandering down the forest lane to the river, was feeling more secure than he had felt in his entire life. These people had welcomed him in, making him feel like one of their family. He had felt the unseen Lord every day since he'd come to the Source. He had even spent a whole afternoon with Edan when he had come up for a visit.

However, Caedmon couldn't hide the sadness when people would ask about his mother and his home. He would freeze up inside, terrified that they'd find out the truth. Remembering his days in the fortress, Caedmon thought of how the people would look at him with concern and then whisper behind his back about his mother. He had hated it.

Gilroy had seen Caedmon leave to go to the river again. He had been with them for three months now, but his guard was still up, and Gilroy could see that there was doubt in his heart. Gilroy had talked to his wife and she had recommended giving him time to adjust to their way of life. However, he knew that Caedmon would be leaving soon ~ he had already mentioned several times that he would like to go to his old village soon to see his grandmother. There was no time to waste.

"Shall I talk to him, Lord?" Gilroy asked humbly.

Gilroy's heart stirred within him and he started down the path to the river. In his hand he held his canteen to fill while he was there. Coming through the trees to the shoreline, he saw Caedmon sitting on a large rock, dangling his feet in the river and singing. Gilroy stopped and listened. He hadn't known that the lad had the gift of song. He was stirred by the melody and the few words that he heard over the rushing of the stream.

Caedmon, feeling someone watching him, turned and saw Gilroy approaching. He quickly drew his feet out of the water and replaced his shoes. Gilroy pulled himself onto the large rock beside Caedmon. Taking off his own shoes, he put his feet into the water while Caedmon stared.

"You mean it is all right to do this?" Caedmon asked.

"Why not? It is our feet that need the most cleansing, because it is our feet that touches this land. The Lord didn't create this river to be worshipped, but to let it cleanse and restore us. This water is for us to use, Caedmon, for our needs and the needs of others. Do not be ashamed that I saw you. If the unseen Lord did not convict your heart that you shouldn't do it, why should I? Besides, I always come here to wash my feet when I come home from an adventure the Lord has sent me on."

Caedmon sighed and said, "There is so much I don't know ~ so much more for me to learn here. It has been good here with you, but I feel I need to go to my grandmother's, and I'd like to see some of the old friends I left behind there."

"I know," Gilroy acknowledged. "Your grandmother has heard you are here. She had been sending out inquiries for information on who I am and where I live. Evidently your mother had sent her word that you were with me. So, I sent her word through Driscoll ~ you know my neighbour ~ that you will be there soon. One of your friends will be coming all the way up the mountain path to meet you, his family is friends with Driscoll. The unseen Lord told Driscoll to tell the young man that you would be coming down the walking path from the river's Source in three days. That was a day ago as he has just arrived back. His name is Teague. Do you know him?"

"Oh yes! He was a close friend at one time. It will be wonderful to see him." He paused. "It makes me remember the other people I have missed all these years. Oh Gilroy, now my heart trembles! I want to go and be with them, but ~ I don't want to leave here." Trepidation entered Caedmon's voice as he spoke.

"I understand fully," Gilroy compassionately replied. "And we, too, don't want you to leave. Though, we must trust that the unseen Lord knows you are ready to leave us. Remember this will always be your home!"

Gilroy looked out across the river and seemed lost in thought. Each enjoying the silent comradeship they shared.

"Caedmon, I need to talk to you and I want to say some things that I believe are truth. I don't want to hurt you in any way ~ you have become like a son to me. As you know, my wife and I have never had children of our own. The unseen Lord has brought many into our lives that needed us. You, like Arthmael, have become like our own."

Gilroy paused and looked Caedmon in the eyes ~ how clear his eyes had become these last months in the village with them. The walls were coming down, and even now he saw no guardedness or apprehension enter Caedmon's eyes.

"Caedmon, first of all, do you know about the unseen armour that the Lord gives?"

"I think I have heard of it. I was told that it could only be given to you if you entered the guardship training."

Gilroy pulled his feet out of the water and stretched his legs out on the rock to let them dry in the sun. It was going to be a very hot day. He quietly asked the Lord to present Himself to them and make the things he was about to share clear to Caedmon.

"When the unseen Lord of the land first came, He came as one of us. We could see Him. He came to show us the way to His Father and what He wanted of us. His Father being the great creator of our land. However the Dragon stirred up the people against Him, even though He never caused anyone harm. Though, I must say, He did not lie or pet the people's ego either. This infuriated some of the leaders of the land. Who, unbeknown to them, had been trained by the Dragon to walk in pride and self-importance."

"Anyway, I know you have heard this, but it bears repeating, the day came when the great battle began. The Dragon had stirred the leaders against the Lord." Gilroy dropped his head in shame. "We know that the Lord was all alone in His battle, and it appeared that

- 90 -

the Dragon had won when the battle was over. The leaders had murdered the Lord. His followers went into hiding for fear they would be next."

"His people were afraid, and in terrible shock, and mourning even though the Lord said He would return to them. Who had ever come back from the dead? Let alone when one's body was mutilated beyond description. However, He did return and many saw Him and rejoiced greatly. During the time the people were grieving over His death, He had actually been in an unseen battle with the Dragon. He took the Dragon's power to kill, and wounded it on the head, which we know made it powerless to those who won't believe its lies. He then proved His power over the Dragon by rising from the unseen place of the dead and came back, but He was invisible to most. He went to His Father to make a new place for those that would follow Him later."

As Gilroy told the story that Caedmon had heard many times before, his heart filled with joy. How he loved his unseen Lord and what He had done for them! Gilroy smiled at him and continued.

"He made the river for them to drink from and be refreshed in the spirit, with strength and patience to wait for Him. He visits personally whenever we call upon Him or even when our heart goes to Him in a silent plea. Before He left to return to His father, He gave each of His followers the most magnificent armour and told them it would protect them from the lies of the Dragon."

"There were helmets, which allowed them to be recognized as the Lord's; they would protect their thoughts. Then there were the breastplates; they protect the heart and our inner desires. When these breastplates are worn, they show that it is His goodness, not our own, that protects us. He gave them armour for their midriffs that was His own ability to discern the truth; this armour protects the truth. He gave them special shoes that truly were wrapped in the wonderful news of the unseen Lord's forgiveness and love for them; these shoes would direct them towards whoever was ready to hear, giving them a courage like they would not have on their own."

Gilroy took a deep breath and continued. "In this land of deceit and hypocrisy, this armour keeps one secure and able to discern a lie when it is spewed on us by the Dragon or its servants. It also gives us the truth to share with others that do not know the unseen Lord. The Lord also gave His true followers some battle weapons to help them win the fight against the Dragon.

He gave them a shield, made of pure gold from His Father's kingdom. In its centre was the emblem of the Lion, representing His victory over the Dragon. This shield, held in the hand of one with their armour on, would protect them from doubt. ~ You will need this in the days to come, Caedmon."

"Finally, there is the sword..."

Gilroy paused and lifted his hand as if he was drawing out a sword. He loving looked at something Caedmon could not see. Then, slowly as Gilroy held up the sword, a faint image of it appeared before Caedmon's eyes. His mouth hung open in silent wonder.

"The sword was taken from the water, and it is to be cleansed there daily. The blade and handle were forged of gold and silver, in the land beyond the mist of the Source, with beautiful gems embedded in the handle. This weapon of war is to be used under the direction of the unseen Lord of the land, and only against the Dragon and its followers. Never, *never* for selfish purposes or it will be ineffective." Gilroy put the sword back into its invisible sheath at his side.

"I wish I had this armour," Caedmon said longingly.

"You do! The moment you met the Lord and gave Him your life, He gave you the armour. You just have never seen it, because your faith has been in man and not in the unseen Lord. Can you understand that?" Gilroy responded carefully as not to offend him.

Caedmon looked down and in the reflection of the sun off the water it was as if he could see the sparkle of gold upon his chest. He squinted his eyes, but it disappeared. He looked more closely.

"Why can't I see my sword, Gilroy? If it really there," Caedmon responded with doubt and a hint of sarcasm in his voice.

"You don't need to see it for it to be effective, Caedmon. Besides, you only need to see your sword; so you can use it effectively when the time comes. The Lord makes sure your other armor is in place ~ you just have to trust Him."

- 92 -

"You will see it when you need it. Are you willing to ask the unseen Lord to show you? What is more important ~ are you willing to do something with it?" Gilroy asked with zeal.

"I think so," Caedmon responded.

Gilroy's voice softened to a whisper, for he knew that what he was about to say might hurt the young man deeply. "Caedmon, you will need to use your sword. You will see the importance to use it because the Dragon has influenced you...it has brought doubt into your heart where only love and trust in the unseen Lord should be."

"Right now I don't feel influenced at all, Gilroy. I've been trying so hard to follow the unseen Lord," Caedmon said, a sob catching in his throat, but quickly turning to defensiveness.

"Son, you will need to talk to the unseen Lord about this. All I can do is tell you that sometimes I see doubt in your heart. I only mention it because I love you."

"I thought we were like equals in our quest of the unseen Lord," Caedmon asked, confused. *Am not I and Gilroy both pilgrims searching for the truth?*

"Oh, Caedmon, I am your servant just like I am a servant of the unseen Lord. He had sent me to you to bring you here and serve you. It is the exact opposite of the Dragon's bidding, that tells the people they need their own identity, their own rights and privileges. I hope that I never came across haughtily to you, Caedmon, or that I know more of the unseen Lord than you do, because I don't believe I do. If what I have shared makes you feel like I do, I am sorry. I was only trying to warn you."

Caedmon looked at his hands. He needed to be alone and talk to the Lord. This was all too much to understand. He was ashamed of the tone of his words, but even more so with his feelings of aggravation with Gilroy. He knew in his heart what Gilroy was saying was true. He wanted to tell this man he was sorry but the words stuck in his throat. He wasn't ready to leave all he had back home for this lonely life on the mountain. He brought his hands up to his face and rested his head upon them, drawing his knees up. He sat quietly for a long time. When he finally straightened to talk to Gilroy, he was surprised to see that he had left. He hadn't even heard him leave.

- 93 -

"Lord, I truly do believe that You have sent Gilroy into my life. However, I need to check out some things first and if they ring true to my heart ~ then ~ I will talk to You again about the Dragon's influence in my life. I hope that You understand, but it is just too much to think that the Dragon could have led me astray when all I have wanted is you."

"All you have wanted is me, Caedmon? Is that true?" the unseen Lord whispered to Caedmon as he got up and headed back to the village. Nevertheless, Caedmon shrugged it off as the wind, for he thought he knew his own heart.

The Dragon grinned as Caedmon came into full view. The vile creature had been hanging around the village for days, trying to find Caedmon and influence him again. Evidently, the young man was more influenced than it had thought, for there he walked in full view with his head held up arrogantly. *He didn't listen to the old man's counsel*, the Dragon thought nastily.

It would keep possession of Caedmon's mind with insinuations and lies. It hurled a blast of slime over Caedmon's head as he was leaving.

~

Gilroy entered the cottage and sat down on a chair behind his wife, who was busy at the fireplace making their noon meal. She spoke without turning around. "How did it go?"

When Gilroy did not respond, she turned and looked at him. He looked so sad it broke her heart. Walking over to him, she leaned over and wrapped her arms around his shoulders, burying her face into the back of his neck. She could feel the roughness of his woollen coat and smell the freshness of the outdoors about him. How she loved this large, gentle man. His wife went around him and knelt down in front of him, looking up into his face compassionately.

"You were right, my dearest. He wasn't ready. I felt the Lord tell me that I had to tell him now, before he left. But I guess I went about it all wrong. I think I upset him, and..." he trailed off. His wife reached up and gently pressed her finger against his lips to stop him.

Passionately, Treva spoke, "If the unseen Lord told you to tell him, then the unseen Lord knows it was time. You must trust the unseen Lord, for He knows what He is doing. Caedmon will listen to Him in time. I know that you love this young man and you want what is best for him, but he has to find some things out for himself. You cannot protect him from his own mistakes. Can you trust him into the Lord's care?"

"You are a gift to me, Treva. Yes, I can trust him into His care. And, thank you for reminding me." He looked adoringly at this small woman with her clear brown eyes and small face framed with heavy dark hair that was feathered with grey. She had always been able to see with more clarity than him, and he was so thankful she had been given to him. *Though at times, her clarity causes me aggravation*, Gilroy thought with a smile.

Gilroy slowly got up from the chair and, pulling her small body up to himself, he gave her a bear hug. Letting out a giggle, she pushed him back. "You better get busy. You will be taking another load down to the valley soon. The storage shed is full of wool, and the villagers have brought their carvings again for you to sell."

With a kiss on the top of her head, he turned and left the cottage. Upon leaving, he met Caedmon coming in. He smiled and greeted him.

"Well, young man, I could use your help after our noon meal to load my wagon. I have more selling to do in the valley. I had planned to take you with me, but now, you will be walking down the old trail to meet Teague. It is a much shorter walk than my long way around into the valley."

"What if I get lost?" Caedmon asked with concern, his conscience pricking him for not trusting Gilroy's advice.

"Oh, you won't get lost. The unseen Lord will help you. Besides, it is a simple trail ~ it does not leave the river. If you come to other trails or forks in the path, stay with the river and it will take you right to Teague. He too is learning to find his way. My friend Driscoll told me," Gilroy reassuringly told Caedmon, his words loaded with heartfelt meaning. As he spoke, his own confidence that the unseen

- 95 -

Lord knew best grew in his heart. Still, he would miss this young man until they met again.

Caedmon looked deep into Gilroy's aging eyes ~ these were the eyes of a father ~ he knew that he was going to miss Gilroy, too.

The Ancients say... "There is a way which seemeth right unto a man, but the end thereof are the ways of death."

Chapter 11

Aine ~ joy

Teague cleared his throat and the women looked up at him. Seanna very quickly dropped her gaze again to her sewing. Teague nervously shifted his weight, and clearing his throat again, spoke. "Seanna, I was wondering if you would want to walk me part-way up the mountain to meet Caedmon. You would not have to go far. But if you don't want to... I don't mind..."

Teague's voice trailed off in defeat as he noticed that Seanna never raised her head to look at him. Turning around slowly, his heart full of dejection, Teague reached for the door to leave.

"Wait, Teague. I would love to walk with you. Would it be all right, Treasa? Though I haven't finished mending these leggings of Cathaoir's yet," Seanna asked, her voice quivering with nervousness.

"Oh my, yes! Yes... Go, have a good time," Treasa said with a smile of relief. "Keelin can help me when she comes in from the barn. Teague, don't forget the lunch I packed for you. It is in your satchel. I filled your canteen from the well this morning. I packed a lot of food. Seanna, I will send Keelin to meet you after the noon meal. Now run along, and Teague, be on guard ~ I have a feeling the Dragon does not want you to meet Caedmon."

~

Teague wiped the perspiration from his brow; he was hot and was not used to walking up the mountain so far. Seanna had been allowed to walk with him as far as the timber line, but then she had to return home. He felt lonely for her. He had never talked to her all alone before. At first they had walked in silence, but then he had tripped on a tree root and fell headlong. Seanna had come quickly to his aid, wondering if he was all right. They had laughed when he replied that if he had been concentrating on the path, instead of on what to say to her, then he would never have fallen.

Once the ice was broken, the conversation flowed freely between them. Teague knew in his heart there would never be anyone else for him, and he had the feeling that she felt the same. All the nervous shyness had left them both, and he had asked her if he could walk with her again. She had agreed, and smiling asked if he would like to come to her home to meet her father. He agreed that it was the proper thing to do, and resolved that when he returned he would walk to the village and see her parents.

The land was becoming steeper. He had never climbed the mountain this high before, even though he loved climbing the hills. The stream, which at one time had been a mighty river, rushed and tumbled beside him. Thirsty, he drank the last few drops of his water from the farm's well. Teague found a low spot on the shore of the river and filled his canteen to the brim with the frigid mountain water.

Sitting down on the soft moss under a large tree, he looked out over the valley beneath him, sipping the water. With shock he looked at his flask, the water had coursed down his body in liquid energy. He took another drink, this time a long one draining his flask, his eyes became bright and his head became clear. Standing, feeling absolutely refreshed, Teague lifted his voice in an exuberant song as he stretched his hands upward and his voice echoed down the valley.

Small animals peeked their furry little faces out from behind the trees, their little hearts responding to this young's man joy. A lone eagle in the sky called out in response to the song as he circled far above. The river seemed to explode into a melody of its own as it joined Teague's song of joy and thanksgiving. Teague brought his hands down to his side and that was when he saw it. In his right hand was his sword; it glittered and shone in the morning light. It was so strange how it would appear sometimes. He felt a slight apprehension. Was the unseen Lord arming him for reason?

Suddenly, he heard a voice speaking to him.

"This is the truth I have given you to share with Caedmon; the Dragon does not want you two to meet. You will need this sword. Use it wisely, My son. It is for your battle that lies ahead," the unseen Lord spoke to Teague as He gently laid His hand upon the young man's shoulder.

Teague stared at the sword and put it in the sheath at his side. His heart felt a confidence like he had never experienced before. Looking back over the last two years, he realized that there was a pattern to him seeing his sword. Every time he was going to have to face the lies of the Dragon, or whenever he was sharing about the unseen Lord with one of the people of the land, the sword would appear. He still wasn't quite sure how to use it; he just *saw* it, that was all. This time, he had the feeling he would need it.

"*Battle!*" That is what the Lord had said. A nervous shudder went down Teague's spine as he anticipated what lay ahead. Trying to shake off his nervousness, he filled his canteen again and started up the path, wanting to meet Caedmon before it got late. Teague knew that the way would be hard, but with this water his energy was restored quickly. Teague tried to smile as he walked along, whistling a forced tune. The creatures of the highlands quietly followed, watching him with curiosity.

High on the mountain, Caedmon, with a walking stick in his hand, had begun his journey. It had been hard to leave his new home and he'd almost reconsidered. Gilroy had left early in the morning before he was even up. They had said their farewells the evening before, and it had been hard on both of them as they knew not when their paths would cross again. Treva had walked the first part of the path with him. He loved this small woman, for even though she was older in years, her heart was like that of a young girl. She laughed and told him stories of her past. He regretted that they came to their parting after what seemed like no time at all.

She handed him some provisions for his journey that she had made for him; he could smell the fresh bread. Giving her a hug and kiss, he turned and left. Looking back, he saw her standing there, waving her hand and smiling. It warmed his heart to know that he had a place and people that would always be there waiting for him, wanting him to return.

Caedmon made good time, enjoying the easy descent down the mountain. The trail was easy to follow and he was always beside the river. He hummed to himself. He was so excited about going to see his grandparents ~ he'd missed them so much.

His mind full of what lay ahead, he had not noticed that he was not hearing as clearly from the unseen Lord as before. Caedmon knew his way and what was expected of him, so he did not even consider that he should be talking to Him. The unseen Lord had left him and gone to Teague to walk with him and prepare him for what would lie ahead.

Caedmon came to the first aqueduct. The ditch was rimmed with stones and was spanned by a small wooden bridge. Caedmon stopped and looked at the aqueduct. It's appearance was so neat, almost natural looking. Long ferns and wild flowers were growing among the stones right down into the water. He noticed a green slime clinging to the rocks close to the water's edge. Caedmon went to step onto the bridge and heard the old boards creaking beneath his weight. He slowly backed up. He could see that his path continued on the other side of the aqueduct winding its way through the forest beside the river's banks. Caedmon looked down the aqueduct's ditch; the water tumbling along looked tamer and more inviting in some ways, and the path beside the aqueduct seemed wider and easier for him to walk on. Looking at the bridge again, he felt his heart tremble with fear. The bridge was high above the water, and if it broke, he would be injured badly.

Caedmon decided that he would follow the aqueduct just far enough to see if there was another crossing further down the mountain. He was also curious about this ancient stream, and wanted to see where it came out in the valley. He had walked a short distance when he realized the path was becoming very steep. Slowing his pace, he came to the edge of a sharp incline. The trail went down through the trees, and the aqueduct's water was falling in a small waterfall beside him. He could not see further down the aqueduct because of the large trees along it. He decided that he would continue just as far as he could see and then turn back if there was no way across.

As he carefully started down the incline, he felt his feet slipping on the loose stones of the path. He tried to slide down on his backside, for the incline had become very steep. Unseen to him, a long, scaly tail slipped out from behind a tree, causing him to stumble. His body began to descend quickly, out of control. Caedmon tried to slow himself by grabbing at small trees and stones, but they just gave way and went with him down the trail. He tumbled head over heels, falling, rolling, bumping into trees and rocks. He cried out to the unseen Lord to help him, and he felt himself come to a sudden stop. He thudded hard against something. Looking up through the dirt that had gotten into his eyes, he could feel the warmth of blood running from his nose and mouth.

A strong hand grabbed Caedmon by the arm and dragged him onto his feet. Blood was running into his eyes and Caedmon was unable to see. He heard a young man's voice say, "Steady, now!"

The man who had stopped his fall carefully guided him down the mountain to the bottom of the incline, from tree to tree. Once there was secure footing, he lowered Caedmon to a sitting position on the ground at the base of a tree and leaned him back against the trunk. Kneeling down, he opened his canteen of water and, tearing a piece of material from his shirt, he wet the cloth and began to gently cleanse Caedmon's wounds. Caedmon's forehead had a nasty cut and his lips were cut and bleeding, and his nose was bleeding from one nostril, there were cuts and scratches down his arms and legs. His shirt and leggings, were torn and dirty and one of his shoes was missing.

"Thank you," Caedmon rasped through his swollen cracked lips. With his eyes now clear of the blood, he was able to look at the young man who had stopped his fall. He was of medium build, with dark curly hair and bright blue eyes. His face was full of cheer. With a shock of surprise, he recognized Edan's brother.

"Gallagher!"

The young man smiled. "I was on my way up to the river's Source. I usually follow the river up, but I felt a strong pull to come this way," Gallagher informed him, "even though I knew it would be more difficult and it is a known fact that the Dragon likes to hang around the aqueducts to cause trouble."

"I am on my way down to the valley. I am going home. I was to be meeting Teague. Do you know if he is coming?" Caedmon looked with hope to his rescuer.

"Yes, at least that is what they told me when I stopped in at their farm. Teague would be leaving later this morning when he was done helping Cathaoir round up their cows into the summer pasture."

Caedmon nodded. "And how are you, Gallagher? It is so good to see you!"

"I have moved back in with my parents for a while, hoping that they would come back to the unseen Lord. They have grown bitter, with all the tension in the fortresses," Gallagher said as he handed Caedmon his canteen of water. "Come, I will help you back up the incline. Maybe we will find your shoe."

Caedmon took a long drink and was thankful that it was water from the Unchanging River. He felt restored and his wounds, he could tell, were healing quickly. However, to go back up the way he had just tumbled down sounded too difficult for him. He tried to get to his feet, and was discouraged when his vision began to blur. He put out his hand to the tree he had been leaning against. "I don't think I want to go back up this path. Thank you though, for wanting to help me."

"Oh, you will be all right. I will help you, one tree at a time. This is dangerous land here. The Dragon lurks around to trip up those that have taken the wrong path," Gallagher said with conviction.

Caedmon had the slight memory of feeling tripped just before his fall. He set aside this line of thought, sure that he was too close to the unseen Lord for Him to have let it happen.

He looked up through the trees that seemed to be growing out of each other right up the sharp incline. He shook his head slowly, and then turning, he saw the wide path going down leisurely through

- 102 -

the trees. It did have the appearance of ease and they should continue on this way.

His conscious began to warn him. He had chosen the easier path before, and look at what had happened to him. He started to feel uncomfortable with himself, realizing that he had not even stopped to ask the unseen Lord for direction, but had been proud and assuming.

"Why did you come this way anyway, Caedmon?" Gallagher asked curiously.

"I have made a terrible mistake, Gallagher, and I am finding it very hard to talk about," Caedmon started hesitantly. "I took this way because of the bridge over the aqueduct. The bridge looked unsafe and this way looked far better to me."

Gallagher slapped Caedmon on the back and laughed. "Well, if that is the mistake you have made let's hope that you have learned from it. Come on, it won't be too hard. We will take it slow and get you back on the right trail. I need to get to the Source's settlement before nightfall. I have a meeting there with one of the young ladies. Her name is Aine, and I hope someday to marry her."

"Yes, I heard of you two up at the Source. I met Aine. She is happy sort of girl. A real treasure, I am sure," Caedmon teased.

Gallagher's face beamed with love and anticipation, making Caedmon feel his own loneliness even more. He was thankful to the unseen Lord for sending him Gallagher, and his heart lifted in silent thanksgiving to Him. He immediately felt the unseen Lord's presence again and realized that he had not felt Him since he had talked to Gilroy the day before.

Again his conscious pricked him. He was beginning to see that he *was* influenced by the Dragon. He gave a shudder and nervously peered into the forest around him, the hair prickling on the back of his neck.

The young men began their laborious climb up the mountain. It was hard going. Both noticed something incredible that they shared with each other ~ when the going was harder they had more energy and clearness of mind, and when the way was easier, they found that they had just the right amount of energy that they needed for that,

- 103 -

too. They came to Caedmon's canteen and satchel with his lunch. Slinging it over his shoulder, Caedmon continued up the incline with Gallagher. They found his shoe, which made him very glad, for his foot was sore and needed the protection from the sharp rocks and roots that stuck out in the bush.

The men were very close to the top when they heard a terrible noise. There was a very great commotion up ahead on the trail. It was the sound of growling and wrestling.

Teague had stayed with the river, but when he crossed the creaky bridge over the aqueduct, his heart began to warn him that something was wrong. He looked down the trail beside the aqueduct and then up the trail ahead. He had expected to have met up with Caedmon by now; something seemed to be wrong. He stopped and, lifting his hands out in a gesture of help, he asked the unseen Lord, "What is the matter with me? I can't go on. I feel a great concern coming upon me for Caedmon. Lord, I need your direction."

The unseen Lord gently turned Teague's head down the wide path beside the aqueduct. Teague's heart went cold. He remembered the warning Driscoll gave when he had come to him from the Source's village, he had told him of the dangers of the paths along the aqueducts. Had Caedmon taken this path?

He immediately felt in his heart, even though there had been no direct word from the unseen Lord, that Caedmon had taken this path and he was in danger. Teague drew his sword from its sheath. It glimmered in the evening light. Night was coming and the sun was laying low on the western horizon. He cautiously started down the wide path, looking this way and that. He had no idea what he might come across and did not even know how to wield the sword. He had to trust that he was ready, or else why would the unseen Lord have told him he would need it?

Teague, peering into the wood, thought he saw something darting along beside him, but when he focused on it, there was nothing there. Teague slowly started walking again. He could feel an icy cold fear creeping over his spine. He tried to focus on the path. However, his eyes kept wandering to look into the forest around him and the gathering darkness. He then had another strong feeling overcome him ~ a feeling that he was acting ridiculous and that Caedmon wasn't even down this path.

"You're crazy! A real lunatic! What a fool you are, for Caedmon would never come this way." The pestering thoughts became so loud in his mind that he swung the sword over his head like he was shooing away buzzing flies.

A loud slicing noise filled the air as his sword connected with the Dragon's slime. Teague, seeing the slime appear, flung it off his sword and out into the bush. The slime slapped against a tree and began to suck the life out of it. The leaves curled up, withering immediately as it died. Teague saw the shadowy form of the Dragon in front of him and realized that it had been what was attacking his mind with fear and doubt. He did not take time to reason; holding sword high, he ran straight at the Dragon, a war cry piercing the air.

"In the name of the unseen Lord and His armies!" Teague cried like a seasoned warrior.

The Dragon leaped back out of the sword's reach just in time, for the suddenness of the attack sent it reeling. It was shocked that Teague had recognized its attack. He must be visible to this man! The Dragon drew back into the shadows, but not before it saw Teague raise the sword again. Teague charged at it, slashing out with his sword like an expert swordsman. The Dragon darted back and forth and grabbed Teague's hand, but Teague wrenched it free. Raising the sword high over his head, he brought it down with precise aim. This time the sword struck the old wound on the Dragon's head. Rearing back and falling over, it curled into a ball and immediately disappeared from Teague's sight. Teague swept the sword several times over the spot where he had last seen the Dragon and laughed out loud. Starting down the path again, Teague carried his sword in his hand, ready for anything that would attack him.

Caedmon and Gallagher were standing, staring in wonderment at the scene unfolding in front of them. Even though they had heard the battle, they had not seen whom Teague was fighting.

Teague stopped and, using his canteen, he poured water onto his sword to cleanse it of the Dragon's slimy lies. Looking up, he saw Caedmon and Gallagher slowly approaching. They were both

- 105 -

looking at him with apprehension. Teague put his sword back in its sheath and it disappeared from their sight. He felt elated and energy surged through his body. He wanted to find the Dragon and slash it again, but somehow he knew that the unseen Lord would not approve. He took a long drink of water and threw back his head in a loud spontaneous ballad of a fight and a victory. When he was done he laughed sheepishly. Reaching his hand out to shake their hands, relief flooded his soul at seeing Caedmon safe and somewhat sound.

"Caedmon! Gallagher!" he exclaimed joyously. He was glad to see that Caedmon was all right, but he was looking rather tattered to be sure.

"May we ask what, or whom, you were fighting? I could see the flash of a sword. Where is it now? Your enemy... What was it? We could see nothing, but we heard the lies pelting us in the face, just like someone was spitting on us," Gallagher said excitedly.

Taking a deep breath, Teague explained what had happened. As he recounted the story, he realized that it was only when he'd hit the old scar on the Dragon's head, victory came.

As they arrived at the junction of the aqueduct, the night drew close around them. The young men decided to camp for the night, even though Gallagher knew he had missed his meeting with Aine. He was glad she had a forgiving heart. They shared Caedmon's lunch and then Teague took his lyre from his satchel and began to strum softly. They sang into the gathering darkness around the small fire, sharing with each other how good the unseen Lord had been with each one of them until their tired eyes could stay awake no longer. Curling up in their cloaks, they fell asleep in the warm summer night's air. The unseen Lord sat on a log beside them watching them, long into the night.

The Ancients say… "The Lord is nigh unto them that are of a broken heart; and saveth such as be of a contrite spirit."

Chapter 12

"Oh, you should have seen the look on their faces!" Teague laughed as he recounted his asking for her hand in marriage to Seanna's family. "I am sure her father thought his daughter would never get married. I was so nervous I wanted to faint. Literally, I mean! Then her father strode forward and took my hand in a hearty shake."

Cathaoir smiled to himself. It was an honourable thing to have his son marry into this family. He had heard that Seanna's father was a good provider and a hard worker. The laughter continued and the talking was mainly of their upcoming wedding. Caedmon slipped out the kitchen door.

"We should mediate for Caedmon," Treasa suggested. She had saw the distraught look on his face as they had all been talking. Cathaoir looked uncomfortable. He had not minded Caedmon's presence around the farm, but he just did not feel any responsibility for him either. *He is a man now. It is time for him to grow up,* Cathaoir thought. But he bowed his head and thought about the work he had to do the next day. The mediating was short but heartfelt from Keelin, Teague and Treasa.

Caedmon walked down the path to his favourite resting tree. He was unaware of his unseen companion. The large ape-like creature laid its heavy arm across Caedmon's shoulders. A non-stop stream of despairing, self-pity words streamed from it mouth as it gradually put more and more weight upon the young man's shoulders. When Caedmon reached the tree, he slumped against it. The weight of his circumstances seemed more than he could bare.

Caedmon lifted his eyes to the setting sun. His heart was so torn. Burying his face into his hands, he leaned back against the large oak tree. He missed the fortress dwellers, but every time he went there, they treated him like an outsider. When he had returned to the village he learned that his grandfather had passed away only weeks before, and sadness filled his heart. His grandmother had left the large fortress and was floating between smaller ones since the loss of her husband. His mother had returned to be with his grandmother, and Caedmon soon found out that he was not happy living with them. His mother and grandmother fought all the time. So he left, to the backlash of both of their anger. Caedmon told them it was only until he could think straight, but they swore he was being unfaithful to their needs.

He had tried to talk to Carew about his father, the old guard ~ Caedmon missed the guard so much. Every time he brought up the subject, Carew would look away and then tell Caedmon he would have to talk to the new guard about it.

He had come out to Cathaoir and Treasa's farm to try to sort out his feelings. They had not pressured him to share his heart, and encouraged him to talk about it when he wanted to. Treasa spent hours with him; he helped her do all her chores, and he did not stray far from her.

He clenched his fists and pulled himself away from the comfort of the tree. He hated feeling so needy, and he was certain he was probably just a bother to them. Even though both Treasa and Cathaoir tried to reassure him that they loved having him around, he could not relax with them. He felt bitterness rise in his heart ~ and he hated that, too. He tried to shake off the dark mood he was slipping into, but even as the sun slipped behind the mountains, his mood, also, darkened with the gathering night. *Why don't I have normal parents? Why am I not really a part of any family? Why was is my family so hateful?* He only wanted normalcy.

He had been finding it difficult to stay focused on the unseen Lord ever since he'd left Gilroy's place. At first he hadn't noticed so much, but he knew that it was getting harder and harder to hear what the Lord was saying to him. He knew that Teague's family was aware of his struggle. They kept encouraging him, but he knew that personally all direction had stopped. Then there was Teague and Seanna's growing relationship, and they had just announced their

- 108 -

betrothal. Caedmon felt so left out. He hated himself for his jealous feelings. He just tried to stay busy to avoid these feelings, but they were his constant companion just lying under the surface.

"Are you there, my Lord?" whispered Caedmon into the darkness.

The chill of the night air was beginning to creep into his being. Sitting down at the base of the tree he drew his legs up to his chest and wrapped his arms around them, trying to stay warm. Caedmon was determined he would not leave this position until he heard from the unseen Lord. The silence was so thick he could feel it pressing in on all sides, just like the darkness.

"You have done your job well, Despondency!" The Dragon said gleefully as he pulled the beast away from Caedmon. The hideous creature grinned with self-satisfaction at this rare praise.

"However, not good enough. He just asked for the presence of the unseen Lord, you fool!" The Dragon's tail coiled around the creature's neck and flung it back away. "See how a professional works. And learn, idiot!"

The Dragon, drool dripping from its gaping mouth, slithered behind the tree and began spouting its lies. "You are fatherless and motherless. It is hopeless! He has left you, Caedmon. Your unseen Lord is gone when you need Him most. You should return to the fortress. Things will be easier there. Return," the Dragon whispered as the drool dripped and ran around the tree towards Caedmon.

"Why, oh Lord, have you forsaken me?" Caedmon cried out into the night.

"May I sit with you, Caedmon?" A familiar voice asked quietly.

Caedmon jumped up on to his feet in one leap, whirling around to see who had spoken. The Dragon recoiled for it had been so intent on its attack of Caedmon that it had been unaware of someone coming. In the dim light of the newcomer's lamp, Caedmon made out Gilroy's face. The Dragon hissed as it felt the unseen Lord approach with this mediator. Wrapping its tail once more around Despondency's neck, it lifted its hulking frame and flew silently away.

"I do not fly!" Despondency screeched.

- 109 -

"You are right, but you do fall! Now go do a better job and find Complacency, Self-centredness, and Greed. Go to Cathaoir's farm and begin to dissemble that mediator meeting place with your lies." The Dragon dropped the screaming creature and laughing maliciously flew to Evergreen.

Dropping his head in shame, Caedmon slumped back down on to the grass that was becoming damp with the dew of the night. Gilroy set the small lamp down on the ground and sat next to Caedmon, putting his arm around the dejected young man. They sat there in the silence together for a long time, neither speaking.

"Cathaoir said that I would find you here. He told me that you come out here every night and sit to watch the sun set over our mountain," Gilroy spoke as he gave Caedmon's shoulders a gentle squeeze.

Caedmon tried to speak, but a lump was forming in his throat. He felt the darkness creeping into his very being. He slowly nodded his head, unable to look at Gilroy.

"Don't you love the silence? It is like a gentle blanket that the Lord wraps around us to hush our fears and tremulous thoughts. I, too, go every night and sit to watch the valley as the sun sets behind me. I have missed you, son," Gilroy's voice had become husky with emotion.

Caedmon's heart was filled with Gilroy's bittersweet words.

"I am sorry about the passing of your grandfather. Gallagher told me when he came to the Source to call upon Aine. He also told me of your mother's return and that you are living with Teague and his family now. Caedmon, the unseen Lord sent me to you. What is ailing you, my son?" Gilroy asked with compassion.

Caedmon, looking up, peered into Gilroy's eyes, and reaching up his hand he gently touched the dear old man's face.

"I feel so estranged from the Lord. He hasn't spoken to me in a long time. After I thought more about what you told me, I asked Him to show me the influence of the Dragon in my life, and He did. I went to the fortress and tried to fit in, but it did not work. For one thing, the people acted so indifferent towards me, like I was a stranger. The new guard there did not have time for me. He told me

- 110 -

to make things right with my mother first. How could I do that?" as Caedmon talked his tongue loosened and the whole story came out. "My mother does not care for me at all anymore. Oh, she says she does, but her actions show that her ale is the only love of her life. She is cruel of speech now, and she will not give me the information so I can find my father. She told me I was selfish to even ask for it and that I was choosing him over her. I felt so angry. I wanted to hit her and I knew it was wrong, so I left," Caedmon sighed.

Gilroy rested an assuring hand on the younger man's shoulder.

"Also, Grandma has become so hard and bitter. She yells, and even curses so loud at my mother and their fighting is almost violent. She won't leave mom in the unseen Lord's hands. She also got mad at me for telling her so. She just keeps nagging her, even though it makes no difference."

"I couldn't understand any of it. I feel lonely because I don't fit in with my old friends very well. I went to go and visit Carew, but he didn't want to see me. And all of my other friends are either getting married or are in a relationship with someone. There seems to be no one for me. I feel so left out and alone," Caedmon hesitated.

"Worthless?" Gilroy prompted.

"Yes! That is exactly it. I want to hear the unseen Lord's voice and feel His love surround me. I have been angry and I think He can't come to me because of the evil state of my heart," Caedmon dropped his head in dejection.

Caedmon became aware that he wasn't cold anymore and that it did not seem as dark outside, either. His heart, which had been so downcast moments before, felt lifted and lighter. Gilroy was sitting quietly, for he knew that he had nothing to say that would lessen the load Caedmon was carrying, and that he had been sent to only listen.

"I feel Him all around us, Gilroy. Do you?" Caedmon asked with relief.

Gilroy nodded as he felt the familiar hand rest upon his shoulder and squeeze slightly. His friend was so faithful to always come when he needed Him.

- 111 -

"Thank you, Lord," Gilroy whispered into the coolness of the night.

"Lord, I am so sorry that I have doubted You. Please direct me in the days to come. I give to You my mother and Grandma, and I give you Carew and all my friends. Take them for they are yours, not mine. I trust that if there is someone for me, that You will bring her into my life," Caedmon breathed out his petition from a tired heart. "Thank you for sending Gilroy. He is my true friend ~ and Your friend."

The unseen Lord laid His hand on Caedmon's head and gently pushed him back against the tree. Caedmon felt the fear and heavy load leave him as wave after wave of peace washed over his soul. The unseen Lord then knelt down in front of the young man, speaking softly to him.

"Caedmon, you must trust Me. That is all I ask of you ~ that you would trust Me. You have a long and dangerous road ahead, but I promise you that I will not leave or forsake you. In three days time you will be leaving with Gilroy to go to a far and distant land. The people there need to hear of me. You will be traveling by wagon to the seaside village of Sunset, and then you will be leaving on a sailing ship. I will show you which one when you arrive there. Enjoy these three days with your new family, and then go to Gilroy's, for he will be ready to leave with you."

"Stand guard over him," The unseen Lord said to his companion. The man nodded and smiled his assent. Wiping his hands on his blacksmith apron, he stood and looked out at the surrounding landscape.

"They left the moment we came, but Despondency will be back. The mediator's had sent for us. Their faithfulness will be rewarded soon." The unseen Lord disappeared from his companion's sight and the strong man kept vigil.

Looking around for Gilroy, Caedmon was surprised to see that he was gone. Gilroy had left the small lamp for Caedmon. Rising from the ground, Caedmon made his way back to the farm house. In the dim light of the moon, he made out Gilroy's wagon going down the road. He would be seeing his friend again in three days, and he was glad for that. However, he was not so sure that he was ready for a journey, a quest!

Although his heart trembled with joy he also felt apprehension to travel to some unknown place. A land over the sea! How exciting! He couldn't wait to tell Treasa, Cathaoir, and Teague. He hoped that he was ready for such a quest. Amazement filled his heart as he realized that one touch of the unseen Lord's hand had changed him completely. In an instant, all of his oppressing thoughts had been banished. Caedmon shook himself. It was almost surreal, this feeling of wellness that had come so suddenly.

With a leap and shout, he ran to the farm house.

The Ancients say… "Deliver me from blood-guiltiness, O Lord, thou Lord of my salvation; and my tongue shall sing aloud of thy righteousness."

Chapter 13

Lana ~ attractive and peaceful

Carew shifted uncomfortably as he sat in on the secret meeting between the guard and the visiting head guard. His mind kept going over what he had done that day. Caedmon had come into the fortress to visit and catch up on things, and Carew had shunned him. Oh, Carew had been polite, but he'd made it obvious that he did not want Caedmon there.

His conscience would not leave him alone. His mind went back over the last months. He tried to stop the negative thoughts, but he could not help remembering Arthmael's cries for mercy and for someone to listen to him. Shaking himself violently, he tried to get his mind around what they were talking about.

Lifting his eyebrow, the guard looked at Carew, saying, "Are you struggling to stay awake, Carew? Please listen, for you will learn something, I am sure. Maybe you should step outside and let the cool air awaken your senses. Go on, we will wait for you."

As Carew left the guard's quarters and was going down the long corridor to the stairway, he remembered he had left his cloak on his chair and it was very cold outside. Returning to the room, Carew saw the door was still ajar, and listening closely he could hear the men talking.

"Carew is a weak-natured young man. He has been seen with those that have left, moreover with a known mediator. I think that he will have to be moved to another fortress. He has still not recovered from his father's death. Carew doesn't seem to realize that we need to instil fear into the people. They need to know that if they

- 114 -

leave the protection of the fortress and its guards, then they will fall into the great deception of the Dragon."

The other man's voice was too low for Carew to hear. Forgetting about his cloak, he turned and fled. Upon reaching the doors, Carew flung them wide and ran out into the night, running to the edge of the precipice over which they had flung Arthmael. He fell onto his knees. The lies of the Dragon were smothered by the cry of his own heart. The questions that he had suppressed for years began to come to the surface. Why could the people not hear from the unseen Lord for themselves? Why could they not trust Him? He had read about the Ancients, and they'd had neither fortresses nor guards...

Why did guards constantly keep the people feeling like they were not good enough? Why were guards elevated above the rest of the pilgrims? If only the people knew that the guards were not really seeking the unseen Lord for them. They were so busy trying to keep the whole fortress together and convince the people of their need to be there that they had no time to seek Him. Even though he, as a guard in training, had time to seek the unseen Lord, he didn't. He had not felt the need to.

Carew began to see things clearly now. The guards had everything they needed ~ the pilgrims fed them. The pilgrims maintained the fortress. The pilgrims sought the unseen Lord and then told them what they had received. In reward, the poor pilgrims were then filled with the fear of being rebellious to the unseen Lord if they questioned the guards. Something was wrong, Carew knew, and he felt powerless to do anything. Carew wished that he could call upon the unseen Lord, but He would not even want to hear from him ~ he had innocent blood on his hands. Carew buried his face into his hands. Perhaps, if the unseen Lord could hear his unspoken cry, maybe there would be a glimmer of hope for him.

The Dragon stroked Carew's back and tried to soothe his questions away. It needed him still to do its work. Carew felt suddenly better and, shaking off the feelings of remorse, he wondered at the negative train of thought he was having. He was ashamed at the strange oppressive feelings that had overcome him, for suddenly he

- 115 -

knew that he was all right. A large sigh of relief escaped his lips as he turned to head back to the fortress.

The unseen Lord walked up to join Carew and the Dragon hissed at Him to leave. "He is mine. See how he throws off your influence?" The unseen Lord never said a word, but only pointed for the Dragon to leave. Turning and sulking away into the shadows, the Dragon made its retreat into the forest around the fortress. Reaching out His hand, the unseen Lord stopped Carew's carefree walk abruptly.

Carew felt a heat pulsate through his shoulder and run down his arm. He stretched out his hand and looked at it as the unseen Lord strengthened His grip. Carew let out a cry as the heat became almost unbearable. Then, in the fading light of the evening sun, he saw the glitter of a sword in his hand. He slowly lifted it and examined the exquisite weapon. His heart felt like it was thumping in his ears, and a dread like he'd never felt before flooded his soul. Then, on the whisper of the wind, he heard Him. "Don't be afraid to fight, My son, and don't be afraid of the questions you were asking or of the feelings of despair. They are necessary if you are ever going to be free and be a warrior for Me."

The breeze suddenly stopped and the sword disappeared.

All the depressing feelings that were previously wiped out by the Dragon came back with a rush. Carew went into the fortress and straight to the guard's chambers. He needed these men of wisdom to help him. Without stopping to listen at the door, he walked right in on them. From in front of the huge fireplace, the men raised their heads from their confidential talk.

"Come to us, Carew. We were just discussing great plans for you."

"First, my honorary guards, I want to tell you of the most extraordinary experience I just had outside the fortress." Carew cleared his throat.

"Hold one minute, Carew. Outside the fortress walls? We all know who would be the mastermind behind that experience! There is no protection outside these walls. But please, go on with your story," the head guard's voice had taken on a critical tone.

- 116 -

Carew suddenly could not share what had happened. His tongue was unmoving in his mouth. He again felt the heat pulse down his arm. He could feel his hand grasping the handle of a sword. Looking down, he saw the glint of the sword, but knew they could not see it. Walking over to the other chair in front of the fireplace, he settled down upon the seat and changed his mind.

"You know, I think it was only the wind on my tired mind. After the fresh air, I feel greatly recovered. Now, what is to be done with these renegade pilgrims that have left the fortress?" Carew asked, trying to sound convincing.

The guard eyed him suspiciously and then went on with the conversation he had been having with the head guard. Carew tried to look focused, but he had become acutely aware that there was not a single reference to seeking the unseen Lord or questioning what He would want them to do.

Inside, Carew felt his heart burst with a sudden expectation of freedom as he let his hand feel the strength of the sword on his lap. The unseen Lord had forgiven him, but how would he ever get out of this situation? Fear gripped his heart, for he could not think of any way to get out of the guardship without leaving the fortress completely. The thought shook Carew ~ leave the fortress? He couldn't! He would be in rebellion and fall into heresy. He slowly felt his courage leave him, and his sword disappeared again from his touch.

The meeting finally came to a close. The visiting guard departed, and Carew felt tired. The evening had torn him in two directions until finally sheer exhaustion took over. His mind refused to consider anything that he had heard or felt. He would deal with it another day he finally rationalized and headed for bed.

Carew's new young wife, Lana, was already asleep in their chambers, and he was thankful he did not have to tell her anything of his evening. Feeling him come to bed, Lana rolled over on her side and watched her husband as the moonlight streamed in through the window. He had been so full of expectations and dreams when they had married, but she now saw him as an empty young man, devoid of passion and care.

Lana heard the heavy breathing beside her, she spoke quietly to the unseen Lord. "Help him, and help me! We both need you so badly. We need you to come to our aid." Snuggling into Carew's side, she too fell back into a sound sleep.

The Ancients say… And therefore will the Lord wait, that He may be gracious unto you, and therefore will He be exalted, that He may have mercy upon you…"

Chapter 14

Wynne desperately needed a drink of ale. Where was Scully when she needed him? She pulled herself from the cot and swayed for a moment until her balance came. Walking over to the window she looked out on the dingy little village. How she hated this place! Wynne's mother had moved out and left her yet again and Wynne had decided that she would not go back to her, even though now she needed money to buy ale. What was she to do?

Upon hearing the creaking of the door, Wynne turned slowly and saw old Scully quietly coming into the room. He carried a small wooden crate with some provisions. Looking at Wynne, he smiled and nodded. *It's good to see her up*, he thought to himself.

"Where have you been, you old codger?" Wynne hissed.

Scully ignored the comment and went to the fireplace to stoke the fire. He set a large kettle full of water on the coals and began to chop up the cabbage he had bought, tossing it into the water.

"I am sick of cabbage stew," Wynne whined. "why can't you buy some meat?"

"There has been no work for me," Scully lied. "Besides, cabbage stew is good for you."

Walking over to the table, Wynne looked in the box. All that were there was two loaves of black bread and a small package of cheese. No ale. She had thought he would have brought her some. Losing control, she whirled around and came at him, shoving him hard against his chest, knocking the old man back. Then, glaring, she snarled at him to get out and go find her some ale.

Scully backed towards the door. Fear gripped his heart as he saw the crazy look in her eyes. At the door, he turned and fled, deciding he would get Nuala, her mother. She would know what to do. At least she was not afraid of Wynne, like he had become.

Scully knew he was her prisoner, but he loved her in his own way, even though he only enjoyed her when she was too drunk to remember. He had been glad to move in with her when she had asked him. They had run into each other outside the bakery when she had got back. She had been glad to see Scully and they became good friends. He would lend her money for food and ale. When her mother moved out he had taken up living and providing for her. Scully felt like her husband and tried to do whatever she asked. In everything they had been through she had never looked at him like that before. Scully had seen that look many times when she was kicking out one of her lovers, but she had always treated him well.

Wynne began to circle the room like a caged animal. Her mind wanted ale ~ her whole being cried out to be drunk. She began to curse everyone she knew, throwing her few possessions around the room. She knew this was her family's fault. If only her son and mother understood her, then they would see that she had needs that only they could fill. They were so judgmental with their high and mighty talk of the unseen Lord. *What has He ever done for me?* she thought, her attack slowly turning to the unseen Lord.

"Deserter! You don't care for me!" she screamed. "I hate You! You never, never have cared for me! I am not good enough for You! You have made it plain to me..."

Wynne felt herself swoon. Sitting down on the bed, she was spent from her outburst. The Dragon watched her, enjoying the sight. It didn't even have to cover her in its slime ~ she was coming out with her own grand attack. *I have trained her well,* it thought.

She looked at her hands. They were aged and yellow, not young and white anymore. They looked like the hands of a very sick old woman. Wynne cringed. She knew that she was not well, but she thought it was because she did not have any ale. After taking a closer look at her hands, she drew her sleeves up and examined her arms. Her arms too were a sickly yellow pallor. The nausea and pain gripped her again ~ they had been her constant companion the last few weeks. Staggering to her feet she looked into the broken piece of looking glass she owned. She had smashed it once in a fit of rage, but had kept this larger piece so she could still fix herself up.

The face looking back at her dismayed her even more. She had not looked at herself in days. Her eyes appeared to be bulging out from her face. Her once fair face was now sunken and drawn, and the whites of her eyes and skin had a sickly tinge of yellow. Sticking out her tongue, she examined it. It was coated and enlarged. She was sick, she realized. Where was Scully now? She had forgotten already that she had sent him to get some ale. Too tired to rail any longer, Wynne laid back down on her cot.

Scully peeked in the door. Nuala had said she would come immediately when her supper was cooked. Seeing Wynne lying down, he felt relief flood his soul and he walked quietly into the room. Finally, she had calmed down.

Wynne looked over at him, and a fresh wave of nausea rolled over her. This time she vomited over the side of the bed. Scully came to her side quickly, grabbing a cloth and washing her face with cool water. He laid rags down on the vomit. He had feared that something was wrong with Wynne, and now he could see that she was very sick and that she had been progressively getting sicker every day.

"Go get Caedmon. I need him," Wynne whispered.

"Don't you remember? He came here yesterday and told you he was leaving today for the port village of Sunset. That he was going to a far land with that friend of his, Gilroy," Scully replied gently.

Wynne forced herself up onto her elbow, the wild look returning to her face. She said, "Go after him! I need him. I think I am dying!"

Wynne fell back on the cot, exhausted, the stench of her vomit filling the room. She felt herself spiralling down into a sick sleep. Scully took a close look at her pale face and ran as fast as his old legs could carry him. Wynne drifted in and out of sleep for a few minutes, and then opening her eyes, she saw someone staring at her. Startled, she tried to get up, but fell back onto the hard straw tick. Terror gripped her heart as the man stared at her steadily. He was stooped down and looking her straight in the face. She tried to pull the ragged cover up to her chin, but her strength was gone.

"Who are you?" she finally stammered out.

"You don't know Me, Wynne? I have known you for your entire life," the man responded tenderly.

Wynne's eyes narrowed. Was the man, the unseen Lord? It could not be true!

"You have finally come to me? I have called to You so many times, but You ignore me just like the horrible family that You have given me," Wynne said grievously.

"I have come every time you called, but you never looked for Me. You were always too busy blaming others for your trouble, and you never took the time to look at yourself. I cannot help you even now if you do not want it," the Lord spoke with an authority that made Wynne tremble.

"You have no idea how hard it is."

Wynne never finished as a fresh wave of nausea swept over her. The unseen Lord gently touched her forehead and the nausea left her immediately. The Lord looked over at the Dragon. Its hulking frame filled one end of the room. It was staring hungrily at Wynne. Wynne felt herself being torn in two directions. She desperately wanted to believe the Lord, but the other side of her hated Him.

"She is mine. She always has been, and You know it, your *Majesty!*" the Dragon sneered, its drool pooling on the floor around its gaping mouth.

Ignoring the Dragon, the unseen Lord looked back at Wynne, remembering the many times He had come to her aid. She would only accept His help for a short while. He gently wiped the perspiration from her brow, and leaning over, He kissed her on the forehead. With that gentle touch, Wynne's heart was forever changed. Her eyes flickered open, and tears coursed down her cheeks.

I'm so tired, Lord. I can't fight anymore," she whispered. "Could you ever forgive me?"

"Yes, you are forgiven, dear one," the Lord spoke gently, as if to a child. The Dragon snarled in the background, but knew enough to keep its distance.

A smile spread across Wynne's face, she felt strength surge through her body as she sat up on the edge of the bed. Rising to

- 122 -

her feet, she took the unseen Lord's hand. Glancing back at her cot she was surprised to see herself still lying upon it, a smile on her face. She looked asleep but Wynne knew that she was not. Looking back to the Lord, she started to walk with Him. The room faded from her sight and as it did, so did the heaviness on her heart. A shepherd was standing holding a door open for her to enter. She walked with the unseen Lord and through it. It was like a thousand pound weight had fallen from her shoulders. She let out a giggle, for she felt young again. Looking down on her simple white dress, she was amazed how spotless it was. The grass beneath her bare feet felt like soft down as they silently walked along.

The Dragon whirled when the unseen Lord disappeared and Wynne breathed her last. *I'm not done with this family*, it sneered. It was her son it wanted anyway ~ he held more influence than she ever could. Whirling, the Dragon lifted its heavy body and flew silently over the village to the hamlet of Sunset.

Wynne's mother came into the room. The stench of vomit hit her in the face, almost overwhelming her. Covering her nose with her sleeve, she walked over to Wynne, and, leaning over, she gently shook her. Fear crept into her heart. Wynne felt so cold and still, although there was a slight smile on her face. Reality slowly flooded Nuala's heart. Sobbing, she drew the limp body to her bosom and cried into her daughter's hair.

Oh, Wynne, you were not ready… her despairing thoughts overwhelmed her as grief covered her soul like a dark blanket.

~

Gilroy and Caedmon leaned upon the railing of the ship. The wind whipped their faces as they looked back on the wharf. The sailors were quickly raising the sails to ease them out of the harbour.

"Look, Caedmon, isn't that Scully?" Gilroy asked.

"Yes! Look, he is waving. He must have come to say goodbye," Caedmon said excitedly, waving back as the ship pulled away. "I never thought he liked me that well. I guess I was wrong," Caedmon said, remaining blissfully unaware of Scully's reason for coming.

~

For the first few days of their journey, the ship rolled with the waves of the sea. Caedmon tried to still his troubled stomach, but he knew he was going to be sick again. Pulling himself out of his swinging cot, he dropped down onto the floor, trying not to awaken Gilroy. He slowly went up the narrow ladder to the open deck, where he saw one sailor in the gloom of the night, leaning against the main mast. Caedmon staggered back and forth with the rolling ship until he reached the railing, which he leaned far over. The bile in his stomach emptied into the murky depths of the sea. Pulling himself back, he turned and sat down with his back leaning on the railing. He felt better again, but he knew it would probably be short lived.

The sailor came over to him, and leaning over, he looked into his face. He reached out and touched Caedmon's forehead.

"You need to eat something," the sailor encouraged. "We have been out at sea for two days now and you have not eaten. An empty stomach is not what you want, my boy. It hurts too bad when you hurl into the sea."

The sailor stood and left, returning quickly with some water and black bread. He handed it to Caedmon. Caedmon could feel his stomach objecting, but he did not want to appear rude, so he took it. As he slowly ate he felt somewhat better, and the more he ate, the better he felt. Looking up at the sailor, he smiled and thanked him. Stopping and taking a sip of the water, he was surprised at how refreshing the water was. It did not replenish his energy like the Unchanging River's water, but it had a familiar taste that made him homesick somehow.

"Where is this water from?" Caedmon asked.

"Oh the captain bought the whole supply from a fortress that was closing in Sunset. They were going to drain the water, but he bought it from them and we put it into kegs for our journey."

Caedmon wiped his mouth on his sleeve, remembering back to when he had pined to drink from the pools in the fortresses. Ever since he drank from the Unchanging River, though, he had not been satisfied with the second-hand fortress water.

Caedmon went below, back to his cot. Carefully climbing onto his cot above Gilroy, Caedmon felt much better, and he whispered his thanksgiving to the unseen Lord. He immediately became aware of His presence in their small room in the bowels of the swaying ship.

"Caedmon, I am here. I came to tell you that your mother is with my Father now. She came home safely," the Lord spoke gently. "Do you mean...?" Caedmon's voice trailed off in disbelief.

"Yes, my son, be strong. Here let me hold you. Cry... Let the tears come."

Caedmon sobbed, his heart breaking. He remembered Scully waving to him frantically. He should have gone back ~ she had needed him, and he had left. Guilt and shame flooded his soul, and the darkness that so often seemed to be waiting to come upon him flooded him like a wave.

"She was gone before Scully got to the shore," the unseen Lord answered Caedmon's unspoken question. "She is safe now, and happy. She wouldn't want you to grieve for her by feeling guilty for what you could not have changed. She made things right between herself and Me, and that is what gave her the ability to walk to My Father in a clean garment. Remember where she is in the days to come when guilt and shame try to steal your life away. The Dragon is on the move. We must move quickly to try to rescue as many as we can. It will try to smother out the light in you. It will try to turn your past and your mistakes against you."

Caedmon's sobs started to subside as he realized that the Lord was speaking the truth to Him. Oh, he had so wished his mother could have been whole here. He tried to stop, but the tears continued to fall unbidden.

"How can I be of any help to you, my Lord? You know my frame, that I am weak, and so many times I have failed you," Caedmon said sadly. He wanted to curl up in a ball and die. His heart hurt so badly.

"It is not your strength that makes you valuable or even your gifts, Caedmon. It is your heart. You have the heart of a warrior, even if you don't know it. Just take a moment and think. Even though your

- 125 -

heart is breaking, you want to know what your quest is, don't you?" the unseen Lord asked pointedly.

Caedmon realized it was true. He not only wanted to know the quest, he wanted to carry on. He felt strangely relieved to know that this was all right and not a result of hardness of heart or even some old bitterness towards his mother. He was a warrior for the unseen Lord, and whether he was weak or not, he must obey.

He felt the unseen Lord leave and Gilroy reached up and took his hand, squeezing it lightly. Knowing his friend had heard his conversation with the unseen Lord comforted his heart. He would not have to explain. His sore heart was soothed from his friend's handclasp and Caedmon fell asleep with tears wetting his pillow.

The Ancients say... "Flee also youthful lusts: but follow righteousness, faith, charity, peace, with them that call on the Lord out of a pure heart."

Chapter 15

Kikeona ~ strong fighter
Pualani ~ heavenly flower

Caedmon sat in front of the fire. The shadows of the palm trees waved in the wind behind him, and the ocean stretched out before him with the moonlight glittering on the rolling waves that washed upon the shore. The others around the fire were sitting quietly, listening to Gilroy. They were a beautiful people. Their skins were brown and their large eyes twinkled with curiosity.

Caedmon marvelled at how long they had been among these people. It had been a month now! At first there had been some conflicts brought on by the Dragon, but the people had persevered and now were reaping the benefits. Many had come to hear from the unseen Lord for themselves and give their allegiance to Him. They did not doubt His presence for they were very aware of His arch enemy, the Dragon. The Dragon had lied to these people for generations. It had convinced them that they were its servants and even required them to offer sacrifices.

Looking over their faces one by one, Caedmon realized that there was no greater joy than what they were experiencing. As his eyes went from face to face, they came to rest upon a young girl, Pualani, granddaughter to one of the elders, who was looking directly back at him. His shock showed plainly on his face. She only smiled and, dropping her eyes, she covered her mouth as she giggled.

Gilroy stopped speaking and asked Caedmon to tell the people of his own personal journey. Caedmon was still staring at the girl and did not hear Gilroy. Clearing his throat, Gilroy nudged Caedmon's side. Even in the flickering light of the fire, Gilroy could see the blush steal over Caedmon's face as he whispered his apologies.

"Why, that is all right my friend," Gilroy responded good-naturedly. Lowering his voice, he added, "I can remember when a pretty face made me speechless." Then, raising his voice, Gilroy said, "Caedmon, would you like to share how the unseen Lord has changed your life?"

Caedmon smiled his thanks, and then, starting hesitantly, he shared about his home life and his first encounter with the unseen Lord.

As he came to a close, the oldest man around the fire stood to his feet. His name was Kikeona, and he was Pualani's grandfather. He had been a great warrior when he was younger and many respected him. Lifting his hand, he brought the attention of everyone to himself, saying, "I am old and have heard many things in my long years. I would have been so glad to have heard this tale many years ago. What a difference it would have brought to me and my village. Today, each of you has an opportunity to bring this change. We have, in these last few weeks, become very familiar with the unseen Lord. Let us dedicate each of our lives to being His pilgrims afresh tonight and start by pouring out any ale that is in our huts. Caedmon, this story you have brought us is very real to us here. The drinking of ale has been going on since the traders first came here with their ships, and it has destroyed our lives."

The people got up and disappeared into the forest to go to their homes to pour out their ale. Gilroy and Caedmon were left alone, except for Kikeona and Pualani. Kikeona sat down again beside Gilroy and began to tell him about how he could feel a great change coming to his village. Three of the four elders were now pilgrims of the unseen Lord, and his heart broke over the fourth, who said he would never stop serving the Dragon.

Caedmon got up and strolled down to the edge of the water, and the low rumble of Gilroy and Kikeona's quiet voices carried over the beach. Pualani shyly got up and followed him. She knew that he had noticed her, but she also knew that she was very young. She had only lived fifteen summers on the earth. Her parents had died of an

- 128 -

epidemic when she was three, and she lived with her grandfather. Her form was fully developed and her long black hair hung like a shiny veil down her back. She was a beautiful girl and many of the village's young men had tried to get her attention, but were very afraid of her grandfather.

Caedmon stooped down and picking up a flat stone, and skipped it across the waves, chiding himself for feeling suddenly shy around Pualani. He could have at least gone over to her and sat and visited for a while. Her beauty was breathtaking. With her dark olive skin and large luminous brown eyes, she reminded him of a royal tribal princess.

He was suddenly surprised out of his reverie when a stone went skipping past his on the moonlit ocean. Turning around, he was shocked to find Pualani, who was aiming another stone to let go across the waves.

"You throw stones well," Caedmon said as he picked up another and let it fly. It skipped many times before it disappeared into the night.

"Yes, my grandfather taught me. He always treated me more like a son, you know. He never had a son and so when his daughter married he had hoped she would have a son. Though, she only had me. When my parents died, he took me in and even though he loves me devotedly, he has taught me the ways of the men of the village. Because my grandfather is highly respected, no one objected. I can fish, mend nets and hunt boars. I can climb the coconut trees and run as fast as the other boys on the beach. It has also stopped them from coming to my grandfather for my hand as well," Pualani added shyly.

"Well, the unseen Lord knows exactly who is to be your husband, and he will give him the courage to speak to your grandfather," Caedmon said with confidence. As he looked down upon her beautiful face, he suddenly became aware that she was close to the same age as Seanna. His heart began to beat loudly in his ears and he wanted to reach out and touch her cheek with his hand. Just at that moment when he did not think he could control himself, he heard a whisper in his ear.

"Go ahead. The men are busy. She wants you to… Look at her, she wants you as bad as you want her!"

Pualani leaned closer to him and then, before he could do a thing, she shoved him back, squealing in laughter as she ran out into the ocean. He quickly recovered his balance and ran after her. She stopped and flung the water up in his face and then ran out of the ocean and to the men at the fire. Her heart was beating wildly and her face flushed with emotion as she flopped down beside her grandfather.

"Hey, you are wet. Move over there," her grandfather scolded. Then he noticed Caedmon approaching and the lad seemed dejected. *What has my granddaughter done?* Kikeona thought. Caedmon's clothes were dripping wet and he almost looked angry.

"Come lad, what did my little flower do to you? She is so wild at times. Pualani, what have you done?" her grandfather's tone took on an edge of authority.

"She did not do anything wrong, Kikeona. She was out-throwing me, that is all. Please excuse me. I need to be alone for a while. I am going to our hut. See you when you get home, Gilroy," Caedmon answered.

"Wait, I will go with you as far as our hut," Pualani said as she jumped to her feet. She felt that somehow she was to blame for Caedmon's darkened mood. "Would that be all right, Grandfather?"

"Yes, if you like, go. That is, if Caedmon wants you to accompany him."

Caedmon only nodded and headed for the trail to the village. The Dragon slithered behind him, letting its drool drip all over his head. "Fool, why didn't you kiss her? She wants you to and you know it. Look at her! See how she lets her arm brush against yours. She could be all yours..." Suddenly a different, softer voice interrupted the Dragon's lies playing through Caedmon's head, and this voice helped Caedmon to see the truth.

"Agggh!" The Dragon hissed as light illumined Caedmon's surroundings. The young man had drawn his sword! The Dragon couldn't believe it.

- 130 -

"Stand back, Pualani. The Dragon is about. And I am going to battle it," Caedmon yelled as he pushed her gently back to a safe distance. Then, with a swing of the sword, he brought it up right under the Dragon's snout. The Dragon reared back in horror as it realized that Caedmon could see it, even though the night was dark. The light from the sword illuminated Caedmon's face as he strode forward like an experienced swordsman, again wielding the sword, only this time at the Dragon's belly. The Dragon spewed its vile spit at Caedmon, who in turn caught it with his sword and flung it back in the Dragon's face. Pualani could not see the Dragon, but she could hear its vile lies screaming at her mind. "He is crazy! Run, he has gone mad! You will be next… He only wants to violate you and then leave you." She quickly reached up to wipe her brow and that was when she saw a sword in her hand as well.

With a scream of delight she whirled around and drove her sword in the direction that Caedmon was fighting. Her aim, though blind, hit the Dragon on his old wound. Falling down and coiling into a snakelike ball, it disappeared from Caedmon's sight.

Running over to Pualani, he took out his canteen and washed his sword, and then had her do the same. As they did, the swords disappeared from their sight. Caedmon then rested his hand upon Pualani's shoulder, saying, "Pualani, I am sorry. It is my fault that it attacked. I should have recognized its lies on the beach, but because I liked what it was saying, I did not take a stand against it. If the unseen Lord had not alerted me just now, I don't know what would have happened. Whatever it was, we would have regretted it for the rest of our lives."

Pualani ducked her head in shame, for she too knew that she had been wanting Caedmon's advances and she had drawn him into it.

"I am also sorry. Please forgive me. Can we start again? And just be friends?" Pualani asked with her hand outstretched. Caedmon quickly took it and shook firmly.

"Yes, we will be friends, and if anything more comes of it, let us leave that up to the unseen Lord," said Caedmon. "For safety's sake, let us not be alone again. That is when we become vulnerable. You are very beautiful Pualani, but more than that, you are one of the

Lord's pilgrims and I must respect that. I will treat you with respect and honour. I pledge that to you," Caedmon concluded as he let go of her hand and turned to go on down the trail.

Coming to the village, he left Pualani at her hut and then made his way to the other side of the village to his hut. People were out everywhere, sitting around fires and pouring out flasks of ale onto the ground. The whole village smelled like a brewery. There was laughing and songs of jubilation. As they saw Caedmon walking by, they saluted him with many words of thanks, as the village cleaned out the dross of their past life.

Caedmon stretched out on his woven grass mat. He had changed out of his wet clothes and put on dry warm ones. Even though the night air there was warm, he still felt chilled. He had come very close to losing a battle tonight, and his heart condemned him for the lust he had nearly given in to.

The unseen Lord spoke, "Caedmon, tonight you have learned a valuable lesson. You could have thrown away your future with one act. It would have been so easy, just like taking that wide path beside the aqueduct all those months ago. You are forgiven. It is not wrong to be tempted by the Dragon, but what you do with that temptation is where you can go wrong. I am proud of you, My friend. You rallied the minute you heard My voice. I will use this to teach Pualani as well. She is beautiful and she is just beginning to learn that she can use that beauty to get what she wants. Tonight she caught a glimpse of the danger in that. You did well in the end. You not only saved your own self from the Dragon, but also her life."

Caedmon felt a quiet satisfaction fill his heart, knowing that he had served the unseen Lord. "There is one last thing tonight, my child. You will be leaving this place in the morning. It is time. Gilroy already knows. Sleep well, My young knight."

Caedmon drifted off to sleep with a feeling of wholeness and victory surrounding his heart. He was thankful he had listened and taken action. His enemy was wily, and he would have to be more on guard in the future.

"Keep careful watch, My friend!" The unseen Lord said to the man of extreme strength. Who's muscles rippled under his white

- 132 -

tunic and his midriff was still gird about with the apron of a black-smith. "He still does not see the significance of all his armour. He has only begun to realize the strength of his sword."

"I will, my Liege," he said as they clasped hands.

The Ancients say… "But in vain they do worship me, teaching for doctrines the commandments of men."

Chapter 16

Tully ~ peaceful one

The air was so still, one could hear their own heartbeat. The gloom of the night was thick around them as they cautiously walked through the dense forest. Occasionally the moon would peek out from behind the clouds and lighten their path, but the young men knew the path well, even in the dark. The soft tread of their leather shoes was muffled by the moss that grew all over the forest floor. Feeling the chill of the night, Caedmon pulled his woollen cape tighter around his shoulders, his heart continued to thump loudly in his ears. He was looking forward to resting. They had been walking the whole day and were close to their journey's end.

Stopping, he lightly laid his hand on his friend's arm beside him as they both sat down on the ground. Edan reached over and squeezed Caedmon's arm, knowing they should not speak. Their hearts were beating wildly, as they were close now to completing their quest. Sitting in the quietness, they tried to relax their weary muscles for what lay ahead. Taking some bread and the canteen of water out of his satchel, Caedmon handed Edan some and they started their humble meal, each lost in their own thoughts.

Caedmon's mind could not really fathom the surreal feeling that overwhelmed him. There had been much that had happened in the last six months. The quest with Gilroy had been exciting to say the least. They touched many hearts, and brought many to know the unseen Lord's love. The thrill of someone hearing the unseen Lord speak to them for the first time would always be the highlight of the quest. Yes, the fights with the Dragon had been exciting, but the fights with the Dragon's subjects were heartbreaking.

Caedmon would never be at peace with the fact that so many were seduced by the Dragon's lies. So often this was where he failed in any quest he was sent on. It was hard to be honest and ~ frank ~ with pilgrims who preferred the fortress over the Lord. When he would try to tell them that they could talk anywhere themselves to the unseen Lord, they, in turn, would accuse him of heresy.

Since he had come home, the Lord's gift to him ~ his ability to see the Dragon ~ had never stopped functioning in his life. He'd asked the Lord to stop it for a while, but He'd reassured him that it was necessary. It had been only two days ago that this quest had begun...

~

Caedmon, finishing his visit with his grandmother at Evergreen, had sat on the ground at the backside of the fortress, his back against its wall. He had kept trying to find a more comfortable spot. He was waiting for his friend Teague. Teague had gone into the village to see Seanna and said he would meet Caedmon at the back of the fortress to walk home together. He finally shifted his weight and looked at the wall to see what was protruding into his back. The large, heavy stone was ancient and it was nestled against others on both sides; a large piece had broken off and the sharp, jagged edge was sticking Caedmon. Reaching over to the mortar, he marvelled at the craftsmanship of the early masons and gently stroked the moss-covered mortar.

Recoiling suddenly, he quickly drew his hand back. Looking at his hand in horror, he saw that green slime dripped from the end of his fingers. Pulling himself away from the wall, he looked intently at the mortar. He could see the veins in the mortar that looked like moss, but it wasn't moss ~ it was oozing slime, almost as if the mortar was alive!

Caedmon remembered that he had seen this slime before, growing along the aqueducts. He recalled what Carew and his father had told him about the construction of the fortresses all those years ago. They had said that the mortar was unique, because it was a special mix of ground stone from the mountain, and water from the aqueducts. However, that had been centuries before. Why had it not dried? Caedmon then had another memory ~ a horrifying one ~ of his battles with the Dragon. The Dragon always spewed green slime at him, and the last battle he'd had, the Dragon had spewed it all over his head. Remembering, Caedmon drew in his breath...

Caedmon had barely been able to breathe, and if it had not been for Gilroy, he would have drowned in the vile stuff. His mind had been bombarded with every lie imaginable, but the one that always done him in was the loudest.

"You are so false! You are misleading others!"

Gilroy had sliced the slime with his sword and flung it from Caedmon's head. Gilroy had raised his sword high and struck the Dragon on its scar. With an agonizing roar from the Dragon, the battle had ended.

~

That was why he and Edan were here, in the forest directly behind the fortress under the cover of night. They had come to find the Dragon and battle it over the mortar. They had discovered that when they won a battle with the Dragon, its lies would retreat with it, giving the people time to think clearly. They hoped that tonight the people in the fortress would have some respite from the constant assault on their minds ~ and from the very structure they had built. The unseen Lord was waiting for them up ahead. He would make His move towards the people when they had finished the battle. No one would ever know they had gone to battle for them, but faceless knights they had become. For that matter, no one would believe them either, but they tried to no longer care for the approval of man, and to only care for their relationship with the unseen Lord.

Edan was an expert swordsman and he wielded his sword with precision. He saw his sword at all times now. His new bride, Tully, could wield the sword expertly as well. The two of them had driven the Dragon's lies far from their families and now were looking beyond their own borders.

Caedmon used his sword, although his gift was the prominent weapon that they all relied on. He had the ability to see the Dragon,

- 136 -

he always knew when it was present. He also knew when the unseen Lord was present, but most of the other mediators knew that too.

Tonight, Caedmon would see for himself what the Dragon was up to. Until now they had only dealt with it when it crossed their path. Tonight they would pursue it ~ they were on the offensive. The unseen Lord had said it was time. He had the mediators all over active for them that very night.

Both young men arose and walked to the edge of the forest, a wide expanse of grass stood between them and the fortress on this side. They knew if they went around to the adjacent side of the fortress where the trees came quite close then they would not be seen. Making their way slowly, to not make a sound, they kept watching the fortress through the trees. It looked large and grey in the moonlight, and very foreboding.

The men shuddered, remembering that at one time they had both thought this was a sanctuary for them. Coming to the side of the fortress, they crept close but stopped suddenly. The Dragon's tail was only two feet in front of them. They did not breathe.

The Dragon was working diligently at something, not realizing in the least that it was being watched. Its arrogant nature underestimated the humans, its pride made it blind to their ability to be victorious. It released another spew of spit onto the side of the fortress and then with the tip of its wing, it worked the spit carefully into the mortar. Finishing that side, it moved to the back wall of the fortress. The young men sighed. It was true then that the Dragon kept its own lies active to keep the fortresses intact.

They both started when someone clasped their shoulders. Standing still and not turning so as not to alert the Dragon, they waited.

They could feel a warm breath on the back of their necks as they themselves dared not breathe. A soft whisper came to their ears, "Hey boys, why did you leave me behind? The unseen Lord fetched me."

Edan let out a relieved gasp as he turned to embrace Teague. The men drew deeper into the wood away from the fortress, bringing Teague up to date on all the evening's events. Teague let out a low whistle. Drawing his sword, he smiled as he raised it above his head. Lifting his shield, he joined his friends as they walked out of the forest onto the lawn.

Standing upright and unafraid, they marched forward to the other side of the castle. They were all amazed as strength and courage infused their beings while they walked shoulder to shoulder. The Ancients said that a three-stranded cord is not easily broken, and the men felt the truth of that statement as they walked, the same purpose leading each forward.

The Dragon was so preoccupied with its task that it did not hear the men come up from behind, though it soon smelled them. Unknown to them, their scent was the scent of the Unchanging River's Source ~ the scent of wild flowers and forest green, with the indescribable odour of the purity of the unseen Lord's presence, saturated their whole beings.

Whirling, the Dragon's eyes glowed red in the dark, and its large scaly frame swung around with an agility that was astonishing. Seeing the three walking towards it shook the Dragon to its bones. It knew all three, moreover, it knew their weaknesses. Although together, they would fortify one another. He knew he could not easily beat them.

It did not wait to battle the three; instead, spreading its wings, it flew over their heads into the gloom of the forest. As it flew in a large arc over the land, the Dragon could see flames flickering in so many homes ~ flames of people awake, no longer sleeping. The mediators were on the move. Throwing its head back in a vicious roar, it flew to the next village and swept into the pool of the fortress there. It would return soon, bringing more of its own army with it.

Caedmon, Edan, and Teague looked at one another in astonishment. Never before had they seen anything like it; their enemy was afraid of them! They began to sing a ballad of a battle that had already been won. The ballad told of pilgrims marching forward and finding that the enemy had fled. They laughed, cried, and sang all the way back to Edan and Tully's flat in the village, where they would stay until morning.

Meanwhile, in the fortress, the unseen Lord walked into Carew's chambers. Walking over to the young guard's bed, the Lord sat down on the edge of it, waiting for him to awaken. Carew rolled over and tried to see who was sitting on his bed. Seeing the Lord in the moonlight that was streaming in the window, Carew cried out in fear. His wife, Lana, groaned and rolled over but did not awaken.

"Who are you? What do you want with me?" Carew said, trying to sound brave, although he could not hide the tremor in his voice.

"You do not know Me?" the Lord implored.

Carew's head dropped. He suddenly knew that it was the unseen Lord, and he was not ready for this meeting. He knew his heart was wicked. He had denied his friends and even gone against his own conscience concerning Arthmael. A low moan came from the depths of his heart. Who would ever believe that he was sorry? No one.

Carew looked up trying to search the face of the unseen Lord as the moonlight illuminated Him in the darkness of the room. The unseen Lord smiled warmly. Reaching out He stroked the hair away from Carew's eyes.

"You must hurry! You have a small door of opportunity to get out. The Dragon has left ~ my young knights have sent it flying ~ but it will be returning in great anger. Disappear into the land as a common worker for a season. You will be restored to Me when you are ready. Call for Me and I will come."

Carew blinked his eyes as the unseen Lord slowly faded from his sight, but he still felt the Lord's presence with him. He knew he must obey, even though it would be difficult to leave. He suddenly determined that he had had enough of the fortress life. Enough of the guard constantly dictating his life. Enough of the people constantly wanting from him something he did not have. Enough of feeling lonely, even though so many lived in the fortress all around him.

The unseen Lord took the hand of a small girl that had accompanied Him. "Keep vigil, Little Fire, keep your arrows handy. The Dragon will want to discourage Carew from looking back."

The small girl stood erect, with one hand on her bow and the other over her heart, and saluted in silent sobriety. The Lord vanished from her sight.

"Enough!" Carew cried, awakening Lana. Packing up their belongings, they left in the darkness just before the early dawn.

The Ancients say... "Look not every man on his own things, but every man also on the things of others."

Chapter 17

Seanna looked again at her reflection in Treasa's looking glass. Her long gown shimmered in the lamp light, and her light brown hair was swept up from her neck, falling in small curls around her delicate face. Turning, she hugged her mother close. It was time to go outside.

Their wedding ceremony would be held in Cathaoir's large yard under the apple trees. They had lit lanterns hanging in the trees, and the beautiful smell of apple blossoms filled the air. Taking her father's arm, Seanna walked out of the cottage into the apple orchard. The light played off her white dress, making her appear ethereal, like a lovely dream or vision. Teague, standing with his father, waited for her to be brought to him. His heart felt like it was going to burst. She was beautiful.

The evening was lovely from beginning to end. After the guests had left, Seanna and Teague headed to their own small cottage that Teague had built for them on the land given him as a wedding gift from his parents. Caedmon, Cathaoir, Treasa, and Keelin relaxed by the big bonfire in the yard, agreeing that life could not be any better, for any of them. As they sat visiting, a cool breeze started to blow. Seanna and Teague had not yet made it to the cottage when the rain began to fall in droves. Laughing, they ran into their new cottage. The rains had come, and not just a shower, but a good downpour.

It rained for days. The land became green and lush, and crops flourished all over the valley. Seanna and Teague settled into their new home, enjoying the shut-in time to get to know each other. They were learning to live together.

Caedmon and Cathaoir fixed harness and worked on the wagons in the barn, using the time off from the fields to fix their equipment.

Treasa and Keelin cleaned the cottage from top to bottom, and Gallagher had gone to the Source to spend time with Aine's family.

The Dragon did not make itself known, staying in the pools of the different fortresses. The beast's slimy lies only worked within the walls of the fortresses and over those of the land that loved to think of themselves and not others. It left its subordinates to cause the havoc necessary to achieve its goals in the land.

The unseen Lord walked daily with His pilgrims and encouraged them to keep mediating for the people of the land. Edan, Tully, and the others met frequently at the farm to encourage one another. Their joyous singing could be heard from afar, with many a neighbour venturing to join them.

Gilroy and Treva became frequent visitors to the farm, and they hoped that one day Cathaoir and Treasa would be able to take a break from the farm to come up and see them.

When the rains finally stopped, the Unchanging River was near its highest banks. Gilroy knew the artesian well that fed it was still low, but the rain encouraged his heart, making him think that everything was going to be all right.

Caedmon was growing in his walk as a pilgrim. He grieved that his grandmother had shunned him, even though, he knew that she did it because she lived in the fortress. He hoped one day she would join him in seeking the unseen Lord and mediating to Him for the people of the land. Though, he determined he would try one more time with his grandmother. *Maybe if she sees my sword!* Despondency was trying out a new attack on his unwary victim.

One rainy afternoon, Shylah sighed as she looked up from her mediating to the unseen Lord. She saw Treasa sitting cross-legged in front of the fireplace with her eyes shut. Opening her eyes, Treasa looked at her friend and smiled. They weren't meeting as much anymore, but when they did the presence of the unseen Lord always came to comfort and strengthen them. Even though things were so wonderful with everyone engaged in mediating, there was an underlying uneasiness growing in the ladies' hearts.

Complacency was looking in the window at them. Its serpent head protruding from the bat-like body, quivered with expectation.

"You know it is not right, Shylah. I keep feeling uneasy since there have been no battles with the Dragon lately. I think I have the wrong attitude and should be thankful instead!" Treasa said emphatically.

"I know what you mean. I think sometimes that I seem to flourish when things are bad, but that is backwards. Just now, I asked the unseen Lord to forgive my rather negative attitude towards life. Do you know what He said to me?" Shylah asked, raising her eyebrows as was her custom when she was surprised.

"I have no idea, but I need to know so I can get myself together," replied Treasa.

Shylah sighed again, and looked off into the distance as if she could see through the wall.

"He told me that our job is not done and that the people of the land need our mediating more than ever. Just because we are not confronting the Dragon personally, that doesn't mean it doesn't need confronting. We have not needed to use our swords daily for ourselves; however there is a need to use them for those of the fortresses and the land. He did not say, 'Oh, its all right. I understand your attitude,' but rather, I felt He was disappointed in us for being too shortsighted in our mediating."

"Well, of course He is right! I was just thinking this morning that our lives are so sheltered at this end of the valley. That we need to think of those deep in the valley who live close to the fortresses and villages. My heart has been selfish. It's time to change, I think!" Treasa thoughtfully replied.

The ugly creature squeezed its displeasure and went to report to the Dragon. These women would not stop mediating whatever they threw at them.

The women felt a renewed vision as Shylah parted. Shylah promised to be back when her family could spare her. Treasa was humming a tune when Cathaoir and Caedmon entered the cottage for the noon meal. Their hearts lifted at the sound, feeling a renewed strength flow deep into their hearts. As the noon meal was close to over, Keelin entered the kitchen. She was returning from the village, where she had taken the wagon to trade their eggs and butter.

She looked nervously at Caedmon. Clearing her throat, she spoke hesitantly. "Caedmon, your father is in the wagon." She paused, waiting for Caedmon's response. Seeing that he had none at the moment, she continued. "I saw a man on the road walking here from the village. I gave him a ride and as we were talking, he told me that you were his son. He wants to see you."

Caedmon stared at Keelin not comprehending what she was saying. Rising from the table slowly he was unable to speak.

Who was in the wagon? Could it possibly be my real father? His perplexed thoughts tumbled over each other. *Why would the man come to see me? I am a grown man now ~ what would he want with me?* Cathaoir put out his hand and grasped Caedmon's arm.

"It will be all right. This must be part of the unseen Lord's plan for your life. Whoever he is, we have to know that this is no surprise to our Lord. Take courage and be the man that you have become," Cathaoir said as he released his arm with a gentle, reassuring squeeze.

Caedmon walked out the door and looked towards the wagon and the man who was sitting in it. The man sat with his head down, and his scraggly hair hung around his face. He looked very dejected. Caedmon strode over to the wagon. Hearing him approach, the man looked up.

Caedmon stopped as shock shook him to the core. Despondency laid his heavy arm on Caedmon's shoulders, he had been waiting for an opportunity.

The man looking back looked exactly like him, only older and very small. Caedmon knew in an instant that it was his father. His father had come...

To See

The Ancients speak of a place ~
Where the Creator
rules in justice.
Where the unseen Lord
walks seen.
Where the warriors war
with kindness.
Where tears are forever kept,
to comfort those
that come.
The Dragon never steps there,
those that listen to its bidding
will never go.
A place of comfort,
strength, and knowledge
to set a pilgrim free.
Where in the forest glade,
pools stay fresh and clear.
Like a looking glass
the water lies.
Peer upon the stillness of the pool,
into the window of the soul
you shall see.

The Ancients say… "There is a river, the streams whereof shall make glad the city of the Lord, the holy place of the tabernacle of the most High."

 Chapter 1

Barris ~ expert swordsman

Treasa looked at her friend, Shylah. *What had happened?* The rains had come and the river rose to the top its banks. The crops had been full and the harvest was exceedingly bountiful. The mediators had become expert knights and had many victories over the Dragon, defeating it time after time. Gallagher had married his Aine, and was settled in the village working as a carpenter.

However things were not what they should have been. Gradually something had happened to the pilgrims. They had slowly lost their desire to go forward into battle. They had listened to the lies of the Dragon, thinking all was well. Slowly, the bickering and feuding had taken over everyone's heart and mind.

Shylah was lying prostrate on the floor in front of the fireplace. She was beseeching the unseen Lord to return to them. Treasa stood and walked to the window. Her daughter was in the other room, alone. Why had all this taken place? Was there any hope for Keelin, her beloved daughter? Her thoughts swept back over the last few weeks…

~

Battles had raged for days, one conflict after another, some of them in the unseen realm and many in the seen world. Neighbour fought against neighbor, brother against brother, townsfolk against the country folk. The worst of the fights were between the fortress dwellers and the Unchanging River's Source pilgrims. Though they all professed to be pilgrims of the unseen Lord, they rose up against each other. The fortress dwellers spread lies of heresy about the

Source pilgrims, and they in turn tried to defend themselves, only to feel confused when it was all over.

Caedmon tried to warn the people that he had seen the Dragon's drool dripping from one side of the valley to the other. However, everyone seemed to have become complacent in their attitude towards the Dragon and its work. Even his close friends had become dull concerning the battle. Caedmon tried to stir Teague and Edan to fight, but his friends said that since their armour had disappeared, they felt that the necessity to fight was over. Now was a time to live quietly and mind their own business. It was more important to seek the welfare of their own families and make their lives comfortable with hard work. Caedmon knew that now was not the time to be complacent or self-centered, for the Dragon was evidently at work. Even though his own heart would not lift in thanksgiving. He could not shake the despair that had entered his soul.

Caedmon had been so discouraged that his father had only stayed a short while. Vaughan had been busier justifying himself than actually trying to build a relationship with Caedmon. Caedmon wondered why he had even searched for him in the first place. *Probably just to appease his own conscience,* Caedmon reasoned.

Vaughan's self-centered, weak nature surprised Caedmon. He so desperately hoped that Vaughan would be the father that he had always needed. Alas, once Vaughan had finished giving every story of his past in his own defence, he left to go back to his second wife and children. He promised Caedmon that maybe someday they would get together again. The whole incident devastated Caedmon, and he had become irritable and restless.

Caedmon had gone to the Unchanging River's Source only the day before, hoping to find strength and encouragement.

Keelin had become involved with a young man named, Barris, who had grown up in a neighbouring fortress to Evergreen. He had become a non-dweller, but he was not a part of their group of pilgrims. Keelin had made it obvious to everyone that she was going to do whatever she wanted.

∼

Gilroy was walking in the forest listening to the song of the trees, when he saw Caedmon coming up the path. Gilroy, too, had found the last months very difficult. It had been hard to sell their wares in the villages, and rumours had been running rampant. Long-time friends and buyers now looked at him with suspicion, and said that they had no one to buy his goods.

In spite of the rumours, he found some who didn't care where he came from, knowing good merchandise when they saw it. For those brave souls, Gilroy was very thankful. It seemed to him that the moment they all had become more aggressive with the Dragon, all things had turned upside down. Their internal bickering was breaking his heart. It was only yesterday that Aine had returned to the Source distraught because Gallagher had become so cruel towards her.

The men clasped hands as they met on the forest trail. Gilroy pulled Caedmon to him and gave the young man a bear hug. Going to their favourite spot on the Unchanging River's shore, they sat on the large rock. Removing their shoes, they soaked their hot, tired feet in the refreshing water. That is when both men saw that the river's level had dropped even more. "Oh, Gilroy, it is happening again." Caedmon pointed to the wet rocks above the water line. " Look, it is drying up fast. How is the fountain of the deep?"

Gilroy looked sad as he replied, "It never increased at all during all the rain. I felt nervous about that, but wanted to focus only on the good that was happening. It is the true Source of the river, not the rain. The rain will feed the river, yes, but it will only last for a season, whereas the fountain is the river's constant supplier. No, it is definitely falling fast. You are right. Look over there, where you pointed."

The wet water mark was two inches higher than the actual river, showing just how much the water level had dropped since they'd come.

"Let us go quickly to the Source, my friend," Caedmon said.

Caedmon put on his shoes and jumped to his feet. He knew he must seek the unseen Lord immediatcly. He knew the river was only a stream now anyway, and with the Source drying up so quickly, it

- 150 -

would soon be no more. Gilroy stood slowly beside him. Laying his hand on his shoulder, he looked deep into Caedmon's eyes.

"I must find the cause, Gilroy. I will seek the unseen Lord and do whatever is required to bring the river back," Caedmon exclaimed with fervour.

"Yes," Gilroy responded slowly. "You must! The unseen Lord told me you were coming. I believe in my heart that He has directed you here. I think, also, that it is time for you to go into the Unseen River's Source."

"Into the Source?" Caedmon asked puzzled. "How can someone get *into* the Source? It is a mighty artesian well. I would be blown into the air!"

Gilroy threw back his head and laughed. The sound echoed through the forest, lifting the oppression that covered the land. The lone eagle that circled high in the sky swept down and flew close over their heads, and his call joined the laughter. Sweeping back high into the sky, the eagle circled and circled, crying out far above them. Caedmon watched him in wonder. Despondency jerked its arm away from Caedmon and slinked into the woods. Its master would need to know about this. Caedmon's felt alive as he listened to Gilroy's laugh.

Gilroy, smiling broadly, slapped Caedmon on the back, saying, "There is much to do. Come, we will prepare for your journey. Don't fear. There is a way into the Source and it is closer than you think. No one goes uninvited, but I feel in my heart that your invitation has come. Oh, Caedmon, what wonders you will see!"

Early the next morning Caedmon and Gilroy left the cottage as a waving, smiling Treva, blew them kisses until they rounded the corner and were out of sight. They walked to the village centre, looking at the Unchanging River's Source and finding that their fears were true ~ the water was only half as high as usual, and there were hardly any rainbows of colours. The rocks around the Source were dry, for the spray did not reach very far and the wild flowers looked badly in need of a drink.

They walked up to the Source and, to Caedmon's wonderment, he noticed a door in the rocks. It appeared that the door went

- 151 -

straight into the fountain. The door was beautiful ~ made of a red wood that had been rubbed until it shone. It was rounded at the top and on the frame a grape vine was growing. Some of the vine was on the outside of the door, but he could see that some of it grew on the inside, too. The door had a glorious golden knob just waiting to be turned. Caedmon stopped and looked questioningly at Gilroy.

"No, Caedmon, the door is not always visible to the human eye. That is why you have not seen it before. If you can see it, then it is time for you to go. The unseen Lord will be with you. He has called you to come." Gilroy's voice had become so quiet Caedmon could hardly hear him over the falling water.

In a final arm clasp with Gilroy, Caedmon turned his attention to the door. Reaching out, he took hold of the knob, and as he turned it, something incredible took place. The knob began to pulsate and the gold spread up Caedmon's arm, as if he were becoming one with it. He felt a gentle pulling sensation, and as he stepped forward, the door's surface became soft like the feel of material against his face. His wonder over the experience kept him from feeling any alarm. He walked into the door, which now had become like the layers of many curtains. At that moment it dawned on him: it wasn't curtains, but the folds of a regal robe.

The next thing he knew, the Unchanging River's Source disappeared and he was standing in a garden. It was wild, yet everything was orderly. A beautiful moss grew on everything, life emanated from every plant, and the rocks themselves seemed to be alive. To his left, he could see the sharp face of a mountain that disappeared into the mist above. There appeared to be ledges cut in the rock ~ slightly basin-shaped. There were cups cut from the same rock surface to one side. From these a small waterfall that descended from cup to cup, as the water gently fell down the side of the cliff. Small delicate leaves grew out from the moss around the cups that were overflowing. Little white flowers were abloom everywhere the water splashed. The ledge was so inviting that Caedmon decided that he would sit there.

Coming closer, he realized that the ledge was much larger than he'd first thought, and that he could lie down on the basin of soft moss. He decided he would rest there for a while when he became aware that he was not alone. Turning slowly, he looked straight into the eyes of the Lord. Caedmon was shocked that in this place he could actually see Him, and they were the same height. The Lord was smiling, knowing exactly what Caedmon was thinking.

"Here in my kingdom, there is no elevation from one another. I am your Lord, but I am also My Father's Son. It is My Father's desire that everyone who comes here is also a son to Him, just like I am. Yes, I am your access to this place, but I also serve you. Follow My example, Caedmon, and you will always find joy." His tender voice filled Caedmon's heart with hope.

The Ancients say... "Wherewithal shall a young man cleanse his way? by taking heed thereto according to thy word."

Chapter 2

Abelio ~ green growing one

As Caedmon's surprise over being able to see the *unseen* Lord finally began to leave him, he remembered his quest.

"Lord, the River! The Unchanging River is dropping and the fountain of the deep is hardly flowing. Everyone's armour has disappeared completely. Why?"

"Come! I have something to show you. Look with Me and you will see My perception of the place where you live. You will see with My eyes, and then you will know the reason."

Caedmon asked the question that was burning in his heart, "Lord, forgive me for being presumptuous, but can anything be done?"

"If you see the cause, you will know the answer. Come, I am taking you to the mist of separation between our two worlds, so that you will see the cause. Caedmon, did you know that your ability to see the Dragon is what I call *discernment?* You can discern between two things ~ two realms, so to speak. You know when it is Me and when it is the Dragon. You need also to be aware that sometimes the Dragon will send his army and they discuss themselves as your own thoughts. When you do not want the gift inside, it makes you unaware of their presence. You have had a companion of the Dragon for a long time. His name is Despondency. So embrace the gifts I have given you. They are not only for you but also for the protection of others. Don't despise it. I know that sometimes you cannot help but feel burdened by it. Though, not wanting it to be inside of you is like despising it."

Caedmon's face fell. He had never meant to disappoint the Lord.

"Don't look so sad, Caedmon. I do not condemn you! I am only correcting you so you will walk a straight line, so to speak, not a crooked one. A crooked path takes longer to get to the destination."

Caedmon followed the Lord and was surprised when they began to climb the ledges. It was like a very steep staircase, and he could not even see the top. Taking a deep breath, he followed close behind the Lord, who would stop occasionally and give Caedmon a hand to pull him up higher. Coming to a very wide step, Caedmon was surprised to see the Lord disappear into the rock in front of him.

Caedmon approached the rock slowly, looking for the place the Lord had gone into, but he found none. Standing there for what seemed to be a long time, he finally reached out his hand and stroked the moss on the rock. An amazing thing transpired, the moss became a curtain and he walked through the many folds into the rock-face.

The light within was dim and he could barely make out the Lord in front of him, walking down the long corridor. Caedmon ran to catch up, grabbing the Lord's hand from behind. The Lord turned around and smiled.

"I wondered if you were going to follow. Don't be fooled by what your eyes show you, Caedmon. Things are not always what they appear to be. Sometimes the most insurmountable looking obstacles are not so insurmountable."

Caedmon smiled and let go of the Lord's hand, realizing that everything he was experiencing was a lesson for his life back home. And yet this was beginning to feel like home in some sort of strange way. He determined in his heart that he would learn his lessons well.

"Yes, learn them well, my friend!" the Lord replied and then laughed at Caedmon's startled expression.

"I know your thoughts, Caedmon. *All* of them!" The Lord spoke to Caedmon's discomfort.

The light in the corridor became brighter as they ventured further in, which seemed quite the opposite to natural laws. There were no lamps to light the way, but the light seemed to hang in the very air itself. As they walked, Caedmon noticed the corridor was becoming wider and that the way seemed quite natural, not like it had been made with human hands, but like it was part of the mountain itself. It was not like a cave or anything like that, but a lovely hallway adorned with swirls of colour from the precious rocks embedded in the walls. He saw streaks of gold and silver, with the shimmer of quartz all around him.

As he looked closer, he could see his reflection in the stone and what he saw surprised him. He could see his armour, his helmet upon his head. His breastplate looked slightly crooked, so he reached up to try to straighten it, but could not. His waist was girded with a shimmering belt that looked too loose and in need of tightening; his shield was hanging limp at his left side. Trying to lift his shield, he noticed that it did not change his reflection in the least, his reflection's arm still hung limply at his side. To his horror he noticed that his reflection's shoes were missing, and his sword scabbard was empty.

"Lord! Where is my sword?" Caedmon cried out in dismay. "And my shoes?"

The Lord did not answer, but strode on and abruptly turned down a side passage. Caedmon again sped up to catch Him, and when he turned the corner, he was astonished. Before him was a huge cavern, like nothing he had ever seen before. The Lord was nowhere to be found. The ceiling of the cavern had large crystals hanging like a million chandeliers. They glowed with a brilliance that lit the entire cave. The walls were of the same many-coloured surfaces as the corridor, only larger, reaching high to the ceiling far above him.

Looking out over the bottom of the cavern, he saw a lone man working at a blacksmith bellows. Taking the long stairway down, Caedmon came out at the man's level. He walked up to him slowly so as not to disturb him.

The man's upper torso was bare and covered with beads of perspiration as he worked the billows that were blowing on the coals of the forge. His leather apron was covered with the blackness of the soot from the coals. He did not look up at Caedmon, but continued to work in silence, his strong back rippling with muscle as he took something out of the coals with huge tongs. Caedmon stared at the

- 156 -

item that was glowing red with the extreme heat. The man lifted it and plunged it into a pool of water to his right as steam billowed up to the ceiling above. As he pulled it out, Caedmon gasped. It was his sword, he was sure of it! Only now it appeared larger and sharper, and more finely honed.

The large man turned, his blue eyes glittering with humour like the lovely sapphires in the walls around him. Wiping his long blonde locks from his forehead, a smile spread across his smooth, shaven face. Taking the sword and drying it very carefully with something that looked like a sheepskin, he knelt on one knee and handed the sword back to Caedmon.

"I believe this is yours, Master Caedmon," the blacksmith spoke humbly as he held the sword up with his head lowered in respect.

Caedmon suddenly felt uncomfortable. *Who was this great man that the Lord had arranged to fix my neglected sword? Why is he acting as my servant?*

"Thank you, but I think it should be *I* who is bowing in deep gratitude, not you," replied Caedmon as he reached out to take the sword.

"Then do!" smiled the man as he looked into Caedmon's eyes. "My name is Abelio, and I am your servant as you are mine. That is the way of the Prince's kingdom, you know. Our joy comes in serving, not receiving."

"Prince?" Caedmon asked.

"The unseen Lord to you, is our great Prince here beyond the mist!" Abelio answered solemnly.

Caedmon knelt down and took the sword gently from Abelio's proffered hands. The sword glistened like it never had before. As he pulled the sword to himself, his last memory of it swept through his being. With shame, he sat back on his heels and bowed his head as the memory flooded him. He was taken back and watched the whole scene...

～

"Grandma, you have to get out of this fortress! Why do you keep returning, when nothing ever changes? It never helped Mom, you know that!" Caedmon pleaded, but as he saw the resolute look on Nuala's face, he became desperate. Surely he could talk her into leaving. He knew so much now. Reaching down, he drew out his sword to show her, and let her see for herself that the unseen Lord had equipped them all personally to fight. That they did not need the false protection of these walls.

Nuala stared at the sword. Reaching out, she hesitantly touched it. It was beautiful in the dim light of the lamp in her room. Looking up, she asked, "Where did you get this? You are not a guard, are you?"

Suspicion filled Nuala's eyes as she took the sword and laid it beside her on her cot. Caedmon fell to his knees in front of her and tried to explain that she too had a sword, only she could not see it because she had chosen man for protection instead of the unseen Lord.

The more he talked, the more suspicious she became. Exhausted he laid his head on her lap. Why could she not believe him? Gripping the soft folds of her dress, he raised his head. Tears streaking down his face, he realized that it was hopeless. There was nothing he could say to change her mind.

Caedmon watched as he got up and left the room. His heart was sick to its very depths at his inability to convince her. Hopeless he left his grandmother's quarters, his heart sinking with each step. He had been so defeated he had entirely forgotten about his sword lying on his grandmother's cot.

Deep in the blacksmith's cavern… Caedmon saw that after he'd left the room, his grandma had quickly rose from her bed, wrapped the sword in a shawl, and left her room. Behind her slinked a strange dark figure. It had the appearance of burned out tree-like object, but he could see it breathing. He heard Abelio's voice.

"Its name is Bitterness. It has grown to quite a size in your grandmother's life. But its days are short. That is all I can say."

He watched as his grandmother took the sword to the guard's chambers. The guard took the sword and patted her on the head like a dog as she smiled up at him. It was obvious she enjoyed the approval ~ Caedmon could see now that it was the first approval she had felt in a long time ~ even though her heart was condemning her.

- 158 -

Caedmon watched, remorse flooding his heart. As the guard took the sword into his large library and sat down in front of the roaring fireplace. He stroked the sword and, lifting it by the handle, he waved it over his head. Letting out a moan, he had dropped the sword and grabbed his wrist as pain shot up his arm. The guard looked in horror at the sword as it disappeared before his eyes.

Then the scene dissolved in front of him...

~

Caedmon, raising his head, looked at Abelio with tears running down his face. Reaching behind himself, Abelio brought out a pair of well worn shoes.

"These are for you," Abelio offered. "They belonged to a valiant warrior of your world. They will fit you. Yours were burned when they purged the fortress. You did not even know they were missing because your heart was so discouraged. You did not notice that they had come off the minute you tried to use your emotions to persuade your grandmother over to your way of thinking."

Reaching out and taking the shoes, Caedmon nodded his thanks. As his thoughts returned to the scene he'd just witnessed, he was shaken to his very core. Had he really become so arrogant as to think he could change people? *Maybe I have always thought that way, and I am only realizing it now.* Trying to divert his thoughts, Caedmon looked at the shoes.

"Why does he not need these any longer?" Caedmon asked.

"He does not walk in your world any more. He walks in the Lord's paradise now. He gave his life for the kingdom. He is honoured highly by all," Abelio answered with awe.

"What was his name? If you don't mind me asking," Caedmon queried.

"Arthmael, a mountain dweller. He is a man of great integrity and love!" Abelio said adamantly.

Caedmon gasped as he looked at the shoes. He did not feel worthy as his own feet felt so dirty.

As if reading his thoughts, Abelio said, "Wash them in my pool if you like. It was created for that purpose. It has washed the dross of metal and the dirt of the world off many feet. Stick your head in, too! You might find it quite refreshing."

Caedmon went over to the pool and, after sticking in one foot at a time, he washed and dried them upon the sheep skin. His feet tingled from the cool water and he noticed that his calluses and bruises disappeared. They looked like the feet of a young child again. Slipping into the shoes, his heart marvelled at the wonderful freshness that came over his body.

Without even thinking about it, he dunked his head into the pool, eyes and mouth open. The water coursed into his mouth and down his throat, his nostrils filled, and a wonderful kaleidoscope of colour swirled in front of his eyes. His mind became clear and refreshed. Raising his head slowly out of the water, he shook the water off like a dog. Taking the sheep skin that Abelio was holding out to him, he wiped the remaining drops off.

When his face was dry, he opened his eyes. Caedmon was back on the step where he had been before entering the corridor. The Lord was standing there, smiling at him, "Are you ready to continue your quest, friend?"

"Lord, can you please forgive me for my feeble attempts to serve you?" Caedmon pleaded.

The Lord grasped him and pulled him into His arms, saying, "You are forgiven. Let us be on our way."

Continuing up the ledges and stopping only to drink from the cascading waterfall beside them. The Lord turned sharply to the left as the trail wound around the edge of the cliff. Caedmon's heart failed him when he saw that the path was becoming narrower and narrower until it disappeared completely in front of the Lord.

The Lord stopped and, turning, said, "This is where I leave you. Follow the path and it will take you to the mist. I will meet you there."

He disappeared immediately.

The ancients say… "if a man have an hundred sheep, and one of them be gone astray, doth he not leave the ninety and nine, and goeth into the mountains, and seeketh that which is gone astray?"

Chapter 3

Treasa was lost in thought. Caedmon had been gone to the Source for many days now, and she wished she had him there to talk to about all that was happening.

Keelin had moped around for days before abruptly leaving home without a word. Cathaoir and Treasa had mourned over their only girl's decision, but she had determined that her life was to be spent with Barris. She had announced their marriage, much to the grief of her family and friends.

Now, she was back at home, broken...

Stumbling, the young woman picked herself up and continued running through the forest. Her long white dress kept catching on twigs and stones, pulling and scratching at her legs. She did not stop running even though she was blinded by the hot tears that ran down her face.

Tripping on the root of a tree, she landed face down in the mud and leaves. Pulling herself up, she crawled over to the trunk of the tree, her dress dripping with mud and water. The beautiful embroidered bodice of the dress was ruined, and the skirt was torn and stained. She rubbed her elbow, which she had scraped and it was bleeding. The sobs shook her slender frame, and, wrapping her arms around her legs, she rocked back and forth. Her mind refused to work; the pain in her heart was more than she could bear. She wanted to die.

"Please, let me die," she groaned.

The day had started with all the joy Keelin could muster. She knew in her heart that she was hurting her parents and friends. Even though her family was not there to celebrate her day, she was in love and knew they would regret their choice to not attend. Barris had swept her off her feet. She did not care that he did not serve the unseen Lord, at least he believed in Him. Her parents had no idea of what she really needed. He was what she wanted and she was glad for it. He was her way to escape what everyone had thought had been the unseen Lord's leading. She was sure they just wanted her to grow into an old spinster. Keelin had shown them; she would marry this young man. Her companion of Rebellion, smiled a sardonic smile. Dragon-like but much smaller than *the* Dragon.

As she had prepared for the ceremony, she felt like a princess in a fairytale. Sobs shook her again. How could he have come in right before the wedding and tell her it was over? How could he say that the feelings he'd had were changed? Keelin had pleaded with Barris, *begged* him to stay. But he, wiping the tears from his own eyes, had turned and left.

Anger swept over Keelin as she looked at her destroyed dress. She got up and began tearing at the fine cloth, but it would not rip. Turning to a tree, she struck it until her hands were bleeding, but still the pain would not leave her heart. Slumping to the ground, she laid her cheek against the tree.

She felt herself being comforted, even though she did not want comfort. Her cold hands and feet became warm. She lay down on the moss beneath the tree and fell fast asleep. The unseen Lord, ignoring Rebellion, looked at her for a long time as He gently stroked her forehead. Humming a beautiful melody, He finally broke into song. He sang of His love and hope for her, and of His knowing what was best for her. The unseen Lord sang of her pain, but also of her recovery and wholeness again. He sang of Keelin coming to Him and wanting to abide by His will again. The Lord's song took on a note of victory as He sang of the influence of the Dragon being broken, once and for all, over Keelin. Kneeling down, the unseen Lord gently picked her up, and, carrying her to the main road. He laid her softly on the grass beside the road. Keelin never

- 162 -

awoke but slept on, for a deep sleep was upon her. Rebellion slithered away into the gloom of the forest. The unseen Lord was the last one it wanted to confront.

Keelin's village friends, had gone out looking for her in the forest after somebody had seen her running that way. Nevertheless, after hours of searching, they had given up hope and returned to their homes. They sent word to the farm about what had happened. Her family and friends went immediately and carried on the searching, but they could find no trace of her. Cathaoir and the rest had returned to the farm in case Keelin showed up there, all except for Treasa, who was still out looking, and calling for her only daughter.

Treasa's own heart was broken, and she did not even know what to ask the unseen Lord for except to strengthen her to keep looking. Coming to the main road to the village, she saw a form lying on the grass beside the road. Running up, she was shocked to see Keelin sound asleep, with her head cradled on the crook of her arm. Treasa fell to her knees and pulled Keelin up onto her lap, rocking her gently. Keelin awoke, but did not struggle to get away as she was too shocked at finding herself out by the open road. How she had happened in her mother's arms was beyond her comprehension. She clung to her mother as fresh sobs tore her.

Treasa kept gently rocking her until she became quiet. Upon hearing the wheels of a wagon behind her, Treasa turned her head and saw Cathaoir driving up in the small cart. With a tear streaked face, she mouthed a "thank you" to Cathaoir as relief flooded her soul, nodding her head down to her slumped daughter on her lap. Cathaoir quickly jumped out of the cart. Lifting his darling daughter up in his arms, he carefully placed her in the back of the cart. Keelin's limp body seemed lifeless. Treasa crawled up beside her, pulling her into her arms. She sat holding her while Cathaoir turned the horse and quickly drove home.

~

Days passed and Keelin never left her room. Her family had tried to help her as best they could. Teague tried singing to her, but realized it had been so long since he had drunk from the Unchanging

River that his song was lifeless. Gallagher and Aine tried speaking to her, but they, too, had not been spending time with the unseen Lord and their words seemed to fall flat to the floor. Even Seanna's words seemed empty, she had been so busy with her own family now that she had forgot to mediate. Shylah mediated to the unseen Lord for Keelin, but He told her that she and Treasa had to wait awhile but He would come to Keelin when it was time.

The family's hearts were broken over the fact that there was nothing, absolutely *nothing*, they could do for her. They showed their love by the food they tried to encourage Keelin to eat, and by brushing her long brown hair. The wedding dress had been damaged beyond repair, so they had put it away, far from her sight, because the day after Keelin's arrival home, Treasa had found her holding her wedding dress and sobbing into it, calling for her lover to come back. It had taken some persuading to get the filthy dress from her.

Treasa, walking alone in the garden, decided she needed to go to the Unchanging River's Source. She desperately needed Gilroy and Treva's counsel. As the unseen Lord walked with her around the garden, she felt an overwhelming peace come to her heart. This was His will; He had told her before that she would go the river's Source.

Striding to the house, with more purpose than she had in months, she told Cathaoir she would be gone for a while. He looked at her for a long moment, then lowered his gaze, knowing that it was time he cried out to the unseen Lord for his daughter.

"I will keep vigil over Keelin while you are gone. I am sorry I haven't been seeking the unseen Lord for her. I've just let complacency be my master. I will seek Him for her, and for me too. Be careful dearest, and stay on the path by the river until you are there. Do you want Teague to go with you?" Cathaoir spoke with genuine concern and brokenness.

"I am going to see if Shylah can come. We both so badly need the water from the Unchanging River. I will fill my canteen. I have been drinking from our own well far too long," Treasa answered with more hope and faith than she had felt in a long time.

In the other room, Keelin rolled over on her bed, grabbed her diary, and tried to write, but her heart felt dead. Laying it aside she stared at the timbers in the ceiling. A faint hope was still in her heart that her lover would come for her yet. Though, she knew it was hopeless… She knew he would not come.

Her heart hurt too much to even be angry at the unseen Lord anymore. Rolling back onto her side, she curled into the fetal position and fell into a depressed sleep. Cathaoir found her like that, after Treasa had left. He knelt down beside her bed and implored the unseen Lord to come to his child. What had happened to them all? When had they stopped living and helping one another? Revelation suddenly came as he realized that it was when they had begun to believe the lies about themselves.

The Dragon had been busy with its lies, spreading insults and gossip about those who had left the fortress. Cathaoir had found it hard to meet any of the fortress dwellers, even on the village streets. He looked back over the time since Arthmael had been murdered and cringed. Yes, it was true. Cathaoir had to face it; he had wished that his family had not stopped visiting the fortress. Even though he had known it was wrong, he did not want to be responsible for his own relationship with the unseen Lord. He had liked the idea that it was up to the guard to do that for him. He *had* believed that they were mistaken and false for leaving.

Stretching out on the floor, face down, he began to sob. "Change my heart, oh Lord! Take me, I am Yours. We need you so badly right now. I need you!" Cathaoir's petition wretched from his soul. Complacency shuddered and left the house.

~

Treasa and Shylah walked in silence for the first part of their journey, each thinking her own thoughts. Treasa was looking forward to seeing Caedmon at the Source, and to seeking Gilroy and Treva's council for Keelin.

When the women came to the Unchanging River, they looked with shock at the low stream that was flowing through the river bed. They could see that the rocks that had once been beneath the water level were now dry, and in some places the river was only a few feet wide.

- 165 -

"What is happening?" Treasa spoke in a whisper to Shylah. "I hadn't even noticed that the river was drying up. Do you think there is any sense in going to the Source when there appears to be no water flowing?"

"I don't know," Shylah spoke with a sob, catching her words in her throat. "What else do we have? We must go on! Maybe the unseen Lord will meet us and tell us what is wrong."

Treasa knelt down and cupping some of the water in her hand, drank from the river. She felt restored immediately and knew she had to go on. Shylah, following her example, knelt down and drank as well. Renewed vigour entered her soul.

Laughing out loud, she slapped Treasa teasingly on the back. Treasa, who had been balanced very precariously on her one knee, fell face first into the stream. Gasping with shock, she regained her focus and grabbed Shylah, pulling her into the water. Both full-grown women began to splash one another, laughing and playing like small girls. The unseen Lord watched them from the bank and quickly ran to join them in the river. The women immediately felt His presence. Laughing hysterically, they all splashed and played.

Dragging themselves from the water, gasping for breath, they lay side by side on the bank, drying themselves in the sun. For the first time in weeks, both women felt restored. That was precisely the moment when they heard it ~ a gurgling, bubbling noise. The river itself seemed to be coming to life. Though it was still a very small stream, it sparkled and glittered in the sun. Getting to their feet, they began their journey with a feeling of hope and joy in their hearts.

The Dragon watched from a distance. This was not going according to its plan! First, Caedmon had disappeared into thin air at the Unchanging River's Source. Now, these two hated mediators were going there as well to seek help for the young woman, Keelin.

The beast could already feel the effect of Cathaoir's supplications to the unseen Lord. And its worthless servant Complacency was too afraid to stay with Cathaoir any longer. The Dragon knew it was losing its hold on Keelin. Turning, it went in a rage down the mountain, intending to spew more of its lies on the girl. *Where is Rebellion when I need him!*

The Ancients say… "He fed them according to the integrity of his heart; and guided them by the skilfulness of his hands."

Chapter 4

As Caedmon looked ahead his head swam. Clutching the side of the cliff wall, he strained to see the path, but it was gone. Looking back, shock and horror filled his heart as he saw that the path had disappeared completely behind him. It appeared that no solid footing was anywhere in sight. His mind began to accuse him of being a fool, but Caedmon's heart rose up and told him that the Lord had never, never failed him before. So, straightening his shoulders, he stepped ahead without looking down, having faith that the Lord would not let him fall.

In complete amazement, he did not fall. He stepped again, discovering that as he walked, an invisible path was under his feet to hold him up. Wonder filled his heart as he looked at the beautiful land that was below him. The valley was so green and the river that coursed through it was as blue as the sky above.

Making his way slowly around the corner of the cliff, he stopped. He was standing on the edge of a beautiful mountain meadow. There before him, sheep were grazing contentedly around a shepherd sitting on a large rock. The shepherd was, in turn, watching Caedmon. In a deep, low voice, he was singing a song about the beauty of a mountain's perspective on life and the joy of caring for contented sheep.

Caedmon, stepping onto the meadow, approached the shepherd. Not wanting the song to stop, he sat down on the grass while the sheep continued their grazing around him. The shepherd's song finally ended and he looked Caedmon over from the top of his head to the sole's of his shoes.

Caedmon was looking the shepherd over as well. He had never seen anyone like him before. His dark eyes were piercing, as if he could see into the very depths of Caedmon's soul. His hair, black as coal, was long and pulled into a tail at the nape of his neck. He had a short-cropped black beard and in his ear was an earring of gold with an engraving on it. Caedmon could not see it clearly, but somehow knew it was a lion's head.

"What brings you to my plateau?" the shepherd asked, lifting one brow in a quizzical way.

"I did not know that I was on your plateau, sir. I am on a quest of the Lord. The Unchanging River has dropped and He is going to show me the cause. I am hoping to fix the problem ~ if I can. The Lord led me this way," Caedmon felt suddenly nervous, like he was an intruder.

"Do not fear! If He brought you to this mountain then there is a purpose. I am a shepherd of sheep. My name is Carden, and I care for the sheep the Lord brings to me. These ones are just about ready to go to His valley pasture. They are full of health now. When they come to me, they are weak and find it hard to eat on their own. I tenderly coax them to try, and as they taste this mountain grass, they soon begin to feed on their own," Carden smiled as he spoke. "It helps them to be up here in the mountain air and to be away from those that want to make them dependent on them. Sheep are not the swiftest animals when it comes to reasoning, but they are affectionate and loyal. Once they know they can trust you, they will love you forever. That is why I sing to them. The song soothes them. They have been yelled at so much in the past. It erases the pain from their hearts."

Caedmon could feel the love that Carden had for his sheep, and he felt inspired somehow to love like this man loved. Looking up at Carden, he spoke before he even thought, "I too have a song. I mean, I suddenly feel like singing to your sheep."

"Go ahead. The sheep will recognize if it is a song of healing or a song out of your own heart. Sing lad, sing!" Carden said, with anticipation. Rising from his rock, the shepherd came and sat on the grass beside Caedmon.

Caedmon began to hum and then the words spilled out of him, like a river gushing through a narrow gorge. His falsetto voice filled the air with breathtaking clarity. The sheep gathered close and

- 169 -

nuzzled at his coat. Carden stared at the young man, never hearing a song like this one. It was as if the Lord Himself was singing out His love for the sheep. The song became low and sad, and the words were for the sheep that did not want to be tended but wanted to stray on their own. Low bleating came from the sheep as they listened. They turned their heads towards Caedmon as if they understood the sadness of the shepherd over his lost sheep. The song took on the sound of authority as the tone changed and the shepherd went to look for his lost sheep. He had his staff in his hand and his rod ready to fight off any foe. A quiet hush came over the meadow as the melody became sweet. Caedmon sang of the shepherd finding his lost sheep and carrying it home in his arms.

Caedmon blushed as he looked shyly at Carden. He had never in his life sang to a stranger before. Carden's eyes were closed and he was sitting perfectly still. A lone tear was glistening on his cheek. One of the sheep laid his head upon Carden's lap and was very still beside him.

Carden opened his eyes, and, looking at Caedmon, he said, "You have been sent by the Lord to refresh my soul and remind me of my own quest ~ to nurture the lost lambs, that He has brought me, back to health. Thank you for the song. It was as if the Lord Himself was singing to me." Then Carden asked, "Now, my young man, what has the Lord given you to take back with you?"

"I do not know what you mean, sir," Caedmon honestly replied.

"What has been given to you? That is, what is it that the Lord wants you to know to equip you for your quest?"

"Well," Caedmon hesitated, then suddenly he knew and spoke enthusiastically, "He has given me new shoes and returned my sword, which, I must add, is in much better shape than it was before. He showed me the condition of my armour, which I know He will improve with time. He also cleared my mind and let me wash my feet. Well, I don't know what he's given me here in this meadow, except maybe a desire to love like you do."

"He has given you a song. As you sing that song you will love, Caedmon," Carden replied.

- 170 -

Caedmon smiled. Nodding his head he asked, "Do you have any idea where I should go to find the mist between our worlds?"

Carden pointed straight out over the chasm that divided this mountain from the next. Caedmon shook his head in disbelief as he gazed at the wide gulf between the mountains.

"Must I go down and then up the other side?" Caedmon asked.

"No, bless your heart. You go straight over," Carden said, "the same way you came on the path. Here, we go where we do not see. Is it different where you live?"

"Well, I guess not," Caedmon spoke carefully, "It is just that in our land, we are asked to do things that we don't know the outcome of. Though, we can see our roads and paths."

Caedmon, speaking more to himself than Carden, added, "I will not let myself be afraid, but go on as the Lord has told to me. We will meet at the mist. No matter what I feel I must go on. There are many who are depending on me."

"Before you cross over, first you must climb higher. Your time here on this mountain is not over." Carden put his hand firmly on Caedmon's shoulder as he spoke. Caedmon felt strength surge through his body as the gentle shepherd squeezed his shoulder. As Caedmon looked around the high plateau, he saw no rise in the mountain. The elevation was already so high that clouds were rolling around the one whole side of the mountain far in front of him.

"The path upward is in the cloud," Carden answered Caedmon's unspoken question. "I will walk with you to the cloud. Come with me! It is a delightful place on the top of this great mountain."

Carden walked with Caedmon to the edge of the cloud. Shaking Caedmon's hand, he turned back to his sheep. Caedmon, taking a deep breath, walked into the cloud.

The Ancients say… "We hanged our harps upon the willows in the midst thereof."

Chapter 5

Aine stood to leave the room. Tears coursed down her fair cheeks. Her long black hair was swept high off her neck. She reached up and tucked an imaginary stray strand behind her ear. She had failed Keelin, somehow, and she could not fix it. She knew that she and Gallagher would soon be leaving, and she knew that in many ways they were not ready for this quest. However, Gallagher had not seemed aware of his insufficiencies or even his complacency. She, too, felt her own worldly desires were greater than her desires for the unseen Lord. Greed dogged her steps, it did not like the tears or brokenness that was evident.

As she walked in the garden by the gate, she pondered where her heart was. She could not remember when she had stopped relying on the Unchanging River for life and the unseen Lord's presence for guidance. Dropping onto her knees among the daisies, she raised her hands in silent supplication to her unseen Lord.

Gallagher had seen Aine leave the room, but he was busy talking to Edan of all that the unseen Lord was going to do through him on this quest. Edan seemed uninterested, and only responded occasionally. Gallagher stood to his feet and left the room to follow Aine outside. He glanced over at Keelin, who sat with her feet curled up beneath her. She was staring blankly into the fire. Even though they were all there to comfort her, she seemed oblivious to their presence. His heart began to convict him of his lack of ability to help her.

Seeing Aine kneeling in the garden, Gallagher went and quietly joined her. Reaching over he took her hand as he thought of how unkind he had been to her ~ the gift the unseen Lord had given him. She looked at him with tears streaming down her cheeks and then, she gently laid her head on his shoulder as they sat there together, basking in the Lord's forgiveness.

"I love you, my joy. Aine, I am so sorry for how I have been so complacent. This whole thing with Keelin has exposed my lack of concern for others, and how I have not wanted to spend time with the unseen Lord. Will you forgive me, my dearest one?" Gallagher's voice broke as he finished speaking. Aine looked long into his eyes and, reaching up, she kissed him tenderly on the lips.

"You are forgiven, my love. Do you forgive me? I, too, have been complacent and selfish. When I should have turned to the unseen Lord, I ran away and sulked."

"Yes," Gallagher answered. "I do forgive you." He then pulled her close and held her for a long time. "Let's ask the unseen Lord to touch Keelin's heart and heal her."

With their foreheads touching, this loving couple made their request to the unseen Lord. They both knew that the only thing they could do was mediate for her. Greed hastened its retreat not wanting to meet the unseen Lord or His warriors face to face. It knew that the Dragon would want to know what was happening.

Gallagher and Aine would be leaving on the morrow. The unseen Lord had asked them to go across the sea to the same land where Gilroy and Caedmon had gone. They were to live among the people there and show them the unseen Lord's love for them. They had been so caught up in the romance of the trip ahead of them that they had forgotten that the only way they could show the unseen Lord's love was to be experiencing it themselves.

Their pleas went straight to the unseen Lord. He came immediately and laid His hands upon their heads. His heart swelled with joy as He knew that they had missed Him as much as He had them. Even though He knew that Gallagher was only partially awake.

~

Edan looked across the room at his wife, Tully. How he wished she would behave herself because he wanted her to be perfect. She looked up at him, as she had felt his eyes upon her. She quickly dropped her gaze again, she knew that he was being critical. She stood and went over to Keelin. Kneeling down, she whispered something into Keelin's ear. Leaning forward she took Keelin into

- 173 -

her arms and held for a long time. When she finally pulled away, she saw that Keelin's eyes were dry, but she smiled wanly at Tully in thanks.

Edan remembered what Treasa had told him ~ that if he demanded perfection from others, that very judgement would come upon him. He had tried to change, but he was still the same, even though he knew that it was wrong. He just seemed to know better than others that was all! He got up and went over to Tully, speaking to her secretively.

"Come on Tully, let's go home. We are of no help here. She needs to get a grip on reality."

Tully looked at him in anger. Leaving Keelin's side, she stormed to the door of the cottage. At times she absolutely could slap her husband's face, but she controlled her temper. Well, he better not think she was going to be loving to him. He was cold to other's needs, and it bothered her deeply. What had happened to the fire they had felt between each other in the beginning?

Tully felt her conscience pricked; she had not exactly been seeking the unseen Lord recently. She had not used her sword against the Dragon's lies in a long time. In fact she had not even *seen* her sword in a long time. Walking slowly out the door after Edan, she laid her hand upon the small swelling in her abdomen. No one even knew she was with child, only Edan. She wondered who this little one would be that she carried within.

Teague arrived at the cottage just after Gallagher and Aine had left. Walking over to Keelin, he bent over and kissed her on her head. She looked up at him and smiled, but did not utter a word. Keelin, looking at the lyre in Teague's hand, straightened in her chair and stood as she quietly walked from the room. Teague looked down at his lyre and ran from the room. Running until there was no strength left in him, he fell on his knees by the Unchanging River. What had happened to them all? His wife, Seanna, had become so indifferent to Keelin lately. Seanna seemed to think that *time* alone would heal Keelin.

Two weeks had passed since Keelin's rejection and there was no change. He wished his mother would get home, because Keelin

- 174 -

needed her, and he needed her. His father seemed to be the only one that was able to comfort Keelin. He, spending long hours with her, talked to the unseen Lord right in front of her. Only then would she talk a little, eat some, and even go for small walks with their Da.

Teague looked at the low river that was exactly like his feelings. It felt like he was drying up inside. Stretching out his hand, he swirled the water with his fingers. Laying his lyre aside, he reached down and cupped some of the water in his hand. Tears streamed down his face as he realized that he could not remember the last time he had drunk from this water.

He slowly sipped the water, feeling his heart break as remorse filled his soul. Instead of life, he felt a deep mourning and longing fill his heart. He missed his best friend, the unseen Lord. He knew that he had to make things right with Him.

"Lord, do you hear me?" Teague cried out, "Come to me, my Lord!"

"I have never left you, Teague, my friend." The soft answer came on the gentle breeze that had begun to blow.

"I know. It was me who left. Please forgive me. Please help me. Help Keelin. She needs You, Lord. I don't know what to do for her," Teague's voice trembled with emotion.

The unseen Lord swept the wind around Teague wildly. Teague tried to hang on, but he felt the wind driving him into the river. He clung to the rocks, but his body slipped into the water and the river drove his head under. Teague quit fighting, letting the wind and the river drive him forward. The rush of the water over his body began to wash away the fear and hopelessness. Coming up for air, he whipped the water from his long hair. Smiling, he dove under the water. Teague could feel the presence of unseen Lord swimming beside him.

Finally, Teague pulled himself out of the river and walked up the shoreline back towards his lyre. He cried, laughed, and felt a song rising in his heart. He knew deep in his heart that things would be all right. Whistling the melody that came flooding over his being, he turned down the road to the farm. His wet clothes were cling- ing to his body. Stopping, he pulled the lyre from its satchel and began to play and sing. He danced ~ twirling around and around. The music became like a rainbow of colours swirling in and about his body. The song rose, floating through the air like the flowing of a spring waterfall cascading over the land.

The countryside disappeared from Teague's vision and he saw a beautiful meadow surrounded by large evergreens. Within the meadow were pools of water, and he could see light dancing off the water in time to the rhythm of his song. He kept playing and dancing among the pools. Teague did not know where he was, but this he knew ~ he was where he was supposed to be. He sang and sang, dancing with all his might. Finally tiring, he stopped and looked into the nearest pool. What he saw startled him. There in the swirling depths he could see his beautiful wife, Seanna. Her head bowed and with a ragged, full sack on her back, weighing her down. He could see his own arm hanging from the sack. He knew immediately what it meant.

Teague began to tremble as he dropped to his knees, crying out, "Oh, Lord what have I done? Help us!" Immediately he was back on the road to the farm with a new determination that gave him energy to do what he had to do.

Seanna was standing at the gate when Teague appeared at the gate. Seeing him, she ran to meet him. Stopping, she looked in shock at his wet clothes. "What have you been doing?" Seanna asked impatiently.

"Swimming," Teague answered with a smile. "Just swimming."

"You went swimming? It is not even hot. And you went in with your clothes on?" She asked incredulously.

"Well, not exactly. Well, I did swim with my clothes on, but I did not jump in ~ I was pushed in," Teague smiled sheepishly as he answered her.

"Pushed in! Who was with you?" Seanna asked nervously.

Teague smiled as he told her what had happened and that he had made things right with the unseen Lord. He also told her that there was going to be a change in their home, and he vowed to help her carry the burden of the household ~ that they were going to both seek the unseen Lord's advice and to hear Him again. He

- 176 -

was not going to allow her to have to carry his responsibilities any longer. He apologized for his indifferent manner he'd had for her lately. Seanna began to cry, and she too apologized to him. She had liked having all of Teague's attention and she had not wanted to have to share him with Edan and Caedmon on their quests. Feeling ashamed of herself, she admitted that she missed their wild music. They held each other for a long time, until Seanna finally pulled away playfully. Selfishness fled from the happy couple.

"I will think that I too have gone swimming if you make me any wetter."

"Let's go in and encourage Da... He has had so much to do. Mama will be coming home soon, the unseen Lord gave me such hope." Teague spoke as he opened the door for Seanna and they entered the cottage.

~

The Dragon had heard enough. Its army had returned distraught. This was not right! It had persuaded the pilgrims to become self-seeking, but this change of heart was not in the plan. It did not like the fact that these farm pilgrims were so connected to the Source dwellers. The Dragon knew that Caedmon had gone to the Source and then disappeared from its sight. Treasa was at the settlement right now on the mountain, and now Teague seemed to be going down the same path...

Fury raged through the Dragon's mind. Why was everyone awakening? The Dragon flew out over the land, swooping down over the Unchanging River. The water seemed alive somehow, though the Dragon had no idea how this could be. Screeching in rage, it flew straight to the large fortress, Evergreen, a trail of slime in its wake. It dove into the pool and the water began to boil, turning a sludge-green colour.

The Ancients say… "Wisdom hath built her house; she hath mingled her wine; she hath also furnished her table. Come, eat of my bread, and drink of the wine which I have mingled."

Sophronia ~ the wise one

Shylah and Treasa, upon arriving at the Source settlement, did not know exactly what to do at first. Gilroy found them sitting by the Source, staring at what was left of the artesian fountain. Tears were streaming down their faces. Their utter dejection stirred something deep within his heart; he knew that the unseen Lord had drawn them here.

"Good day, ladies," he greeted them.

Treasa, lifting her face, looked up at him. Smiling, she replied, "Oh, Gilroy, it is so good to see you! We felt compelled to come to the Source, but now that we see the state of it and the little water that is coming out, we do not know what to do. Our hearts are broken because…" She was not able to finish her thought as a sob rose in her throat and choked the words away.

Shylah put her arm around her friend and pulled her close. Looking up at Gilroy, her friend's sobs made her own tears start again.

"Keelin is in a bad way. We came to the Source to seek the unseen Lord for answers about what to do for her. Now we do not know what to do. We tried calling to Him and we even waited silently, but He does not seem to be answering us."

Gilroy's eyes grew wide in wonder and he pointed to something behind them. Both women turned to look at the fountain. Rocketing high into the air from the very centre of the Source, crystal columns of water were suddenly spurting forth. All three looked with amazement at the water, which seemed to be under extreme pressure as it shot up into the air. Rainbows of colour appeared in the spray, and small flowers around the base of the large pool began to turn a living green again, their tiny wilted heads beginning to rise to face the sun.

Pilgrims from the village came running out and stood in awe. Their beloved Source was returning ~ they could feel it. Some felt deep sorrow as their hearts convicted them of their self-centered ways. Still others began to dance, sing and twirl around. The children ran into the pool and played in the falling water, their innocent hearts revelling in their simple devotion to the unseen Lord. The noise of the people was like a tumult; some were laughing, and still others were singing at the top of their lungs.

Treasa and Shylah, felt almost guilty over their heavy hearts for Keelin, as it seemed to be stealing the joy of the moment. Standing quietly, they both turned and walked into the pool with the children. Their sombre faces made the children retreat to their parents. Both women walked straight into the fountain, knowing that this was what they were to do, and disappeared from the villagers' sight.

They must be heading into the Source. It must be their door, Gilroy thought. Dropping to his knees, he petitioned the unseen Lord to guide them to the wisdom they both so desperately sought.

Caedmon had been gone now for many days already, and Gilroy wondered if they would meet beyond the mist. His old heart longed to go after them, but knew that his place was here. He needed to comfort the ones that the unseen Lord sent him to. His day to cross over between the two kingdoms was coming, but he also knew that in his case, when he was called he would not return. His trip would not be just beyond the mist but beyond the veil of no return.

As she traversed the fountain, Treasa looked around with surprise. She was knee deep in mud. Standing beside her was Shylah, who was also deep in the mud. How they arrived there was a mystery. One moment they were walking in the fountain, enjoying the refreshing water falling on their aching heads, and the next moment they were knee deep in mud. The women stood still baffled by the suddenness of the change that had befallen them ~ not even knowing that they had passed through the mist into the unseen Lord's kingdom.

- 179 -

"Look, Shylah," Treasa said as she pointed to their right. "It appears that someone is waving to us."

Shylah turned her head and looked, but as she did, she lost her footing ~ falling sideways into the large mud pond. She shrieked in surprise, then began to laugh. Mud splashed all over Treasa, who was trying to avoid the splashing mud. Slipping, Treasa fell onto her knees as her hands flayed out in front of her to catch her fall. Shylah's laughing did not please Treasa, who now could not move at all, with both hands stuck fast in the mud.

"Where do you think we are?" Treasa asked stiffly.

Letting out another nervous laugh, Shylah answered, "I do believe we are stuck in the mud."

"Shylah!"

Treasa screeched as she ripped her hand up out of the mud, flinging a handful of mud in Shylah's direction. Before she could help herself, she too began to laugh. Thinking to herself that only hours before they had been playing in the Unchanging River with the unseen Lord. They had felt so clean, she had no idea why they were now wallowing in the mud like a couple of sows.

Shylah was sitting in mud that came up to her waist. As she examined it, she saw that it was of the most beautiful colour ~ like gold, but the texture of cream pudding. She wiped her hand across the surface of the mud and felt the drawing quality like a large poultice. Treasa pulled herself up to sit beside Shylah and wiped the mud from her splattered face. In doing so, she streaked a large smear across her top lip, which resembled a moustache. Shylah had a pile of mud situated right on top of her head, flowing down into the tendrils of hair that hung freely by her face. She smiled at Treasa.

"I wouldn't say anything if I was you," Treasa teased, "until at least you look at your own reflection."

"Look at this stuff, Treasa. It is like gold dust made into pudding. See the glitter and sparkles? Doesn't it look like the purest gold pudding?"

Treasa examined the mud and let out a resigned sigh. "I think it only *looks* like gold, Shylah ~ like so many other things that have appeared around us," she said warily. This is exactly what her circumstances had seemed like lately ~ like she was stuck and couldn't change herself or help those around her. At the same time, she knew that these circumstances had been drawing out something deadly that had been lying dormant within herself. Like a large poultice drawing out the infection. *Complacency! Self-protection!* These thoughts pounded in her heart.

The women suddenly knew that the unseen Lord was working on cleaning them up. *This is a pretty upside-down way of doing things!* Treasa thought with a smile as she played in the mud with her fingers.

Looking up, she could see that the pool of mud was only about the size of a very small pond, and around the edges of the pond was the tallest bull rushes she had ever seen. The bank of the pond rose high above the mud, with a forest of large fir trees standing like silent sentinels.

Looking over, she was surprised to see that Shylah was now lying on her back, floating on the mud with a contented smile on her face. Her eyes were closed and a faraway look was upon her face. Tears were making little rivers down the sides of her muddy cheeks, washing the mud away. She looked beautiful in her mud bath with the glitter of the mud shining in the daylight.

Treasa stood and looked towards where she had seen someone waving at them. A woman was sitting under a tree. Her head was leaning back against it and her eyes were shut. Long black hair hung down around her shoulders like a veil, and her white face was one of the most gorgeous that Treasa had ever seen.

Treasa reached down and, pulling her one foot free of the mud, stepped ahead and did the same with her other foot. Shylah, sitting up, followed Treasa's example. Both women finally made it to the shore and pulled their bodies from the mire. As they walked towards the woman the mud began to dry, cracking and falling off in small chunks.

"Welcome, ladies. I am so glad you have come," the woman's melodious voice filled the air.

Treasa walked up to her and stretched out her hand, but withdrew it quickly as she saw the half-dried mud clinging to it. The woman smiled and, reaching out, she grasped Treasa's hand despite the mud.

"I am not afraid of getting this lovely mud on myself. I am the one who has been appointed to mix it and keep it available for the unseen Lord's people from beyond the mist," she told them with a serious note entering her voice. "Sometimes, those who come will fight and kick, screaming that they are drowning. Those ones are returned to the other side of the mist, because we cannot help them. They have let their circumstances *rule* them instead of perfect them. There are others, like yourselves, who learn to enjoy and even desire the mud. Evidently, you two have been learning not to kick against your circumstances."

Seeing the shocked look on their faces, she smiled and added, "You never know what the outcome of your circumstances will be while you are in the them but your hearts, whether you know it or not, have grown stronger through this time of testing. Or, as I like to call it, *'time of poultice applying'*."

Treasa and Shylah laughed wholeheartedly, instantly warming to this mysterious woman. Treasa told her how this lesson was one she was just learning. It was evident by her attempt to free herself from the mud and then, having to take small steps out of it.

"My name is Sophronia. I know your names well. Treasa, which means strong, and Shylah, your name also means strong. You were named well by your parents. Come! I will take you to my cottage and there you can bathe," she said as she turned and began to walk away down the forest path.

The women fell into line behind her, following down the path. The huge branches reached high above them like a beautiful canopy blocking the direct light from the sky. The light around them had the appearance of the reflected light of an emerald. On the floor of the forest every fern and bush imaginable grew. The lush carpet lay as far into the woods as they could see. Here and there they could see wild yellow daisies shining like bright little faces interspersed in the green foliage. Birds of every colour darted among the trees, their beautiful voices filling the air with music. The women slowed their pace, letting the peace of this lovely land soak deep within their beings. Their hearts came to rest from the cares that had driven them there.

"Caedmon is here," Sophronia spoke softly. "He, too, had to learn much for what lies ahead. Here you will gain the wisdom you need for your quest. The unseen Lord only invites those that are seeking Him ~ and only Him ~ to find answers. I have been appointed to feed you and let you bathe. Our food here is your kingdom's insight."

Coming out into a glade, the women were surprised to see a small cottage that seemed to be part of the very forest itself. Sophronia went before them, opening the door to invite them in. The women stood stock still in the doorway, utterly speechless with mouths gaping open. Stepping through the doorway they were overwhelmed, for on the inside it was a magnificent mansion. Their sense of perspective was completely thrown for a turn.

Sophronia led them up the winding staircase to a long corridor that had many doors down both sides. Coming to a door on the left, she stopped and opened it. Treasa and Shylah followed her into the beautiful room. The high ceiling towered far above their heads with shimmering curtains, which were hung on the walls, fluttering as if a breeze was gently blowing them. In the centre of the room was a table spread with all kinds of fruit and delicate cakes and, the smell of fresh bread wafted through the air. Upon the table, a large loaf of fresh bread was set beside two lovely wine goblets, filled to the brim with a sparkling purple drink.

"This is where you will come to eat when you are done bathing. The door there on the left is for you, Shylah, and the one on the right is for you, Treasa. Enjoy your bath and do not leave until you are absolutely sure that every speck of the mud is washed from you. You must be ready for your next set of circumstances without the old still hanging onto you," Sophronia quietly spoke to them.

Treasa walked to her door and went through, and Shylah went to her door and walked through. Both women were suddenly feeling very vulnerable from being alone, but knew in their hearts that this next experience had to be a personal one. Treasa looked about the room, which turned into a garden as she stepped inside. The lovely carpet became soft grass beneath her feet, and the walls became weathered stone. What had appeared to be a large bathtub turned into a lovely pool with water lilies blooming upon the surface of the shimmering water. The water sparkled and shone in the daylight, and the branches of tall blossoming trees hung over the wall, their fragrance filling the air. A small path led to stone steps that went down into the pool. Approaching with sheer delight, Treasa removed her soiled clothes and stepped down into the pool. As she looked back towards her pile of clothes, she was shocked to see that they had disappeared. Hanging on one of the low branches were clean clothes. She smiled to herself because she had never in her life felt so pampered and special.

The water swirled around her legs as its warmth drew her in deeper. She lowered her tired body into the pool, and the water swished around her slowly. She began to wipe at the mud on her face and it dissolved, slipping from her skin. She then slowly began to wash her body with extreme care. This was going to take awhile, so she settled herself down on one of the steps in the water to begin her meticulous bath. She noticed that what she had thought to be water lilies were in actuality floating washcloths. She took one and used it to wipe her skin. As she wiped herself she smiled with pleasure. The fabric felt so soft on her body.

Finally finished, Treasa took her fingers and combed the knots out of her wet hair. She stepped out of the pool, walking unashamedly to the clothes hanging on the tree. Even though she had nothing on her body she felt entirely covered and protected and clean. Her body dried as she walked over to the clothes. Taking them down, she put on the simple undergarments and dress, which had beautiful embroidered roses on the bodice and a full skirt in lovely folds to her feet.

She could see her armour appear over the dress looking polished and new. She carefully drew out her sword and lovingly stroked the polished gold of the blade. She wondered why she had quit using this mighty weapon against the Dragon's lies.

Feeling someone come up behind her, she turned and looked straight into the eyes of her beloved unseen Lord. She was not surprised to actually see Him. 'Twas only natural to see Him here.

- 184 -

He smiled, slowly drawing her into an embrace. She let herself lean heavily on His chest. *How I need His comfort at this time. He is here, and He cares.*

~

Shylah stepped through the door to bathe her muddy body. She looked around herself in utter amazement as the high ceiling of the room faded from her sight. A blue sky rolled into view, with light fluffy clouds slowly moving across the expanse. Looking around her, the walls slowly transformed into the high walls of a cavern. On the other side, a beautiful waterfall was gently falling into the pool. The walls of the cavern were naturally adorned with every gemstone imaginable and swirls of gold and silver.

Shylah stepped down into the bubbling water of the pool. The water felt as smooth as silk to her skin. Quickly stepping back out, she undressed, laying her clothes aside carefully. As she did they disappeared right before her eyes. She gasped in shock and dismay. Looking all around, she wondered how she would ever cover herself. Seeing nothing, she dove into the pool.

The water pulled at her tired body and began to wash off the mud. Shylah came up for air and found herself beneath the water-fall. The water was only knee deep, so she stood to allow the gentle falling water to wash the rest of the mud from her hair and body. Lifting her hands in joy, she felt strength surge through her whole being. Walking back into the depths of the pool, she swam back towards the edge. Beneath her, Shylah could feel steps cut into the rock below the gurgling water. She slowly rose out of the water as she climbed the steps, no longer feeling unclothed, just clean through and through.

Looking down, she was surprised to see that she was fully covered in a white tunic with lovely lilies embroidered on the sleeve. The dress flowed like the purest satin around her form. She also could see her armour again. It had been a long time since she'd last seen it, and relief flooded her soul.

Shylah thanked the unseen Lord for bringing her there, and she could hear His gentle answer.

"You have been a faithful friend to Treasa and Keelin. You will not go unrewarded!" Shylah felt a gentle kiss upon her lips, so pure and innocent. In all her life she had longed for that kiss but she had never known it until it was given. It made her feel unconditionally accepted and loved. Even though she could not see Him, she knew Him. Falling down onto her knees, she spread her hands out in silent surrender to the unseen Lord, the lover of her soul.

The Lord's gentle voice wrapped itself around her heart, "I love you very much and I have found you faithful. Come in the strength of my Father."

Looking up she saw an outstretched hand. Taking the hand, she arose and looked into the eyes of the Lord. Her faith became sight in an instant. Then He was gone, but His smile still warmed her heart.

Shylah slowly walked back into the room where the table was spread with the lovely meal. Sophronia was sitting quietly waiting for her to return. Rising she greeted her, saying, "Did you enjoy your bath?"

"Oh, yes!" exclaimed Shylah.

"Come, sit and enjoy your meal. You have been cleansed and now you will be strengthened for what you need when you return beyond the mist," Sophronia said to her with an inviting smile.

Sophronia bowed to her and turned and left the room. Shylah became uncomfortable that Treasa had not returned. So, wrapping some bread and fruit in a large napkin, she went to the door through which Treasa had passed to bathe. Upon opening it, she was surprised to find the forest path that had led them to Sophronia's cottage. Looking around the room one last time, she stepped out onto the forest trail, feeling odd that she had been in the second story of the cottage and somehow now she was on ground level. *What a strange land this was!* She thought.

Shylah looked behind her to find that the cottage was gone. Where it had stood was only a large oak tree. Shrugging her shoulders in puzzlement, realizing there could be no turning back now. She needed to find her friend.

The Ancients say… "I remember the days of old; I meditate on all Thy works; I muse on the work of Thy hands."

Chapter 7

Aithne ~ little fire

At first, Caedmon seemed to know his direction, but then as the cloud wrapped itself around him, everything disappeared. He stopped and slowly put his foot out in front of himself, and feeling the path, he stepped ahead. The air was becoming thinner as he slowly climbed the path. Several times he felt nothing but thin air beneath his feet. Knowing he was near the edge he would slowly move his foot until he felt the path again. Finally lowering himself to his hands and knees, he began to crawl up the steep path, using his hands to feel the way in front of him.

Caedmon struggled forward and upward for hours. He realized that the day would soon be at its end. The wind came up and tore at his clothes as the clouds swirled around him. Soon, he felt the sting of rain pelting his face. His clothes had become wet, and he shivered with the cold. Stopping, he lay down upon the path, burying his face in his hands. He cried out for the unseen Lord to help him, for the way was too hard for him.

He then remembered Carden's last words to him. "It is a delightful place on top of this great mountain." Pulling himself back up to his feet, he decided he would go on. He knew that the unseen Lord would not have led him astray, though he shuddered to think of falling off the edge of this mountain.

Finally, he *felt* rather than saw that the cloud was thinning and the rain had stopped. The wind had died down as well. It was so silent that he could only hear his breathing and the soft crunch of the gravel beneath his feet. A beam of light pierced the cloud and fell directly upon him, warming him instantly. He lifted his face and let the light warm his entire being. He had never longed for something so simple before, but to have longed for it so desperately made the actuality of it coming all the more wonderful.

As he came out of the cloud, the evening sky shot beams of glorious light all around him. The heavens looked to be on fire with colours of orange, gold, and crimson. It appeared that the sun had slipped behind the mountain out of sight, but its warmth still filled the air. Caedmon let it embrace him and comfort his heart.

Looking around himself, amazement filled his soul. The top of the mountain was very flat and there was a high wall all around its edge. Grape vines, laden with fruit, were growing upon it. Caedmon went across the top of the grass-covered mountain to the wall and there in the wall was an opening, no taller than himself and no wider than his width. It was as if it had been made just for him, but when he tried to go inside, he did not fit. Puzzled, he took off his cape and tried again, but still he did not fit. He slowly removed all his clothing ~ including his wet tunic and leggings ~ and trying again he found that he nearly fit. Looking around himself, to make sure he was alone, he slowly stripped off his undergarments and passed through the opening stark naked. His desire to cover himself was overwhelming. He tried to use his hands as best he could, but the feeling of vulnerability was almost more than he could bear.

The opening in the wall led into a corridor; he reached out and touched the inside of the wall. He then saw a small alcove in the wall, and suddenly a lamp was shining there. A pile of clean clothes was neatly folded in the alcove, and above them, etched into the wall beside the lamp, was a very ancient script that read:

"To the one who is brave of heart and will
expose their own being...
These clothes are for thee."

Caedmon carefully unfolded the garments and put them on. They fit him perfectly, and they were very finely made of the most magnificent material. As he looked down at himself, he saw that his armour was there and had never before fit him so perfectly. Tears of gratitude fell from his eyes as he realized how close he had come to covering himself with his old clothes and retreating back down the mountain.

As he walked ahead, the new clothes seemed to strengthen him. The fit of the clothes did not hinder him; it was as if they were part of himself, not merely garments hanging upon him. Looking out through the opening into the walled enclosure, Caedmon stopped.

Before him was the most beautiful garden he had ever seen. The trees were laden with fruit of every description, most of which he did not recognize. There were paths and small, beautifully carved benches beside bubbling fountains. In the middle of the garden was a large pond with a pair of beautiful white swans swimming among the lilies that floated on the water's surface. Seeing him, the swans flew towards him, their feet skimming the top of the water as they swept across its surface. Stopping close to him, they bowed their heads. Swimming back into the middle, they dove out of sight. Caedmon waited breathlessly as he saw ripples forming in the middle of the pond. With a loud splash the two swans came flying straight up, out of the water and into the air. With a swoop over his head, they disappeared into the cloud around the mountain.

Caedmon stood looking after them for a long time; somehow they had given him the desire to fly. The cloud was turning a lovely shade of pink. It had the appearance of a flock of sheep all around the top of the mountain.

Caedmon heard a startling sound ~ the trill of a child's laughter. He turned and saw the prettiest little girl he had ever beheld. She appeared to be about six years old with golden curls tumbling down her back. Her blue eyes sparkled like the pond behind her. Her dress was a simple white tunic with a golden sash. Her small bare feet danced back and forth. Upon her back was an archer's quiver full of arrows and over her shoulder was slung a bow. Her lovely little face was full of the most innocent goodwill that Caedmon had ever seen.

"My name is Aithne, which means 'little fire'," the girl giggled out as she danced about. "Do you like my pets?"

"Oh, the swans? Yes, yes indeed! They were magnificent. They are your pets?" Caedmon asked incredulously. Never before had he spoken to someone so absolutely innocent. It left him with the feeling of not being clean enough.

"I will let you rest here, but we do not sleep here. Did you know that?" Aithne asked.

"Well, no, I did not. Then again, I do not feel the slightest bit tired," Caedmon realized as he spoke. In fact, he was disappointed that the day was closing. He had the feeling he could have kept living this day forever.

"We all rest here, and while you have a rest, you will realize how much you need it. It is only your mind that is active but your body is needing rest."

Caedmon immediately did feel the true condition of his body and realized that the climb had been terribly hard on him, both physically and emotionally. He suddenly wanted to sit down and have something to eat. Looking around he saw a small table spread with all kinds of fruit. He wondered why he had not seen it before. Beside the table were small couches covered with a material that looked very much like the down of the swans.

Aithne went before him and sat on one of the couches. With a small wave of her hand she beckoned him to sit on the other couch, which he did. The couch felt very much like his clothes ~ like it was part of himself. Never in his life had he rested upon something so wonderful. Caedmon laid his head back on the couch and looked at the streaks of colour in the sky, they were ever changing before his eyes, from crimson to brilliant gold and lavender. He also noticed that the sky was not getting any darker.

Watching his gaze, Aithne responded, "There is no darkness here, or sun either. That is why you did not see it on your climb. What a funny look upon your face!" Aithne squealed with delight. "The Lord's Father lights this place with Himself. I don't know how He does it, but I love it. Sometimes, when I am sent to the other side of the mist where you live, it is in the dark. His light surrounds us so we can see to complete our quests."

Caedmon could not help himself; he had to laugh with her, even though he did not know what was so humorous. This little girl was not what she appeared to be, he recognized. She came to his world on quests, and she was outfitted with an archer's weapons, which she never removed from herself, even as she sat and watched him eat. *What exactly were her quests,* he wondered. *Maybe I should ask...* But he again had that strange feeling of not being her equal and was hesitant to question her.

"The Lord told me that when you arrived, I was to give this to you." As she spoke, she drew out an archer's bow and quiver full of arrows from under her couch. Smiling, she arose and slung them over his shoulder.

"You see, these arrows are the Lord's truths that bring hope. Sometimes, when His people are so discouraged that they can't go on, He sends me to them to pierce their hearts with an arrow. So usually I am sent in the night, when everything is the darkest. Then they remember what the Lord had spoken to them in the past and their hope is rekindled. You know, like a small bit of fire that warms the heart and lightens the darkness." Aithne giggled again. "My name means *little fire*! Get it?"

Caedmon smiled broadly. "Yes, I get it. The Lord wants me to use these arrows as well?" Caedmon asked.

"Oh, you must. Truly, you must. He needs to have His people remember His promises to them. They have almost forgotten. They will listen to you much better than they do to me now. You see, they've been sleeping so heavily since they became complacent that they do not hear me in the night. They barely dream at all any more ~ only horrible *"Dragon"* dreams that terrify them, and those they usually block out of their memory." Aithne spoke very seriously for the first time, her small fists clenching and her eyes turning to a hard cold blue. As she leaned forward her whole form seemed to change before his eyes. She was a small child still, but he could sense the warrior she truly was.

He drew out one of the arrows; the shaft had the appearance of ivory. The arrowhead looked like a large ruby that had been intricately cut, and the feathers were beautiful and white like those of the swans. Inscribed on the side of the arrow was one word in a beautiful script:

~ Remember ~

Caedmon put the arrow back in the quiver and examined the bow. It was carved with a lion's head at the top. The wood was almost as black as ebony and polished as smooth as glass; the string was tight and shone in the twilight. The handle was laid over with gold filigree, and it was very beautiful.

The sky suddenly lit up like the most brilliant of sunny days. The colours fled as the deepest blue that Caedmon had ever seen spread out like a great canopy over the mountain. The cloud evaporated into nothing, and Caedmon climbed to the top of the wall and looked out over the valley far below, surveying the way he had come. The mountain trail he climbed looked like a winding staircase without steps. The trail went around and around like the coil of a rope. It was as if the top of the mountain was floating in the sky and the path was like a lovely ribbon connecting it to the plateau of the shepherd, Carden, below.

Caedmon's heart trembled as he remembered climbing that path. How afeared he would have been if he had known how it was suspended in the air. He now was very thankful for the cloud and the storm that had blocked it from his vision.

Aithne, joining him on the wall, waited for him to speak. Her presence was so comforting, for he knew that she too was a servant of the unseen Lord, just like him. He watched silently with her as the two great swans flew towards them from far below, circling ever closer. They alighted silently beside them on the wall.

"Farewell, Caedmon. I will meet you in your dreams," she spoke quietly.

"Farewell, small one, though I know that on the inside you are a great warrior. I will forever be grateful for your service to me. Now I ask of you, how do I get to the mist that separates our two worlds?" Caedmon asked with a small bow.

Aithne pointed straight out in front of her, just like Carden had done. Then, slipping on to the back of one of the mighty swans, she flew away. He could hear her musical laughter fade into the blue as they flew out of sight.

Standing, Caedmon took a deep breath. Could he do this next step? Looking back at the garden and the shimmering pool, he saw where the one swan was swimming. He knew that he was too close to winning over his fears to go back the way he had come.

The Ancients say… "I have taught thee in the way of wisdom; I have led thee in right paths."

Chapter 8

Caedmon turned and looked out straight in front of him, his heart failing him as he considered stepping off into thin air. As he stepped closer to the edge of the wall, the presence of the chasm seemed to draw him downward. Taking a deep breath and without thinking, he stepped ahead. As his foot plunged his body began to fall forward, stopping his heart. Suddenly, his foot thudded against something hard. Shaking terribly, Caedmon found himself standing stock still on an invisible bridge. His knee was twitching violently from the plunging sensation of falling. Leaning over he rubbed it, willing the spasms to stop.

Straightening, his heart slowed down as the twitching in his leg ceased. Looking ahead to his destination on the other side, he continued, one step at a time. He could hear the hollow sound of his steps on the invisible bridge and his confidence grew. He began to realize that his whole life had been like this walk on the bridge in a sense: one foot in front of the other, never really knowing what lay ahead but trying to trust the unseen Lord with his life and his very next step.

Finally reaching the halfway point of the bridge, Caedmon looked down. He could see the river, which looked like a tiny thread far below. He could see far down the valley and a small lake in the distance. Then again, he thought, maybe its not so small. It could have been just his perspective from up there.

He started walking carefully again, when suddenly the whole landscape changed. Instead of standing on the bridge in a wide chasm, he found himself in front of a rustic cottage. It had plastered mud walls and small windows that shone clean in the sunlight. The thatch roof was as neat as a pin, almost as if someone had laid every blade of thatch one piece at a time. Smoke gently wafted into the air out of the stone chimney. A lovely morning glory vine grew over one side of the cottage, and its bright pink flowers were nodding in the breeze. The cottage looked like it was part of the forest it was set in. The large fir trees behind it sounded like the ocean as the wind swayed them back and forth.

~

Treasa, upon finishing her leisurely bath and meal, had ventured back down the winding staircase, hoping to find Sophronia. Maybe she would know where Shylah was. Finding the large banquet room, Treasa saw a beautiful meal laid out on the large table. Sophronia entered, carrying a loaf of fresh bread.

"Come in and sit by the fire," she said.

"I will join you in a short time. Though, first I must prepare for another guest," Sophronia added with a smile. Treasa went into the room and settled down in front of the fireplace with her back to the table. The high-backed chair hid her from view.

Upon nearing the cottage, Caedmon could smell the most wonderful of all smells ~ that of bread baking. Realizing that he was very hungry, he walked up to the front door and knocked. Hearing the light footsteps of someone inside coming to answer the door, he waited expectantly. The door opened and the full aroma of the bread greeted the hungry Caedmon.

Looking up, he saw one of the tallest women he had ever seen. Her entire being radiated peace, from her green-hazel eyes to her long brown hair. She smiled when she saw Caedmon, and with a simple wave of her hand she welcomed him into her home.

Caedmon was amazed as he came into the cottage, for instead of it being small and quaint, it was one of the largest interiors he had ever been in. The inside of the cottage was a grand palace, with tapestries and beautifully carved furniture. A winding staircase led up to a second storey, and large windows that let in the glorious light at the far end of the room.

The woman led Caedmon to a side room which was an ornate dining room with real glass tumblers and dishes that gleamed in the light. The long table was set with a beautiful bouquet of flowers in the middle, and bowls of fruit and berries. There were plates of cheeses and small dollops of butter. Best of all at the far end was the largest loaf of fresh bread that Caedmon had ever seen.

The woman went to the far end of the table and motioned for Caedmon to follow. Smiling, she pulled out a chair that was very close to the bread. Caedmon knew that she wanted him to take the seat. He sat down and waited for her to speak, but she seemed to be in no hurry to talk to him. She took the seat opposite him and cut off a large piece of bread. Delicately laying the bread upon a plate, she passed it to Caedmon along with the plate of cheese and butter. Handing him the bowl of fruit and berries, she happily noticed the generous portion of butter and thick slices of cheese he was spreading onto the warm bread.

Looking up at his hostess, he was surprised that she wasn't eating ~ she was only sitting and watching him closely, a smile upon her face. He smiled back with the sudden realization that he did not feel the need to talk to her. It was as if she knew what was inside of him and they were communicating on a deeper level than he had ever experienced before.

As he took a bite of his bread, the taste filled his mouth and was wonderful. It was as if his mind was clearing and his senses sharpening. Caedmon remembered that he had felt a similar sensation the first time he had drank the water from the Unchanging River. He slowly finished his sandwich and sipped the bright red berry juice. It, too, was refreshing as the flavour filled his mouth with the most wonderful fullness.

Caedmon wiped his mouth on the delicate cloth napkin laid by his plate. Pushing back from the table, he arose. The lady of the home stood and walked to the three chairs in front of the large fireplace.

"Are you full?" her strong, musical voice broke the stillness of the moment.

Caedmon looked up, replying, "Yes, thank you. I feel very satisfied. I was very hungry but did not know it until I smelled your bread."

"Yes, it is strange how people do not recognize their hunger. It was your hunger that finally drew you to my cottage. I have called to you for years now. Sometimes you have listened to me, but mostly not," her voice did not accuse, but only stated the facts.

"I've never seen you before. I don't even know your name," Caedmon answered incredulously. The lady raised her eyebrows in surprise, shrugging her shoulders.

"My name is Sophronia. Some who know me, in your land, call me *"Wisdom"*. I have called to you many times. I have called to you above all the distractions around you. Try to remember."

Caedmon realized that she had been the voice of reason that had come so many times in his life. Those times when he had wanted to do his own thing or run on some wild emotional cycle when things were bad. Looking at this beautiful woman as she took a seat in front of the fire, Caedmon thought she looked royal ~ yet there was a humility about her just like Aithne, Abelio and Carden had possessed. Sophronia turned and looked deep into Caedmon's eyes. Dropping his gaze, he felt suddenly ashamed of himself.

"Yes, I heard you. You came to me many times, but I would be so caught up in my feelings that I did not listen to good sense. I did not want to calm down or do the required thing. I wanted to listen to my own reasoning. I am sorry. Will you forgive me?" Caedmon asked quietly.

Her musical laughter filled the air as she replied, "My dear young man, I do not have the power to forgive ~ but my Lord does, and He will. Listen, I have been called to minister to *your* needs, not my own. You do not offend me when you do not listen to me. You offend the One whom has sent me, our Lord."

"Just the same, I am sorry! I can see that I would have been saved from much heartache if I would have listened to the voice of Wisdom and to not the voice of human reason and emotion." Caedmon stood there, wondering if he should take a seat beside her at the fire, but was waiting to be invited.

"By the way, the bread was wonderful. Did you bake it?" Caedmon asked.

"Yes. I'm glad you liked it, because here you eat my wisdom as bread. The sweet wine I gave you was made from berries that are only found on the *Mountain of Meeting*. This wine cleanses your mind and makes it new. Your conscience will become sensitive the more you drink, to the point that you will know right and wrong in even the most intimate and complicated details of your life. In your world, the wine is the words of the unseen Lord. Hold them dear to your heart," Sophronia taught Caedmon. "Come join us at the fire, Caedmon!"

Caedmon heard laughter as he went to sit down and to his surprise a laughing Treasa was smiling up at him.

"Treasa! What are you doing here?"

"Hello, dear Caedmon. I, too, have learned from Sophronia's home and presence," Treasa said. "I did not mean to be eavesdropping. I was just waiting for an opportune time to make my presence known. To answer your question. Shylah and I came here through the mist to find some answers and now I don't know where she has gone. Maybe we could find Shylah together."

"Shylah is missing?" Caedmon asked in amazement.

"No, she is not missing," Sophronia interjected. "She has gone on ahead of you two, that is all. It is the Lord's will. If you take the forest trail, it will lead you to *The Glade of the Forest Pools* ~ a lovely place, and a necessary place for you to meet her. She will wait for you there."

Caedmon knew that it was time to leave, but he truly wanted to stay with her and learn more. She looked at him, telling him with her green eyes that he must walk in the wisdom he had gained here before he would receive more. Caedmon nodded silently, understanding.

Sophronia held Treasa for a long time, in a warm embrace.

"Be strong, my friend! You just watch what our great Prince will do on Keelin's behalf."

Taking their leave, Caedmon and Treasa headed down the only path that led from the cottage. After a few paces, they turned for one last look. They were surprised when they did not see the cottage, or mansion, or anything like it. There was only a large oak tree that towered above the firs, its leaves hanging like umbrellas, sheltering the forest floor. The light shimmered green all around the base of the tree, and Sophronia was sitting on a low branch waving to them. They waved and turned to head on their way. This was a really strange, but truly wonderful, land. Things were not what they appeared, and yet Caedmon knew that if anything had really changed here, it was him.

The Ancients say... "When my soul fainted within me I remembered the LORD: and my prayer came in unto thee."

Chapter 9

Eammon ~ the hidden
Briant ~ strong, he ascends

Shylah had the feeling she had walked for miles, and still there appeared no end to the tall forest. She wasn't tired and the feeling of invigoration still clung to her from the wonderful bath and lunch she had enjoyed at Sophronia's. She wondered how she had fallen so far behind Treasa. However, she did not worry or fret, for this place seemed to annihilate all those feelings from her.

The soft moss on the trail made the treading of her shoes almost noiseless and comforted her feet. The brightly coloured birds they had seen earlier now, darted all around her, chirping their beautiful little songs. Shylah had noticed that there appeared to be no sun in this land. The sky was still as light as it had been earlier in the day, only perhaps a little redder, like the sun was setting somewhere far beyond. One little yellow bird alighted upon her shoulder. Stopping, she turned her head slowly to not frighten it.

His little head had a red streak down the top, and the bright yellow feathers on his wings were delicately tipped in black. He cocked his head to one side and stared back at her, his sparkling black eyes looking into hers steadily. With a chirp he flew up and around her head and then off into the forest. Soon returning, he came back and alighted on her shoulder again. He repeated this little parade two more times, but each time his chirping seemed slightly more impatient.

"Do you want me to follow you, my little singer?" Shylah giggled. With that, the little bird flew up into the air, did some rather daring acrobatics, and flew off into the woods again. This time Shylah was quick to follow him, this way and that, through the maze of under-growth and wild daisies.

They soon came out into a beautiful meadow that opened up in the centre of the forest. The entire floor of the meadow was covered in pools, and each one had the shimmer of a different colour. The water looked as still as glass, and the moss that was all over the forest floor grew right down into each pool. They were perfectly round with no forest undergrowth surrounding them. The blanket of soft green moss had lovely, tiny blossoms of white violets in small patches scattered among the pools. The little yellow bird flitted back and forth, inviting Shylah to come into the glade, chirping his little song into the still air. He came to settle on what appeared to be a large rock in the middle of the meadow glade.

Shylah stepped into the glade and walked around the pools towards the rock. The rock began to shift in shape. Shylah stopped in mid-stride and watched in wonder as the rock stood up. The moss-covered rock was in actuality a man covered in a green robe that hung to his feet. He had been sitting with his head resting on his knees, but as he arose, the hood of the robe fell from his head. Shylah stared in shock. His hair hung in heavy waves to his shoulders and was the colour of the sun, and his face was as black as ebony. Out of the darkness of his skin shone the brightest blue eyes Shylah had ever seen. She had never beheld anyone so beautiful or so rare, like a precious gemstone.

The man smiled as he strode towards Shylah. His hand out-stretched to shake hers in greeting. She felt like she knew this man somehow. His appearance was ancient, but young at the same time, all wrapped together in a robe that seemed to be part of the very glade they were standing in.

"You have come at last," he said. "Shylah, the Lord's strong one! The others will be joining you soon. But you have been called here first because you need to see for yourself what is in the pool that has been created for you."

"Why thank you, sir. I feel honoured. Who do you mean by *others*? I only came with Treasa, and no one else," Shylah asked shyly.

"Caedmon met Treasa at Sophronia's, and they will both be coming soon. There is much for you to see, so come ~ I will show you to your pool."

"Do I know you? You seem so familiar to me," Shylah asked, though she realized that if she had ever seen this man before she would have never forgotten him. Perhaps it was his voice that was familiar.

"My name is Eammon. I am keeper of *The Glade of Forest Pools*, I have called you here many times when you have mediated, but you were afraid of what you would see. So you retreated back to what was familiar to you. I know you well and have called to you often!" Eammon earnestly replied.

Shylah did not understand. She really couldn't remember any time that she had been afraid to see something when she was mediating. However, she knew that in this place beyond the mist of the Source, deceit was not a part of anyone, so it had to be true.

"You will see what I mean when you look into the pool, fair one. Come and look. This is your pool," Eammon said, as he laid his hand upon her arm to direct her to the pool. There she saw her reflection. Her arm became immediately strengthened and she found that she was suddenly holding her shield. She looked down at it; the lion's head upon the front looked like it was on fire. She raised it up and let the light reflect into the forest.

"Amazing. Simply amazing!" she cried.

"Yes. When one comes to the pools, their own defence becomes stronger than when they try to mediate in their own understanding. Do you understand that?" Eammon asked.

"Yes, and no. I see that these pools must be the unseen Lord's perspective on the things we are mediating for. Is that correct?" Shylah asked.

"Yes. The pools are also His Father's desire for whoever you are mediating for as well. You know that our Prince's whole purpose for coming to your land was to reconcile the people with His Father. His wonderful Father! Our very breath is from Him. He is our maker and our life, and yours as well," Eammon said, as he stopped and looked intensely into Shylah's eyes.

"I am afraid I do not know much about His Father, only what the ancients wrote. I am walking in His land here, am I not?"

"Yes, this is His land ~ but so is your land. He has made all things. He is the grand architect of all things."

"Will I see Him here?" Shylah asked, hopeful.

"No, you will not see Him here. He has chosen to reveal Himself to you through His Son, the great Prince. The one you call the "unseen Lord". You will see His Father upon *The Mountain of Meeting*. Here, look closer into your pool, which is right beside Treasa's pool."

Shylah smiled at the thought. The pool, was rather small and looked not unlike any other pool in the glade. Shylah had not expected more, but then again, maybe she had...

She shook off the feeling of disappointment that tried to rob her of the joy of the moment.

"It is all right," Eammon laughed out as he shook back his heavy blonde hair from his shoulders. "It is not the *size* of the pool that lets you know how to mediate, but the *depth*. And your pool is very deep, dear one. Kneel down and intently look into it. I will leave you now and go prepare to meet your comrades." Eammon turned to leave and disappeared immediately from Shylah's sight.

Kneeling down she carefully leaned over the perfectly still pool. The water, Shylah noticed, did not reflect the forest and, instead of being green like the forest around it, it was a beautiful shade of pink. The top of the water looked like glass with iridescent shades of colour, very much like mother of pearl.

As Shylah stared into the water, the swirls of pink began to separate to the outside edge of the pool, leaving the centre looking dark and void. Suddenly, Shylah could make out the shadows of people milling about in a small, confined area. They looked like they were in a dungeon or maybe a prison. They were trying to get out, but then, tiring, they would go and sit in the middle of the area looking very dejected. After a while they would return to the walls again and try to chip away at the mortar to loosen the stones so they could escape, only to give up again and return to sit.

As she looked at this group of people, she recognized one fairly large man in the middle of the room. His head was hung low and his shaggy, dark brown hair hung down around his face, hiding it from her view. His shoulders were massive, but seemed to have no strength as they slumped forward. She did not need to see his face to know that she knew him.

She gasped and sat back on her heels. The pool immediately became a swirl of colour. Pinks and reds with vibrant blues were swirling and moving, never stopping. The look of the pool made her feel dizzy, and so did the fact that the person she saw was none other than her husband, Briant.

She tried to steady her emotions. She loved this man, but she also disliked him greatly. He said he was a pilgrim and she believed him, but he seemed to be stuck in his own life and purposes. She had to admit that she envied the other pilgrims whose mates were right there with them, wanting to obey the unseen Lord, wanting to reach out to others and change the land, wanting to mediate.

With a rush she realized this is what Eammon had been talking about ~ this was what she had not wanted to see. She had not wanted to mediate for Briant from the Lord's perspective; she was too bitter over her husband's indifference. She began to weep, and as the tears fell she noticed that the little river of tears streaming down her face ran straight into her pool. As the tears joined the pool's water, the colours in it settled down and became very still, resembling a beautiful rainbow that arched out from where she was sitting.

She felt someone's presence beside her, and, thinking that Eammon had returned, she reached out her hand to grasp his ~ it was not Eammon's hand she held, but that of someone much larger. Looking down, Shylah saw the massive hand, underneath her small one, that had the appearance of burnished bronze. Shylah slowly turned her tear-streaked face towards the person. He was the unseen Lord.

His hair looked as white as wool and His close-cropped beard had little golden flecks that sparkled in the light of the day. His large brown eyes looked as if the expanse of the universe were in their dark depths, and He was looking adoringly at her. Shylah dropped her head in shame and she hesitantly pulled her hand away. Before she could stand, the Lord grasped her hand and pulled it onto His chest, holding it close. He then lifted and opened it, placing a gentle kiss upon her palm. Shylah's shoulders shook in sobs as He pulled her close. She felt so small and protected as she snuggled into His side.

"My Prince, I have been so concerned about myself, in regards to Briant. I have not wanted to see him the way you do. I am so, so sorry. How could you ever find me faithful to mediate for anyone else when I have not considered coming here before?" Shylah sobbed out.

"Shylah, this is not a place that is easy to come to. Very few have come here before, and only today Teague came here for the first time, although to him it did not look like this place. I understand what you are saying, and you are forgiven, but it is time for all the mediators to come here. This is your only real protection from the Dragon when you are mediating, for it cannot infiltrate this place of personal truth and reflection. We can bring anyone that wants to come here to show them what We see. When you see what We see, then We can show you how to truly mediate. Sometimes it is in words, but at times it is in actions."

Shylah was sobbing silently. She knew that her actions had been wanting lately.

"Hush now. There, there. You are forgiven sweet heart. Rest awhile and then I will tell you what must be done so that Briant can live up to his name ~ *the one who ascends*! He too will ascend here, if you just ask me to bring him," the Prince said.

"Yes, oh yes, please rescue him, and the others that are with him as well. They are locked within walls that they have created themselves. Set them free! For their sake, not mine, and for Your sake, not mine," Shylah said with renewed strength. Again she felt the handle of her shield.

The unseen Lord spent many hours with Shylah and told her of the things she could do to bring deliverance to her husband and family. He then reached right inside her, she gasped as she saw His hand disappear inside her chest. She could feel His hand squeeze her heart and she let out another gasp as He slowly drew out His hand. He was holding a very old bloody knife. He threw the knife into her pool, and it exploded into a million diamonds as it hit the water's surface. Shylah reached her hand up and felt her chest. She knew that the anger and bitterness she'd felt towards her husband's inadequacies were gone. Her heart felt like it was quivering within her.

"Now you will feel My love for your Briant. *My* Briant." With that He disappeared and the sky above the trees immediately shone with all the colours of a sunset again.

The Ancients say… "Lean not unto thine own understanding. In all thy ways acknowledge Him, and He shall direct thy paths."

Chapter 10

Treasa leaned over to tighten the lace on her shoe. When she straightened, Caedmon was gone. She looked around herself, but he was nowhere to be seen. One minute they had been talking and laughing, and the next he was gone. What a strange land this was! She was rather liking the unpredictability of this place, for she could rest assured that Caedmon was safe. He had probably just wandered off a short distance to investigate something.

She began to hum a tune that was dear to her heart. It was one that Teague had composed. Joy bubbled up inside of her as she laughed out loud, and then, skipping like a young girl, she headed down the path into the forest.

She heard someone on the path behind her so she quickly darted out into the forest and hid behind the nearest tree. Trying to stifle a giggle, she planned her attack on Caedmon. She loved startling people!

The sound of the soft footsteps was right beside her and she leaped out, squealing out, *"hello, there!"* to her unsuspecting prey. However, it wasn't Caedmon. Eammon laughed out loud at Treasa's shocked look as her surprise ended up on her own face.

"I am so sorry, sir. I thought you were someone else," she breathed out finally.

"Don't apologize. I love a good joke!" Eammon's ebony face shone with joy and laughter as he reassured Treasa. "Come, I am Eammon, and I am here to take you to *The Glade of the Forest Pools*. My Prince, the Lord, wants you to come and learn of Him there. Caedmon and Shylah will meet you there as well, but not until you have experienced your pool."

Treasa looked at this beautiful man. Just like Shylah, she was taken by his appearance of extremes. His beautiful eyes were still sparkling with humour, like tide pools of the sea within the darkness of the midnight sky. Treasa obediently followed him off the beaten trail into the shadows of the forest until they came to a glade. Lovely pools were lying in the open meadow, surrounded by the forest which was like a great green wall hiding them. Large boulders were scattered here and there in the meadow beside the pools, all covered in a soft lovely moss.

Treasa noticed that Shylah and Caedmon were nowhere to be seen, but her curiosity over this beautiful place removed all worry from her mind.

Eammon brought her to the edge of a pool and motioned for her to sit on the large boulder beside it. Sitting down, she awaited what would come next. Eammon smiled at her and then spoke to her in a sober tone. "This is a place you have come to before, occasionally. Where the Prince shows you what to mediate for. You have relied on your own strength in the past, and lately you have let your fretting be your ruler. Now you will rest in His strength and let Him guide you."

Treasa lowered her head in shame, for it was true, and she could not deny it. Even though she knew that she'd had the leading of the unseen Lord in the past with her mediating, she had recently been thinking that He had left her, and that her time as a mediator was over! Though really, it had all been because she had stopped coming here in her heart. To now see this place with her eyes was incredible. No wonder she was filled with rest when she had mediated from here. To think she had avoided coming here lately!

"Do not be afraid to look in," Eammon told her.

She smiled in response. *To know something is wonderful, but to see it just goes beyond comprehension.* She added, "I suppose this is the difference between inspiration and revelation. With inspiration I feel something and it stirs my intellect, but with *revelation* I have this exploding of knowing and seeing all at once."

Eammon laughed and nodded his head in hearty agreement, then said, "I suppose that is one of the best definitions I have ever

- 208 -

heard for this place. Now I'll leave you, for you clearly know what you are meant to do here. I must go and usher in our young warrior, Sir Caedmon."

Treasa was surprised to see him fade into the very green that was all around her, his long green robe becoming one with the landscape. Treasa squinted her eyes, but she could not see him.

Turning, Treasa looked long and hard in her pool. Leaning closer she saw her own self looking back. The pool's surface was as black as the sky at its darkest hour in the night, and she suddenly realized that that was how her soul had felt since Keelin's heart had been broken. She had wished she could take her pain, but in the midst of all that, she had taken on a worse pain ~ the pain of despair. She had blamed the unseen Lord when He had not answered her pleas.

Tears of repentance slid down her face and dripped into the pool. Wherever a tear fell a golden ring formed and shone like the noon day sun. The golden rings began to move and spread across the surface of the pool until the entire surface shimmered like a beautiful mirror of gold. Her reflected image slowly turned youthful and her face was full of peace. She even looked a little pretty again, and blushing she tucked a stray strand of her auburn hair behind her ear. Stroking her chin, she wondered where the years had gone, it seemed like only yesterday that she had been the young bride of her handsome Cathaoir.

As her reflection slowly faded, she could see deeper into the depths of the pool as the golden surface slowly moved to the edges, leaving the centre looking absolutely empty and void. Slowly, she could see stars shining in the depths of the pool. Then suddenly, Treasa felt like she was flying down into the pool at a very high speed. The stars flew past her, and she could feel her hair flying out behind her like ribbons.

Beginning to become afraid, she suddenly stopped above her own dear farm and could see into Keelin's room in the cottage. Keelin was lying on her bed, curled up on her side, her small arm cradling her head as her tears were wetting her pillow. As Treasa watched, Keelin stood and walked to her parents' bed. Kneeling down and reaching far under, she drew out her ruined wedding dress. Treasa gasped, shocked that her daughter had found it. She thought she had hidden it well. Keelin was carefully unwrapping the folds of what was left of her dress, piece by piece. Inside the folds lie a broken bleeding heart.

Treasa's own heart was breaking as she watched the scene. Suddenly she realized that she was seeing with the unseen Lord's eyes and that she had never left her seat by the pool. What she thought was a rock she was leaning against was a pair of loving arms. She was sitting upon the lap of her Lord.

Laying her head back upon His chest, she drew her legs up onto his lap as He sat cross-legged under her. He had been there all along ~ she knew it, for she would never had been strong enough to see what she had seen without Him.

She felt a delicate hand take her's and kiss it. Startled, she looked beside her and there was none other than her dear friend, Shylah.

Smiling through her tears, Treasa asked, "Shylah did you see?"

"Yes," she answered quietly. She, too, was wiping away tears from her own cheeks.

The Lord spoke to them both. "My daughters, My friends. I have shown you into the very heart of Keelin's pain. Now you need wisdom and love. A sprinkling of patience will be needed as well," He added with a smile. "I will be doing things in the future that both of you will struggle with, but My purposes will be accomplished as you mediate for her."

Treasa and Shylah nodded in silent understanding.

Treasa spoke hesitantly, "I have been caught up in the fact that Keelin made a mistake and now it is time for her to get over it. I knew that she needed Your healing, but I am afraid I did not know the extent of her broken spirit. She appears to have truly loved that young man very much. I think I have treated it like a school girl crush. I have definitely seen now the extent of her pain, and we wait for Your guidance in the days to come."

The Lord smiled and squeezed her tight.

"So do you like the looks of this place?" the Lord asked.

"Yes," they both said in unison, laughing at their own joke.

"You spend so much time together you even answer together!" the Lord laughed.

Treasa could not stop laughing and Shylah, who found it easy to laugh, joined her even though it really wasn't that humorous. The deep rumble of the Lord's laugh joined them until all three were laying side by side, totally still with great smiles upon their faces. Treasa knew that this place was where she belonged. She would be ever grateful to her blessed Lord for being patient with her and bringing her back. Shylah lay there, thinking of all she had seen as another unbidden tear fell. She again saw Keelin's heart lying broken and bleeding in her wedding dress.

The Ancients say… If a man be overtaken in a fault, restore such an one in the spirit of meekness; Bear ye one another's burdens, and so fulfill the law of Christ."

Chapter II

ammon found Caedmon sitting beside the road, looking very bewildered. *Where had Treasa disappeared to?* Caedmon thought. He looked up slowly. There seemed to be an imperceptible rustle in the forest in front of him. Suddenly, he realized that he was seeing a large man whose green robe seemed to flow and meld with the moss-covered trail. As Caedmon's gaze came up to his head, he too had the same reaction as Shylah and Treasa ~ wonder and amazement at the man's beauty. Eammon's brilliant blue eyes sparkled out of his dark face from under his hood.

Knowing his thoughts, Eammon spoke. "You know the Grand Architect, the Father of our Prince, your Lord. He made me to stand out among my fellow servants in appearance, but sometimes I am the most hidden of all. Oh, I love Him!" Eammon said with a flourish, reaching out his outstretched hand to help Caedmon to his feet.

"I am sorry for staring, but you are rare, that is for sure!" Caedmon laughed as he took the proffered hand and leaped to his feet. "I was just contemplating how on earth my travelling companion, Treasa, disappeared right after I found her! I thought she was just waiting to jump out and scare me, but now I think she's truly gone ~"

Eammon's laugh cut off Caedmon's discourse.

"How right you are! Only it was me she jumped out at. Only, I don't think it was me who was more startled!" Again Eammon's laughter rolled out.

Caedmon smiled broadly. Oh, how he would have liked to have been there! He thought of all the times Treasa had startled him when he had lived with her and Cathaoir.

Eammon spoke, waking Caedmon from his reverie. "Come. I will take you to your friends, Shylah and Treasa."

Caedmon followed Eammon through the forest, wondering how the man in front knew his way even though all the trees appeared alike and there was no path. When they finally broke out into the opening of the glade, Caedmon stopped, taking in the breathtaking view of *The Glade of the Forest Pools*, it was lovely! Across the glade he could see Treasa and Shylah coming towards him.

"Go to them," Eammon said. "They will take you to your pool. This is what the Prince desires. You will need your friends with you while you look into your pool."

Caedmon turned to thank Eammon, but was surprised he was gone so quickly. Treasa and Shylah met Caedmon with hugs.

"So glad to see you finally made it, young man!" Shylah teased.

"Yes, I heard you ran ahead. I also heard that someone was trying to cause me a fright," he said mischievously, sneaking a glance at Treasa.

"Hmm...wonder who that could have been?" Caedmon said with a wink at Shylah. "I hear it fell upon their own head."

Treasa took a playful poke at Caedmon as he jumped out of the way, nearly falling into a pool. Its water was a boiling red mass of ripples and bubbles.

"That is your pool, Caedmon," Treasa said nervously, then added, "You are to sit and look into your pool and the Prince, our unseen Lord ~ will show you how to help someone in our land. You will then know how to mediate for them. It is not difficult once you do it Though, I warn you that both of us were shocked by what we saw."

"The Lord wants us to sit with you and hold your hands while you look and mediate for you."

"Will this pool bring me to the mist of separation?" Caedmon asked, a bit confused about what was going to happen.

"No. Not exactly," Treasa told him.

- 213 -

Shylah interjected excitedly. "When you are finished here, we are to go *The Mountain of Meeting*. Eammon, the man who brought here, will take us to the edge of this great forest and he will show us the path to the mist between our two worlds. From what I understand, the path to the mountain will lead us right beside the mist. Did you know that we will see the Lord's Father there?"

"No, but I have heard about Him from a great warrior who I just met," Caedmon said, thinking of Aithne fondly.

"That He is beyond what I can even imagine." Caedmon said as he sat down cross legged on the grass. Then, raising his hands, he added, "Come ladies. Sit down and hold my hands."

As all three waited, Caedmon searched the pool as the water churned and bubbled. The water was so red it appeared to be blood, but the aroma coming from the water was the strong fragrance of lily of the valley, with a mingling aroma of the spicy fragrance of nard. The water gradually settled down, but every now and then a bubble would come to the surface and pop like soap suds. The women sat silently, mediating from their hearts for their young friend. They petitioned the Lord to give him the grace he needed to see whatever was within his pool.

As Caedmon watched the pool, he noticed that he could see the shimmer of shadows within its depths. He leaned forward to try to make them out. Sure enough he was seeing someone moving around in a small circle, almost as if his one foot was nailed in place or tied to something in the ground. As the pool settled, Caedmon saw clearly that the man had a large manacle on his ankle and the chain from the manacle was fastened to a large iron ring that was secured in the ground. The man continued to walk around and around, oblivious to the fact that he was getting nowhere. His ankle was raw and bleeding. His armour lay on the ground beside him. Immediately, Caedmon saw himself in the room, reaching out for the man to come with him, but the man looked at him blankly and continued his circling.

Caedmon became so caught up in what he saw that he yelled. "Hey are you a lunatic? You can't go anywhere! Take off the manacle!"

- 214 -

Caedmon's sudden outburst startled both woman, whose eyes were closed and could not see anything in Caedmon's pool. They kept their eyes closed and began to mediate harder for Caedmon as he squeezed their hands until they hurt. *What is he seeing?* They wanted to ask, but knew that he would tell them when it was over.

Caedmon did not even realize that he was yelling until he felt the women's hands wiggle a little to loosen his grip. Relaxing his hands, he looked back into the pool. The man was now taking off his manacle and going to a table where he ate some bread and wine. Finishing his humble meal, he got a heavy blanket to lie on. Returning to his manacle, he secured it firmly on his ankle and laid down upon the blanket. After he laid there for a moment, two small boys came into the room. They went to the table to eat without even a glance to the man on the floor. When they were done eating they looked over at the man, who Caedmon assumed was their father. They were calling to him. The manacled man opened his eyes wearily and waved for them to leave. Then a woman came in and she too ate. Caedmon could see that she was angry, for she was yelling at the man. He awoke a little and waved her away as well. She grabbed a small blanket and wrapped some belongings in it, then left the room. The man slept on.

Caedmon, with a sudden understanding he had never felt before, could hear the thoughts going on in the man's head.

"Why can't anyone understand me? I work hard to look after my family, but they are so selfish. I was a good husband, but, she was not a good wife. She has left me! I work hard! Can't they see that?"

The man's thoughts had a familiar ring to it. Caedmon leaned back and looked into the forest, tears streaming down his face. The man was his father, Vaughan. Caedmon tried to get his hands free from the women's grip, but they held on.

"What did you see, Caedmon?" Treasa asked soothingly. "Don't be afraid. You've seen this so you will know how to mediate."

"Why would I want to mediate for *him*?! I ask you this; how can you mediate for someone who only cares about himself? Someone who makes excuses and never takes responsibility? What I saw gives me no insight ~ it only opens an old wound. I know why my mother

- 215 -

left him now. He only cared about his work!" Caedmon cried with sudden understanding as he shook free of their hands and rushed to his feet. As he did so, his pool began to shrink at a fast rate, becoming smaller and smaller. The beautiful aroma took on the putrid odour of rot. The lovely red water began to turn brown as both women watched in horror.

"Caedmon, look!" Shylah said as she pointed at his pool. "You better sit and ask the Lord what He wants you to do with the information you have received. Quickly! The water is almost gone completely."

Caedmon, realizing the truth of her words, sat back down between the ladies. When he took their hands, the water began to rise and change back to its former colour and smell.

"I know this is hard," Shylah went on to say. "I too saw something I did not want to mediate for. It made me angry. The person I saw, in my pool, was also in a prison of selfishness that he had made for himself. However, if I don't mediate for him, he will never get out. He does not know how. I know He wants out, I saw him trying to claw his way out, but now he has given up." She then explained everything she had experienced at her pool. Treasa then told him her experience.

Taking a deep breath, Caedmon told the women what he had seen, and then together they asked the Lord to remove the bitterness from his heart. As Caedmon asked this, he instantly realized that he too had been caught in the same trap as both his mother and father ~ the trap of blame. He saw that as long as he blamed someone else for his own circumstances, there would be no room for him to change.

He bowed his head over his knees and quietly asked the Lord to show him how to mediate for his father. Looking again in to the pool, he saw himself go into the room, and this time he pointed at the manacle on his father's ankle. His father grabbed his blanket and tried to hide his leg from Caedmon's view. Caedmon then strode over and removed the blanket. His father tried to grab it back, but Caedmon threw it out of his reach. Vaughan swung his fist at him, but Caedmon ducked and stepped back out of the way. Vaughan lunged ahead and, coming to the end of his chain fell head long forward. It happened so fast that he could not catch himself.

Caedmon saw himself run up to his father to help him up, but Vaughan brushed his hand away and yelled. "You tripped me! I don't want you here. Go!"

Caedmon was not moved by the yelling, for it appeared to make the manacle shine brightly. Vaughan sat up and watched his ankle in shock. It was as if he was seeing the chain for the first time, even though he had secured it there himself.

As Caedmon removed the manacle, he saw that there was green slime all over the iron loop. It was dripping onto the floor. It had to be the Dragon's work, but it was his father who had chosen to wear it. Vaughan sat still and continued to watch Caedmon in silence as his son gently washed the raw wound and wrapped it in clean cloths. His father slowly and hesitantly reached forward to touch Caedmon's cheek as tears began to wash down his old, tired face. The image faded from Caedmon's pool and the water took on its former boiling and bubbling. The beautiful aroma filled the entire glade.

Caedmon relaxed, feeling as if a large stone had been removed from his heart. He would need strength to confront his father's bondage, but he knew now that if he mediated, free from bitterness, the day would come for him to set his own father free.

Turning he hugged first Shylah, then Treasa, saying, "Well, ladies, this is a place where one should come often. I do believe that everything will be all right now. For the first time in my entire life, I saw with my own eyes what the Lord sees, and I don't feel overwhelmed or hopeless. If we see with His perspective, then we can mediate properly and get our own hearts right at the same time. I think it is time I took the manacle off my own foot. Shylah, it is time for you to get out of your own dungeon. And Treasa, you must not keep your broken heart tucked away, but rather bring it out to be healed. Let us decide now that we will never return to our old ways!"

The women nodded in hearty agreement.

"Come let us be going. I can hardly wait to see what is through the mist." Caedmon said.

All three stood up and walked across the glade. As they passed the moss-covered boulders beside the pools, they saw that they were not boulders at all, but others who were looking into their own pools! What appeared to be moss over them was a green robe, just like Eammon's, that seemed to camouflage them from prying eyes.

Stopping suddenly, Shylah pointed at one of the green clad pilgrims ~ it was Tully, Edan's wife! Her long red hair hung down about her and tears of joy were running down her enraptured face. Her hands were stretched out towards the edge of the pool as she knelt there beside it. They could see her lips moving as she was mediating for whoever she was seeing in her pool. She looked more beautiful than she had ever appeared in their land.

They walked by her silently and then, seeing Eammon striding towards them, they joined him.

"Come with me," he whispered. "The others are beginning to arrive here as well. Soon the glade will be opened further and more of the hidden pools uncovered. They are here among the trees just waiting for their pilgrims to open them."

With that said, the glade's magnificent keeper silently turned and led them into the forest. They had not walked far before they reached the edge of the forest and saw a great grassland laid out before them. To their left, a wide road wound through the tall prairie grasses and the brightness of the sky made them blink.

"There is your road. Until we meet again," Eammon said as he raised each of their left hands in turn and kissed their palms. When he released them, they all felt the handle of their shields within their grasp again.

"Farewell, friend," Treasa spoke. Turning back into the woods, he was gone. *He truly was like his name ~ hidden,* Treasa thought. *What a joy he was when you found him!*

- 218 -

The Ancients say… "Awake thou that sleepest!"

Chapter 12

arris wiped the sweat from his eyes. What had he done? He had defiled Keelin by promising something he was not fit to give her.

He continued to work on the mill's gears. It was his work. He travelled all over the valley fixing any mechanical part on all the different grist and lumber mills. He had even been called in to fix one of the catapults used at the fortresses. This had bothered him deeply. These war machines had not been used for years, but now everyone was repairing their old machines. They would fire off large boulders at anyone who seemed to be a threat to them. Wiping his brow again, he walked over to the water bucket and, scooping up the water dipper, took a long drink. The water in the aqueducts was becoming stale since the river had been drying up. The water had a foul aftertaste.

Finishing the job, Barris received his pay and made his way home. He lived with his mother, and knew that there would be a hearty meal waiting for him. On his walk, Barris could not get Keelin off his mind. Why had he done it? *Fear,* the thought came unbidden. Yes, it had only been fear, but the pain he had inflicted on her. He had been even too much of a coward to tell her the truth. He was afraid he could not serve the unseen Lord.

He knew deep in his heart he loved her and should try to reconcile with her, but he was afraid of her parents and family. He had behaved like a scoundrel right from the beginning ~ not at all like someone honourable. The unseen Lord laid His hand heavily upon Barris' shoulder, squeezing it slightly. Then, leaning into him, He whispered, "It is time to behave like a man and do the honourable thing!"

Barris stopped dead in his tracks. Who had spoken to him? There was nobody else around! The hair on his neck prickled as he walked

- 219 -

the rest of the way home feeling the weight of his guilt upon his shoulders. The unseen Lord walked quietly behind him and kept both hands placed firmly on him. The Dragon hissed and hurled its slime at Barris, but it hit an invisible wall and pooled harmlessly at Barris' feet.

"He is mine!" The Dragon screeched.

"He is not yours, and you know it!" Authority rang in the unseen Lord's voice as He spoke. "He is mine! He gave himself to Me when he was but a youngster, and I won't give him back. You know the rules. I will always be able to speak to My own, even if they don't want to listen or obey. He will obey because you have not been able to defile his *heart,* only his mind. Now be gone, you slithering liar, before I strike you again on the head!"

The Dragon squealed like a stuck pig as it vanished from the village street. Barris sighed. Suddenly he felt lighter even though he knew a hard task lay in front of him.

~

A soft knock came to the door and Cathaoir got up from in front of the fire to go see who was coming so late in the evening. He walked slowly, for he was tired. He missed Treasa. She had been gone for days and he needed her badly to come home.

Standing in the doorway was Briant. His hair looked dishevelled and unkempt, and his clothes appeared like he had not changed them in days.

"I am a wretched man, neighbour. May I come in?" Briant spoke so quietly that Cathaoir could barely hear him. He quickly stepped aside and motioned for him to enter.

Walking back to the sitting area in front of the fireplace, both men sat down facing one another. Keelin was sound asleep in her bed chamber, so they would not be disturbed.

"How is Keelin tonight?" Briant asked.

"Well, I do think she is getting a little better. She even, laughed today when she was playing with the kitten I gave her. The unseen Lord has been ministering to her through our mediating and I know that Shylah and Treasa are mediating as well ~ and many others," Cathaoir replied.

"I have not... I have not mediated for anyone. I just think about myself and I don't know how to stop. I worry about the crops, I worry about the drought, I worry that there won't be enough. The only mediating I do is for myself, and it has not helped at all. I want my children to be good, but I do not know how to discipline them. Now that Shylah is gone, they have become belligerent towards me. Maybe they always were, but I would just let Shylah deal with it. I want to be angry at her for leaving me with all this worry, but I know the unseen Lord told her to go. Why can't I think of others? I cannot even think of Shylah for her sake. My thoughts are always how she affects me, not how I affect her,"

Briant's story, once started, kept tumbling out. For over an hour he talked on about his own faults and did not blame a single other person. Cathaoir sat in silence, his own heart feeling the truth in Briant's words. They hit home for him too. Very close to home, for his own heart had convicted him of the same crimes when Keelin had first become broken. Finally, the story ended and Briant slumped forward in his chair, utterly defeated.

"Listen, friend," said Cathaoir. "I, too, was exactly like you only a few short weeks ago. There is only one cure. Only one! You must tell the unseen Lord what you have told me. I cannot change you, but I can direct you to He who can. Take it to Him. He is changing me, that's for sure. I got into my self-centered mess over time, and it is taking time to get out. I mediate for others now, not myself. I think of Keelin and Treasa before myself. Sometimes, I have to shake myself hard because there are days I want to get mad that Treasa is not here when I think I need her. However, you know, if she had not gone to the Source, I would not be the man I am now. She would be the one attending Keelin, but in her absence I have had to do it. It has been good for me," Cathaoir spoke straight and firmly to Briant.

His neighbour nodded in understanding. "It will be hard, but it is harder living the way I have been," Briant answered honestly. "I better get home and talk to my children about a few things. I think I have some confessing to do on the way home with the unseen Lord. Thank you, Cathaoir, for listening and for not condemning me."

As the men walked to the door, Cathaoir slapped Briant on the back and said, "Condemn? Now, wouldn't that be the pot calling the kettle blackened. Have a good talk on the way home. I feel His presence with us already."

As Cathaoir turned from the door, he saw his sword and shield in his hands. His heart raised in thanksgiving, for he hadn't seen them for many weeks now. Kneeling in front of the fire, he mediated for his wayward neighbour and friend.

~

Barris walked up the lane to the farmstead. His resolve was slowly evaporating as he saw the small cottage nestled in the trees. Someone was at the well fetching a bucket of water. Chickens were scratching and clucking all over the front yard. He saw a neat garden to one side of the cottage, with a large barn on the other side built of stone and thatch like the cottage. Cows were milling around in a pen beside the barn and he could hear pigs rooting in the dirt as he came closer. Whoever had been by the well had disappeared into the cottage and he was glad, for it might have been Keelin and he wanted to talk to her father before he saw her.

Just as he was about to step up to the door, it swung wide open and a startled Keelin came stepping out with the water bucket in her hand. Her hand went to her throat as she stared in unbelief. Tears spilled up and over her tired eyes. One sweep of his gaze told him that she was very thin. She did not look well.

"What do you want?" she croaked out.

Clearing his throat, Barris spoke, before he lost courage and fled. "I have come to ask your father if you can be my bride. That is, if you will have me. I know that you must hate me now but I cannot sleep, or eat, or do anything else until I know for sure that there is no hope for us. I have been a coward, and I want to ask your forgiveness. I was full of fear that I could not serve the unseen Lord. That I could not provide for you ~ crazy fears! I have asked the unseen Lord to forgive me and He assured me that He has. But I have to

- 222 -

make things right. Please, Keelin, I love you. I know that I have not shown it in any honourable way, but I do."

Keelin began to tremble violently and, setting down the pail she wrapped her arms around herself. She nodded her head, unable to speak. Turning she quietly walked into the house. Barris stood there, uncertain of what to do, again feeling the pressure on his shoulders. He somehow knew that the unseen Lord was with him to give him support. He stepped up to the door and went inside. Keelin was nowhere to be seen, but he heard someone off to his left in what he supposed was the kitchen.

"Is that you, Keelin? Did you get lost going to the well? Come on girl, hurry. We want to get these dishes done and I need more rinse water," a male voice boomed out.

Barris tried to breathe, but found that his breath stuck partway up. Before he could reconsider, the weight of his conduct pushed him forward into the kitchen. Cathaoir turned, smiling, to greet his daughter. His hands, dripping, water holding a dish suspended in mid air. He stood there frozen to the spot, staring without even blinking at the young man before him.

"Excuse me, sir," Barris finally said. "My name is Barris and I need to confess my great sin to you."

Cathaoir turned slowly back to the pan of dishes and lowered the plate into the sudsy water. *Lord, help me,* he silently petitioned. He felt a familiar peace wrap itself like a blanket around his being, for his Lord was present. He could do this, even though everything within his mind wanted to send this young man packing.

"Please sit down by the fire. I will dry my hands and join you," Cathaoir said firmly without turning to look at him. Barris quietly went and sat in one of the soft chairs in front of the open fireplace. There were only coals in it, as it was near midday and the air was already hot outside.

"Go ahead, lad," Cathaoir said as he took a chair opposite him.

Barris shifted uneasily in his chair. He did not know where to begin. "Well, first of all, I want to say that I love your daughter. I know I don't deserve her and I know we did everything wrong, but I want her to be my wife and I promise I will look after her. I

- 223 -

will understand if you send me from here without a word," Barris spoke quickly to get it all out. He let out a deep sigh, as if he hadn't breathed since he came into the room. Then, shifting his weight again, he forced himself to look Cathaoir directly in the eyes, waiting for a response.

"Well, that took much courage. I don't think you could have done this without the help of the unseen Lord. I felt His presence when you came in. I have to tell you right now, if He wasn't present I would have asked you to leave. I know that my wife will struggle with this, but I consent on one condition… that Keelin wants you." Cathaoir was surprised by his own response.

Barris's eyes widened in amazement. The man's response was what he had hoped for, but had never expected it.

"Keelin, please come here. It is time to deal with this. Now!" Cathaoir, for the first time since her heartbreak, raised his voice with commanding authority to his daughter. She quietly entered the room and came and sat at her father's feet. Her head was bowed and she was still holding herself and trembling. Cathaoir reached down and stroked her hair, then spoke gently, "What do you want, my dearest?"

She looked up at Barris, her eyes wide in shock and unbelief. This was exactly what she wanted, what she had dreamed of! She tried to speak, but the words choked in her throat. She knew her mother would not understand, for Treasa had never approved of her feelings for Barris, but she had to do this. She had given her heart to this man and it would be his, no matter what anyone said or did.

"I want to be Barris's wife, and I forgive him. I know that he was afraid, but he has shown much courage by doing the right thing now. I only hope that you and mom will forgive both of us and welcome us back into the family."

"Keelin, you have never been excluded from this family. Remember, it was you that left us, not us you. We have only wanted the unseen Lord's will for you, and we all hope that this is His will revealing itself now. You will always have mine and your mother's love, and Teague and Seanna's too. Everyone has proven that to you these last few weeks. Your mother might have left, but only to seek

- 224 -

the unseen Lord for you. We have to believe Barris's presence here is due to her mediating at the Source."

Barris slowly rose from his seat and knelt down in front of Keelin. Taking her hand, he placed a gentle kiss on the back of it. Softly, he spoke to her.

"I will return and do this right. We will plan our wedding here, where it should have been in the first place. I love you, my Keelin."

"And I love you. I will be awaiting your return," Keelin said as she stood and went to her room. Cathaoir showed Barris to the door and then went back to his dishes in complete wonder over all that had happened in the days since Treasa and Shylah had left. He felt a little nervous about how they would take this change in events, but he felt certain that the unseen Lord was guiding them.

As Barris walked down the road back to his village, he felt the heavy weight lift off his shoulders. Joy welled up inside.

"Thank you, Lord. I owe you much," Barris breathed out in great relief.

"Thank you, Barris, for being a man. A man of honour. I am pleased, but you will need to rely on me in the days to come, for not everyone will be so easily moved by your change of heart. To prove your merit to them, you must let your own life be true," the unseen Lord spoke to Barris on the breeze.

Barris dropped to his knees with his hands stretched up in surrender. No one would ever tell him again that the unseen Lord did not speak to His pilgrims.

The Ancients say, "My soul thirsteth for thee, my flesh longeth for thee in a dry and thirsty land, where no water is."

Chapter 13

The tall grass waved in the wind and the wild flowers coloured the land with yellows, blues, and reds. Treasa, Caedmon, and Shylah continued on the path through the wide grassland, taking their time. They knew suddenly there was no rush. The Lord would have told them to hurry if there had been a reason for speed. Caedmon came to the realization as they sauntered along ~ he was always in a hurry. He had thought that everything depended on *him*! He had been so wrong, so self-reliant, and finally he was beginning to see the truth.

Caedmon looked ahead of him and was shocked by what he was seeing. He could see a desert with the sand blowing. It was like he was standing upon an invisible line that was between the desert and the lush green of the prairie.

"Look, ladies! What is that? It looks like a desert has been cut right out of this lovely green prairie!"

The women stopped, also mesmerized by the blowing sand and the extreme change in the landscape. There was a slight mist falling between them and the desert. The unseen Lord appeared next to them and stood looking into the desert also. Together they saw a woman begin to appear, coming toward them through the burning sandstorm. Her hair blew across her face and her loose garments blew in the wind around her slender form. She looked as grey as the sand that whipped around her. Caedmon felt he was seeing a spectre. She was moving towards them, almost as if she was floating and not walking at all. Caedmon could see glimpses of her face, and the appearance was of someone dead, utterly expressionless.

Her long hair kept whipping across her face, but it did not seem to stop her advancement toward them. Caedmon stepped back as her foot came forward and stepped onto the prairie, only inches from him. He could feel the heat of the desert emanating off of her. Looking down at her foot, he noticed that it was slowly taking on a healthy, pink colour. The colour was slowly climbing her leg as she came forward through the mist. Reaching out her small delicate hand towards him, the blush of colour travelled up her arm. Soon the grey pallor had left her skin completely and lovely pink flesh replaced it, spreading quickly across her cheeks. She suddenly stopped mid-stride, stuck between two worlds. She seemed half alive and half dead.

"Lord, should I take her hand and help her through?" Caedmon pleaded.

"No. You cannot help her through, Caedmon," the Lord spoke quietly.

"Who is she, Lord? She looks so familiar to me. Wait a moment..." Caedmon gasped as the hair blew back from her face.

Treasa let out a small whimper, while Shylah just stood there in complete shock. Before them stood Keelin. What had happened to her?

"Keelin?" Treasa whispered, not wanting to believe her eyes.

Then they saw the forms of others through the sandstorm. Some were talking to one another, while others appeared to be doing their daily tasks.

"Yes, it is Keelin," said the unseen Lord. "This is what I see when I look to your land. The people's hearts that once knew me and talked to me have become preoccupied with life. The very pilgrims that I once called friends have forgotten their need for the Unchanging River ~ and their need of Me. That's why the Source has started to dry up. So you see, the reality of their condition is much worse than what you had thought. This is the way they truly are." The Lord spoke softly as He waved His arm toward the desert.

Caedmon had to speak. "Can I not help them? I so want to pull her forward to this place. I have tried to stir them, but they seem so complacent with things the way they are. The Dragon has stirred up so much dissension and persecution that everyone has retreated into their own lives." Caedmon's voice was full of exasperation.

"You cannot, Caedmon, but I can. I have been waiting for someone to ask Me, for someone to want Me to intervene. Even you thought that it was something that *you* could do alone. You can do nothing. Don't you see that? The Dragon knew that if it could get everyone thinking that they could battle it on their own, then the beast would win. It would cause a drought so devastating that no one would survive. My mediators, listen to me. Can't you see how your old self is too ready to go along with the Dragon's schemes and pride?"

Caedmon, Treasa, and Shylah looked far out into the desert, squinting their eyes against the hot sun and blowing sand. They could see the forms of people coming into view in the blowing sandstorm, their bodies grey and lifeless looking. Caedmon suddenly saw himself out there, and that is when he noticed something ~ that his hands and feet were a healthy colour. Teague too was wandering amidst the sandstorm, and his face appeared blushed with life. Gallagher's arms were full of life as he was helping someone along a dusty road. Edan's eyes were bright and sparkling, and Tully's lips, cheeks, and neck were full of colour. Shylah saw herself. She, also, was full of life in her heart area, but her arms and legs and head were grey with death. What did it all mean?

"Every one of you still has My life in you, but sometimes your complacency takes over and forces that life and joy from your beings. Keelin here is learning to live in joy again this very moment! That is what I brought you here to show you ~ how to bring life back to yourselves through joy. When you go back just be yourself. Love! Laugh! Live! Be everything I have called you to be, and talk to Me and use what I am about to show you in every situation and watch life spring up all around you," the great Prince laughed out this final decree.

His laughter filled the air, and the rocks of the valley walls rang with it. It grew louder and louder. Caedmon could not help himself, for the laughter was so contagious that he joined until he was rolling on the grass, holding his sides. They laughed and laughed, and Caedmon felt all fear and anxiety leave him and in its place was a feeling of great contentment. He lay quietly for a long time, his eyes closed, enjoying the warmth of the daylight on his face.

Suddenly it came to him ~ understanding from deep inside. He knew what was required of him now. It was so simple that he had entirely missed it before!

Caedmon looked at the Lord who was lying beside him on the grass. Rising to his feet, he stretched out his hand and helped the Lord to His feet. Looking into the unseen Lord's eyes, his own eyes filled with tears.

"I have no love in my heart for Keelin. I ask that you allow me to love her and the others, and take away my frustration with them. I ask that you would reach out, to her and the others, and draw them to yourself," Caedmon spoke with an openness that he'd never before felt.

"You have discerned correctly, my friend," the Lord said, reaching out his hand to touch Caedmon as He spoke.

Caedmon felt a deep alteration, as if someone was pulling out something lodged deep inside himself. Memories flooded his being ~ bad memories, memories of rejection and humiliation. Then, as abruptly as they had come, they stopped. He felt as if a soft rain was falling in his soul, cleansing away the hurt and shame. Wonder of wonders, he felt a genuine love, of a kind that he had never felt before, pouring out of himself. It was the kind of love that requires nothing from anyone ~ the kind of love he received from the Lord. It flooded his soul in great waves until he thought he could not bear it any longer because it almost hurt to love so unconditionally.

Shylah and Treasa watched in wonder at the transformation in Caedmon. They also could feel a change happening inside of themselves. They realized that they had not loved Keelin unconditionally. They needed to lose the disappointment and sad faces around her. It was time to go on. *And* to let Keelin go on with life as well, encouraging her with joy!

Caedmon stood to his feet and joined the women. The Lord joined them, almost as if He was waiting for them.

"Lord, we ask You to bring her to Yourself," Caedmon asked, with a certainty that he had never felt before. Treasa and Shylah watched in astonishment.

The unseen Lord turned from them and walked over to Keelin. He gently took her hand and pulled her toward Himself. As she came through the mist, life flowed into her entire being. Her whole face shone with a radiance that made her beautiful. Her dress glistened such a pure white that Caedmon had to blink from the glory of it, and her hair tumbled in brown cascades down her back. The dust and sand seemed to have disappeared from her completely.

When Keelin saw who had pulled her through, she let out a squeal of delight, throwing herself into the Lord's arms. Lifting Keelin high off her feet, the Lord twirled her around and around, and they laughed in the purest joy. He gently sat her back on her feet. Reaching into His cloak, He drew out a golden flute.

"This is my gift to you," the Lord spoke with such a tenderness that Keelin's eyes misted. "This flute will heal those who have been injured by the Dragon's lies and those who cannot resist the beast any longer. I will teach you to play songs of deliverance to restore them."

The three spectators felt that everything was going to be all right. They looked down, away from the intimate scene before them...

Keelin was holding something as she came quietly into the sitting room. It was past the midnight hour and all was still. The fire crackled low in the fireplace, and its glow danced upon the walls. Kneeling down in front of the fire, she gently tossed in the rolled garment. It was her soiled wedding dress. Bowing her head, Keelin stretched her hands out, saying, "I'm sorry, Lord."

A single tear slipped down her cheek and fell in slow motion to her lap. As it splashed against her nightdress she opened her eyes and saw a page of the ancients lying on her lap. In the light of the embers she read the single line that was written upon it:

~ You Are Forgiven ~

~

When they finally looked up, the three of them were back on the path in the grassland. The desert was gone and they knew that they had been to the mist of the Source between their worlds.

Now they must go on to *The Mountain of Meeting*. Each was quiet in their own thoughts. Shylah kept rubbing her heart, at least it was still alive. Caedmon wondered at the sudden change of his heart. All it took was his honesty and the Lord's touch. He knew that he would need to be reminded of this in the future. Treasa thought about her daughter and joy flooded her like the great waves of the sea.

Incredible ~ simply incredible, she thought with jubilation.

The Ancients say… "Whether we live therefore, or die, we are the Lord's."

Chapter 14

Dei ~ shining
Brina ~ protector

Treva straightened and stretched her back. She was tired and sore from hoeing in the garden, as it was backbreaking work, the ground was hard and dry. She knelt down beside her carrots and tried to coax a little life into them, as she scooped the fresh hoed dirt over them to protect them from the scorching sun.

It had been one week, and still there was no sign of Gilroy. He had taken a load of merchandise into the neighbouring valley and said he would be home in five days. She wondered what could have waylaid him for the additional two days. Reaching up, she wiped a stray strand of greying hair from her eyes, leaving a streak of dirt across her brow.

Getting up off the ground, Treva headed into the cabin to get a drink of water and rest for a while. She did not like the fact that she was getting older and it was taking her longer to move. She could not work as long before she needed rest. However, she was thankful to the unseen Lord for her good health.

Gilroy too, had slowed down since Arthmael's death. She wiped a tear from her eye as she settled down on one of the large cushions near the window. She recalled the times when she, Gilroy, and Arthmael had sat down in this small sitting room, laughing and telling of their day to one another. Fond memories. Good memories.

Treva remembered how her mother had taught her that one is always making memories, so they might as well be good ones. She missed her mother, she had been a good woman ~ a hardworking pilgrim who'd lived at the Source, raising her brood of children.

Treva was the only one left at the Source from her immediate family. Her brothers and sisters had married and moved away years before. She only had one sister left living, and she lived in the village of Sunset near the sea. Treva had been there years before to visit her and it had been wonderful. Her father had died only ten years ago. He had been ancient and wise. He had lived with them the last few years of his life, but he had not been a burden. Even though his eyesight was dim, he still would peel her potatoes or help her hoe in the garden. He had been a true pilgrim of the unseen Lord.

Treva could still hear her father's mediating in her memory, as clear as if it had been only the day before. He never tired of mediating for the fortress dwellers. His love never wavered, even though he had been shunned by many of them. She knew that he had influenced Arthmael greatly with his love and tenderness. He'd always treated Arthmael with such respect, even when Arthmael was a small child.

Treva rested her head upon the crook of her arm and fell into a peaceful sleep. The afternoon slipped by and the shadows were long across the floor when she was startled awake. Treva looked around bewildered as she had slept so soundly that she did not know where she was at first. Then, remembering, she smiled to herself and went into the kitchen to fix herself supper.

A little bread and cheese was all she needed, with maybe a little of the beef broth she'd boiled that morning. As she prepared her supper she could not shake the feeling of uneasiness that kept coming over her. Giving herself a good lecture about how thinking negatively was not good for one's soul, she sat down to her simple meal.

"Lord, is something wrong?" Treva asked after she thanked Him for His provision of food. Again, she felt an uncomfortable uneasiness that made her heart beat more rapidly. "Please Lord, answer me. I feel unnerved about something and I don't know what it is."

"Treva, I am with you," the unseen Lord whispered gently into her ear. Laying his hand firmly on her shoulder, He said, "You will need to be strong. Do not fear. I will not leave you alone."

"It is Gilroy, isn't it?" Treva asked just before a knock came to her door. Rising from her chair, she went to it. Their good friend

- 233 -

Driscoll was standing there, his hat in his hand. He was shifting his weight uncomfortably from one foot to the other.

"Gilroy is in my wagon, Treva. He is very sick. Come, for I don't think we should move him." As he spoke, he took Treva by the hand and led her to his wagon on the road in front of their cabin. Finally comprehending, Treva let go of his hand and ran to the wagon. Grabbing the side, she scrambled up into the box. There lay her beloved, his face ashen white and his eyes closed. Sobbing, Treva flung herself upon his chest, willing him to live.

"I found him laying by his wagon on the road through the forest. Some of the men have gone to get your wagon and horses. He hasn't awakened. Treva, I am so sorry..." Driscoll could say no more as a sob rose in his throat for his dearest friend.

Gilroy slowly opened his eyes, raising his hand and laying it gently on Treva's shoulders. Gasping, she raised her face and looked into his adoring eyes. "My precious darling, I am afraid I do not have much time here left."

"Don't, Gilroy..." Treva began. Gilroy put his hand to her lips to silence her, then he clasped her hand upon his chest.

"Please listen, my Treva. I have loved you since the first time you pretended you did not see me looking at you. Do you remember that? You were a little kitten with the hiss of a wild cat! My, how you have enlightened my life. Please dearest, don't cry. I am going to the kingdom of our unseen Lord. It is my turn. I have known for some time, and so have you." Gilroy stopped and drew in a long, laborious breath.

"Oh Gilroy, you can't go! I cannot go on without you! You are my strength and my song. The unseen Lord gave you to me so that I could be strong. I love you..." Treva tried not to cry, but her sobbing came wrenching out again. "No, Gilroy, no!"

"Hush, my little one. The unseen Lord will provide for you and we will be together again soon. But, there are still things for you to do for His kingdom here. And there are things for me to do over there." As Gilroy spoke, his voice took on a faraway sound. He looked past Treva, to something she could not see. Suddenly raising up on his elbow, he spoke forcibly, "Look Treva, the mountain of

- 234 -

the great Father of all! Look, my dearest, there is Arthmael! He is coming for me. Can you see him? He's with your father."

A long sigh escaped his lips as he lay down again. His eyes shut one last time, only to open in the land beyond the veil. Treva lay upon his chest. She did not think she could breathe. Her life felt like it had been squeezed out of her. Driscoll finally coaxed her to come down from the wagon, and his wife, who had arrived, gently took her into the cabin. Driscoll, with tears flowing down his face, drove his wagon home to care for his beloved friend's body. The people of the village slowly came out, each one crying, following the wagon to Driscoll's cabin.

Driscoll's son, Dei, came and helped his dad take Gilroy into the cabin to prepare his body for burial. What would they all do without their loving shepherd? Each was lost in their own grief.

~

The days passed and Treva went through the motions of living. Driscoll's son, Dei and his wife, Brina, had moved in with her for company. Brina was a sensitive young woman and she helped Treva in the garden and the cabin. Treva kept hoping that Caedmon would return soon.

The day came for them to go through Gilroy's things. It was a hard day, but also a good one. They laughed and cried about the different memories his clothes and belongings brought to them. The settlement had come to a halt with Gilroy's passing. No one knew how they would go on without their faithful servant. He had done all the merchandising for them, though he had taken Driscoll and his son with him many times. Driscoll knew that he and Dei would have to carry on for the settlement if they were to continue to get supplies.

Brina, her long brown hair hanging loose around her face, sighed as she examined the lovely walking stick that Arthmael had made. Looking up at Treva, her eyes were luminous in wonder.

"I have never seen carving this beautiful in all my life. The carving of the other villagers is fine, but this almost looks like it grew this way!"

- 235 -

"Yes, he was talented. Some said the unseen Lord spoke through his carving. Gilroy encouraged Arthmael to carve, even though he personally never cared for carving. Gilroy loved to be out traveling and that is what he did well," Treva said with a distant look in her eyes and a smile on her face. Then she added, "And he is still traveling, I would imagine. It will be hard for the unseen Lord to settle him down, I am thinking."

"You amaze me, Treva. You are so strong," Brina said.

"Well, I am not strong. Though, lately I've been amazing myself, you know. Though I know it is the presence of the unseen Lord that has strengthened me. You know, if anyone would ever have told me that I would be able to go on without Gilroy, I would have laughed in their face. But look at me. Oh, I still cry and sometimes I feel as if the wave of grief will never lift, but then it does. The light breaks through for a moment and I know that I will make it," Treva spoke quietly. Then she added, "I want to thank you and Dei for living with me. I love you being here, and I don't have any family now."

"I do have Caedmon but he is not really mine. He just felt like it. Do you think they will meet? Caedmon is beyond the mist of the Source?" Treva asked.

"I don't think so. I believe that even beyond the mist there is a place for those that passed over where we cannot go to. Not until we pass there to be with them. Caedmon is not dead, Treva," Brina reflectively spoke. The women continued to work sometime in silence, sorting through Gilroy's things.

"Dei and I want to thank you for having us. Our cabin was so small with only one room, and with this little one coming..." Brina trailed off, a faint smile appearing on her face.

Treva's eyes opened wide and she exclaimed, "Little one coming! Oh, Brina, I did not know! The unseen Lord has provided for us both. I have all these rooms to myself and now I can share them with your family as long as you want to stay with me. Let this be your home now. I am going to move into the small sleeping room and you and Dei can have the large one."

"No, you can't! You mustn't ~"

Treva's hand came up to stop Brina's response.

- 236 -

"Yes, I can. And I will. I don't like sleeping in there anyway. I have been coming out here and spending the night on the floor cushions. This will be better for me as well."

"Do you ever wonder what they are doing right now?" Brina abruptly changing the subject, as was her habit.

"Who do you mean?" Treva asked raising her brows in wonder.

"Treasa, Caedmon and Shylah. They have all been gone so long," Brina answered.

"Yes, it has been long. I wonder, too, now more than ever, with Gilroy gone." Treva answered slowly. Both women finished their job. Then quietly started supper feeling a comfortable comradeship with each other. This day had drawn them very close.

The Ancients say… "Judge not, and ye shall not be judged: condemn not, and ye shall not be condemned: forgive, and ye shall be forgiven."

Chapter 15

Briant and Edan talked long into the night. They had been friends off and on since the fortress years. Even though Briant was much older than Edan, they seemed to relate well with one another. Briant had been sharing with Edan the error of his ways and what he planned to do about it. He told Edan that since Shylah had left to go to the Source, he had allowed the unseen Lord to deal deeply with him. Briant's heart had been laid bare. He had to admit he was a selfish man and that he did not like what he was. He had never liked it, but had seemed unable ~ and unwilling ~ to change. Now he was crying out daily to the unseen Lord to forgive and change him.

Edan had listened uncomfortably. He, too, wanted to change, he told himself, but he was so busy thinking about how others should change that he never really addressed his own issues.

Briant had finally stopped talking and looked intently at Edan. "The reason I asked you to come was that I felt the unseen Lord had prompted me to tell you something."

Edan let out a nervous laugh as he shifted in his chair. Then, trying to sound encouraging, said, "Well then, tell me! I am sure it is not anything that I don't already know."

Briant did not expect this response and dropped his head. This was going to be harder than he thought, but taking a deep breath, he went on ~ "That is exactly the problem ~ you seem to know everything and it makes you unteachable. I don't want to hurt you, but unless you hear something first for yourself, you are not interested in learning it from another pilgrim."

Briant saw immediately that his words had cut deep into his young friend. He continued, "Don't be offended, Edan. I was the same and look at where it has got me! I have become imprisoned in my own little world, but I am determined to get out now! The unseen Lord wants you to be sorry for your judgements and harsh thoughts of others. He wants you to return to Him with a tender heart like the one you had before. He wants you to listen to Tully. She has been mediating for you, and that is how this word has come to me. It was her mediating that has moved the unseen Lord to ask me to come to you."

"Well, why hasn't He come to me? Why did he have to go through you?" Edan took a deep breath, not liking the bitter taste in his mouth. Then he squared his shoulders, but inside he could not stop the trembling, as he said, "Briant, I thought you were my friend."

"I am! Did you not ever read what the Ancients said ~ that when a friend wounds you it is out of faithfulness, but when your enemy kisses you it is only for heaping upon you? I don't want to hurt you, but, if that is necessary then I will be obedient to the unseen Lord and hope for the best. Come on, Edan, let's mediate together. Then you can ask Him if what I have said is true," Briant entreated Edan earnestly.

"You're right. I hate my arrogance, but I seem to be stuck somehow. I have tried to protect myself from criticism to the point of becoming obstinate. I know that I have hurt Tully with my judgements. I don't like feeling needy and weak, but I don't like feeling isolated and alone, either." Edan buried his face in his hands and leaned forward on his chair. A groan escaped his lips. *Why am I so proud?* His heart overwhelmed him with the truth of himself and he groaned again.

Briant got down in front of the fireplace and began to mediate for Edan in his heart. He knew that only the unseen Lord would be able to help him now. Immediately, Briant was upon a high mountain. He could see far around to the outlying countryside. Turning all around he felt a rush of exhilaration flood his being. Lifting his hands high, he turned around and around. The wind began to blow, as if it too was dancing on the mountain top. Along the path were large stones burning brightly, and, looking down at himself, he saw

- 239 -

that he too had the appearance of a bright burning stone. He was amazed, but not alarmed. Energized, but calm. His mind felt so active, but still.

Briant settled down on the ground and looked around his marvellous surroundings. He was neatly in line with the row of burning stones, and right in front of them was a path. He could see the backs of three people walking along.

It looks like Caedmon, Shylah and Treasa, he thought. Shylah was dressed in a beautiful gown and her hair was hanging loose down her back. She was carrying her shield and sword, which were glittering in the light of the burning stones. Caedmon was approaching a large throne and the women waited, behind him, standing still. Then, they all knelt down. Briant could feel the presence of the unseen Lord all around him. He felt exhilarated with new strength.

Bowing forward, he worshipped the Being on the throne, for he knew in his heart that He had to be the unseen Lord's Father. He lay that way for a long time, and let his heart become perfectly at rest. Becoming aware of the floor again he looked up and saw Edan lying prostrate, face down on the rug in front of the fireplace, sobs shaking his shoulders. Briant leaned over and laid his hand lightly on his friend's shoulder, surprised by the tears that were streaming down his own face as well.

~

Edan tried to focus on his mediating, but his heart kept confusing him. He wanted to justify himself so badly. He watched Briant, who seemed to be in his own little world. Briant had risen to his feet and was twirling around and around, laughing right out loud and then stopping and kneeling. Then he bowed down and became quiet. Edan had never seen anyone act so bewildering before, but he didn't say anything. He knew in his heart that Briant was truly seeing something the unseen Lord wanted him to see.

Suddenly Edan felt heavy, so very heavy. He slipped to the floor under his weight, and finally sprawled face down on the rug. The weight increased and increased until he felt like he was being crushed beneath the load. The unseen Lord knelt down in front of him and whispered in his ear, "Edan, those are the judgements that you have made of others. It is your pride and arrogance that you have used to protect yourself from being wounded by others' opinions. I am letting you feel their true weight." The unseen Lord paused, and then seriously added. "There is no way for you to remove them. A judgement made will stay with you forever. There is only one remedy."

Edan began crying, his heart breaking under the weight of the load, his mind bombarded with every judgement he had ever made.

"Help me! Please, Lord, I am so sorry."

The unseen Lord grabbed Edan by the shoulders and pulled him to his feet in one sweep. The rubble fell off Edan's back with a loud rumbling, crashing noise. The Lord shook Edan until he thought his bones would never be the same. Pulling Edan close, He hugged him until Edan thought he was being crushed again, only this time it felt good.

"That was all it takes to be free ~ just ask for help. Admit your weakness. I will always help those who are honest with me. Come, I have something to show you."

Edan immediately found himself in a forest glade. He could see the shimmer of pools all around him. A soft green light was shining upon him, and the leaves of the trees above blocked the sky from his view. Off at the far end of the glade he saw Tully. She was kneeling, looking into a pool, tears falling from her delicate face. His heart smote him, for he knew immediately what she was seeing. This place was the place of mediation ~ he knew it. It was as if at one time he had been there before.

"Tully comes here often. It is the only place that has kept her at your side. Tully was going to leave you many times, but she would come here instead, and I would show her who you really are. She would then mediate for you, asking Me to help you. She never judged you, and she was always trying to respect your place as man in the home. Tully is here right now because she is worried that you have not come home. It is late in your land and, she has been up all night, mediating for you," the unseen Lord informed Edan. There was no condemnation in His voice, only compassion.

- 241 -

"So is that why You had Briant ask me to come here?" Edan asked the unseen Lord.

"Yes. His heart is so sensitive right now because of his own recent return to me. I knew that he might break through to you because of his own personal struggle. So I had him send for you last evening, and now you must arise and go home. Make things right, my young warrior! You are a Dragon slayer, not a Dragon's puppet."

Edan lay on the floor. He felt Briant lay his hand upon his shoulder. Rolling over, he looked at his friend through the pools of tears that formed unbidden in his eyes.

"I have been such a fool. I am going home now. I have much to do to make things right. Thank you, friend," Edan said quietly, as he rose to his feet and made his way to the door.

Briant gave Edan a one-arm hug around the shoulders and the two parted without saying another word. None was necessary.

But unto the Son he saith, Thy throne, O God, is for ever and ever: a sceptre of righteousness is the sceptre of thy kingdom."

Chapter 16

The three pilgrims had resumed their walk across the wide grass prairie. A slight breeze was blowing, fanning their faces with the most wonderful of all fragrances. To Treasa it seemed as if the wind was holding rare spices, to Shylah it was the lovely perfume of flowers, and to Caedmon the fragrance of tree-ripened fruit. The perfume only was slight, not heady, making them want more. "How long do you think we have been in this land?" Shylah's voice broke the silence.

"Well, I am not sure," said Caedmon, "How long was I away before you joined me? It seemed like only one long day."

"Oh Caed, you had been gone for a few weeks!" Treasa exclaimed. "We were beginning to think you were not coming back. I wonder if they are worried for us back home? We must have been gone for quite some time now."

"I am sure that time is not of importance here, and that the unseen Lord will have it all synchronized exactly how it should be by the time we get back. I have this feeling, though, that we are near the end of our journey. I have learned so much here," Shylah said with a relieved sigh.

"Look, over there! Is not that a shepherd with his sheep?" Treasa pointed off to their far right.

Caedmon, a smile breaking forth on his face, spoke up. "It is Carden! Come, ladies, he is worth getting to know." Caedmon again felt the stirring to sing rise within his heart.

"Carden!" he called out.

Carden raised his head, his black hair blowing in the wind. His face broke forth in a huge smile. Striding over to them, he grabbed Caedmon and placed a kiss on each of the younger man's cheeks. "Well, lad, I was hoping to meet you again before you went back.

You have been gone for a long time. Look, the sheep are ready to feed on their own. I have brought them down to their grassland. Don't they look healthy and fine?" Pride ~ the good kind ~ filled Carden's voice as he looked at his flock.

"Carden, these are my friends; Shylah and Treasa," Caedmon introduced the women, who in turn curtsied to Carden. Carden nodded and smiled at them, "I know you well. There have been many times I fed you and sang over you to comfort you. When you were not even aware, I was the one who would whisper the Ancient's words to you. I would remind you of the Lord's words in times of despair."

The women looked at the sheep who were feeding contentedly behind Carden in the field. Caedmon said, "We are supposed to be taking this road to *The Mountain of Meeting*, but we do not even see any mountains. Are we on the right road?"

"Well, Caedmon my friend, you know what I think?" Carden spoke with a glint of humour in his hazel brown eyes. Then, answering his own question, Carden said, "If you cannot see, then ask to see. Remember, this land is different from yours. We see what is not visible and do not see what is truly there. We live in a land of knowing, and the seeing comes forth from our knowing. We *know* the mountain is right there in front of you, so therefore we do not need to see it. Not seeing is not really not seeing when you know." Carden began laughing at the bewildered looks upon the pilgrims' faces. He decided to confound them even more.

"Look at those sheep! Are they really sheep?"

The three looked at the sheep closely and then, in amazement, they saw that a group of them that had at first appeared to grazing in a circle facing one another, were in actuality a group of people sitting cross-legged in a circle, talking and reading very old parchments. They could see Cathaoir, and Briant. There was Keelin and Teague, Seanna, Edan, and Tully. Even Barris was there. They were looking at the parchment papers intently, then sharing with one another, smiling. They were all surprised to see Barris there, but knew from what they had seen at the mist between the worlds that something good was happening back home. They knew without

- 244 -

even speaking to one another that their mediating was working! The pilgrims were walking in a relationship with the unseen Lord again. Tears of gratitude fell down their faces as they bowed down and worshipped the unseen Lord.

It was finished, what they had needed to learn ~ all three felt it in their hearts as they arose, one by one. Carden and the sheep were no longer visible, but they knew they were still there.

Walking down the road, they felt that the ground was rising drastically under their feet. Then, as if scales had fallen from their eyes, they saw the winding path going up the face of a mountain right in front of them.

The mountain had no trees upon it. It was rocky and bare. Along the path were rocks that glowed in the dim light. Looking around they saw that a great cloud of darkness was upon the mountain and the path led straight into it. Not even hesitating, the three ascended the mountain, the glowing rocks lighting their path into the cloud. The climb was steep, but not difficult. They could see the path plainly in the light from the glowing rocks. Stopping and kneeling down, Treasa looked intently into one of the rocks. They appeared to be like living balls of fire. Reaching out, she gently touched one of the stones and the fire leapt into the air. She withdrew her hand quickly, astonished that the fire was not hot, but very bright.

"They are living," a familiar voice spoke to her. Looking up she saw the Lord standing with Shylah and Caedmon.

"Those stones are pilgrims that walk with us. They light the path to my Father. That way, many can come to this place to meet Him. The stone you touched, Treasa ~ that was you! That was why there was such a reaction. Look intently at yourself. Don't forget what you see."

Treasa turned again to the burning stone and looked intently into the fire. She was not prepared for what she saw. She saw a tall young woman, fully dressed as a knight, with bright shining weapons. Her auburn hair was blowing in the wind and looked as if the fire of the stone was shining from the locks that fell around her shoulders. Her hand was raised high with her sword firmly grasped in it. It was her, only with none of the age of her land upon her. She carried no worry, no fears, no regrets. *Is this how the Father sees me?* she wondered. Seeing her own strength, she felt her heart leap within her, and a heavy weight that had been upon it slipped away. She was safe, and she was known by the Father for who she truly was. It did not matter anymore what others saw when they looked upon her. He knew her!

As Treasa rose to her feet, and turned, to see Shylah also looking intently at a rock of fire. Her long golden hair was falling around her fair face, and tears were slipping unbidden from her sky blue eyes. She also was known! Caedmon stood talking with the Lord in hushed tones. It was time. They must go and see Him who had called them here.

The three started up the path again, into the ever-darkening cloud. The Lord joined them, but no one talked, as the solemnity of the moment was too great. Coming to flat ground, the cloud broke away. Before them, on a large rock that shone with the colours of the rainbow, sat a throne. Upon the throne, they could make out a figure whose appearance was more like light and fire all melded together. The light was ever moving in a random manor, but at the same time it appeared to the eyes to be moving like music sounds. The Prince put out His hand and halted them.

"This is where you can stop. The day will come when you will go right up to Him, but for now, as long as you live in your land, I will approach Him for you."

Putting His great hand upon Caedmon's shoulder, the Lord led him slightly closer. The women knelt down in homage and waited. The great Prince, the unseen Lord, the best friend he had ever known, gently pushed Caedmon down onto one knee. As Caedmon knelt there with his head bowed, he heard a beautiful song coming from the throne...a song about him! A song about Caedmon becoming a knight!

The three heard the whirling noise of a sword slicing through the air. They all looked up and saw the Prince dancing around Caedmon. He was dancing a war dance, whirling and spinning, raising His mighty sword high and then swinging it low, just missing

- 246 -

Caedmon's neck several times. Caedmon did not flinch, but knelt there transfixed by the song and the dance that moved around him.

Then as abruptly as it started, it ended. Caedmon saw the head of a lion glow from the front of his shield, like it was on fire. The Lord gently laid His sword upon each of Caedmon's shoulders. Then, with a booming voice, He spoke, "Enter into the knighthood of pilgrims who walk in your land and in Ours. You will know them when you see them, even as they are known and seen."

Caedmon looked back at Treasa and Shylah, who had their shields raised. The engraved lion heads upon them were pulsating with great light. He was now a knight! Caedmon would never have believed that he was worthy.

"Obedience has made you worthy, my young friend!" the Lord's soothing voice broke into Caedmon's thoughts.

Caedmon stood and embraced Him. He was so surprised to see they were the same height again. The throne and the cloud were gone. They could see for miles from their high vantage point. Just below them, in a small hollow of rocky land, there appeared to be a lake. It was swirling like a large whirlpool. Walking down the path to the lake, the foursome noticed that the burning rocks only looked like ordinary rocks now. They were no different from the other rocks on the mountain.

"It is my Father's presence that makes your true selves dance with life. Burn! Friends, remember that. When things get dark and you can't find your way, just ask for His presence and you will see again."

The Lord pointed into the distance to the shimmering lake. "There is the mist of the Source of the Unchanging River. The Source is full here, but I must tell you that the days ahead are going to be very bleak in your land. Things are going to change. Prepare your hearts! Now, go into the lake. It will take you into the Source. I bid you farewell for the moment. I will come to you soon!" The Lord became the unseen Lord again, and they saw only the rocks around them and the lake before them.

The three joined hands as they walked into the swirling water. Nearing the centre, they felt themselves being sucked under. The next thing that they knew, however, they were not being sucked down, but were flying upward at an incredible speed.

The Ancients say… "I will even betroth thee unto Me in faithfulness: and thou shalt know the LORD."

Chapter 17

The water swirled around them. Like they were rushing up through a living well. It was as easy to breathe as if they were out in the open air of the mountain. The three did not let go of each other's hands as they slowly came to a stop, suspended in mid-air ~ or, more accurately mid-water. The water was moving gently around them and then, as if a curtain was drawn up, they could see through the water in front of them. They saw what looked like of a large stage ~ like they were watching a play, but it was real life. They watched in amazement as the story unfolded before them…

~

The soft padding sound of slippered feet could be heard coming through the forest. The mountains towered high above like silent sentinels guarding their precious pilgrim. Soon a young woman came into view through the thick underbrush of the trees. Her hair was hanging in long tangles about her lovely face. She had scratches on her cheeks where the trees had whipped at her tender skin. Her dress was tattered as she clung to the shawl that was wrapped around her shoulders, trying to will warmth into her tired body.

The sun broke over the mountains, sending its morning rays all around her. She stopped to bask in the warmth and to try to get her bearings, for she was lost again. Slumping down on the ground, she waited. They would be soon upon her. Would she ever be free?

After a few moments, an army of men and women came out of the trees and surrounded her. She did not even lift her head as her strength had left her. The Dragon had many workers, both of the seen and unseen, in all reaches of the realm. Sometimes the pilgrims would think they were battling the Dragon itself, but it would in actuality be one of its cohorts.

Within the realm of the unseen on their very small planet, lived a host of wicked creatures. These creatures all served the Dragon to do its evil work against the unseen Lord's Father. Caedmon, Shylah and Treasa saw the shadows of these evil creatures of darkness now. Many were stroking the heads of this army, while others were running in glee around them, and even riding upon the armies' backs. The watchers exchanged nervous glances at this revelation. *So that is how the Dragon seemed to be in many places at once!* Caedmon thought.

A loud voice boomed out, "When are you going to learn, Princess? You need to stay in our protection! Why are you so rebellious? Get up! Back to the dungeon for you! Maybe then you will learn to submit to our protection."

Caedmon gasped, as he saw the man that was speaking was the head guard who had visited his old fortress years before. They watched in silence as the man roughly took the young woman by the arm and dragged her to her feet.

Who is she? they wondered.

The three pilgrims slowly began to rise through the water again. When they slowed to a stop again, they found themselves in front of another curtain. As the curtain rose they watched the soldiers put the princess in the dark dungeon of a large fortress on a hill. She did not try to struggle, but sank down on her small cot and curled her legs up beneath her skirts. The head guard shut the large wooden door and locked it securely, smiling contentedly to himself as he strode down the long corridor with the only light in his hand.

The dungeon became as black as ink. They could hear the soft sobs of the princess. A very soft light began to glow in the middle of the cell. The light continued to get brighter until they could see everything clearly. They saw the Lord standing in the light in the middle of the room with her. She looked at Him blankly. It was as if she did not know Him, or maybe she couldn't even see Him.

The Lord reached out His hands towards her, but she slowly dropped her head again, looking at her clasped hands upon her lap.

The light slowly faded from their sight as the lady curled up on her side on the cot. In the gathering gloom, they heard her cry, "Why won't you come to me, my beloved?"

Treasa, Shylah and Caedmon began to rise through the water, only to stop again shortly. The curtain rose, and now they could see the princess sitting in front of a window. She was looking out at the scene below, watching people milling around a village. She appeared to be in a high tower room. It was a beautiful room, with tapestries that hung to the floor and a large raised bed with gorgeous curtains that hung down from the posts on the corners. She was brushing her waist length, blonde hair over her shoulder.

They could see her plainly now in the bright daylight. She was one of the most beautiful women they had ever seen with skin brown like burnished bronze. Her large almond-shaped eyes were grey with flecks of green, and her long blonde lashes fluttered over her cheeks as she blinked back tears. She had not tried to escape for days, but she longed to be free. The princess wondered if there was any such thing as freedom to do as one willed.

The Lord walked into the room and stretched His arms out to her, but again she did not seem to be aware of Him. He called to her gently.

"My princess, my bride-to-be, come to me. I will give you freedom."

She went on brushing her hair, looking out the window, apparently not hearing Him. The head guard strode into the room, walking right by the unseen Lord, unaware of His presence. He put down a large platter with a silver food cover on the table beside her.

"Here are your rations for the day. Are you comfortable now?" he asked.

"Yes, thank you. But I am a little tired of eating your leftovers... Is there any thing fresh from the cook?" she asked, pleadingly.

"You should be thankful for what you get. I go without, so I can feed you," the head guard said over his shoulder as he left the room. She gracefully took the silver cover off the platter. The picked-over meal did not look appealing to her, but she tried to eat a little. She found a scrap of bread to the side of the plate and spread a little of

- 251 -

the leftover jam upon it. Then she sipped the stale, tepid tea to wash down the bread.

She often wondered why she had come to the fortress for protection. *Have I ever known the answer?* She could not remember anymore. The princess had so liked feeling protected back then, but now all she wanted was to remember what it had been like to be free.

The princess looked out the window again as a dreamy faraway look came into her eyes. She'd had the same dream for three weeks now. A handsome prince had come riding up to the fortress on a magnificent white horse. He had rescued her and she had ridden away with him, his arms holding her securely and safe. She would awaken every morning with her heart racing and the feel of his strong arms around her. Maybe he would come for her! Maybe it was a sign from the great Creator of the land. She hoped so!

The three pilgrims began to rise through the water again. Their hearts were breaking over the fact that the princess did not know that her Prince had come to her many times, but she had not recognized Him.

Stopping again, the curtain rose. The fortress was laying in ruins with the Dragon standing on top of the rubble. It threw its large head back and spewed slime towards the retreating pilgrims, who were following the Prince on His white horse.

As the scene closed, Caedmon turned to look at Treasa and Shylah. He smiled as he looked at their strange appearance. Their hair was lofting around them in swirls in the water. They looked like mermaids. As he laughed, bubbles floated up all around his face. Both women joined the laughter. Then, sobering, they looked back towards where the curtain had fallen.

"Do you think that the princess could be us?" gurgled out Shylah, giggling over the strange sound of her voice under the water.

Before anyone could answer her, they began to travel up again through the ever-moving water. They were slowly being revolved around and around, in perfect sync with the whirling water. Music began to play and they heard the quiet singing of a man's voice. The song was of a captive princess and a devoted lover, her Prince. The song was about how the Prince never stopped loving her, even when she would go with other lovers. The ballad spoke of His love and His increasing determination to have her for His own. He came for her and she finally saw His love for what it was ~ pure and unconditional. She finally surrendered to Him. The song rose up in the romantic melody of love fulfilled.

The three felt the love of the song bring tears to their eyes and all three knew in a moment who the princess was ~ it was *them*, and all the pilgrims.

As abruptly as they had found themselves rising in the water, they appeared before a door, perfectly dry. It was the very door that had led Caedmon into the Source all those many, many days before. It opened on its own before them and they were back at the Source. Behind them the water spewed high into the air like a great geyser, raining down around them. Those that were near the Source saw and ran to fetch the others.

The three pilgrims walked out of the water into the light of the day, the villagers stood waiting for them, eager to hear about what brought on such a magnificent flow of water. Then, suddenly, the geyser stopped. The Source had quit flowing completely, and all was silent...

The Dragon, standing back in the forest, looked with glee at the dry Source. Things were definitely moving in its favour. With a vicious laugh, it flew back down over the valley, his bedraggled army scurrying along on the ground beneath its shadow.

The Ancients say to know
is good,
Above all things we need to know,
    but even greater is to be known.
And when one sees
    what they know
        they will begin to be.
When one sees
    that they are known
        then they are.
There is a land where the Creator dwells,
    and knows those that are.
His Son the Prince waits for them,
    as they in turn wait for Him.
Those that are realize one thing
        they are His Bride...
    the Princess,
        His true love,
Warriors each one!

The Ancients say… "And the parched ground shall become a pool, and the thirsty land springs of water: in the habitation of dragons, where each lay, shall be grass with reeds and rushes."

Chapter 1

Arlynn ~ pledge, vow
Caiomhe ~ gentleness, beauty and grace

Treva picked at her supper as she remembered back to Caedmon's return. The young man had not been able to comprehend that Gilroy was gone. She had held him for hours. She had not wanted him to leave, but knew he had to obey the unseen Lord. She had wished with all her heart that he would have been allowed to live with her for a while. Though, she knew she wasn't just thinking about Caedmon only but herself as well.

Dei looked across the table at Treva and Brina with concern as they had been without water for two days. He knew that if he did not get water soon, they would perish. Pushing back from the table, he stood. Walking around the table, he hugged his wife and put a reassuring hand on Treva's shoulder.

"The unseen Lord knows all things. Remember what Treasa, Shylah, and Caedmon told us. The Lord is coming soon, and we are to prepare ourselves. I believe that He will lead me to water. Let us ask Him," Dei's voice held such hope that both women lifted their hands in unison, fully surrendering.

Treva's voice took on such strength as she shook off her doldrums about Caedmon, and petitioned, "Oh, my Lord, you hear the cry of your people. Forgive us for doubting. Here you tell us to prepare ourselves and we have been so busy being afeared that our hearts have become full of despair. You have never once left me or forsaken me. Show Dei what to do. You know we need water, so we do not ask for water. We only ask this day show us how to believe in You."

Lowering her hands, she saw her sword glittering in the firelight of the open kitchen fireplace. Brina was weeping silently, her head bowed over her shield that she had laid on the table in front of her. Dei stood, and his helmet glinted with gold light. His breastplate shone in the early light of the morning. With a sombre look upon his face, he walked out the door.

"All is well," Treva spoke soothingly, as she put her arm around Brina's shoulders. "Look, our armour has made an appearance! I always *knew* it was here, but now I see it. Our unseen Lord is here as well. He knows what we have need of, and He will care for us." She thought momentarily about Caedmon and knew he would be looked after as well. Then, she said, "I believe He already has spoken to Dei, although Dei has not yet realized it because of the fear that was reigning in our hearts."

Brina looked up through her tears and a smile broke out on her lips as she gasped and held her stomach.

"I do believe someone agrees with you!" she exclaimed, and then added, "I also believe my time is near. Someone is getting eager to make an appearance."

She said this with another gasp, for another contraction had seized her abdomen. Treva jumped to her feet. Helping Brina to stand, she led her into their sleeping room. In all her childless years, she had never had the joy of seeing a human life being born.

"I will run and get us some help. I won't be long... I will get Dei's mother, Arlynn. She will know what to do. Be at peace, my daughter, this is a good day. A day of new joy and hope!" Treva ran from the cabin, anticipation flooding her being.

Dei never heard the commotion, for he was in the back yard. He had retrieved Gilroy's shovel from the shed and was digging like a madman. Dirt was flying high in the air. He had already dug a hole that was four feet across and two feet deep. Perspiration sparkled on his brow, his helmet was tipped back from his face, but was still clearly visible. His breastplate shone in the morning sun, and the lion's head on the front glistened in the purest gold.

When he stopped and looked around, he saw Treva and his mother, Arlynn, running towards the cabin. He continued to dig, for his heart compelled him that expediency was necessary. The presence of the unseen Lord filled the entire yard, encouraging him to go on. Treva came out the back door and looked in wonder at Dei.

"The time has come, Dei. Today you will be a father!" Treva announced, her voice full of joy. Dei dropped the shovel and began to climb out of the hole.

"No, don't stop!" Treva spoke with authority, adding, "We will need water, Dei. Brina and the baby need water. I will keep you informed on how things are. Mediate while you dig!" With that said, Treva turned and went back into the cabin, silently mediating for this young couple and the little one that would soon make an appearance.

Dei dug all morning, and by noon the well was at least six feet deep. He was now putting the dirt into a large wooden box that had four ropes attached. When the dirt was heaped high, he would go up the ladder and hook the ropes to his horse and pull the dirt up to the surface. He could here the cries of Brina coming from the cabin. He felt helpless as he wiped the perspiration from his brow.

"Oh Lord, how long?" Then he heard it ~ the cry of a new born babe. Running into the cabin and straight to their sleeping room. Dei tried to wipe the dirt from his hands as he ran.

Brina looked up at him. Her dark brown hair lay tangled around her shoulders. Her face was drawn and white, and the little infant was resting in her arms. Arlynn came to him and taking his hand, she said, "My son, meet your new daughter."

Dei walked over and tenderly picked up the wee infant. Her tiny fist was curled under her chin and her long dark lashes lay upon her wet cheeks. He realized then how much they needed water. First to bathe this little one and his darling Brina. Reaching over, he wiped Brina's tangled hair from her brow.

"You did well, my love," Dei spoke tenderly and with hesitation turned to go. "I have to go back and dig our own well. The unseen Lord spoke to me and told me that. This is a time when every pilgrim must dig their own well and He will fill them. Mother, could you tell Da that, he needs to get word to the men of the settlement. We also need to send someone to the men of the valley." His mother

- 260 -

nodded her head to him. Then giving him a hug and Brina and the new one a kiss, she left.

"I will be back soon to hold you and our darling daughter," Dei called over his shoulder. Once in the yard he leapt in the air and clicked his heels together as joy flooded his soul.

Dei looking into the hole, and he was amazed. The water glistened and sparkled. The well was full! Falling to his knees, he lifted his hands in thanksgiving. Hearing his joyous cries, Treva joined him, unbelieving until she saw the water.

That evening around the table, the newest member of the family lay sleeping in her little cradle beside the fireplace, the three sat in contented silence. One day had changed them all so completely. The morning had begun with fear and trepidation, and now their hearts were full of faith, joy, and hope.

Brina looked over at Treva, her heart filling with a deep gratitude. "Treva, Dei and I have decided that we want you to name our little babe. If it had not been for your conviction, where would we be today…?"

A sob stopped her as her emotional day finally loosed a torrent of tired tears. Dei reached over and grasped her hand. Then, rising, he walked around the table and gently picked up his wife like a small child, carrying her to their sleeping room. Treva followed with Brina's plate and sat down beside her on the cot.

"You have had a long day, my dear child. Now eat your supper and try to sleep. I would be honoured to name your little one. For now you need rest because before you know it, a little cry will awaken you for feeding time. Here, sip this tea," Treva said encouragingly as she handed Brina a cup of hot tea made from special herbs of the mountain to induce rest.

As the sun set and the darkness of the night came upon the cabin, Treva sat on the old bench on the porch. *Wouldn't Gilroy have rejoiced for this day?* Realizing that he probably was rejoicing right now at their great victory, a tear rolled down her cheek. Wrapping her shawl tight around her shoulders, she looked up at the first twinkling stars that were appearing.

"Could you greet Gilroy for me, Lord? I miss him so," Treva whispered to the sky. The unseen Lord sat on the bench beside her and pulled her close. A lone tear rested upon His cheek. He felt her pain, and with comforting arms He held her close. Feeling His presence, she let her own tears fall until the sadness finally lifted.

Standing, Treva walked into the kitchen. She stoked the fire and then made her way to her small sleeping room that had been Arthmael's and then Caedmon's. She hoped Caedmon was doing well, she would put him up in the sleeping room in the loft, if he came home.

As she settled under the down-filled blanket upon her cot, a name came to her. The name of her own dear mother, Caiomhe. She knew that the meaning of her name, *gentleness, beauty, and grace,* that was everything that had happened to them this glorious day.

The Ancients say… "God setteth the solitary in families: he bringeth out those which are bound with chains: but the rebellious dwell in a dry land."

Chapter 2

Finna ~ fair

Cathaoir went to the cistern in the back yard to draw some water for Treasa to bathe. He lowered the bucket into the well, but he did not hear a splash of water. Lowering it down farther he felt, rather than heard, the thump of the bucket hit the bottom of the cistern. Pulling up the rope quickly he was shocked to see only a muddy sludge in the bottom of the pail. Leaving the bucket, he ran to the river. Standing, out of breath, in shock looking at the river. It was dry. The hot, late afternoon sun beat upon his perspiration-laden back. There were only muddy spots left here and there in the river bed.

Falling down onto his face, Cathaoir sobbed out for the unseen Lord to come to their aid. He felt a firm hand grasp his shoulder and he was pulled to his feet. Looking around he saw no one.

"Lord, is this You?" Cathaoir whispered.

"Yes, it is I," the soft reply came like the gentle breeze blowing in the grass around him. "I've tried to let the people turn to me in genuine friendship. I supplied all the water for this land, but it was only wasted. You, yourself haven't even come to the Unchanging River for a long time. You did not even know that it had dried up. Did you not know that it is supplied from the Source? They told you that the fountain of the deep had stopped." He paused and sighed.

"Supplying all your needs did not awaken you. I have heard all your mediations for Keelin, but still you do not see your own need. Do you even know what your real need is?" the Lord asked quietly.

"No. I know that ~ that there is like a hole in the middle of me that I cannot fill. That is all I know," Cathaoir bowed his head in shame.

"Your need is Me. I want to be your strength. I want to be your first source when difficulties rise and you need an answer. I love you pilgrims so desperately, but I know that being a fair weather friend is not what you need. You need Me there all the time in order for that hole to feel filled. It was created on purpose by My Father to be filled with a relationship with Me. If you are serious about your love for Me, then wait and see what I am about to do!" the unseen Lord's voice rose and echoed across the valley.

~

Cathaoir, tired from digging all day, finally came into their cottage for a rest. Word had come through Driscoll that they were to dig a new well and the Lord would fill it. He had believed the word because he had no other hope. He examined his heart. He wondered if he would have believed if they still had some water in the old well? *Probably not.* He bowed his head in silent humility.

Lifting a tired hand, he pushed his hair back from his dusty face. Treasa had gone to Shylah's that morning to talk about Keelin's wedding. That day was approaching quickly, for it was to be in one fortnight. His darling wife had taken it well, considering that she had been left out completely of all the decision making. *She was altered by her time beyond the Source, no question about that,* he thought.

The last of their water had been gone for three days now and they drank of their wine supply sparingly. His thoughts jumped around in his head, from one subject to another. He was too tired to try to control them.

Deep in thought, Cathaoir tried to lick his cracked lips, but his tongue felt thick and large. Keelin still was not herself completely, but he did notice that she seemed more at peace. He missed his old daughter, she used to be so carefree and humorous.

However, things would never be the same again, he reasoned. Stretching back on the chair, he closed his eyes and rested his tired muscles.

- 264 -

His mind strayed back to last month when Treasa, Shylah, and Caedmon had returned from the Source. What an experience they'd had! Their clothes had a glowing appearance about them, so clean and flowing. He remembered that first night, when they had gathered the mediators in their sitting room to hear of their adventure beyond the Source.

Caedmon had lifted his voice and a song came rolling out like the waves of the sea. The song told them everything that he had learned beyond the mist. They saw the flash of his armour and the shine of his bow. Caedmon's voice rose and fell with the emotion of his experience as the ballad swept around them like no other song they had ever heard. His voice was barely audible when he sang of Keelin and the state of the land. His voice was so sweet, yet so powerful. They could hear the voice of the unseen Lord harmonizing with him. After the song they had sat for a long time with their eyes shut, lost in the presence of the unseen Lord and His mystery.

Treasa shared next, with Shylah interjecting. Both were laughing as they told of their experience.

"We were not given anything specific. What we did receive, is hard to put in words. Except maybe our mud-bath and a thorough washing with new clothes," Shylah commented at the end of the discourse.

"Oh, do you not understand?" Cathaoir replied and then went on, "There is nothing more powerful than a clean heart, with no condemnation, no regret, and no living the past over. You have been given an opportunity to live life fresh, without the old hanging onto you. This, too, I am jealous of. I will ask the unseen Lord to cleanse me of all past circumstances. I must let them go and be cleansed from the pain. It is time for me to wash off the testing."

Caedmon drew out an arrow and aimed it at Cathaoir. Before anyone could speak, he let it fly. It struck Cathaoir in the heart, piercing deep into his chest. He slumped forward in his chair, a look of shock spreading across his face. Treasa ran to him. Shocked silence filled the room as the pilgrims struggled to understand what had just happened.

Caedmon slowly rose to his feet. Striding over to Cathaoir, he pushed him back upright in the chair. The arrow disappeared into his chest, and then Cathaoir opened his eyes. He slowly looked from face to face. Tears of joy were slipping down and dripping off his chin. Rising to his feet, he began to slowly dance around the room. They could hear the rhythm of the music filling the air. When the music faded away, Cathaoir sat down again in his chair and stared at Caedmon.

"Well, my boy, I thought you'd killed me. When that arrow pierced my heart I felt myself fall into a deep sleep. I truly thought I was dead, but then every good thing that has ever happened to me flooded my heart. Life like I'd never felt it before surged through my entire being. Every word that the unseen Lord has ever spoken to me became like the music of a dance. The next thing I knew, I was dancing to the music," Cathaoir said with passion. As he spoke he felt a dark blanket of grief leave him and he straightened even taller in his chair.

"I don't know why I did it..." Caedmon whispered. "All I know is that I have been given a gift to use. The arrows are to cause the Lord's people to remember so that they will awaken. Before I had time to think it through, I let it fly. I must say that I, too, thought I had killed you," Caedmon finished with a sheepish grin.

That night the mediators spoke of the many others who were joining with them in mediating. Many, especially those in the villages, were coming and living on farms where they could dig their own wells and build their own houses. The water in the drying cisterns in the villages was very defiled. They felt it was time for them to stop drinking what was left of the water of the land.

Cathaoir and Treasa were expecting Edan and his family to join them soon. Going outside to the hole, Cathaoir began to dig again with renewed zeal.

~

Edan looked lovingly at his wife, Tully. She had been such a comfort to him this last while. When news came of what had happened to Keelin after she had been rejected by Barris, he realized how weak he had been. Then, Barris had proved he was more of a man by doing right with Keelin than he had been with his own wife. He realized that he should have tried harder to help Tully minister to Keelin. He had only been mad at her for trying, and wanted Keelin to snap out of her depression.

Leaving their small flat in the village, he made his way to the well to fetch some water for his wife to bathe their little girl, Finna. Coming to the well, Edan saw a loud group of people milling around. He weaved his way through to look at what they were staring at. A man grabbed him and yanked him out of the way, speaking harshly.

"Wait in line. First come first serve! Get back!" As he spoke he shoved Edan down to the ground. Edan heard the stories of the drought and death from all sides as he lay there.

Edan pulled himself to his feet and went to the back of the milling crowd. He listened to what the people were saying. The new well was running dry and news was coming from all over the valley that everywhere the Unchanging River was completely dry. Even in the twilight, Edan could still feel the extreme heat of the day ~ He walked away. They still had water to drink, and they would have to use what they had sparingly. He decided to go to the fortress and see if they had any water to spare. He had helped them so often in the past that maybe they would help him now.

He stood in front of Evergreen on the outskirts of the village, knocking on the large door. A small window opened in the door and Edan recognized the face of the man who looked out at him. It was the guard of the fortress. The man stared at him blankly, then spoke before Edan even had time to state his request.

"Go away!" he spoke gruffly. "There is only enough water for us. You do not live here, anymore!"

Edan began to protest, but then slowly turned and went back to Tully and his child. He needed to seek the unseen Lord. Edan realized that no one in this village would even want to seek Him. He only knew of the pilgrims at the farm and at the Source who would seek Him. Cathaoir had told them to come to the farm and dig their own well, and Edan decided that he had put it off long enough ~ it was time.

Once he got home, Tully helped him pack their belongings. They put the little water they had in canteens, loaded their wagon, and left the village without a backward glance. They could hear the low rumble of mad distraught voices fade behind them as the drove out into the gathering darkness.

As Edan drove, he again felt his hopeless condition, just like he had that night at Briant's. Tully had her head upon his lap and was sound asleep, their child was sleeping in a little crate at their feet.

"Lord… Do you still hear me? This is Edan. Come to me please, I need You. My family needs You. The people of this valley need You."

Edan did not hear Him, but could suddenly feel hope rise in his heart. Eammon walked beside the donkey directing the beast. Edan's eyes grew accustomed to the dark and he clucked to their faithful donkey to pick up the pace. Early in the morning hours, Eammon directed the donkey down a side trail off the road. Edan did not know, as he had fallen fast asleep and was sitting hunched over his wife.

At the base of a tree was a small, clear pool. The tired donkey drank long from it, then lay down in his harness on the cool moss of the forest floor and fell fast asleep.

The sun was high in the air when Edan awoke. He tried to gain consciousness, but he felt all turned around. Looking around himself, he realized he had no idea where he was. His faithful little donkey was still sound asleep on the moss. Quietly, so he would not awaken his family, he walked to the pool. Edan fell onto his stomach and drank of the sweet cool water.

When he had splashed some water over his head to awaken himself, he went to the wagon and pulled the large barrel out of the back. After carefully scooping the water into the barrel and then fastening on the lid, he rolled the barrel up the plank into the wagon. He filled all the extra canteens they had, and as he did, he thanked the unseen Lord for prompting him to move his family out of the village.

Tully, awakening, washed herself and the baby. Edan had let the donkey loose to graze, and when they had finished eating a small breakfast of black bread and cheese, they harnessed him again to the wagon. Snuggling close to Edan on the wagon seat, Tully felt hope rising in her heart again.

"You know, Tully, all is going to be all right. The unseen Lord is caring for His people. He will give us springs in the dry land. I had a dream. He came in the dream and said that we were to wait and see what He is about to do," Edan spoke reassuringly to his wife.

"I also had a dream," Tully said. "However, mine was not so comforting. People had their pockets full of thorns. They would pull the thorns out and stab one another. As they walked, the thorns in their pockets would prick them, and making them more angry. One of their thorns came at me and it stuck in my hand. Upon it was written *Accusations*. I reached into my pocket and pulled out a thorn and tried to use it to dig out the other thorn from my hand. Written upon it was the word *Self-justification*. Then I began to cry and cry."

Edan nodded slowly as he realized that there was truth in his wife's dream.

"I asked the unseen Lord to take the thorns away from us. I heard the Dragon laughing at me. I tried to call out, but my voice could not be heard over the hideous laughter," Tully shuddered as she went on hesitantly, "I even tried to wake myself up, but could not. Then I heard the Lord's voice. It wasn't in my ears, but deep down inside me, like my own conscience ~ but it was His voice. He quietly told me to throw down my own thorns. As I threw them down I felt vulnerable, like I had no defence against those throwing thorns at me. At that moment another thorn hit me, and instead of hurting so badly, it only pinched me. I asked the unseen Lord to forgive me of what I was being accused of, and the thorn disappeared."

"What kind of accusations?" Edan asked, truly interested.

"Some were true things I had done. However, sometimes the accusations were false and mean, and yet when I asked the Lord to help me not throw any back, they too disappeared. The Dragon stopped laughing and I could hear it flying away, hurling insults at me, but I did not care."

The two travelled in silence as they pondered their lives. They passed many farms that lay desolate. The owners had fled from the drought and left everything behind. Tumble weed laid strewn around the deserted yards. It all looked so hopeless and sad. They would arrive at Cathaoir's farm soon. They passed over a bridge that went across the Unchanging River and, true to reports, the river was dry. The grass looked dry and lifeless along the road as the dust rolled up behind their wagon in the burning sun.

The Ancients say... "Cursed be the man that trusteth in man, and maketh flesh his arm ~ he shall not see when good cometh; but shall inhabit the parched places in the wilderness. Blessed is the man that trusteth in the Lord."

Chapter 3

Arienh ~ an oath

Keelin and Barris were married on a hot day. The heat would have made it impossible for there to be any joy at all, but Cathaoir had set up pavilions of bright material to shade the guests. The ribbons that Treasa had used for her own wedding were brought out of storage and hung from the corners of the pavilions, making the whole farmyard look festive and bright.

The happy couple, oblivious to any anxiety on the family's part, left to go to their own little farm that was next to Cathaoir's. Treasa and Cathaoir stood with theirs arms linked and watched the wagon fade into the swirling dust in the evening sun. Their little girl was someone else's responsibility now. They sent up their silent mediation with tears glistening upon their cheeks.

When the newlyweds had left, talk amongst the guests quickly turned to the topic on everybody's mind ~ water. News of the well digging spread like wild fire among the pilgrims, but those within the walls of the fortresses only scorned the information. Their own supply of pool water was running low, but they had begun to join with the other fortresses to share their water supplies. It was amazing how this drought had caused the fortress dwellers to forget past differences and to learn to share. Yet the Dragon was the ever present in their midst, stirring up some guard to think that his fortress was not getting its fair share. The pilgrims were beginning to tire of the constant innuendos that were being dropped in their assemblies. They knew in their hearts this was not a time to be critical of their neighbours in the other fortresses, though they would never say anything openly for fear of being in rebellion to their appointed guard.

The Dragon slithered in their midst, leaving a trail of green slime behind its huge frame. It seemed that someone different was falling in it every day. Many people had left the fortresses, not to join the pilgrims that had already left, but to join the villagers in their pursuit to find water. The villages of the valley had dug many wells and the water would last for about a fortnight, then slowly dry up. The people tired from the constant work and fear. They would clench their fists and shake them at the unseen Lord for causing the horrible drought.

No one in the villages or fortresses even recognized that the drought was of their own making. They had forgotten that the Ancients had said that to be thankful would open flood gates of provision, but greed and self-seeking would close up every blessing. However, the fortress pilgrims very seldom consulted the writings of the Ancients any longer.

All the pilgrims who had their own wells would share their water with anyone who asked. The land began to turn green again in small places, where the people painstakingly watered the ground by hand. Such was the garden of Seanna and Teague. They had a little girl now, Arienh, who was just learning to walk. Seanna would take her out to their small vegetable garden while she weeded. Teague would carry buckets of water from their well and carefully pour it on each plant. He had noticed that the pasture lands around their modest cottage seemed to flourish, even though no rains had come. He knew the unseen Lord was watering the fields from hidden sources underneath, and for this he thanked Him profusely. Cathaoir also noticed that his crop of wheat had grown and even though it was short, the heads were filling out fine.

Caedmon, whistling a merry tune, walked down the road to Shylah and Briant's farm. He had been hired by them to help them plant the crop. It had been painstaking work with the soil so dry, but they had persevered and now they were amazed to see the lovely crop blowing in the wind.

The strange phenomena of the crops growing without water was bringing attention from the neighbouring farmers who did not know the unseen Lord. Some were encouraged and responded to the unseen Lord's call, but others were jealous and spewed out threats against the pilgrim farmers. Caedmon was enjoying living with Briant's family ~ the children were boisterous and would follow him around, so glad to have someone listen to their non-stop chatter.

Caedmon remembered his last visit with Edan and Tully before they had moved out to Cathaoir's. Edan had shared with Caedmon how he had seen the Dragon sulking around the fortress. The beast had looked much larger to Edan than it had in the past. He had drawn his sword on it and, hearing the whirl of the blade in the air, the Dragon had flown, dropping slime all over the massive stone walls of the fortress, as it flew out of sight. Shortly after it had left, the guard had come around the corner and asked Edan what he was doing there. Edan told the man what had happened, but he only eyed Edan suspiciously and asked him to leave the property. Edan had felt anger and he knew that he should have felt sadness for the deluded man.

Why could not the fortress pilgrims believe it? The Dragon was running around in their midst... Its lies were so obvious ~ how could they not know? These were the questions that had filled their conversation.

Caedmon had reassured Edan that as far as he knew, from what he had learned beyond the Source, the unseen Lord would speak to the pilgrims within the fortress, too. All they had to do was mediate for them, not judge them or even be angry at them. Definitely they shouldn't be trying to convince them of anything, for that was up to the unseen Lord to do that.

Caedmon smiled to himself. *The unseen Lord, the Prince.* What a wonderful thought. He was coming soon! Caedmon could feel it inside every time he mediated ~ this expectancy of seeing the unseen Lord again. He felt that special orders were going to come for them. *Maybe it will even be today,* Caedmon thought.

~

Treasa laughed at Shylah, who in turn was looking very perplexed.

"I don't think this is funny!" An exasperated Shylah said in a high-pitched voice. Flour was everywhere ~ all over Shylah and the floor around her. On top of her head, a pile of flour sat like a cocky little hat.

"Well, I can't keep myself from laughing! I will help you clean it up," Treasa said, trying to sound consoling.

"What on earth were you doing anyway?" she added as another giggle escaped her lips.

Shylah was moving slowly to her kitchen door. As soon she went into the back yard and she began to dust the flour off she disappeared in a white cloud. Much to her disdain she heard Treasa laughing. Entering the kitchen, she saw her friend sweeping the flour up into a pile on the hard stone floor. Shylah quietly joined her and held the dustpan while Treasa swept in the flour.

"I was holding up the flour over my head to see if I was as strong as I used to be, and the sack split and down over my head it came." She then started to laugh, thinking of how crazy that explanation would seem to Treasa.

"Let me explain…"

Caedmon's step on the doorstep stopped Shylah's explanation. Entering, he saw the women covered in flour dust, sweeping and talking.

"What happened, Shylah?" Caedmon said laughing. He stopped abruptly when he saw the slight shake of Treasa's head warning him.

Shylah sighed and, pulling out a chair from the table, she sat down. Taking another deep breath, she looked up at her friends. "You know, it all started when I began to ponder that I needed to get in shape for the great battle."

"The great battle?" Treasa asked.

"Yes, you know, the unseen Lord has been preparing us for His return and the great battle with the Dragon," Shylah said, and then, looking at their blank stares, she went on. "I have been mediating for the defeat of the Dragon in the fortresses. I have heard so plainly to prepare my heart for a great battle. Have you not heard it?"

Caedmon, pulling out a chair, joined Shylah at the table. Treasa, after taking the last dustpan full of flour outside, came back and joined them.

"I have not heard specifically about a *great* battle. Have you, Caedmon?" Treasa asked.

Caedmon, resting his chin upon his hand, leaned onto the table. "I knew in my heart that I was knighted for battle, and I have to admit that I thought it would be a large battle with the Dragon. I have to say, though, I have not heard anything specific. Please Shylah, tell us more." Caedmon reached over and squeezed Shylah's hand to encourage her to go on.

"It started the day we got back from beyond the Source. I kept feeling the weight of my armour. As I mediated, the unseen Lord came to me in a dream and told me to prepare for the great battle. So, because my armour feels so heavy lately, I decided to build up my strength by lifting the sack of flour over my head several times a day. Well, today when I lifted it, the old sack tore and, well, you see the rest..." Shylah's sigh ended in a giggle.

Treasa came to Shylah and hugged her shoulders tight. "I was beginning to think you had lost your sanity... but I don't think it is *physical* muscle building you need. Shylah, you are a dear friend, nevertheless at times you are ~ a laugh!" Treasa said, then added, "Well, we are all here so let's mediate right now and see if the unseen Lord will tell us how to prepare for battle."

The three became quiet and soon they all stood in *The Glade of the Forest Pools*. One large pool stood in front of them, and, kneeling down they looked in together. A swirl of colourful water like moving rainbows filled the pool. As they became very still ~ waiting ~ the water cleared and the colours shot up into the air like beams of light. Glittering stars, every colour of the rainbow, fell around them like a soft rain of light.

They saw a pilgrim walking down a long lane through a desert land. The sand was blowing, and the hot sun was beating upon his back. His armour glinted in the sunlight, and his shoulders were bent forward and his arms dragged his sword and shield behind him. He would try to lift his sword, but they could tell from the man's apparent struggle that it was too heavy.

Stopping, the pilgrim lay his armour down and did some strenuous movements, lifting his arms high in the air and lowering them. It was as if he was stretching out his tired muscles. Then he took heavy iron rings that were lying beside the road and, lifting his sword carefully, placed them down the blade and against the handle. He put two rings on the sword and then, placing two around his wrist on the hand that held his shield, he picked his shield back up. It seemed strange that this man was making an already difficult situation worse.

As the three gazed down the road, ahead of the man, they saw the Dragon. It was carefully placing the iron rings in neat piles every furlong. As they looked closely they could see words inscribed in the rings, in ancient looking script. The words were plain to them...

WORKS ~ RESPONSIBILITIES ~ COMMITMENTS ~SELF-IMPROVEMENT

Many other such words were written, and on one of the rings that the pilgrim had placed on his sword was written, *BODILY DISCIPLINE*. The Dragon seemed to enjoy that the pilgrim didn't realize that it was behind these *good* things.

As the pilgrim started his journey again, he seemed to appear frustrated that his sword and shield were even heavier. All his armour was becoming heavy and his sword was too heavy to wield. The pilgrim lowered his weapons to the ground and, lying down, he curled up in a ball, tears falling from his face onto the hardened path.

The three looked at each other in shock. What did it all mean? They turned back to the pool, looking for answers.

They then saw the Lord walk up to the pilgrim. Kneeling down on His knees, He gently lifted the pilgrim onto his feet. He pulled the pilgrim close and held him for a long time. Releasing him, the Lord lifted the sword and carefully removed all the rings, one at a time. Slime dripped from His hand, and when He was finished the Lord carefully took a flask of water and washed off the Dragon's drool. Handing the sword back to the pilgrim, He then removed the rings from the shield-bearing arm. The man stared in disbelief at the Lord.

"But Lord, this is the way I serve you! I need to take on those burdens or I will be of no use to you. I will not be prepared for battle," the pilgrim's pleas shocked the three mediators.

The great Lord looked at him tenderly. Then, looking straight up through the water of the pool, He said, "You don't understand, yet? Well then, let Me tell you. It is not what you do that makes you a warrior, but what I do *through* you. If you learn to wait upon Me, I will strengthen you! I will direct you! I will cause you to do greater things than anything you have ever imagined. Stop working, stop committing yourself to things that I have not appointed, stop beating your body."

Then, turning to the pilgrim in the pool, He said, "Look at Me! Look to Me!"

The pilgrim looked up at his Lord and, he lifted his sword high above his head in salute. The three then saw the Dragon hurl the iron rings at the pilgrim's head. The first ring hit its target and the pilgrim tumbled back from the Lord as his head was shaken, but his helmet stayed fastened upon it. Straightening his shoulders again, he raised his sword in salute. The Dragon hurled another ring, this time hitting his chest. Knocking the wind out of him, he fell onto his back. His sword and shield clattered beside him. The Lord continued to watch silently...

The pilgrim slowly rose to his feet, sword and shield in his hands. The gold on his breastplate shone in the sunlight. Again the Dragon threw a ring, this time at the pilgrim's feet, but before it collided into him, the man leapt high in the air. As the ring hit the ground beneath his feet, the pilgrim came down and with the tip of his sword, he picked up the ring and flung it back at the Dragon. The Dragon tried to recover the ring as the pilgrim charged toward the Dragon, a blood-chilling cry escaping his lips. The Dragon flew high in the air and disappeared from their sight. The three gazed at the pool in amazement.

"I am stronger than I have ever been. Thank You, my great Lord," the pilgrim said as he knelt in front of the Lord. He lifted his sword up to Him, and with head bowed, he waited on Him. The Lord took the sword and slowly laid it upon each of the pilgrim's shoulders. They knew then that he had been knighted.

~

Shylah, sighing, looked down at herself. There was still the dust of flour on her clothes. Smiling, she reached across the table and said, "Take my hands, my friends! I have tried to prepare myself without the guidance of the Lord, and look where it got me. Could you please help me to guard myself from the enemies' weights?"

"Well, that depends," Caedmon spoke with a twinkle in his eyes, "We will, if you will also help guard us. And if ~ from now on, you only use flour for baking your good bread."

With that said they all laughed as Treasa got up to put the kettle on the fire for some tea, while Caedmon and Shylah finished cleaning up the mess.

The Ancients say… "all my bones shake; I am like a drunken man, and like a man whom wine hath overcome, because of the Lord, and because of the words of His holiness."

Chapter 4

Aine was tired. Gallagher had not stopped to rest for a couple of hours as they battled the dense jungle path. Bitterness walked beside her and twirled its long finger in her mind. The distorted looking plant creature gave off a vile stench of burnt garbage. *Why did he constantly revert to his coldness?* Aine's jumbled thoughts increased in turmoil.

Here they were on this great quest for the unseen Lord and now it was all about Gallagher. He would do well for a short time, showing some care and concern for her, and then as if an invisible cloud had descended upon Gallagher's mind, he would frantically try to make everything about him. She loved this man dearly, but the emotional ups and downs he constantly lived in were hard to bear. They had not mediated together in a long time and she could feel her strength slowly seeping from her.

"Hurry up, Aine. We have far to go before nightfall. You know the wild beasts like to feed in the night," Gallagher said impatiently. Stopping, he turned and looked at his wife. She looked tired and angry. He stiffened his neck, in his resolve to move forward, against his better judgement to stop and let her rest. Aine had become a burden to him, moreover a constant reminder of his own insufficiencies. He resented that.

Aine finally caught up to him and putting her hand into his, she squeezed his palm. His heart smote him as she so needed his reassurance, so why did he struggle to give it? He linked his arm in hers and slowed his pace to better suit her.

"It is not much farther. Kikeona told me it was just through this stretch of jungle."

"Oh, won't it be lovely to meet with all the pilgrims at last! Pualani shared with me that the unseen Lord had met with many and had told them that we all were to meet with them in the large meadow. Pualani and Kikeona have already left for there this afternoon. Many are there now, and we are to dig a large well. There is supposed to be sweet water, enough for us all," Aine said. The drought had even struck this far forgotten land. "Gallagher, do you think that there is a drought back home, too? I guess that's silly. We have always had the Unchanging River." Aine felt talkative, as all her bitterness had flown away the moment Gallagher had shown her a little kindness. But the grotesque tree like creature kept close beside her.

Gallagher smiled at her. He too was feeling better inside for being patient for once. He wondered why he always seemed to be in a hurry, but was still always late no matter how hard he worked to be on time.

Gallagher felt the weight of his sword in his hand. Glancing down, he saw the shine of the steel in the waning evening light. *The Dragon must be close by*, he thought. *Or else, one of its evil servants.*

The unseen Lord had been teaching the pilgrims of this land about the enemy's tactics and its creatures of darkness. It was one of these ugly creatures that was following Gallagher and Aine right at that moment. Gallagher felt the hair stand up on his neck. He did not see the cloven hoof ~ of the part cow, part snake beast ~ that wiped his neck. A red ooze was dripping from the creature's forehead. The substance looked like the slime of the Dragon except for the colour. Wiping at the ooze with its hoof, the creature dabbed it on Gallagher's neck.

Fear began to creep over Gallagher like a living thing. He shook himself, but the feeling kept mounting. He wanted to run, flee...

Shaking his arm free from Aine and raising his sword, Gallagher looked this way and that in the gathering gloom of the evening. His sword seemed heavy, beyond his own strength to wield it.

Whirrrr! The sound of a sword slicing the air whipped behind his head. Spinning around, Gallagher saw in an instant that the creature was lying with its head half cut off, and then it disappeared.

Aine was standing over it, her eyes bright from the fight. She was carefully washing her sword with water from her canteen. Looking up from her task, she smiled at her husband. Gallagher, still shaken from thinking it was himself that the sword was aiming at, slumped to the ground.

Aine put her sword in her sheath and ran to his side. Bitterness backed away slowly into the gloom. Pride was a greater warrior than it and it knew to flee before it was decapitated.

"Gallagher! What is the matter? Are you all right?" Aine's cry became desperate when Gallagher did not respond.

He sat there staring straight ahead, his eyes slightly glazed over. His sword and shield lay beside him, and his hands lay lifeless in his lap. Aine shook him and then pleaded for him to come to himself. Gallagher only sat there, gazing at the spot where the beast had lain.

Picking up Gallagher's sword, Aine felt its immense weight immediately. Examining it closely, she saw iron rings, like the rings of a chain, delicately woven into the handle. Each link had an inscription.

BOASTING~ SELF-MOTIVATION ~
PERSUADER ~ GREAT THINGS

Aine tried to remove them, howbeit they were woven right into the handle. As the night began to fall, like a heavy blanket, Aine fell onto her knees and began to mediate in concern for her husband. Looking up, she saw Gallagher slowly rising to his feet as if someone was picking him up from behind. His body was completely lifeless. He was suspended in mid-air. His feet were slightly curled in, his arms hung limp to his sides, and his head lay at an awkward angle upon his chest. Tears fell down Aine's face as she watched, too stunned to speak or move.

Gallagher's head gradually lifted. He tried to slowly stand, but his feet were suspended several inches from the path. As he came to, his arms began to flail and his feet kicked this way and that.

"Aine, help me! Someone has a hold of me! Get your sword and whack it away from me!" Gallagher cried in anger. Aine remained

- 281 -

where she was, staring in utter shock. Her husband was powerless. She took Gallagher's sword and handed it to him.

He tried to lift it, but it seemed heavier than it had ever been. Another couple of iron rings were on the handle.

ANGER ~ CONTROL

A soft light started to fall all around Aine, like a gentle rain. As the light fell in sparkles of reflection, Aine felt strength like she'd never experienced before course down her arms into her hands. Wrenching Gallagher's sword from his hand, she began to pry the rings off the handle.

"What are you doing to my sword?" Gallagher cried.

He was still suspended mid-air, and again tried to free himself from the invisible hands that held him. However, instead of becoming free, he was shaken like a naughty dog until his teeth rattled. He quickly quit trying to free himself.

Aine finally finished removing the rings. The handle of the sword looked marred and ugly. Most of the precious gems had come off with the rings. She looked at her husband in the gloom of the night. All around her the soft light still fell, illuminating her and casting its beams toward Gallagher. Aine, with her head slightly bowed, waited for directions from the unseen Lord.

"I will do fast work for your sake, my lamb," the soothing voice of the unseen Lord whispered like a calming breeze upon her ear.

She looked again at Gallagher's ashen face that was contorted, and great sobs were coming from deep within him. She slowly walked around him, laying his sword down by his feet beside his shield, and continued up the path to meet the others.

"Aine! Aine!" Her husband's desperate calls followed her. She continued on, having no fear for leaving him behind, for she knew that he was in the unseen Lord's care now.

The unseen Lord walked over to Gallagher and looked at him for a long time. The rings on the sword had been strong, but not as strong as the chains the Dragon had put upon Gallagher's heart.

"Do you love me, Gallagher?" the unseen Lord spoke.

Gallagher looked up. Shock filled him as he looked straight into the unseen Lord's eyes. He thought he had been utterly left in the dark by Aine, but a glorious light illumined the path all around him. The largest man he had ever seen was looking him straight in the eyes. It was the unseen Lord of the land, he knew it.

"Yes, Lord, you know I do!" Gallagher said with confidence. Then he was again shaken like a tree in the wind.

"Do you love me, Gallagher?" the Lord asked again, quieter this time. The Lord was slowly fading into the light around Him.

"Lord, you know all things. Yes, I do, I do! I mean I will. You know I want to love you! I will love you, Lord," Gallagher pleaded, fearing another shaking.

"Drop him, Abelio!"

Gallagher dropped to the ground in a heap. Crawling on his hands and knees to the unseen Lord, he grasped the edge of His robes.

"Please, Lord, forgive me! You are right! I have been more concerned about *me!* I have loved myself more than Aine, You and others! Don't go! Please! I am sorry..." Gallagher's pleas trailed off. The Lord continued to fade from his sight.

Gallagher becoming desperate, screamed, "Lord, change me! I am a wicked, self-centred man! I have tried at times to change, however no matter what I do, I stay the same. I want my own way, I am like a spoiled baby and I want to be a man! Really I do! Please, Lord, make me different! I cannot..."

All his strength left Gallagher as he sighed out his final plea. Slumping down he lay prostrate before the Lord.

"Take him to the mountain, Abelio. Throw him in the pool of dross cleansing. And, my faithful servant, will you refashion his sword as well?" the Lord asked.

"Yes, my Liege, I have already sent it to the forge," Abelio said as he lifted Gallagher to his feet. Drawing the limp man's arm out he put it over his own shoulder. Clasping Gallagher around the waist, Abelio helped him walk, and the two disappeared from the light. The unseen Lord disappeared as well, but the light that had

- 283 -

emanated from Him continued down the path towards the meeting in the large glade.

~

The sombre pilgrims sat around a huge bonfire in the middle of the glade. Aine had arrived and sat down beside Pualani. They had become dear friends.

"Where is Gallagher?" Kikeona asked her across the flames.

Smiling at him, she replied, "He was in a personal meeting with the unseen Lord the last time I saw him."

"That is good, very good. He has needed this meeting for a long time. I have mediated much for him," Kikeona said.

Turning his attention to the large group around the fire, he went on, "Tonight we start to dig. We will make shifts of people, five in every shift. The rest will sleep. We must start tonight, for our canteens are nearly dry. Obedience is of great importance!"

The pilgrims immediately began to mill about, deciding on who would dig first.

Aine went to sleep with the sound of shovels hitting the dry earth. As she lay by the fire, the unseen Lord sat next to her and watched over her. Carden walked up to them. Laying his hand gently upon her brow, He tenderly sang the Shepherd's song over her tired soul. She, too, had relied upon Gallagher more than upon the unseen Lord. She was young and she had proven herself faithful to the Lord when the time came to choose between obeying Him or Gallagher. Aine had learned that only He would be able to change her husband. She would become a magnificent warrior in the great battle.

The unseen Lord and Carden, looking around the group, watched lovingly as they worked carefully and diligently. Some thought these pilgrims were savages, but they were the most loyal of all His pilgrims and definitely the most humble. They did not even realize the great honour they had in the unseen realm. They would win many battles one day soon.

Late into the night, Gallagher, wet and tired, walked into the firelight. His heart felt sore, but new. The feeling of cleanness that clung to him was nothing like he had ever felt before. Spotting Aine asleep by the fire, Gallagher sat next to her. Sophronia had arrived and sat behind them, smiling at their new found joy.

"Thank you, Lord, for looking after my Aine and me." The unseen Lord nodded His head and then He and Carden disappeared. Sophronia stayed for she knew that they would need wisdom if they would make it together. Snuggling down beside Aine, Gallagher pulled her close. Awakening slightly, she looked up into Gallagher's face. Suddenly feeling his wetness she squirmed away.

"Gallagher, you're wet!"

"My precious girl, I am *clean*. I am a new man!"

They fell into a peaceful sleep, with Aine cradled in Gallagher's strong arms. And Sophronia keeping vigil. She took a large loaf of fresh bread from the folds of her tunic and laid it beside the couple.

The Ancients say… "For the redemption of their soul is precious."

Chapter 5

Walking away from the village, Caedmon's head hung low. Why couldn't his grandmother see? She refused to listen. She still believed that the only truth was found within the fortresses, even though she herself did not live in one or even attend their gatherings that often. Her old heart hung onto the past, refusing to let the light of this day shine in her heart.

"Lord, I am so weak when it comes to my own family. Why?" Caedmon pleaded. His heart wretched within in him as he cried out. He felt an arm rest across his shoulders, and, looking beside himself, he saw the Lord. Stopping his walk he flung his arms around the Lord's neck.

"My Prince!"

"Caedmon, I am here. Remember that I am at work. Nuala knows Me and My voice, although she has forgotten. I will call to her. I have been calling to her through you, but it is not working. It is not you she has rejected, but Me. When you speak My word do not take it so personally when you are shunned. Try to remember Who is really being rejected. You have mediated for her and I have come." The unseen Lord spoke the words of comfort as He slowly faded from Caedmon's sight and touch.

~

Caedmon's grandmother, pulled herself from her bed. She felt so alone. Nobody in the village spent any enjoyable time together any more. Everyone was talking about the shortage of water. She had attended the gathering at the fortress and everyone was suspicious of one another and kept to themselves.

As Nuala walked home after the gathering, she felt the stare of her neighbours and the whispering behind her back. She had always been so good to the pilgrims in the fortress, and now they were treating her like an outsider. *Even my own grandson is showing me disrespect, trying to dictate how I should act and think!* She'd had enough of this place. She decided that she would leave, although she knew not where she would go.

Nuala began to slowly pack a small satchel with a change of clothes and her empty canteen. Her water had run out the day before and the guard would not give her any at the fortress. His excuse was that it was reserved for those that lived in the fortress.

Nuala's parched mouth and tired body made her head feel fuzzy and out of sorts. She walked down the old creaky stairs to the ground floor of the decrepit old rooming house. Stopping at the landlady's room, she left the last of her money to pay for her rent. The old landlady felt sorry for her and gave her some bread and a small flask of wine for her journey.

Nuala walked out of the sleepy little village and headed for the open road. She felt utterly lost as she stumbled down the road. She just wanted to die.

Why won't the unseen Lord let me die? She stormed within, but it was short lived. She was too tired to even care to fight or justify herself. That was when she heard it...

Nuala nervously looked about herself. Then she heard it again, but this time she knew it was only the breeze blowing through the trees along the road. She raised her head and looked down the road, past the forest to the rolling farmland. Not knowing what else to do, she decided she would go to the Unchanging River and see for herself if it truly was dry. The wind gently blew across her face as a wisp of her grey hair fell loose and tickled her chin. She reached up and tucked it behind her ear. The wind then blew playfully again, and this time a whole cascade of grey curls fell down around her face, fluttering in the wind. Nuala sat down and grumpily pulled her hair back from the wind and secured it tightly with her pins. Reaching into her bag, she pulled out her bonnet and tied it onto her head.

Standing back up, Nuala began her trek again. She looked nervously around. The wind was whirling around her faster and faster, and then in a dust devil it took off out into the trees. Then it completely stopped.

"If I did not know any better I would think that the wind is trying to get my attention," she spoke out loud to herself. At that moment the wind began to blow again and picked up the edge of her skirt and pulled it towards the trees. She quickly patted it down with her hand.

"I think I am mad!"

She looked into the forest where the dust devil had gone. It was exactly the same direction that her skirt was being pulled. She looked down at her grimy clothes and hands; there had not been enough water to even wash with. She was glad that she had not drunk the wine, or she would think she was drunk.

The wind persisted in pulling at her. *What would it hurt to take a look into the forest?* She reasoned with herself.

There was no one around to mock her. Carefully she went into the tall dark trees and again she felt the breeze, this time like a quiet breath gently pushing her from behind. Nuala let out a giggle like a young girl. This was so exciting and she was actually enjoying herself for the first time in a long while.

The breeze stilled, so she, too, stopped. Then she heard it ~ a faint whisper.

"Nuala…"

She stood still and, straining her ears she listened. All seemed silent. Nuala walked in the direction she had heard her name being called. She walked for some time, weaving her way through the dry undergrowth ~ that so badly needed a drink ~ just like her. Stopping, she strained to listen. Then she thought she heard it again.

"Nuala…"

This time it came from somewhere on to her right, so she turned and walked in that direction. She did not know how long she repeated this procedure, though it was growing late in the day. Instead of getting tired, she seemed to be gaining strength. When she did not hear her name whispered, the wind would pull or push Nuala gently along.

Nuala finally became so thirsty she could not bear it and she sighed out to the unseen Lord, "Do you care if I die of thirst, Lord? I know that I have lived a dry old existence. I ask that if You give me a little sip of water, then I will never again return to my old ways."

At that moment, a beam of late-afternoon sun broke through the branches overhead and glimmered off what could only be a pool of water. She picked up her skirts and ran to the edge of pool that was surrounded by the loveliest small white forest flowers. A deer, startled by her coming into its domain, leaped away, its small white tail waving like a flag as it disappeared into the forest.

Nuala knelt down and even before she took one sip, she began to cry. She thanked the unseen Lord over and over again. She began to tell Him of all her short-comings and the wicked things she had done, pleading for forgiveness.

"You are forgiven, my daughter... Drink, for you will need it. Pour out the wine and fill your flask with water for your journey. It is a matter of the heart. Be encouraged!" the unseen Lord's voice was as clear as if He was standing over her.

Nuala drank for a long time, then poured out the wine and rinsed out her flask. After filling it to the brim, she tucked it carefully into her packsack. She then washed her body and wiped some of the grime off her clothes with the cool refreshing water. She did not waste any time, but worked in a quick, nervous manner. She was heartened that the unseen Lord thought she could accomplish a task of the heart.

She picked up her sack and headed back to the road. She walked long into the night by the light of the moon. Finally stopping to rest, she took a long refreshing drink and laid down her tired body in a little hollow beside the road. Lying her head on the crook of her arm with a contented smile upon her face, she fell fast asleep.

$\sim$

Nuala awakened in another place. She thought she was dreaming. Wynne came running up to her and hugged her and kissed her repeatedly.

"Oh, Mother, how I have waited for this day! You look so beautiful! Come, there is so much to show you… The Lord's Father has been preparing a large banquet for an upcoming wedding," Wynne's excited chatter caused Nuala to laugh aloud at her daughter. Looking over her shoulder, she was surprised to see a wonderful river flowing behind her. It was wide and glittered in the light, it looked very much like a river of diamonds that sparkled and dazzled. The river was so wide that she could barely make out the other side of it. She squinted her eyes and saw the forest she had been walking beside just the night before.

As she looked she saw the road she had been on and there lying in the hollow appeared to be an old woman. It was her! She looked in surprise at Wynne. Had she passed over the veil and not even known it?

"Yes, mother, you are home. Your journey is over. Come, you are young again and there is much to do," Wynne said encouragingly.

Nuala looked down at her body and was surprised to see the form of a young, beautiful woman. A stray wisp of hair blew across her face. She reached up and caught it, examining the black tendril carefully. Letting out a giggle, she began to follow Wynne away from the river. As she did, strength like she had never felt surged through her body. Picking up the skirt of her white dress, she bolted past Wynne.

"Catch me if you can!" She laughed out as she darted down the path in front of her daughter. As she ran, the life that had seemed so hard fell from her shoulders and her heart lifted in exultant jubilation.

She was alive…

Truly alive!

The Ancients say… "He hath put a new song in my mouth: many shall see it, and fear, and shall trust in the Lord."

 Chapter 6

The Dragon, and the host of evil it had gathered, wanted to find out why the pilgrims were gathering at Cathaoir's farm. They had been coming all day, in wagons, on horseback and walking. They were a bedraggled lot to the common eye. However, the Dragon saw them for who they really were ~ warriors of the unseen Lord. It could see their armour glinting in the bright light of the hot sun. The Dragon hissed out its anger and slapped a creature that was crouching by its side.

"But master," it drooled, "we have been careful to keep a watch and we do not know why they are gathering. You know that it is hard to hear them anymore… Their speech has become so garbled." The creature ducked, missing the Dragon's blow.

"If I ask for your excuses, then give them. If not ~ then shut up ~ you fool! Don't you know the Lord is on the move? I can feel it! I thought we were winning when the Source stopped flowing. I thought we had caused this drought! But all it has done is caused these cursed pilgrims to unite with the mountain dwellers! Now, the pilgrims from over the sea, are also awakening!" As the Dragon spoke, its anger rose higher and higher until the last words came out like a screech. Turning its hulking frame, the Dragon moved through the ranks. The group slithered and clambered back to make a path.

Every ugly creature imaginable had gathered with the Dragon, bringing their reports from all over their small world. The pilgrims were on the move and their need for water was being supplied by their own well digging and faith in the unseen Lord. They were wearing their armour and wielding their swords. A creature came forward, that had the body of a man and the head of a beetle, its huge eyes bulging out the sides of its face, and bowed before the Dragon. It lifted its huge bear-like paw in a salute.

"My Honour, we have discovered that the divisions between the guards and the pilgrims has become wider. Now is the time to try to turn the hearts of the pilgrims back to their guards, or we fear they will all leave the fortresses. The great fear held over them by the guards will be broken. Give the command and we will go and do it."

The Dragon looked long and hard at this high general of its army. It was true ~ it knew that the pilgrims had become restless and unpredictable. *I need to weaken the pilgrims individually as best I can.* The Dragon thought of how it could use Nuala's recent death to cause bitterness in Caedmon.

Unfulfilled promises, that should work, it mused. Flying over the ranks of evil, the Dragon let its drool drip over the its herd of creatures. As they turned their faces upwards in glee to listen to their commander's orders.

"Go! Cause a false sense of obligation! Make sure the guards become sweet and agreeable to win the favour of the people again. You must cause their false leadership to raise up the old inquisitions. No one will dare leave them when I am through!"

~

The pilgrim warriors and knights ignored the presence of evil around them. They only had eyes for the Lord in their midst. He was crouching down on His ankles in the middle of the gathering crowd of pilgrims. He, too, ignored the Dragon's creatures of darkness. The enemies slowly went to do their assigned tasks, for the fear of the pilgrims was leaving them, as they now had a plan of attack.

The Lord stood to His feet and began to speak. The enraptured pilgrims sat still. Their unseen Lord was now visible to every eye. They hung on every word. His voice travelled like the wind to even the last pilgrim walking down the road.

"I have gathered you to tell you that in the days to come, things will be different. *Much* different. Your own purposes will become one purpose, and that will be to bring in the kingdom of My Father.

The Dragon is on the move ~ but it will be the last move concerning you, My blessed followers."

Dei pulled his wife close, their little Caiomhe in her arms. Treva stood up and walked closer. The tears fell unbidden down her cheeks, how she wished Gilroy could be with her!

The unseen Lord, looking into her eyes for a long time, finally spoke to her.

"Treva, my faithful girl, I have some things for you to do yet. Gilroy is doing well! Try not to long for the things that cannot be. I know your pain. Take comfort."

Caedmon, a sob halfway up his throat, tried to comfort his own heart. At times since they had come back, he would suddenly remember that Gilroy was gone, and at those times he had thought his own heart would break in two.

"Caedmon," came the Lord's gentle voice. "Be still, my young knight. You will be with your true father before you even realize it. Don't look so startled ~ I don't mean you are going to die. Things are changing quickly, and the land beyond the mist will invade this land. Things will change. And before you know it, it will be time for you to walk beyond the veil. Gilroy awaits your reunion with joy."

Caedmon wove forward through the people, his tears washing down his face. His sobs tore at all their hearts. Crawling up to the Lord's feet, he clung to the edge of His flowing robe.

"Help me, Lord!"

Kneeling down, the Lord wrapped His arms around Caedmon and pulled him close. He rocked him like a small child for a long time. Then, releasing him, He returned His attention to the pilgrims.

"Whether you remain here or go beyond the veil, remember this one thing ~ you are always alive in My Father's kingdom, whether here or there. The day of being joined with those that have gone before is closer than you can even imagine."

All eyes were fixed on His face. His beautiful dark eyes were illuminated with love. His hair, as white as wool, blew out slightly from His broad face in the wind. The Lord's royal blue robe was gird about with a golden sash, and upon His head was a simple,crown of twisted gold with a single diadem on the front. They were in awe,

- 293 -

for few had ever seen Him before with their eyes, and even though He had called them together, they had never expected to see Him. Every one of them had their heart in their throats as they waited in expectancy for His next words.

Sitting down again, the Lord leaned forward and looked each one full in the face. "I must tell you of My Father's desire for you and for His chosen ones. I know that each one of you is His chosen one, but before the Ancients were here, there was a people who walked with Father ~ long before I came to battle the Dragon. It was among and through this people that I was born a man, and I tried to persuade them of the Father's love for them."

The pilgrims listened silently to the story they had heard many times before, but never from this point of view.

"They became hardened over the years. They believed more in their own ability to do His bidding than in having a relationship with Him. So that was why He sent Me ~ to reconcile them to Himself and to defeat the Dragon's lies over them. He wanted everyone that He had created to know Him. That, too, made some of His people jealous. So the few who believed in Me became the scribes who wrote the parchments for everyone who wanted to see Me and know Me."

Taking a deep breath, He pulled His knees up and rested His massive arms upon them. Looking at the faithful pilgrims, He went on.

"However, now My Father is stirring their hearts again. I have been sent to many in that far-off land of my birthplace. I have been calling, and many are listening to My voice. I have found many that intermingled with those of other lands. They too are preparing to come and join us in the great battle against the Dragon." A gasp of shock came from the pilgrims.

"Do not fear. Remember, our battle sometimes does not look like a battle to the eye, but each one knows what it is like to have the Dragon's slime steal from you. Its lies have even taken some of your lives, but the Dragon cannot take your breath."

"In the days to come there will be some who will lose their lives in this realm, but do not fear ~ one moment you will be here, and

- 294 -

the next moment you will be beyond the veil. I will strengthen you then."

The pilgrims looked at one another, nodding and smiling, giving one another courage.

The Lord lifted His head and, shaking back His hair from His face, He began to sing. The song was the song of a battle where the warriors walked in peace and the enemy fell before them as the pilgrims went forward in unison.

It was calm and still in the yard, and no one seemed to be breathing as the song wove around them. Like a wind that was gently blowing, the words swept by each one and that pilgrim's armour would begin to shine and sparkle in the daylight. Strength and purpose flooded each heart. The song spoke of the defeated enemy and of loved ones returning.

Cathaoir looked down at Treasa, who sat still at his side. Tears were falling down her face. He knew she was thinking of their daughter and her new husband. Treasa's eyes were shut tight and her hand was holding the base of her throat, which was her habit when she was stirred deeply. He drew her close and whispered in her ear, "I love you. You are precious... she will return. Take comfort, He has promised."

When the song finally ended, each one had their head bowed and sat in perfect rest. Even the children were still. After a few minutes of silence, a loud clap of thunder over their heads startled the pilgrims. Looking up, the Lord had disappeared and storm clouds were brewing on the horizon.

Rain!

Scrambling to their feet, they began to gather their families quickly and head for home. Treasa and her family, with Caedmon and Tully and Edan in tow, ran to the cottage. Rain! Rain!

He was sending rain to strengthen them and to fortify their belief in Him. Joy flooded their hearts as they began to sing songs of thanksgiving. The rain pounded all that day and into the night. Treasa and Cathaoir made room for everyone in the cottage. It was wall to wall with sleeping pilgrims and their small ones.

- 295 -

Teague, his head resting on his hand, looked down at Seanna, who was asleep with their precious little girl nestled in her arms. He spoke. "You have been faithful to me, my Lord. Thank you for my family. Please, Lord, protect them in the days to come. Protect them from the enemy."

Teague could feel his own fear and he did not like it. He did not want them to experience any pain. He wanted to protect them from any attack that could harm them. He knew that the song had stirred him deeply. He could not even remember the last time he had sung. Again he felt the fear rise up above him, coming down like a smothering blanket.

Creeping slowly from under their blanket on the floor, Teague went to the door. Holding his cloak over his head, he darted to the barn. Running into the barn, he was surprised to see Edan sitting there on a pile of hay, with a candle burning. Edan had his head buried in his hands. Hearing Teague shut the door, he glanced up. Tears were streaming down his face, mixed with the raindrops. Teague strode over to Edan and took a seat beside him on the straw.

Edan spoke first. "I want my song back. When I heard the Lord sing today it stirred me so deeply, but I feel so full of fear and inadequacy. I don't know if I could die for Him. And, I am afraid that maybe my family will die in the battle."

"Me, too. I felt driven from the house. I did not know you were out here."

"I came out right after everyone settled down. I just don't like this fear. Everything within me wants to avoid this battle, but I know it is time. I need to be the man that the Lord created me to be," Edan shuddered as he finished speaking.

Reaching over, Teague turned the candle over so they could burn the other end. "Well, I came out here to sing. Even if it doesn't sound ~ " Teague was cut short by the sound of the barn door flying open. A very wet Caedmon came darting into the barn.

"Come and join us, Caedmon! Are you afraid, too?" Edan asked with a grin.

"Well, I don't know about being afraid, but I knew if I did not start to sing I would burst," Caedmon breathlessly said.

He handed Teague his lyre, saying, "Here, I know that I do not play as well as you. Would you two like to make some music? I brought my flute." He looked expectantly from one to the other.

"Yes, but I haven't sung since I washed in the Unchanging River. Oh, how I miss the river. Isn't it strange how sometimes you don't know how important something is to you until it is taken away?" Teague asked.

Edan answered Teague, "Yes ~ or you feel the fear of losing it."

The three sat in silence, and then Teague began to whistle and strum on the lyre. Edan joined him, singing words that spoke of his longing for bravery. The lovely melody soon joined them as Caedmon played upon the flute. The three sang long into the night, not even aware that the rain had stopped and the sun was beginning to rise.

~

Seanna stretched and reached over to awaken Teague. She was surprised to see he was gone, Tully walked over and kneeling down she whispered, "Edan is gone as well. I would not be surprised if Caedmon is as well. Maybe they are on a quest."

Seanna smiled up at her friend. Her little one stirred, their darling Arienh. She was such a good little girl, though Seanna knew she always had to keep a close eye on her for she was very active.

"I think they must have left in the night... I am glad, you know! I remember when I was jealous of them spending time together, but then when it stopped, I so missed it. Is Finna sleeping? Arienh is such a sound sleeper."

"Yes, she is asleep, though I am afraid she will stir at any minute," Tully whispered. "Let's get up and make the morning food for Treasa and Cathaoir. I heard them say that Barris and Keelin were coming today."

They went over to the window and looked outside. The entire yard looked like a lake. The ground was baked so hard the water just lay on the surface. They had had a good rain in the night. The Lord was so faithful to all the people of the land. Tully's heart raised in grateful thanksgiving to Him.

- 297 -

Stoking up the cooking fire, the young women soon had a gruel cooking and thick slices of Treasa's bread toasting on the open flame. The aroma filled the house. Waking, Treasa smiled at Cathaoir.

"Well my darling, I do believe that I am being spoiled this morning. Do you smell that heavenly aroma?"

After the meal, Cathaoir headed to the barn to do the chores. Entering the barn, he was surprised to see a pail of milk sitting on the bench and the cow munching contentedly on her fresh hay in the manger. Checking the hogs and chickens, he realized that all the chores were done. He knew that his helpers must have been Caedmon, Teague, and Edan, but there was no sign of the three young men. Lying on the bench was a candle that had been burned at both ends and the satchel for Teague's lyre.

Cathaoir wondered where they were off to as he carried the milk to the house.

The Ancients say… "Be sober, be vigilant; because your adversary walketh about, seeking whom he may devour."

Chapter 7

"Caedmon, where are you going?" Teague called out from the open barn door to the retreating back of his friend.

"To Evergreen. When I arrive there I will be told what to do," Caedmon said over his shoulder, not slacking his pace. "I am to arrive alone, nevertheless, I think you two might be joining me later."

Teague and Edan looked at each other quizzically.

Their music had chased every fear and inhibition away. They felt renewed and strengthened by the songs. It was almost as if a dam had broken inside of them and all the pent up longings that had been trapped within had gushed forth in great release. Their armour shone in the early morning light. They were ready!

Drawing their swords they followed their friend at a distance until the crossroads, then they went down the trail along the aqueduct. It was a longer road to the village, but they felt compelled to go that way. Some murky water lay in the bottom of the aqueduct from the rain, though most of the rain was seeping fast into the dry cracks in the parched ground.

The men stopped and listened because every time they walked they could hear the crunch of someone's step behind them ~ following them. When they stopped, the steps behind them stopped too.

Without a word, Edan took off at a fast run and Teague darted to the left, jumped the aqueduct and ran the other way. Then, jumping back across the aqueduct, he ran straight up the road he had already travelled. Meanwhile, Edan stopped and, turning abruptly he ran straight back the way he had just darted. Teague and him were coming at one another at a very fast pace, swords drawn and faces set like flint. It appeared like they would collide into one another.

However, just when they were a few feet from each other the Dragon appeared.

Turning its head first to Teague, then to Edan, it sprang straight into the air ~ but not before Teague's sword swiped the Dragon's tail. Smoke and slime oozed from the gash as Edan leapt into the air and drove his sword into one of the beast's wings, tearing its bat-like sinew as he fell back down to the road.

The Dragon cursed them. Flying high above them, it dove down on their heads, spewing a volume of green drool upon them. Edan back-flipped away from the falling mass of ooze, and Teague swept his sword through it and flung it into the aqueduct.

"Be gone, Dragon! We come in the name of the Lord and His armies!"

Teague yelled out at the Dragon as it flew again over their heads. With a screech, it flew out of sight in the direction of the village.

The young men stopped and looked at each other. Then, grabbing one another about the shoulders, their laughter filled the air. The Dragon stopped in mid-flight and listened, not liking what it heard. *What is so humorous?*

"We better hurry! Caedmon is in danger!" Teague began to run down the road.

"Stop, Teague! Remember, this is the Lord's quest. He knows what He is doing. We should wait for Him to call us!" Edan called out after Teague.

Teague stopped. *This is true,* he thought.

He waited for Edan to catch up and said, "You are right, my friend, though I do feel an urgency. Caedmon is going to be taken inside… I can feel it in my bones. We must be prepared to fight, only this time it will be pilgrims that we will encounter, not the Dragon itself. I feel sick in my heart at what the unseen Lord has shown us. It has begun ~ *the* inquisition! Did you hear it as well?"

"Yes, just before we fought the Dragon, the Lord was preparing my heart for what lay ahead. Then I heard Him say, *'Inquisition'.* It made my blood run cold. We have heard of the inquisitions of the past, and about how brutal they were, all in the name of truth. You

- 300 -

are right, though, we must not tarry. Caedmon will need us, and sooner than he thinks. Lord be with our families, please!"

Both men felt a hand rest upon their shoulders and knew the unseen Lord was walking with them, and telling them it was time to join their friend. Encouragement rose in their hearts immediately. They could and would do whatever was required of them. They were not alone and they had their armour. They had seen Him, they had heard Him, and they knew that He was with them right at the moment. *Look at what had happened a few minutes before,* Edan thought, *We didn't have a plan, but we executed a precise plan instantaneously to overthrow the Dragon's attack. It's amazing!*

Straightening their shoulders, they lengthened their strides to the fortress.

~

Seanna and Tully helped Treasa clean up after the morning meal. Little Arienh was still asleep. Seanna went into the sitting room and knelt down beside her babe. The little girl had not moved at all, and her face looked blotched with crimson. Seanna reached out and touched the small cheek, and her hand jerked back in shock ~ Arienh's face was hot as coals.

"Treasa, come!" Seanna screamed. Her scream did not even stir the sleeping girl. Treasa and Tully ran into the room and fell on their knees beside the child.

"She will not awaken and she is so hot! I cannot get her to wake up! Help, oh Lord, help!" Seanna began to sob uncontrollably. Treasa flung the blanket off the wee girl and, lifting her up carried her into Keelin's sleeping room. Tully ran for cold water and cloths. Seanna just sat on the floor, rocking back and forth, helpless with grief.

"Seanna, you need to be strong," Tully said as she passed her. "Come, we must help Treasa break the fever." Just as she disappeared into the sleeping room with Finna cradled on her hip, Cathaoir came in.

Seeing Seanna rocking and crying on the floor of the sitting room, he knelt down beside her. "What has happened?"

- 301 -

"Arienh is sick. Really sick, and we don't know where Teague is," she sobbed out.

He quickly helped her up and took her into the sleeping room. He fell onto his knees to mediate when he saw the lifeless face of his beloved granddaughter. The women worked, wringing out cloths and applying them to her hot little body. Seanna, finally joined Cathaoir on the floor and began to plead for her child's life. Looking at the babe from her kneeling position, she saw the shadow of something moving over her baby's body.

Becoming very still, she whispered, "What am I seeing Lord?"

As if a veil was split, what had been a shadow became totally visible. A huge, spider-like creature was hanging onto her daughter's body. It looked at Seanna, and a dark purple pool of drool dripped from its huge gaping mouth. The slime was covering Arienh's body and face.

Seanna let out a gut-wrenching scream. Tully and Treasa dropped their cloths in surprise. Cathaoir quickly pulled himself up off the floor. Seanna, pointing above the child, yelled as she drew her sword.

"In the name of the Lord and His armies," she cried. With an upward slice of the sword she flung the creature from her daughter. It instantly disappeared.

Arienh let out a little cry, "Mama... I tirsty!"

The entire room let out a sigh of relief.

"What was it?" Treasa asked.

"It had to be one of the Dragon's creatures of darkness. It was drowning Arienh in its drool of sickness," Seanna said as she picked up her little girl and wrapped her in a blanket.

Cathaoir ran from the room to get the wee one a drink of water. All three laughed and cried when she took the glass and looked from one face to another and said very primly, "Time to git up, Mama?"

~

Caedmon looked around the guard's quarters. Another new guard had been put into this position. He wondered how many had been there in the last few years. His quarters were extravagant. It seemed that every new guard had spent much money on improvements.

- 302 -

Caedmon had been brought there by one of the pilgrims who had let him into the fortress and told him to wait until the guard could see him. Caedmon heard the door open behind him. Turning in his chair, he was surprised to see the head guard of the fellowship of fortresses.

Looking at Caedmon his face lit up in recognition. "Caedmon… It has been a long time. How are you doing? Come, let me see you," the guard looked so friendly that it took Caedmon aback for a moment. As Caedmon came forward, the man embraced him.

Caedmon was speechless. Why had the Lord sent him here? Caedmon made himself relax; *this man is obviously glad to see me.*

"Hello, sir. I was in the area and thought I would stop in and see if my grandmother was here. I thought I would see how things were going. Some of my fondest memories are of this place," Caedmon spoke earnestly as the men sat down. Caedmon on one side of the massive desk and the guard behind it. Caedmon looked at the guard, and his heart filled with that old feeling of wanting this man to accept him. Suddenly, a shadow began to move behind the man and Caedmon recognized its form.

"No one sent word to you?" the guard asked.

"*Word?*"

"Yes, word… Oh my, I see they have not. Nuala, your grandmother, disappeared from the village a few weeks ago. We would have sent out a search party, but you know how things are. Your grandmother did not want to live within the protection of these walls, so it was her choice, not ours. We can only help those that will help themselves," he said with the same old condescending tone in his voice.

Caedmon felt his anger rise in response to the coldness, and the colour drained from his face as he wondered what had happened to his grandmother.

"If you had been keeping in touch with your grandmother, you would have known this. Maybe you should check into it yourself. We have heard all about how great you have become with the renegade pilgrims… and that you have seen the unseen Lord." The man did not even try to hide the mocking in his voice.

"Now, if you will excuse me, I have things to attend to," the guard quickly lost all the false kindness he had first shown. Caedmon saw the Dragon's shadow rise from behind the chair and overshadow the man, almost engulfing the guard in darkness.

Reaching for his sword, Caedmon began to draw it out. The glint of the steel shone in the Dragon's eyes. Screaming out, the Dragon hurled a ball of slime onto the head of the guard. The guard quickly pulled a long cord on the wall and Caedmon could hear the hollow sound of a bell somewhere below him in the fortress.

"I welcomed you as a friend, and now you draw that cursed sword against me!" the man became irrational as he slurred out the words. "We know that you use the power of the Dragon… and we have you now! Caught in the very act of trying to kill me."

Caedmon, looking in horror at the wild man, quickly put his sword back in its scabbard and it disappeared. He looked for a way of escape, but three large men ran into the room, stopping him. They had on crude man-made armour, and their faces were hidden behind their helmets.

"Take him to the dungeon. Watch him closely! He tried to kill me with the Dragon's power. He has one of those cursed invisible swords. We know that only guards receive swords from the unseen Lord. He is an impostor and a fraud. He tried to infiltrate the fortress to spread the Dragon's lies." The guard wiped drool from his mouth as he spoke. The tallest officer hated it when this new guard became a lunatic, but he hated these wayward pilgrims even more.

The Dragon appeared to Caedmon as the men bound his hands behind his back. Spitting the green slime into Caedmon's face, the creature laughed at him. Its laughter turned to hatred when it saw that the slime had disappeared, and Caedmon's face was shining with light. Taking a long talon, the Dragon tore it down Caedmon's cheek. At that very moment, one of the officers struck him on the face. Blood spurted from his nose, and his lip began to bleed.

"Apologize to our guard," the officer blurted out and then added, "beg for your life, traitor."

Caedmon looked at the man, tears glistening in his eyes. What could he say? The unseen Lord had sent him here for a reason, and he had to trust Him. He could feel his eye beginning to swell shut from where he had been struck.

"Get him out of here, before he gets blood on my floor," the guard spat out. The men began to drag him out of the room and down a back corridor.

"Don't let any of the pilgrims see him! You know they don't understand that we are protecting them," the guard ordered as he turned and became occupied with what was on his desk. Again the tallest officer felt his conscience stir, but he quickly set it aside.

Taking Caedmon down into the dark recesses of the fortress's underground, they came to the ancient cells. Caedmon looked around in shock. He never knew that a prison was underground! *What had it been built for and who built it?* He thought confused.

The men thrust him into the cell and locked the door behind them as they departed. Caedmon was left alone in the inky black darkness of the cold cell. Stumbling across the floor, he tripped over something. He heard the low moan of someone.

"Who is there?" Caedmon whispered.

The Ancients say… "If one prevail against him, two shall withstand him; and a threefold cord is not quickly broken."

Chapter 8

Liam ~ determined guardian

Teague and Edan, finally stopping to rest, saw the old woman laying still on her side in the hollow by the road. They knew she was dead, for the aroma of death clung to what remained of her. They began to dig a temporary grave with their hands in the soft shale by the road. Wrapping the body in Teague's cloak, both young men were surprised to see that it was Caedmon's grandmother, Nuala. She must have been there for many days.

The men finished their gruesome task, and then they drove a stick in the ground to mark the place so that they could move her to a proper burial place when they'd told Caedmon.

"Don't you think it strange that no one found her?" Teague asked.

"No, Not really!" said Edan. "I believe that is why we felt compelled to come this way. Maybe the Dragon wanted Caedmon to find her, so that he would never be able to get that picture out of his mind." Clenching his fist, Edan exclaimed, "But we found her! She looked so at peace, just like she had crossed over in her sleep. We can tell that to Caedmon."

"You are right, Edan! I would wager that the liar was guarding her body, hiding her from view, just waiting for its opportunity to cause some sort of distress to Caedmon," Teague answered enthusiastically.

The men washed their hands with some of the water from their canteens and continued down the road. They would be at the fortress soon, and as they drew closer, they felt the need to mediate. Leaving the road, they went to a small meadow in the surrounding trees. Kneeling down, they mediated for direction and for Caedmon. Silence wrapped itself around them. Suddenly they were standing on a high mountain top and a beautiful walled garden stood before them. A small child, a beautiful, golden-haired girl, sat on the wall and was looking inquisitively at them. The men stared in shock, trying to comprehend what had just happened.

"Welcome friends!" her voice sang out like a little melody.

"Well, hello there," Teague greeted back.

"You will never know how long I have waited for you two. I was given gifts for you a very long time ago, but alas, you never came for them." Her small face became so sad that it broke their hearts.

Before the men knew what was happening they were both crying like babies. She jumped down from the high wall so lightly that at first they thought she was flying. She walked over to them, handing Teague a long package that was rolled up in a cloak, and to Edan, she handed a very small, ornate alabaster box.

"Don't cry. See? I am happy now!" She giggled and then she drew out an arrow from her quiver and slapped, first Teague, and then Edan, across the face.

Jumping back, as the sting of the arrow shaft startled them. They were equally startled by the clearness of mind and energy that filled them afterwards. Rubbing their whisker-covered jaws, they both knew that something had taken place deep within them. It was as if the past had rolled off their shoulders, and every mistake they had made evaporated in the twinkling of an eye. They suddenly remembered every word the unseen Lord had ever spoken to them.

"Thank you, miss. I definitely needed that, but I must say that I was not expecting one so small to have such a mighty blow," Edan said as he continued to rub his jaw, even though the sting was gone.

"My name is Aithne. *Little Fire.* I am one of the messengers of the Great King. You were sent to me; I wanted to come to you, but the Prince said I was to wait until you came to me. Oh, it has seemed so long…" Another giggle escaped her lips. "Come, I will feed you a little and you can look at your presents."

Both men realized then, that the Lord's messengers should not be judged by outward appearances, for they knew in their hearts a mighty warrior walked in front of them. They were glad she did not shoot them with the arrow. Then they remembered Caedmon's story and him shooting Cathaoir.

"I could have shot you, you know." She laughed at their shocked faces. "But I like variety. These arrows do their job well. I have hit you before with them, but you were always sleeping then."

She began to giggle so hard that she had to stop and lean against a tree. Both men began to laugh as well, and just like Caedmon's experience they had no understanding of what was so humorous. It was one of the most infectious laughs they ever heard.

They came to a bench beside a pool, and on the bench were two plates laden with fruit. The men realized then how hungry they were. They had left on this quest without eating. Sitting down on the soft grass beside the bench, they began to partake of their feast. The fruit was unlike anything they had ever eaten. It made them feel happy and fulfilled all at the same time. Wiping their mouths on their sleeves, they slowly opened their gifts.

Edan gasped when he saw the beautiful ring. A lion's head was engraved in the gold, with small diamonds that glittered all around the entire ring. He slowly put it on and, wonder of wonders, it exactly fit.

"Of course it fits!" Aithne responded, reading his thoughts. "Abelio knows your size. He made it! Isn't it lovely? It is to help you always remember whose son you are! You are now and forever a son of the King."

"Understand?" she giggled out.

Edan nodded his head as his tears fell down his face unashamedly. A son...

A real son...

Of the King!

He knew that he did not deserve it, and that it truly was the ultimate gift. Teague was slowly unrolling the cloak, and it looked like his own cloak that he had wrapped Nuala in just minutes before.

"Yes, the cloak is for you as well. You will need it for it is very cold where you are going!" Aithne said emphatically.

Inside the cloak lay the most gorgeous carved walking stick. It looked similar to the stick that Arthmael had carved for Gilroy, only made of a wood that Teague had never seen.

"This stick will support you when you do not know where you are going. It will be your eyes when all is dark and you cannot see. It will be your strength when you feel you cannot go on," Aithne lowered her eyes for a moment, then with a sober face, went on.

"Caedmon is in prison. Down in the dungeon of the fortress. You will be put there, too. Don't despair ~ the Lord is with you, but first you will suffer. You will be a sign to some of the pilgrims there, and their eyes will be opened. Oh yes, Edan, you will be tested concerning not judging people before you know what the unseen Lord knows. You must be on your way now. Do not forget your gifts!"

The men immediately were standing on the road again, and they shook their heads. *Did this just happen?* they wondered. Then Edan felt the ring on his hand and Teague felt the warmth of the new cloak on his shoulders and the walking stick in his grip. Looking nervously at one another, they walked the last furlong to Evergreen.

~

As Caedmon slumped down against the wall, he heard the moan again. He felt in both directions with his hand. The floor was definitely made of stone, and it was damp and cold. Slowly inching himself along the wall, he kept feeling with his hand. He soon felt a rough cot. He let his hand move over the cot that had a few rags on it, that was all. Then, still seated on the floor, he eased himself along the cot and came to the corner, and kept inching along until he came to the door where he had been pushed in. Further along the wall he came to a rough table. Reaching up, he felt the table top and was shocked to feel a few candles and a flint.

Relief flooded his heart. Rising to his knees, he struck the flint and with the spark lit one of the candles. The soft light illuminated the cell showing that the room was very small and made entirely of quarried stone. He put the candle on the holder and carefully examined the room again. The light was dim from the candle, but he could make out another cot on the other side of the room. Lying

- 309 -

in the middle of the floor was a man, and beside him on a crude pan was some black bread and a flask.

Caedmon carefully went to the man and knelt down. He gently rolled the man onto his back and was shocked to see Carew. He seemed to be barely breathing. Caedmon loosened Carew's tunic from his throat and tried to awaken him, but his old friend seemed to be out cold. Checking the flask for water, Caedmon poured a few of the precious drops on the edge of his tunic and used it to wash Carew's face. The shock of the water seemed to awaken him and he looked, his eyes glazed, into Caedmon's face.

"Is that you, my friend?" His voice sounded old and cracked.

"Yes, it is I. What is wrong, Carew? Can I help you in some way?" Caedmon tenderly asked.

"They would not let me tell my wife and mother I was all right. I gave up, I did not even bother to light the candle any longer. Here in the dark, I do not even know how long or how many days I have been here. I have quit eating and drinking. I want to die," Carew's face contorted in agony as he turned his face away from Caedmon.

"Try to eat a little. The Lord sent me to you. He will get us out of this place. Teague and Edan are to follow me." Caedmon's heart began to stir with excitement at the possibilities that were in store for them. "Here, let me help you. I will soak the bread in a little water."

Carew, shaking violently, tried to sit up. Caedmon quickly helped him up onto one of the cots and then laid him gently on the rags. He began to feed Carew a chunk of the black bread soaked in water. Lifting the flask to Carew's lips, he let him drink his fill. Carew fell back onto the cot and went sound asleep as he whispered softly, "Thank you, Lord, for the light…" Caedmon blew out the flame to save the candle as his friend slept fitfully.

After what seemed like an eternity, Caedmon saw a light shine under the crack of the door. The door creaked open and, through half opened eyes, Caedmon saw the tall officer come into the cell, a candle and loaf of bread in his hand. The man looked in surprise at Carew on the cot and the bread that had been eaten. He looked over at Caedmon, who pretended to be asleep. Quietly, the officer

- 310 -

went out and came back in with a basin, a pitcher of water, and some cleaning rags. He then brought in another candle and laid it on the table.

Looking skyward, he said, "Remember me, Lord. I want to be your servant!" The man's hoarse whisper moved Caedmon's heart… truly there were His servants everywhere.

~

Later that night, a great commotion outside their cell awakened Caedmon and Carew. The door flung open and two men were pushed inside. The one leaped to his feet before the cell closed and stuck his foot in the crack of the shutting door. The other jumped up and grabbed the door, swinging it back open. Two more officers ran toward them and, with the end of a club, pushed the men back inside and slammed the door shut.

"I told you, tie their hands! These men are savages ~ wild men! The sooner they are taken from here the better, is all I can say. And you, Liam, can feed them in the morning if you are so kindhearted to traitors."

"I am not kindhearted to traitors. I just want to serve the unseen Lord, and we were taught that He is kind to all men!" the tall man blurted out.

"Oh, shut up until you get your guardship! Until then, we listen to the one that has been commissioned to protect us," the surly voice answered. The captives could hear their retreating steps down the corridor.

Caedmon felt his way over to the table to light one of the candles. Upon striking the flint and lighting the candle, the small flame illumined his friends' faces. Edan had a swollen eye and Teague looked very dishevelled. They definitely had not come peacefully.

"My friends, what took you so long?" Caedmon said with a smile. Setting the candle on the table, he walked back to the cot and sat down. Carew had pulled himself up on the cot and was sitting there, looking very sheepish.

"Well, we ran into a few obstacles on our way here. Well, not our way *here*, but we all ended up here, didn't we?" Edan said through

- 311 -

his swollen lip. Teague looked at Carew with awe, but did not say anything. He had news that couldn't wait.

"Caedmon, we found your grandmother, Nuala. She has passed over the veil, and the look of peace on her face was beautiful. We buried her temporarily until we can move her. I am sorry, Caed," Teague said compassionately.

Tears of sorrow and relief fell down Caedmon's face as he spoke, "I am glad she looked at peace. She never has had much peace in her life. She is with mom now…"

His sobs broke off the end of his sentence. Teague and Edan, one on each of his sides, tried to comfort him the best they could.

"I am sorry, Caed," Carew spoke quietly, then added, "and I am sorry Teague and Edan. I treated you so badly. I helped murder Arthmael and I will never forget his pleas. The unseen Lord has forgiven me and He told me that Arthmael has forgiven me too, but I cannot forgive myself."

The Ancients say... "Our soul is escaped as a bird out of the snare of the fowlers: the snare is broken, and we are escaped."

Chapter 9

The whiz of the arrow sliced through the air. Carew slumped forward on the cot and then fell face first onto the stone floor. Caedmon stood, his bow still pulled taunt in his hand. Teague and Edan rushed to Carew on the floor, and a girlish giggle filled the room.

"You are present, Little Fire? Aithne?" Caedmon asked as he strode over to Carew.

"Yes, I am, Sir Caedmon," Aithne replied from somewhere above them. The men could hear the swooping noise of wings above them, as if they were in the open field and not in a closed-in cell.

"That was a direct hit to the heart. I see that you have learned the bow well, and a true knight and archer you have become. I had come to strike Carew myself, but you have done the job well. He will sleep the night and be fully restored by morning. Cover him with your cloak, noble Teague. I must be gone," Aithne's voice trailed off as they heard the swan's wings sweep her away.

"I have never met anybody like that little one in my life," Teague said passionately as he covered Carew with his cloak.

"She is a blessing from the unseen Lord. Remember how I told of my first meeting with her. However first, we must plan our strategy," Caedmon spoke. The three men blew out the candle and talked into the night, each knowing that they had been sent there for a reason. They all came to the consensus that it was to come and rescue Carew and to mediate for Liam, the officer.

Carew, stirring on the floor, rolled onto his side. They could hear him sigh, long and slow, followed by a low chuckle as he continued to snore. Edan finally laid down one way on Caedmon's cot and Caedmon the other way, feet to face. Teague took Carew's cot and all three fell into an exhausted sleep.

~

Seanna and Keelin worked quietly in the garden. Arienh, her grubby little hands holding a rag doll, was playing in the dirt at the far end of the garden. The women had decided to put in a garden together to save work. The garden was growing well. The short rain they had two days prior had cleaned the leaves of the plants. But the rainwater had quickly disappeared down the large cracks in the baked earth.

"It's amazing, you know, how the fields and gardens grow despite the drought, isn't it?" Seanna asked, breaking the silence.

"Why, yes it is! Barris and I were talking of that last night. How good the unseen Lord is to His pilgrims."

Keelin standing stretched her tired muscles and ventured hesitantly, "Seanna, are you worried about Teague?"

"No, and yes. I know that they must have heard from the unseen Lord," Seanna replied then, adding as an afterthought, "Do you think that they went to the fortress?"

"Do *you* think so? Well, if they did, we know it had to be the unseen Lord leading. I do not think they would go there on their own bidding," Keelin answered.

"What made me think of the fortress was when we were all together at the Lord's gathering. Carew's wife, Lana, and his mother were there, but he wasn't. I talked to them and asked where he was and Lana became quiet and dropped her head. I could barely hear her as she said that she did not know and that he had disappeared after he went to make things right at the fortress. That is when she had started to mediate and call on the unseen Lord for herself, and why she came to the gathering," Seanna replied.

"I don't know. It is a mystery. The unseen Lord spoke to Barris that He is working and that Barris is to prepare himself for testing. Maybe this is a test for us to keep trusting despite what we feel," she answered Seanna.

"Maybe you're right. Would you look at that little child? She is so dirty! Oh my, how she loves playing in the dirt. She never stops talking to herself either. She is our little bundle of activity," Seanna said as she arose from the ground and straightened her sore back. "Let's go in and help your mom make lunch. I am so glad that your parents have let us stay here while Teague is gone."

The women walked to the cottage with little Arienh between them, one grubby little hand in each of theirs.

~

It had been three days since the men had been imprisoned in the dungeon. They had tried to talk to Liam every morning when he came with their bread and water. He would become very nervous and leave quickly, but they did notice that on the third morning he had left them a loaf of fresh bread instead of the hard black bread, as well as four pieces of cheese. Turning to leave their cell, Liam told them that he was mediating to the unseen Lord for them, that was all he could do.

The men waited until early evening to finish their meal, trying to make it last for what lay ahead.

"He is mediating on his own? I wonder if he knows that is frowned upon," Edan spoke as the men slowly ate the cheese and bread. It tasted like a grand feast after what they had been eating. When they took a drink from the flask they were surprised that it was a delicious wine instead of the stale water they had been given previously. The liquid had coursed through their veins, energizing and alerting their minds.

"I feel like we are feasting!" Teague replied, and then added, "I do believe that Liam is starting to know the truth and is afraid of it. Let's mediate for him right now, men."

The four men began to beseech the unseen Lord to meet with Liam, and for them to see the man's heart and not to hold any of this crime against him.

As they poured out their entreaties, Abelio walked into the cell. "Hello, my friends!" he greeted the astonished pilgrim knights.

He handed each of the men a new sword from a bundle he held under his arm. The swords gleamed in the dim candle light. They

- 315 -

were much larger and sharper than their old swords. When the men reached for their scabbards, they were amazed that they were empty.

Abelio, flinging his long blonde hair back from his shoulders, laughed. "These *are* your old swords! I took them last night to refine them even more for your battle ahead. The Prince is on the move this day, so prepare yourself. Liam will be joining you in the battle. I have polished his sword as well, though he has never seen it before. Remember your gifts and use them wisely. The Dragon is on the prowl in the corridor outside right now, but I have shielded your conversation from its ears. It doesn't know that I am about!" With those words, Abelio disappeared.

Carew looked down, and upon his lap he was surprised to find an intricately woven satchel. Golden threads woven on the flap were in the image of a lion. Beautiful purples and blues were woven together making the bag look like the morning sky just before the dawn. Carew opened the satchel carefully, and inside he saw four loaves of bread, a flask of water and a large piece of dried meat.

"This satchel will satisfy your needs as you have them," a voice spoke out from the walls around them. "If you will always share what is provided, it will always be replenished, my lamb!"

"It is Carden! Hello, my friend," Caedmon called out to the shepherd.

"I am waiting on the other side of the mist, Caedmon, for another song. Sing men, sing the song of the Shepherd for His sheep. Be brave and strong, but above all things, don't let anything steal your song," Carden's voice faded as if he was walking away from them.

"He is the shepherd beyond the mist I told you of. He is one of the unseen Lord's great ones. Carew, what a marvellous gift he that has given to you. Now we have everything we need for our escape," Caedmon said.

"Except one," a quiet female voice spoke out. The all turned and there stood the beautiful Sophronia.

"I have come to give you counsel. The things you have been given must be shared. And also, they are not for your own personal use but for the furtherance of the Lord's kingdom. Bless His sovereign name forever. Carew, you have refused my counsel in the past but as

- 316 -

you eat this bread that I baked. And allow Carden to shepherd you, you will begin to take my counsel in the future." She disappeared.

Before they could respond a long, eerie cry came from outside their door. The men quickly stood to their feet and blew out the candle. A soft light came from Edan's ring and illuminated the room around them. They could hear the gruff voices of the officers.

"They are not criminals, I tell you. The unseen Lord spoke to me and told me that they are His knights and we are not to do them any harm ~ " Liam's speech was cut short by a hard blow to the side of the head. The officer stopped and looked long and hard at Liam.

"You would do well to stop your false ways, noble officer. I will let it go this time, for we need your help to subdue them. But if I were you, I would recant quickly what you just said." The officer's steely voice could be heard over the Dragon's continual wailing.

"Don't you hear that noise?" Liam asked through his swollen lip.

"Shut up, Liam," the other officer spoke. "The only noise we hear is your continual whimpering." He reached for his keys and the slime of the Dragon dripped all over his hands as he opened the heavy cell door.

They were not expecting what they saw next and they let out a howl of pain and shock, grabbing at their eyes. A light so bright it blinded them as the door opened and threw them back on their heels. Edan's ring was on fire, and the light seemed to be growing brighter by the second. Teague, with his sword drawn, walked out to face the officers.

"What do you want of us?" Teague himself was surprised at the authority in his voice.

"What do you mean by being so rebellious? You would question us?" The surly officer replied gruffly as he strutted into the cell. He tried to sound like the one in charge, even though his knees were shaking and his eyes still stung from the bright light coming from Edan's hand. He walked over to Edan and tried to rip off the ring. A hot flaming pain went through the officer's hand; crying out, the man jumped back.

"What kind of Dragon magician are you?" he screamed as he ran out of the cell and locked the door. Heaving, he looked at Liam

- 317 -

in terror and said, "I am going for the guard. Watch them closely! Don't let them escape. They are mad, I tell you!" Flinging his commands over his shoulder, he disappeared down the corridor taking their light with him.

Liam stood still in the dark corridor, the hair prickling on end upon his neck. His breathing was ragged, and he felt terrified almost to the point of fainting. The inky darkness seemed to be closing in around him, heavier and heavier. Leaning against the door of their cell with his back, he tried to regain his composure.

"Help me, Lord!"

A firm hand clasped his shoulder and his heart froze. Then he heard a whisper in his ear. "Why would He help you here? You have been serving me, not Him. You have enjoyed my presence and power, haven't you?" The eerie whisper felt wet against his ear.

Reaching down, Liam felt the handle of a sword on his side. Surprised at the discovery he dropped his club from his right hand, he reached over and drew out the sword. The blade glistened in the darkness, illuminating the form of the shocked Dragon standing behind him. Liam struck out suddenly and the Dragon leaped back, out of the blades reach.

"Amateur. You have never used that before! I will devour you for trying," the Dragon shrieked as it dove its ugly snake head over Liam, preparing to drown him in drool.

Liam yelled, "In the name of the unseen Lord and His armies!"

With an upward thrust, he struck the beast in the jaw and, hitting bone, he twisted the sword hard. Smoke and slime oozed from the wound as the Dragon disappeared. Not sure if it really was gone, Liam sliced at the air until his arm tired.

Turning towards the cell door, he was surprised to see Teague and his friends standing in the dungeon hallway, watching dumbfounded.

"How did you get the door open?" Liam asked.

Teague held up the walking stick. "No door is locked before me when I hold this within my hand. It is the guidance of the unseen Lord. Look at Edan's ring ~ his sonship ring lights our path. We are leaving now. Come with us!"

- 318 -

"I would, for my wife left me months ago and joined the pilgrims at the Source. But I don't know if she could ever forgive me. I just couldn't leave to follow her. I felt trapped by my loyalty to the guards somehow. What I have seen these last few weeks has broken my heart, but I convinced myself that we were in the right. We needed to protect this great place in order to protect the pilgrims. I have lapped their feet like a dog for attention and respect. Here I was serving the Dragon all along! I am so ashamed," Liam's speech broke off in sobs.

Caedmon put his arm around Liam and comforted him.

"It wasn't easy for any of us. We all have failed, but that is the beauty of it! Even despite our failures, our great Lord wants us in His army. Come, Liam! Join us. What an adventure awaits you!" Carew put his hand on Liam's shoulder, speaking softly to the distraught officer. The man slumped over into Caedmon's arms.

The men looked up as the guard came striding down the corridor with four officers. All five men drew their swords and stood ready for battle. The guard stopped and eyed the men, then in a rage spoke, "You wouldn't dare! I represent the unseen Lord! If you have any respect for what is decent, then you will put those swords away."

Caedmon put his sword back in his scabbard and, taking his bow from his shoulder, he drew out an arrow and pointed it at the guard's chest.

"We not only *don't* respect you, but we are also not afraid of you. You are a poor, deceived man, and I pity you. You have lived so long under the Dragon's influence that your conscience does not even function anymore. If there was ever a time when you heard from the unseen Lord, I hope that you will remember it," Caedmon said and then let the arrow fly. It hit its mark.

The shocked Guard grabbed the arrow and pulled it from his chest. There was no wound, not even a dent. Snapping the arrow in half, the guard threw it from himself disgustedly, like a piece of refuse. A look of hatred reddened his face as he ordered the officers forward to disarm the men.

"Liam, what are you doing?" the guard yelled as Liam struck the club from the first officer's hand with his sword.

Teague and Edan ran into the foray and quickly disarmed the other three officers. Then they ran past the raging guard, who hadn't joined the battle, but had stood to one side shouting orders. The officers lay bewildered on the corridor floor and watched the backs of the pilgrims as they ran down the corridor out of sight with Liam.

"This way!" Liam said as he made a quick turn to the left and instead of running up the stairs. The men ran through a narrow, secondary hallway until their sides hurt. The corridor wove this way and that, they felt totally lost. However Liam knew exactly were he was, for he had studied these corridors and knew them by heart. He had spent many lonely hours down here since his precious wife had left him heartbroken. He hoped she would forgive him for being so blind and obstinate.

Coming to a door, he asked the men in hushed tones, to wait for him. Opening the door, he got down on his hands and knees and crawled in.

The men stood nervously looking around. What if they had just fallen for a trap? The corridor was completely blocked by broken and fallen rocks in front of them, and the only way out would be to go back the way they'd come and they knew they would be lost.

Suddenly they felt the floor beneath them begin to shake. Trembling, they waited as the very ground beneath quaked.

The Ancients say… "All the bright lights of heaven will I make dark over thee, and set darkness upon thy land, saith the Lord."

Chapter 10

Liam crawled through the small tunnel and came to a room about the size of a well. Standing, he felt along the wall and found the candle holder and flint on a ledge. Lighting the candle, he quickly began to turn a large wheel on the wall. The wheel was connected to cables that disappeared through a hole in the floor. Finally, coming to the end of the cable, he stopped and locked the wheel with a bar that was fixed to the wall. Crawling back through the tunnel he came out at the pilgrim's feet through the small door. The pilgrims were standing there looking down at him, slightly bewildered.

"Is this a trap, Officer Liam?" Carew asked, with that old edge of arrogance in his voice.

"Look up, Carew. What do you see?" Liam asked as the four men all looked up. The ceiling was gone and the darkness of the night sky spread out before them, the stars twinkling their silent greeting.

Liam walked past them to the pile of rubble and began to climb the ruined wall where stones were precisely set as footholds, like a secret ladder. He disappeared over the top and the others were quick to follow. Liam walked over to a large stone and, rolling it over, he quickly pulled the chain that was coming out of a large hole beneath it. A moss-covered stone floor slipped back into place over the corridor as a ceiling.

"Took me a long time to find this, but somehow I felt compelled to keep exploring the tunnels. I guess the unseen Lord was preparing me for this night." He smiled broadly at the pilgrims, feeling the full weight of freedom. His face becoming serious, he looked around himself. "It has gotten dark early tonight. That is strange. It is only the first watch," Liam said as he looked up at the sky.

"The unseen Lord is on the move!" Teague said. "We must hurry home to the farm. Come, Carew and Liam, we can notify your wives from there."

Teague took off at a fast walk through the forest to the main road. Edan was on his heels, and the rest followed quickly. A shadow blocked the starlight as the Dragon flew overhead, watching them flee. Swooping back into Evergreen, it went straight to the guard's quarters. Walking through the wall, the beast squeezed its large body into the chamber and drooled all over the floor.

The guard sat in front of the fireplace looking dazed, but still angry.

He began to think about how he should have dealt with Caedmon years before when he'd had his chance. His thoughts became darker and darker as he pondered the battle with the pilgrims in the dungeon. They were of the Dragon, he knew it deep within his mind!

Not once did he feel the slime that dripped from his face as the lies ran down the front of his tunic. The Dragon knew that this man was his. This guard had never once heard the unseen Lord, nor even cared to. He believed every lie the Dragon had carefully planted in his mind over his lifetime as a guard.

The man justified himself out loud. "I am head guard of all the fortresses in the area! They are so blessed to have me guarding Evergreen. I do not need to hear from the unseen Lord! He has made me to be His servant, and He chose me because of my skills. I am one of the best!"

His arrogance inflated the Dragon until its hulk filled the room.

~

The men arrived at Edan's small cabin on the edge of Briant's farm. Quietly entering the kitchen living area, the men talked in hushed tones to Edan and then quietly left him and went on to Teague's farm.

Tully stood in the sleeping chamber, holding a large club raised above her head. She had started sleeping with the club when Edan had disappeared. This night she was thankful she had, for she had been alerted by the furtive noises coming from the kitchen.

Edan walked quietly into the room and Tully swung the club. Edan saw the weapon sweeping toward him and dropped to the floor, rolling out of the way just in time.

"Tully! Its me!" Edan yelled, his voice so high pitched he sounded like a girl.

Tully dropped the club and fell onto her knees beside Edan, trembling violently. Edan slowly got up on his knees and pulled her close.

"I am sorry, my love. I did not mean to startle you. We have been on a quest and I have lots to tell you. Here, don't cry. Shhh… It is all right now," Edan soothed Tully like a parent soothing a vexed child.

Tully pulled away slightly and began to giggle. "Fortunate for you I picked too heavy a club, or I am afraid I would have been able to swing it harder and maybe even killed you. I have tried not to be afeared while you were gone, but the nights have been terrifying. Then, when it went dark so early this evening ~ I thought our world was ending."

"I believe it has to do with the unseen Lord. He is coming! Can't you feel it? Let us sleep and tomorrow I will tell you all," Edan said as he helped Tully to her feet.

~

"Where you going, Caed?" Teague asked as Caedmon turned to leave them.

"I need to get home to Briant's," Caedmon said, "Shylah will be worried, and they have been so kind to let me board. I feel in bad need of my own cot." The men bid him farewell and headed on down the road to Cathaoir's farm.

A while later, Teague slipped into his cottage and felt the cold. The fire was out. Lighting a candle, Teague peeked in their sleeping room and saw that it was empty. *Seanna must be at my parents' farm.* Turning, he ran and caught up to the others on the dark quiet road.

"Seanna must be at my parents' farm. The house is cold and no one is there. Come, let's all go to my father's and bed down for the night," Teague said.

As the men settled down on the straw of Cathaoir's barn and ate from Carew's satchel, Teague made his way to the cottage. How he loved this dear old farm. The Lord had been good to them as a family.

Upon reaching the house, he saw a candle light coming from Keelin's old sleeping room. Walking quietly to the door, he drew back the curtain and looked inside. His wife, Seanna, was sleeping with their little Arienh cradled in her arms. He was surprised to see his little girl, her eyes bright and open, looking right back at him. Walking over to the cot he knelt down and kissed her on the forehead.

"Mama is sweepin'. Be quiet, Da…" her loud whisper stirred Seanna. Her eyes flew wide open when she saw Teague in the dim candlelight. She quickly sat up and hugged him to herself.

"You are all right, my dear? I was frightened. We heard that Carew was missing, for Lana has joined the pilgrims at the Source. He disappeared after he went to the fortress. We started to think that the three of you had gone to find him," Seanna explained. Cupping his chin in her hands, she examined his face carefully, then kissed him tenderly on the lips.

"That is a homecoming worth coming home to," Teague smiled as he spoke. "And yes, Carew is asleep in the barn, though we had no idea we were going to rescue him. I will tell you about it in the morning, but I need sleep. I am bone weary."

~

The pilgrims all over the valley and mountain felt an anticipation rising in their hearts that night. The darkness had become so thick that one could actually feel it.

The Dragon slithered around its host of wicked companions. They could not see one another, but their high pitched-squeals as they jostled one another were deafening. Finally, the Dragon barked out a command for silence. The mob stood still and listened.

"The unseen Lord is up to something. This darkness is not from us. We have no power over the sun or moon, only over the minds of the people," the Dragon whispered loudly. "Now go, all of you, and bring discord and fear upon the hearts of many tonight. Hit the mediators hard. They will be thinking that this is from the unseen Lord! Bombard them with fear and let them think it is I, not Him, who commands the sky!"

There was a commotion of huge grunts and squeals as the Dragon's army made its departure. The Dragon spread its bat-like wings and headed for the Source. It had plenty of drool to spill upon the unsuspecting pilgrims. It knew that if it could get the pilgrims to fear, they would be incapable of becoming involved in the Lord's plan.

Landing in the forest right behind Dei's cottage, the Dragon listened for stirring within. Sure enough, it could hear someone mediating. Coming closer to the cottage, the beast looked inside. In the dim flicker of the candle, Dei was standing. He had his hands outstretched in silent plea and a look of sheer joy upon his face. The Dragon spewed slime out at him, and Dei fell to his knees. The slime dripped down over his head and shoulders, but Dei never stopped mediating and the look of contentment never left his face.

Just as the Dragon was about to spew more upon him, Dei spoke. "Who am I to fear the assault of the Dragon? There is only One to fear ~ He who rules my soul and life. To Him I give myself afresh."

With that final statement, Dei turned and looked right at the Dragon, seeing it for what it was. Reaching up, he wiped the drool from his head.

"Get out, liar! I know you and your kind! In the name of the unseen Lord and His armies, leave our village now!" Dei yelled on the top of his lungs. The Dragon's serpentine body recoiled. Then, striking like a viper, the beast lunged at Dei's head. Dei, using the helmet upon his head, head-butted the Dragon squarely between the eyes. The Dragon fell back, writhing in pain, holding its eye and squealing like a pig.

"Get out, I said!" Dei yelled again as he drew his sword and advanced toward the fallen Dragon. The Dragon quickly rose to its feet and flew straight into the air, circling high above the mountain and finally disappearing over the crags above. Dei sighed and wiped his helmet clean.

The night had begun early, and now it was still dark even though it was going into the morning. No sunrise. And the stars had disappeared as well.

What does it mean? Dei wondered.

～

The rooster's crow awakened Carew. Stretching out his long frame upon the hay, Carew tried to make out his surroundings, but it was still black as ink. He pondered his life and what had happened the last few days. He heard Liam stretching beside him.

"It sure is dark! Wonder what it means," Liam spoke into the stillness.

"I think it is a call from the unseen Lord," Carew answered thoughtfully. "It is like a test, somehow..."

"Will we trust Him even in the darkest time of our lives, or not? I know in the past I did not. Every time things got too rough, I wanted an easy way out. Things are different now. I want to be able to stand for the unseen Lord, no matter how hard it is."

Carew stopped speaking suddenly and both men listened. "Did you hear that noise?"

There was a heavy breathing over their heads up in the loft area. Fear like a steely hand gripped the men's hearts. The hair bristled on their necks as they heard the breathing getting louder, almost like it was floating in the air right above them. Liam's mind became confused and he felt like he was suffocating.

Reaching down, he drew his sword. Rising to his feet, he whirled the sword over his head. Carew stood and raised his shield high in the air. Light shone from the lion's head on his shield, casting its rays all around them, illuminating the entire barn.

They saw a large dog-like creature with the face of a man and horns that curled out the sides of its head like a ram. The creature was suspended in the air above them and seemed unaware that they

- 326 -

could see it. It continued to hover there and hiss out statements of fear and apprehension, trying to cast doubt on their unseen Lord.

"You are such a liar! Be gone, you foul thing from the Dragon's lair. We know your purposes!" Carew spoke, authority filling his entire being.

The creature looked stunned at first, and then it began to plead with them to let it stay or it would get in trouble. Dumbfounded, Liam stepped forward, slashing his sword just inches from the beast's belly. With the sound of a gust of wind, it was gone.

"I do believe that the Dragon's hosts are afraid of the darkness. Hmmm, it makes me wonder! Let's go into the cottage and see what the others think."

The Ancients say… "A light that shineth in a dark place, until the day dawn, and the day star arise in your hearts."

Chapter JJ

Bairrfhoinn ~ a marksman
Ide ~ thirsty

Cathaoir and Treasa fed the livestock by the light of their torches. It had been dark for two days and even now there was no sign that the sun would rise today. The air was cold and still.

Wrapping her shawl closer around her shoulders, Treasa walked back to the cottage. Cathaoir was going to check in on Teague and Keelin's homes, and he thought he would probably go to Briant and Shylah's as well. Treasa waved as she saw Cathaoir leaving in the wagon, the torch burning bright to light the road in front of him. He had put it in a special holder that he made on the side of the wagon.

Liam and Carew had left the day before to go to the Source. They had been excited, but also fearful. What if their wives would have nothing to do with them? Howbeit, they had to go, they were compelled. Treasa and Cathaoir, with Teague and Seanna, had mediated with them before they left.

Drawing their swords, they had walked out the yard following the light that emanated from their shields. Teague had sung a ballad of broken pilgrims returning to the unseen Lord and of them being turned into warriors of great stature and power. The departing men heard the song until they were out of range, their hearts rejoicing in the words and melody.

Treasa walked into their cottage and tried to look around. The candle light was so dim, she found it hard to work. Work she must, for there was their morning meal to prepare and dishes to wash from last night. Kneeling down in front of the fireplace, she stoked the fire and then, prostrating herself face down, she lay quiet.

"My precious Lord, You are Prince of this land! What is happening? The drought was awful, though I must say You have provided for us abundantly! However now, this darkness is so thick I can almost feel it. The neighbours are so fearful they won't leave their homes. The Dragon and its creatures of darkness have been very active instilling fear. We know, oh Lord, that You are in control of the weather and the light. Please come to our aid…" Treasa's pleas ended in a sob.

The unseen Lord walked into the room; with Him was Eammon. The two were talking quietly to each other. Stopping, they looked down at Treasa. They had just been at Shylah's, where she too had been mediating about the darkness and her neighbours. They had strengthened her and called her to come to Treasa's home.

It was time…

~

Shylah knocked on the door lightly, and when there was no answer, she let herself in. She had extinguished her torch outside and left it beside the well, so it was hard for her to make anything out. Finally, she could see Treasa in the dim candle light, lying on the floor in front of the fireplace. She felt the dust from the dry road clinging to her clothes, and she was cold.

Walking over to the fire, she knelt down beside Treasa and warmed her hands on the hearth. The firelight was throwing lovely flickering patterns on the wall around them.

Shylah gently laid her hand on her friend's shoulder. "The unseen Lord sent me to you," she whispered into the stillness.

"I know," Treasa mumbled, her face still resting on her arm for she had not moved. "He told me that you were coming and that Eammon was going to take us to *The Glade of the Forest Pools*. I have longed to go there again, but I have been so preoccupied with the darkness around me that I forgot about the place of light." Treasa slowly pulled herself up onto her knees and sat down beside Shylah on the floor.

- 329 -

"Caedmon left for Sunset this morning," Shylah told her. "He went with Driscoll. They are to meet the ones who are coming by ships. The unseen Lord told them it was time. But time for what?"

"I don't know. Don't you have this expectancy inside about all this?" Treasa asked enthusiastically, as she looked her friend in the eyes. She then broke out laughing.

"What is so funny?" Shylah asked in dismay.

"You are my friend. First you had flour for a covering, and now you have dust. You should see yourself! You look like a spectre," Treasa feigned fear as she laughed out loud at her friend.

Reaching up, Shylah wiped at her face. Sure enough, her face was covered in a fine layer of dust from the road. Treasa went to the kitchen and, wringing out a rag from the water pail, she brought it back for her friend to wash herself. Shylah smiled and gave her face and neck a thorough cleansing. The coolness of the water made her shudder. How she missed the sun and its warmth! She remembered how she had complained of the heat and the drought. She suddenly became aware of something.

"Treasa, do you remember how awful the drought was? Day after day of insufferable heat, with everything turning brown around us. The despair of the neighbours that their crops had withered in the fields. We did not think anything could be worse than the sun beating down mercilessly on our heads. In all our complaining, in words, and in attitude, we never once sought the Lord for the *purpose* of the drought. Maybe we were not thankful enough that we had been provided for during it. Remember how He watered our crops from beneath and gave us new wells to drink from and share with those who had none?" Shylah sighed and then went on. "I know that we were a *little* thankful, but now that the sun is gone, it's got me thinking…" Shylah's eyes took on a faraway look. "Oh, how I miss the warmth! I could use a good hot day again to warm my bones!"

Snapping back to the present, she said, "Do you think that our ungrateful attitude could have anything to do with this darkness?"

Treasa sat for a long time and mused over her friend's counsel. *Yes*, she thought. She had been thankful, although she had also been

- 330 -

sick of the constant heat and dryness. She had longed for life and greenness again. Oh, the crops had been fair, but their yard looked like a dust bowl. The garden had brought them some provision, however it had been a sad looking amount of vegetables. She had not seen what was good for the most part ~ she had been too busy thinking about what was not there. How right her friend was! Now, with the sun gone, she too had longed for a hot day, but not once had she apologized for her ungrateful attitude.

Nodding her head slowly at Shylah, tears streaming down her face, Treasa said, "My dearest friend, you have exposed my heart. I have not only been ungrateful, I have also taken all this wonderful creation the Lord's Father made for us for granted, as if it was my due. You know, yesterday I went to Bairrfhoinn's farm to visit Ide, his new bride. He met me at the door and raged about the drought and darkness. He said that it was the unseen Lord's fault."

Shylah drew in a sharp breath. She gently touched Treasa's hand urging her to continue.

Treasa took a shaky breath and then went on, "I tried to reason with him, but he told me to leave. I left the basket of bread for Ide. As I was leaving the yard, she ran after me and told me not to be angry at Bairrfhoinn, for he had almost surrendered to the unseen Lord when he saw that our crops were being looked after. When none of us shared with him, he thought that we were not worth his time. He thought if we were the unseen Lord's people, then why did He not have us tell him how to remedy the problem. He became bitter and now he wants nothing to do with us. I never felt so stricken in my heart. I asked for her forgiveness."

Shylah dropped her head in shame, for she too had not spoken with her neighbours of the Lord's provision, even though she had reached out to them with some of her harvest. She had been too silent, which was just as bad as being ungenerous. She knew it was because her heart had not been full of thanksgiving.

"Ide forgave me, you know. She told me that she had become so thirsty for change that she had cried out to the unseen Lord and He had come to her. He had told her where to dig a well, and they had. The water was sweet and good. She knew that Bairrfhoinn was angry and wanted to lash out at something other than his own self. She told me not to fret, but only mediate for him. We both cried and she thanked me for the bread and I left."

Both women began to mediate and immediately they were in *The Glade of Forest Pools*. Eammon was sitting there, waiting expectantly for them. His long blonde waves were pulled into a tail at the nape of his neck, and instead of his long green robe he had on a sky blue tunic. His face shone like ebony and his sparkling blue eyes twinkled.

"Welcome, ladies. So glad you came to join me."

Shylah and Treasa looked around in wonder. The whole place seemed alive and light. It almost hurt their eyes, for they had become accustomed to living in the darkness and gloom. They could see many others mediating around the pools. Some they knew and others they had never seen before.

"Yes, there are many new mediators," Eammon said to them. "They have joined the ranks since the great darkness was revealed."

"Revealed?" both women asked in unison.

"Why yes!" Eammon replied and then went on to explain, "First the drought, as you know, was the condition of men's minds being shown that if you rely on your own understanding, you will dry up and blow away, so to speak. Now the darkness is revealing men's hearts. An ungrateful, self-centred heart is none other than a cold heart of darkness. The unseen Lord had to show this to the people and His pilgrims to prepare them for the day that is about to come. Your hearts must be ready and your minds prepared."

Shylah sighed, nodding in sudden understanding. She walked over to the pool beside Eammon. "Shall I gaze into the pool?" she asked.

"No," said Eammon. "The Prince did not call you here to look into a pool to see the people in your world. He called you here to mediate for them," Eammon answered as he pointed to the other mediators. That is when the women noticed that the pilgrims there were not really mediating, but were distracted from their purpose. Some of them were walking around going from pool to pool and not waiting or looking into any of them. Others seemed to be preoccupied with their fingers or picking at the dust upon their clothes. Still others were lying in the grass beside the pools and appeared to be sleeping.

"Their hearts are in the right place, but their strength is gone. They cannot seem to focus or stay with anything until it is through," Eammon said. "That's why you have been brought to mediate for them. They can't seem to hear me ~ they are so young in this. You two have become seasoned warriors. Did you know that? Well, you are, and the Lord thinks highly of you. He will answer your mediation for these, His faithful pilgrims." With that said, he disappeared from their sight.

"Look at that young woman over there, Treasa. She appears to be afraid to look into her pool."

"Look ~ it is Keelin!" Shylah exclaimed.

Sure enough, there was Keelin. She would walk up to her pool and begin to kneel down, but rise and step back away from it again.

"Oh, Lord, help her!" Shylah cried out. "Give her courage and help her to do what you have called her to do. We ask on her behalf."

Immediately they saw the Lord behind Keelin. Reaching out, He pulled her into His arms. She relaxed and looked with pleasure up into His face.

"Keelin, do not be afraid to look into your pool." The women could hear His gentle voice coming like a summer breeze. "This is what I want you to do. Take your flute and begin to play it towards your pool and see what happens. Don't be afraid, my dearest one. I am with you."

Keelin pulled her flute from her pocket and, kneeling down, she began to play a soft melody over her pool. The water began to spin up like a small fountain. It swirled and bubbled to the music. The music became playful and Keelin, rising to her feet, began to dance and play around the pool. The water jumped and danced with her, around and around. The water seemed to take on the form of a young girl, leaping like a ballerina. Keelin finally stopped playing and knelt down by her pool as the water became quiet and still before her.

- 333 -

Treasa and Shylah turned away from Keelin's private moment, but not before they saw great tears rolling down her cheeks and a smile upon her face.

They spent the rest of the morning mediating for one after another of the mediators at the pools. Never before had they felt so fulfilled as they saw their mediation answered before their very eyes. Cathaoir came into the room and saw the women lying face down in front of the fire. He could hear their petitions and he quietly joined them, lifting up his neighbours and family to the unseen Lord of the land.

The Ancients say… "If therefore the light that is in thee be darkness, how great is that darkness!"

Chapter 12

Bricriu ~ poisoned tongued

Caedmon and Driscoll had driven the wagon slowly to Sunset. They could hear the groans and complaints of those on the road. They had Caedmon's torch to light their way, but many appeared to be just stumbling in the darkness without a light of any kind. *Why would they stumble around in the dark if they could easily acquire a light of some sort?* Caedmon wondered. This puzzled both men as they heard the constant complaints towards the unseen Lord.

"It's amazing, isn't it Caedmon?" Driscoll said. "They don't want anything to do with the unseen Lord of the land when things are good, and then when things are bad, they shake their fist at Him. We are a strange lot, us people!"

"Yes, we are," Caedmon responded. His mind went over the fact that even though he hadn't voiced it, on the inside he was so sick of the darkness that he had been questioning the unseen Lord about it himself.

"I, too, have been upset with the Lord about this darkness," Caedmon confessed. "I am ashamed to admit it. I might not have shaken my fist on the outside, but on the inside I have."

"You know, that's myself as well," Driscoll said after he thought for a moment. "Just because I haven't been angry, I haven't been thankful, either. Thankful that we have torches and armour that lights our path, and His presence to lead us. Thankful that we have water to drink and homes to live in, and loving family and friends… the list goes on and on."

"Look over there!" Caedmon said suddenly as he pointed to his right. Driscoll looked and was amazed as a long line of torches appeared far off into the hills.

"It must be the pilgrims coming!" Driscoll said in excited anticipation. The line of torches could be seen slowly moving up and down as the pilgrims walked steadily on to Sunset. As Driscoll and Caedmon drew closer to the line, they could see that it was about thirty people wide and they were all walking in unison. Their faces shone in the torch light. Driscoll pulled the wagon to a stop.

"They are beautiful," Caedmon said, adding, "Look at their armour. It is like ours, but different somehow." That is when both men saw that the pilgrim's shields were glowing red like they had been dipped in blood. These pilgrim's faces and purpose seemed so much more steadfast. They truly had their faces set like flint to their destination. Their ranks did not falter in the flickering torch light.

Driscoll saluted the first row that came abreast of his wagon. They, in turn, saluted back. "Greetings pilgrims!" He heralded.

"Greetings to you as well, pilgrim," a small woman called back from the second row.

"You must be coming for the gathering of the unseen Lord's pilgrims," Caedmon spoke out.

"Why yes, we are," she responded. "We are of His own people. He finally awoke us and here we are. We have travelled far from His earthly homeland. We are combining forces with His pilgrims here to wage battle against the Dragon. I must say we find this darkness very oppressive."

"Yes, it is, but it is from the unseen Lord. He has been trying our hearts and preparing us for battle. He has also made it very evident for those of the land to come to the light if they want to," Caedmon said.

The pilgrims marched silently beside the wagon to Sunset. As they approached the port village they camped on its outskirts. Their torches lit the entire countryside, and people came out of the village and watched the pilgrims. Some children ventured close and spoke to them, and their young voices filled the air with laughter. The children loved the light of the torches, and they danced around them. A few brave souls that came out asked questions regarding the gathering. Then many locals returned to their homes and gathered a few belongings to join the pilgrim camp

Caedmon and Driscoll went down to the port and waited for the ship to arrive. Gallagher and Aine should also be arriving soon, according to the unseen Lord. They had felt His presence on their entire trip to Sunset, though now as they waited at the dock, the very air seemed alive with Him.

The water lapped against the pier and they could make out the tops of the waves reflecting in their torch light. No one else was at the dock, for the people hardly left their homes and all trade and commerce had stopped. The men had left their team of horses at the abandoned livery stable. They had fed and watered them and walked to the dock to wait.

"Do you miss Gilroy?" Caedmon asked.

"Yes. He was the dearest and most loyal of all friends. There are times when I just long to go to him, but I know that day will be here before we know it and we will all be together again," Driscoll replied quietly as he leaned against the rail over the water.

Caedmon tried to feel as confident, though the darkness was pressing in too hard on him and he could feel it entering his soul.

"I want to believe that. Though, this darkness has made me feel despair. Sometimes I wonder if it is all true or just a myth. Then I remember the encounters I have had with the unseen Lord and my time beyond the mist." Caedmon's voice trailed off as he tried to explain his feelings.

"Yes, this darkness has been a trial. Everything that I took for granted has been taken away. The crops are dying and we don't have much food stored. The gardens were producing fine, but now it seems that they too are struggling. They need the sun! I have learned to think more of the big picture than my own small existence lately," Driscoll replied. With a sigh, as he tried to peer across the open water, he said, "Caedmon, it does not appear they are arriving tonight. Let's go back to the livery stable and sleep. Tomorrow will bring much activity and we will need our strength."

"You go on ahead without me, Driscoll. I will be along shortly," Caedmon answered and sat down on the pier and looked down at the water shimmering in the torch light. "I know my way back. Don't worry. Take the torch with you. I can feel my way along and if it gets too overwhelming I will draw my sword. It will show me the way." Driscoll looked unsure, but then, shrugging his shoulders, he walked away, leaving Caedmon in the inky blackness.

Time slowly passed and Caedmon enjoyed the stillness. The only sound was the quiet lapping of the water against the pier.

"You don't really believe this is from the unseen Lord, do you?" A soft, gentle whisper came like a breeze in the stillness of the dark.

"He would never cause such chaos…"

Caedmon at first thought he had imagined the voice, and then reasoned within himself that it sounded like Eammon. He hadn't been in mediation for such a long time that he had even forgot about Eammon until now. He wondered what was happening at *The Glade of the Forest Pools.*

"Eammon, is that you?" Caedmon asked into the darkness, trying hard to see.

"No, I am not Eammon. You don't know me, Caed? That hurts…" the voice took on a contrite note that touched Caedmon's heart with regret. Caedmon began to shiver as he felt the soft drops of rain beginning to fall. Reaching up, he wiped his face and recoiled at the feeling of not rain, but *ooze* dripping off his fingers.

"You liar, Dragon! It is you! Leave me in the name of the unseen Lord and His armies!" Caedmon's voice rose in defiance, but he did not stand or even draw his sword. The Dragon stepped back and watched the young man. When Caedmon did not move, the beast moved in closer and tried a different tactic. Extending one of its long talons, it began to submerge it into Caedmon's mind and then slowly stir it around.

Caedmon, feeling confused, tried to rise to his feet, only to fall back again. What was the matter with him? He struggled to rise again, but despair like he had never felt before overwhelmed him. Why had he not gone with Driscoll? Why had he come to Sunset in the first place? He hadn't heard from the unseen Lord for many days. Maybe he had only made it all up.

The more the thoughts whirled in his head, the wearier he became. What was the point? He wasn't of any use to any of them. With those hurtful thoughts pounding in his head, he rolled onto his stomach and rose slowly to his feet. Like a drunkard, Caedmon staggered into the darkness, with the Dragon walking slowly behind him and continually stirring his thoughts with despair.

Caedmon came to a large building. He could see a light shining out from underneath the door. He could hear music and laughter coming from within, with the delicious smell of mutton stew wafting through the air. Finding courage, he knocked loudly on the door.

A small wiry man opened the door a crack, asking, "Can I help you? Oh excuse me, you are a traveller. Come in, come in! Boys, make room for this lad at your table ~ he's a foreigner, I can tell. What brings you to my door on this dark and ominous night?"

"I am lost," Caedmon shyly answered.

"Ain't we all... and that is a fact! Ain't we all!" the man responded. "My name is Bricriu. I am a man of my word around these parts. Now where are you going? Maybe I could help ya!"

Caedmon took the bench that was offered to him and began to eat of the stew that was set before him. Looking around, he was surprised to see that the light in this tavern was coming from a pool near the hearth. It was only two arm lengths wide, but looked deep, like a well. "I am waiting for someone to arrive on a ship, but my friend and I are sleeping at the livery. It is deserted."

"No one is around there, that is for sure," Bricriu answered and the men in the room laughed as if something hilarious had been said. Caedmon stopped eating and looked up bewildered.

"Don't be baffled boy, don't be!" Bricriu went on, "Look, we all be a little vexed about this darkness. Now what kind of unseen Lord would let this happen to decent folks anyway? You know those pilgrims are always spouting off about how good their unseen Lord is. Well, I tell you, this is not good, is it?"

"No, it is not," Caedmon conceded.

"I know that it will work out in the end," he added with more confidence than he felt. Hidden in a corner, the Dragon smiled and the drool from its large gaping mouth ran into the pool.

"Sir, why does your pool shine with light?" Caedmon asked.

"Oh, that is a remarkable pool, that is. The darker it gets outside, the brighter my pool becomes. People from all over come for my advice and as I share with them, my pool get brighter and brighter. It is a pool of man's wisdom it is, that it is!" Bricriu answered with a large bow and tip of his hat.

Caedmon felt himself relax a little, but his conscience kept reminding him of another pool he had gazed into years before. It too had given off a green, iridescent light, but there was no wisdom to be found in it ~ only lies and despair.

"Finish your stew and stay the night. In the morning we will direct you to the livery stable. You can take some of my pool in a glass and it will light your way."

"Oh, I have my sword to light my way," Caedmon answered innocently.

The little man rose high on his heels and let out a long, eerie howl. The other men rose to their feet and closed in around Caedmon. The Dragon began stirring its talon madly in Caedmon's thoughts. It needed him to relax and forget about his sword.

"What do you mean, *sword*? Are you one of those beastly pilgrims? I heard they are gathering on the outskirts of our village this very night! They are up to no good, I tell you! I be telling you that you better not be one of them." Bricriu's voice was full of malice, but Caedmon could also hear the fear in it.

Caedmon slowly got up and backed away from the table. "Your pool is none other than the pool of the Dragon, and it feeds it with your lies. The more you elevate yourself and your wisdom above the unseen Lord's wisdom, it glows brighter. However, it is a deceptive glow and it will not be able to permeate the darkness outside. If you don't believe me, try it. Go on ~ if you are so brave, then take some and try it," Caedmon's voice rose with authority and the confusion began to leave him. The Dragon leapt from behind Caedmon and sprang to the side of Bricriu.

"All right," Bricriu said, "and when it shines outside, I will be back and me and my friends will rip you limb from limb!" Bricriu filled a glass flask with the pool water and stepped through the door. The men inside ran to the window to watch, but Bricriu had disappeared from their sight into the inky blackness. Caedmon drew his sword and the men whirled on him. The sword shone a magnificent red light and blinded the men. Grabbing their eyes, they cried out in pain and pleaded with Caedmon to put it away.

"Not until you acknowledge the Lord and denounce the Dragon!" Caedmon bellowed.

"We denounce the Dragon! We do! There is only one Lord, only one! The unseen Lord!" As the men yelled, a wonderful peace filled the room and the light in the pool faded. Caedmon walked over to a lamp and lit it. Then he put his sword back in its scabbard. The men fell to their knees with tears falling from their faces.

The Dragon whirled from the room. "I will get you yet, Caedmon!" it hissed.

"I don't think so, Dragon. I am not yours to get. I already have been found by He who will never leave me, even if I leave Him. Be gone, you reptile of evil," Caedmon spoke with authority as he drew his sword again. The Dragon hissed and squealed as it darted up and out of the tavern and flew over the village, looking for its servant, Bricriu.

Caedmon told the men where the pilgrims were camped and invited them to join him on the morrow. They agreed, but were still too shaken to talk much. Caedmon left them and walked down the narrow street with his sword drawn. Out of the corner of his eye, he saw the shadow of lurking creatures run for cover down dark alleys, away from the light of his sword. Finding the port, he retraced his steps to the livery stable. The glow of the torch light met him and warmed his heart. *How easy it is to fall away,* he thought. *One only has to concentrate on what we don't know, and what we do know quickly fades from our hearts and minds.* Caedmon smiled as the thought reminded him of Sophronia.

"Yes, I am here, Caedmon," she said.

"I have made a terrible blunder, dear lady," Caedmon hung his head in shame.

"Yes, but then you made a wonderful recovery! The wisdom of this world seems light and wonderful when we have become lost, but it is not the way out! Remember, when you feel lost, Caedmon, to ask the unseen Lord for wisdom and He will send me to you. I will always come to those who ask." Sophronia smiled as she spoke and then, squeezing Caedmon's hand she disappeared from his sight.

The Ancients say... "The Sun of righteousness arise with healing in His wings."

Chapter 13

The glow of the torches aboard the ship shone across the waves to the dock. Driscoll and Caedmon waited anxiously for Gallagher and Aine, hoping that they would be on board. Soon the ship slipped close to the dock and the ropes were flung and secured. Able sailors deftly swung down onto the dock. The gang plank was lowered and the pilgrims came down the plank carrying their torches and few possessions in bags slung over their shoulders.

Caedmon spotted Gallagher and Aine and rushed through the crowd to hug him tightly.

Aine let out a laugh at his side. What about me ~ don't I count?"

Caedmon turned and, bowing, he kissed her outstretched hand.

"Yes, you count, fair lady. Come, we are traveling to the outskirts of the village where many pilgrims from the Lord's homeland are already gathered. Did Pualani and Kikeona come too?"

"Yes ~ there they are! Pualani, come this way," Aine called over the heads of many of the island pilgrims.

Kikeona strode through the people and embraced Caedmon. Pualani lowered her eyes and a blush stole over her face. "Oh, we were so hoping that you would meet us, our young friend. Were we not, Pualani?" Kikeona enthusiastically spoke.

"Why yes, grandfather! That is true. I am so glad you came to meet the boat, Caedmon," Pualani's raised her eyes to Caedmon's as she spoke. Caedmon smiled and relieved her fears. He held nothing against her ~ she knew it in an instant ~ but then why would he? She knew him to be a man of the unseen Lord and that his integrity was known to all.

Caedmon took Pualani's bag and then the five led the large group of pilgrims through the dark streets to the camp. When they arrived, the greeting was one of joy. The Lord's own people greeted the newcomers with genuine concern and welcomed them to their fires to eat a hearty meal. They all knew they would need their strength for the inland march to meet with the rest of the pilgrims before the battle.

As the pilgrims finished their morning meal, light began to glow in the sky on the horizon. Beautiful colours of pink to crimson were shooting high into the air like dancers around a fire. The glorious sight became brighter and brighter until a cheer could be heard coming from behind them in the village. The sun was rising and spreading its rays of warmth and promise over the land!

The people began to throng out of the village and join with the happiness of the pilgrims. The sun was rising! Everyone was rejoicing.

Caedmon and Driscoll stole away to the hillside outside the camp and there they fell to their knees. They raised their swords high above their heads while the tears streamed down their cheeks. The sun came into full view and chased the last traces of the darkness away. The warmth of the rays felt wonderful on their upturned faces.

Not able to find the words to express their gratitude to the unseen Lord, they just smiled and let the light warm their faces with their eyes shut.

"You did well, My faithful servants," the unseen Lord spoke gently to the men.

Caedmon began to sob and bowed himself to the ground. He could not lift his face because of the great shame from the night before and his walk into the darkness. The Lord laid a hand gently on his shoulder, but Caedmon shook it off. Leaping to his feet, he ran down the hill and through the camp.

"What is wrong with him, my Lord?" Driscoll asked with concern.

"He has let shame separate himself from Me. He must not forget that I died so he would not have to be shamed," the unseen Lord said. "He has always been able to find me and talk to me when he has desired. He has been one of my most enthusiastic pilgrims! But this understanding he lacks ~ the ability to admit his error and then leave his shame and come to me. However I will not leave him. I will send Carden after him right away."

"Carden?" Driscoll wondered aloud.

"Yes, one of my generals. He is in charge of my sheep, especially the wayward ones. He has shepherded you many times in the past. When you have felt that I was far from you and did not hear you or care for you. I would send Carden to sing over you and encourage your heart to believe."

"Yes, I remember those times," Driscoll said in awe. "I would suddenly feel better, like I could go on. The most recent was when you called Gilroy beyond the veil ~ oh, how I needed those shepherd songs then. Thank you, my Lord, thank you for sending your shepherd to Caedmon. Caedmon has been a good friend and we need him desperately right now. I did not even know that he had fallen," Driscoll replied with mixture of sadness and relief.

~

Caedmon ran until he could run no farther; his sides hurt and he slowed to a walk. He was far down the road that headed back to his valley. Many had called to him as he had run by, but he had ignored them and kept going. He wanted to be alone! Why wouldn't they just let him be alone in his pain?

The trees came quite close to the road and Caedmon felt eyes watching him from the forest. *Probably the Dragon,* he thought. What did it matter? He was acting like he was one of the Dragon's any way. He felt more than heard someone walking behind him, just behind the trees to his left. Stopping, he held his breath. He slowly turned and looked intently into the forest and saw someone standing, looking right at him. It was Carden!

"Caedmon, my lad! Why are you out here on this lonely piece of road? Are you lost, my friend?" Carden asked, with a smile playing at the corners of his mouth.

"You know very well what I am doing out here," Caedmon responded dully and turned to walk away.

"So now you are angry with me? What have I done to cause you such discomfort and pain?" Carden asked earnestly, "Let's see, was it because you made a mistake and now you blame me for it?"

Caedmon stopped and looked at Carden, "What do you mean? I am not mad at anyone! I just want to be alone… To sulk, I guess," Caedmon added this last statement with a sad note in his voice. "I am a coward. I let the darkness overwhelm me. I failed!"

"It seems to me that you *won*," Carden said. He put his hand up to stop Caedmon from responding, and then walking closer, he laid his arm across Caedmon's shoulders.

"Let me tell you what we saw beyond the mist in *The Glade of the Forest Pools*. We saw two women doing mediation for you. We saw you going down into the blackness and then suddenly you drew your sword. Do you understand that at that exact moment, those ladies were crying and doing battle against the Dragon for you? They saw you ~ the Prince let them see you ~ and they did not judge you, but went to battle for you."

Carden stopped by a large rock and drew Caedmon down onto it to sit. Caedmon buried his face in his hands, and his shoulders slumped under the great weight of shame.

"They saw my shame? I can never face them again!"

Carden began to sing. His song was the story of a little goat that used his horns to get his own way. Caedmon looked up in surprise at the childish tune, but held his peace when he saw the serious look upon Carden's face and that his eyes tightly closed.

The song painted the lovely picture of green pastures and this playful little goat frolicking and playing with his friends around the goatherd's feet. As the little goat grew, so did his horns and he began to see that he could make his own way in the pasture and did not have to rely on the goatherd's staff to protect him. Then one day he went off by himself. A wolf came and told the little goat how big and strong he was. The little goat threw back his head and bleated loud, telling the wolf to leave or he would ram him with his horns.

The wolf pretended to be afraid and started to come forward slowly. The little goat ran straight into the jaws of the mighty wolf and the wolf grabbed him and flung him over his shoulder. The little goat let out a bleat of surprise and pain. The goatherd had seen that his little goat was missing and he was out searching for him. When he saw the wolf leap onto the fallen goat, he let out a war cry. The startled wolf tried to flee, but the staff of the goatherd caught it on the throat and sent it hurtling into the air. The wolf hit the ground to move no more.

Carden's song took on a hushed tone like a lullaby.

Gently, oh so gently, the goatherd picked up the wounded little goat and wrapped him in his robe. The little goat looked afraid because he had run away from the only one who could truly protect him. However, the goatherd held the goat close to his heart and carried it back to his home. He wrapped its wounds and calmed its fears, because he loved his little goat.

Then Carden sang of the unseen Lord's love of his own dear pilgrims, especially the ones who, through their own carelessness, had become wounded and ashamed.

The song finally ended and Caedmon raised his tear streaked face to Carden.

"How long since you have sung a song, Caedmon?"

"I have no song to sing, Carden. My song seemed to disappear in the darkness, or maybe in the dungeon of the fortress. I do not know when I lost it, but there is no song within me. I have tried to sing, but it is a hollow sound. That is all I can seem to make," Caedmon answered truthfully.

"You might be surprised. I think your little horns were getting in the way of the song," Carden answered, and his laughter filled the air with joy.

Caedmon looked up in shock, but Carden was gone. He sat for a long time and looked at his hands ~ the hands he had dedicated to the unseen Lord. He got slowly to his feet and started to walk back to the camp.

"Lord, I am sorry. I need you. Please cut off my horns!" Caedmon called out into the morning air. A woman's laughter stopped him dead in his tracks. Looking first one way and then another, he searched for the source of the laughter, but there was nothing or nobody to be seen. He started on his way, but again he heard the

- 347 -

laughter. She sounded so familiar. Like the trilling of a little girl, yet mature like a woman. Aithne!

"Yes, Sir Caedmon, it is I! I have come to let you have a good arrow to the heart, but I see that you have chosen to humble yourself and cry out instead," Aithne's childlike voice held the authority of a soldier.

"Well, you might as well strike me anyway," Caedmon said, still unable to shake the feelings of worthlessness.

"Waste of a good arrow it would be," Aithne replied and jumped down from the high limb from which she had been watching Caedmon on the road.

"There you are, my little friend," Caedmon said and stuck out his hand. Aithne darted to him and gave his hand a good shaking. "Have you come for the great battle with the Dragon?" Caedmon asked the fierce little warrior.

"No, I am afraid not. I've come to prepare the pilgrims for the battle. That is what we do, you know. We prepare you and then you do the fighting," Aithne giggled this out and drew her bow out and carefully stroked it.

"Though I must say, I like a good fight."

"I am sure you do!" Caedmon could feel the gloom leaving him as he spoke with this child warrior of another realm. He heard the flutter of wings and knew that she would be leaving him soon. "Aithne, have you been to the valley?" Caedmon asked, thinking of his friends back home.

Aithne nodded her head and her blonde curls bounced in the wind.

"How are they? Has the sun risen there as well?" Caedmon asked, realizing that he had been so focused on himself that he had forgotten about those who meant so much to him. He had not mediated for his friends at all, and for that he felt truly sorry.

"They are struggling with their own issues, but overall they are doing well and preparing for battle. They long for your return, though. Yes, the sun has risen there this morning ~ in fact, just now it is coming over their mountains. What rejoicing will be sung there!"

Aithne leapt onto the back of the swan that had landed beside her and, with a giggle and a blown kiss, she was gone.

The Ancients say... "He shall turn the heart of the fathers to the children, and the heart of the children to their fathers."

Chapter 14

aedmon knew that he had to face the bitterness that kept surfacing in his heart. His thoughts kept returning to his experience in *The Glade of the Forest Pools*. It was time to go to his father and speak of what he had closed up inside for years. Maybe then his heart would finally be free to serve the unseen Lord wholly.

He hurried back to Driscoll and told him that he had to go to his father's village, but promised he would meet up with them before they reached the river's Source. Driscoll held him at arm's length for a long time, looking deep into his eyes.

"Yes, it is of the unseen Lord," Driscoll finally spoke. "Go! I will mediate for you. Until we meet again, dear boy."

The men clasped arms and Caedmon nodded his head as he turned to go. For the first time in a very long, long while, Caedmon felt strength and purpose enter his entire being. This was right, even though in his heart of hearts he knew that it would be very difficult.

The hot sun beat down on the dry earth and the dust blew across the land as Caedmon walked to his father's village. It was in the same valley as Sunset, so he knew that he would arrive there by evening.

After many hours of travel, his feet ached so badly that he finally stopped and sat on a large boulder by the road. Taking off his worn shoes, he rubbed his feet while he rested. No one was coming along the road as far as he could see. He knew that the Dragon was close by because he could feel the heaviness that clung to the beast, but he tried his best to ignore it. He had his sword and shield ready. Rubbing his hot, tired feet he remembered when Gilroy and himself would sit on the river's bank and let their feet rest in the cool, refreshing water of the Unchanging River. A sob caught in his throat at the unexpected memory. How he missed his dear friend and those precious times! Life had changed so radically in the last few months.

The Dragon became alert as he noticed Caedmon wipe a tear from his eye. Warily, the beast snuck up on Caedmon from behind and stroked his forehead with his long talon. Thoughts of self-pity swirled suddenly in Caedmon's mind. He leapt to his feet, and, drawing his sword, he whirled and slashed in one smooth movement. The Dragon felt the hot sear of the steel slice its chest. Screaming in anger and pain, the Dragon flew up in the air.

Caedmon cried out, "Come back, you spineless beast! I command you in the name of the Lord and His armies, stop your worthless lies! I know you and I know your tactics!"

"If you know me so well, then why are you crying like a babe?" the Dragon hissed in reply as it spewed green slime.

"I have nothing to say to you of the workings of my heart!" Caedmon roared. Then lifting his shield over his head, he flung the descending slime to the ground.

The Dragon swooped down with its talons outstretched to tear the shield from Caedmon's hand. Wrath was boiling over inside the hulking frame of the beast. Caedmon ducked down to the ground and rolled out of the way. Then, jumping to his feet, he again swiped as the Dragon tried to ascend quickly from its missed attempt. Caedmon's sword struck the talons of its back legs. The beast, losing its balance, crashed into the ground and disappeared from Caedmon's sight.

Caedmon, brushing the dust from his clothes, put his shoes back on. Laughing almost hysterically, he recognized that his worn shoes were really Arthmael's shoes. His eyes had been opened to the unseen realm during the attack of the beast. He took his canteen and carefully cleaned his sword and put it back in the scabbard on his hip. Taking his sleeve, he polished his shield until the Lion's head began to shine in the sun a brilliant red. His precious armour.

As he thought of his wayward time of doubt and despair, a song began to rise in his heart. Flinging his shield up over his shoulder and straightening his helmet, Caedmon began his journey again.

The song whirled inside his heart, until finally the music came and the words poured forth.

~

Teague, feeling overcome with loneliness, walked down the road to the Unchanging River. The sun had come back this morning and with it warmth, but also the knowledge that the land was still dry and parched. The rain that had come when they met the unseen Lord seemed to have been soaked up by the dry earth like a sponge, leaving very little moisture for the plants and fields. What would become of their farms?

Teague missed Edan and Caedmon. Kicking at a stone, he dropped to his knees beside the dried, parched river bed. Memories of times past flooded his soul.

He remembered going to meet Caedmon and his first battle with the Dragon. He remembered his commissioning from the unseen Lord. He remembered the unseen Lord telling them to prepare for the great battle. His heart began to pound in his ears. *Why,* he wondered, *was his heart racing?*

The skulking frame of a small raccoon-like creature sat behind Teague. Its bright yellow eyes and long ears twitched with anticipation. Teague finally sat back and looked up at the sky, letting out a long sigh.

The ugly creature rose on its hind legs and began to come closer to Teague. Its belly looked like the belly of a reptile, and the long striped tail wound around itself like it was a snake. As it moved closer, a strong smell of sulphur began to fill the air around Teague. Turning, Teague saw the creature, who falsely thought itself invisible.

Teague, pretending that he hadn't seen the Dragon's messenger, lay back on the dry ground and watched a lone cloud fly across the sky. It looked like a flying swan, and the thought made Teague smile, even though there was a slight apprehension growing in his heart. The creature was moving in on him ~ he could feel it. It moved right next to Teague and, reaching out its front paw-like hand, it tried to take off Teague's helmet.

- 352 -

Just as it reached for the helmet, Teague's hand came up suddenly and grabbed the creature by the wrist. He quickly wrenched the wrist down, pinning the creature to the ground. It began to howl and shriek.

"Tell your master that there will be no sneaking up on the Lord's army any longer!" Teague said through clenched teeth. Then, giving a final twist to the wrist, he let it go. The creature let out a long scream and disappeared.

"Good fighting, my friend," a musical, voice trilled out. Teague looked up to see Aithne. A smile broke out over his face and he quickly got to his feet.

"What brings you to our world, my young warrior?" Teague asked as he stretched out his hand in greeting. Aithne took the offered hand and shook it firmly. Teague winced from the grasp of the strong hand that was more like the hand of a seasoned warrior than the hand of the child she looked like.

"Well, as far as young goes, in your years you would not even be able to imagine my true age. In regards to my being here ~ the battle is about to begin. The enemy has sent many spies into the Lord's camp of warriors, just as you have just experienced. I have been sent to tell you to get everyone to the go the Source. The Lord will meet you there." Aithne gave the orders in such a way that it did not seem like orders at all, but more like an exciting anticipated celebration invitation. She went on, "Caedmon and Driscoll will be returning soon with the army from beyond the sea and the Lord's *own* people's army. Many others will meet there to prepare for battle as well."

Aithne went on, "Caedmon needs your mediation. You must get the others to mediate today for him. He is going to wake... or should I say undo... No, let me say he is about to..." Aithne trailed off incomprehensibly.

Teague looked at her with raised eyebrows, waiting for her to finish.

"For the first time I am at a loss of words," Aithne giggled. "Caedmon is going to meet with his father and speak the truth to set him free. And by him, I mean both of them."

Teague looked on amazed as Aithne leapt upon her swan and disappeared. *So it was a swan, not a cloud,* Teague thought, smiling to himself.

Striding down the road to home, Teague straightened his shoulders and began to sing a warrior's song of victory. The enemy's horde shuddered as he walked up the road. They had been marching to Cathaoir's farm to cause havoc among the mediators who were meeting there. Hearing the song and seeing the glint of Teague's armour, they thought better of it and left to find the Dragon. They were afraid of Teague when he was alert and seeing.

The raccoon-like lizard shuddered as it ran into the midst of the pack, holding its wrist in agony.

~

Caedmon reached his father's village just as the sun was low on the mountains. The village, not unlike any other village that Caedmon had been to, was grubby and smelled foul. Human refuse and litter was everywhere, but in the village square everything was neat and tidy around the well. Caedmon made his way to the well and sat on the stone bench that circled it. He knew that eventually someone would ask him his business.

A small man, vaguely familiar to Caedmon, approached cautiously. "Scully!" Caedmon cried.

Stopping abruptly, Scully whirled to run, but Caedmon had already run up to him and held onto him firmly by the arm.

"Why are you afraid of me?" Caedmon asked him.

Scully squirmed to free himself from Caedmon's iron grip. Finding he couldn't, he finally resigned himself and stopped struggling. "I was afraid you would blame me for your mother's death. I tried to get to you on the ship to tell you that she was ailing, but you had already left. When I came back, she was dead. She was awfully sick. She had been crying out for me to get you."

"I know, Scully, I know. I saw you when I was on the ship, but I thought you were waving farewell. The unseen Lord came to me on board the ship and told me Mom had passed over," Caedmon's voice trailed off in sadness.

- 354 -

"Then you are all right with things then?" Scully asked incredulously.

"I suppose so, yes! I know that she could not make it in this world. She was so weak, but in her heart she wanted Him. The Lord knew that and in her weakest moment He came to her to take her home…" Caedmon smiled, thinking of the unseen Lord. "He never stops reaching out to us even to the end," Caedmon finished. He stared at the wizened old man, and his heart went out to the old reprobate.

Scully dropped his gaze and moved slightly back from Caedmon, who had released the man's arm. He did not like the way Caedmon was looking at him ~ his old suspicious mind could not believe anyone could care for him for nothing in return.

"Why did you come here?" Scully asked, still looking down at Caedmon's feet.

Caedmon decided to be honest with Scully and ask him where his father lived. "I am looking for my father. His name is Vaughan. He probably works in a mill. He has two sons and I do believe his wife has left him."

"Yes, I know where he lives. Over the baker's shop where I work. He is alone now… his sons have grown and left him. He is a miserable man, though, I am warning you." Scully gave all this information quite indifferently. Caedmon could tell he did not care for his father, but then he had not cared for him either.

"That is where we first met, Scully?" Caedmon said, referring to the bakery. "Sometimes life does make full circles, doesn't it?" Caedmon spoke with a genuine smile on his face as his mind swept back to his young days at the bakery.

"Yes, I suppose sometimes. The door on the side there leads to the flat up above. Good luck, lad." With that, Scully ducked his head and scurried away into the dwindling crowd in the square.

Caedmon, squaring his shoulders, headed for the door by the bakery. In front of the flat's door, Caedmon stopped. "Are you here, Lord?"

"Yes, my friend. Do not be afraid. I will not leave you, but this is something you must do. Your friends are mediating for you right now in *The Glade of the Forest Pools*."

Caedmon, with renewed purpose, wrapped on the door in front of him. After a moment, he heard heavy footsteps coming down the stairs.

"Who's there?" a grumpy voice yelled from beyond the door.

"It is me, Caedmon, your son. I have come to see you," Caedmon spoke loudly through the closed door.

He could hear scuffling inside and the door opened a crack. His father peeked out at him and then, opening the door wide, he invited him in. They climbed the stairs to Vaughan's small flat. "Sorry for the mess, but that wife I had provided so much for has left me. So have my sons. No one appreciates what you do for them. I work and work... Oh, sit down." Vaughan moved the pile of clothes off of the bench. His hair was pulled back in a greasy tail at the nape of his neck. His hair was white and his face lined from bitterness and worry.

Caedmon, taking the seat offered to him, wondered what he should say or how he could start the conversation. However, his father spoke first. "So, after all this time you've come to see me," Vaughan could not keep the sarcasm out of his voice. "And I here was the one that reached out to you first."

"Reached out to me first?" Caedmon sprang to his feet incredulously, anger rippling through his being.

"Where were you when I was growing up with my ale-addicted mother? Where were you when I needed you most desperately? Reach out to me ~ you are one of the most self-absorbed, selfish men I have ever met. I thought maybe, just maybe, there was hope for you. I felt the unseen Lord wanted me to come to you, to warn you of your ways and to let you know He is on the move and the great battle is to begin..." Caedmon sputtered to a stop.

The invisible grip on his shoulder tightened. He knew the unseen Lord, was wanting him to be honest and forthright.

Before Vaughan could respond, he went on, "All you have ever cared about is your work and how someday you would have

- 356 -

everything to prove to everyone that you really are a big man. You and I both know that it is not what a man *does* that makes him big, but who he *is*. He must think of his family first, then himself. He must seek the unseen Lord and His will, not his own!" Caedmon's voice rose in passion.

Vaughan's jaw hung open and he tried to sputter a response, but no sound came out.

Caedmon continued. "You never even tried to get my mother and I to return. You were not willing to change your ways even a little to make me ~ your son! ~ a home. You have complained to everyone about how horrible your wives and children are, but did you ever consider that you were a horrible father? No! It is all about you and *your* work and *your* life!" Caedmon finished and sat down.

Vaughan stared at him in shock, his mouth still gaping open. He slowly sat on the edge of his cot and began to ring his hands together, trying to think of a way to justify himself.

Caedmon reached up and squeezed the hand on his shoulder, feeling spent but very relieved and almost joyous.

A quiet whisper came to Caedmon's ear.

"Invite him on your journey to the Source. Don't be moved by what you see! I am with you."

"Da…" Caedmon waited for his father to respond, and when he showed no signs, Caedmon went on, "Would you like to go to the Source of the Unchanging River with me? I want you to come and be in the unseen Lord's army. He wants you to come. He sent me here. He is here now, too."

Caedmon waited quietly for some response, and when none came, he got up and walked over to his father. Laying his hand gently on his father's bent head, he began to implore the unseen Lord out loud to intervene in his father's life.

Vaughan jerked away and then, rising to his feet, began pacing the floor. Tears streamed down his face. Everything was screaming out inside himself to get rid of his son, to throw him out of the flat. The Dragon's emissary was stalking behind him. The small reptilian creature kept poking Vaughan in the back, causing pain and discomfort to his soul.

Caedmon, seeing the creature's shadow, drew his sword and began to wipe it across his sleeve. The beast immediately became aware of the sword and hissed out its displeasure. Caedmon, seeing the creature fully now, raised the sword and pointed it straight in the creature's face. It squealed in anguish and disappeared as his father fell to the floor and began to thrash and roll about. Caedmon strode over and taking out one of his arrows from his quiver, he drew his bow and let loose the arrow at his father's chest. Vaughan became still as the arrow penetrated his heart and disappeared within his chest.

Caedmon sat down on the floor beside his father and waited for what seemed to be several hours. The light from the window had left a long time before and the only light in the room was from a dim lamp on the table. Finally Vaughan opened his eyes and stared about himself. He reached his hands toward the ceiling as great sobs shook his frame.

"I am clean! I am forgiven! He has forgiven me!" Vaughan repeated the statements over and over in quiet wonder. Caedmon, getting up from the floor, walked over to the window and looked out on the darkened village square. In the dim lights coming from windows, Caedmon could see the clutter and debris of human waste around the square and could not wait to get to the Source away from the filth of the village.

"Will you come with me?" he asked again.

"Yes ~ that is ~ if you will forgive me, my son!" Vaughan said hesitantly.

"I forgive you, Da. I did a long time ago. I knew after the unseen Lord showed me that if you did not face your own failings honestly, then there would be no hope for you. So I came. I am so glad that you made things right with the unseen Lord!" Caedmon said.

"Now pack lightly. We must be off tonight. Do not look alarmed; our swords will light the way and if not, the unseen Lord will direct us in the dark."

Vaughan left some coins on the table to pay his rent for the month and then quietly slipped through the doorway, following his son.

- 358 -

The Ancients say… "Thou fool, this night thy soul shall be required of thee."

Chapter 15

Scully crept up to the loft above the stables where he had a room. How dare that Caedmon speak so high and mighty to him? He rubbed his chest, for the soreness was spreading. He would have to go see his boss about a few days off. He was so tired.

Rolling onto his side, he tried to find a comfortable spot on his straw tick. The dingy room suddenly was full of light. Scully sat up and rubbed his eyes wondering if he was dreaming.

"Who's there?" he croaked out.

"It is I," the unseen Lord spoke gently. "I have come to ask you something. Are you ready?"

"Ready? Ready for what?" Scully asked insolently. "I am ready to go to sleep and mind my own business. I haven't hurt anyone or murdered or lied. I just live a quiet life. Why would you ask me that, anyway?"

"I care for you deeply and I have made it possible for you to be free from all the gossip and hurtful things you have said about others," the unseen Lord replied softly.

"What?! That is ridiculous. I have not gossiped. I am a man of my word and I only share the facts. Better to learn the facts about people before someone tells you lies. Gossiping is about lying, and I don't lie!" Scully's voice rose in agitation.

"When one tells something about someone else based on what he has heard, it is gossip. If one only has interest in the information for selfish reasons and has no care for the individual that they are talking about, it is gossip. If one gathers information for the sole purpose of telling others they are a gossip," the Lord said emphatically.

"You don't know me. Go away!" shrilled Scully.

"Are you sure? Your time is at hand," the unseen Lord answered earnestly.

"Yes, I am sure. My time… Right… Right! As if you know when my time was up. I am fine, just a little tired. Go away!" Scully responded as he turned his back to the light. The light began to fade from the room and soon it was in utter darkness.

Scully could feel someone looking at him and slowly turned over in the dark. A pair of red glowing eyes was staring at him.

"Now what do you want?" Scully said sarcastically.

Realizing it was not the unseen Lord, he said, "Who are you?"

The Dragon laughed at the audacity of the little man. Scully was not moved by the evil chuckle. He began to breathe laboriously and hold his chest as the pain was getting sharper. He wished the visions of the night would leave him alone.

"Just leave me alone!" he cried out as he tried to sit up and get his breath. He fell back on the bed gurgling and gasping as the Dragon spewed slime on the small man. Taking one final breath, his eyes flying wide open, he sighed, "Just leave me alone…"

The Dragon pulled Scully from the room. As Scully looked back, he saw his body lying on the straw tick.

"No!" he screamed to the deaf ears of the Dragon.

His time *had* run out.

~

More people gathered during the night at the farm, and among them was Shylah and her family. The little water, that they had, they barrelled and put on their wagons. Some came with only their packs on their backs, others brought their horses to ride.

Early in the morning they all left, starting out to go to the river's Source. There was little talk as they could feel the seriousness of the time they were in. They had listened to the Dragon's lies for so long that they did not trust themselves to even share what they had heard from the unseen Lord of late. Instead they just enjoyed the quiet companionship, knowing that they were all in the same state. No one more right, no one more wrong. Tully had shared her dream she'd had when they moved to the farm, about the thorns and the bitterness. The pilgrims, one and all, felt stricken to the heart, it was time to let go of the thorns.

When they got to the crossroads, they could see the army from Sunset coming down the road towards them. Their armour glinted in the hot sun, and there were smiles on their faces. As they reached each other, a great commotion broke forth. They greeted one another and fell into rank to go up the mountain road together.

Driscoll found Cathaoir and told him of Caedmon. He was hoping that he would catch up to them soon. Cathaoir silently mediated for Caedmon and the hard thing that lay before him, knowing it would be difficult for Caedmon to face Vaughan, who had never shown any type of love or affection for his son. Cathaoir felt uncomfortable, for he knew in his heart that he had not given the young man what he had really needed ~ the love of a father.

Striding ahead on the road, Cathaoir went into the forest on a side trail. He wanted to be alone. He needed to seek the unseen Lord, and he was ready to face his own failings. The unseen Lord had required him to love ~ love like a father ~ not only his own children, but all the ones that He had sent to him. There had been Caedmon, Edan, Gallagher, and his own son Teague. Why hadn't he taken the time to take them fishing or exploring or even just sitting and sharing? He was always so busy thinking about the future and trying to look after the future for his family that he had somehow forgotten about the present. Now they were all grown and he could not get back the years...

Falling to his knees in the deep recesses of the forest, Cathaoir confessed soberly to his Lord and Friend.

"The past is gone, My son," the gentle voice of the One he loved rolled over his sore soul.

"I know," Cathaoir brokenly whispered, "but how does one go on with it lying so heavy upon the heart? I remember every opportunity I passed up on ~ to just love! I have tried to excuse my behaviour, but there is no excuse…" A sob caught in his throat cutting his confession short.

"Yes, it is true. You did make some wrong choices and yes, others did suffer from your neglect. Now you are sorry and I forgive you.

Not only are you forgiven, but I also have the power to rectify in their lives what you have failed to do. Listen to me, Cathaoir ~ look at me!" The unseen Lord spoke sternly and Cathaoir jerked up his head. To his surprise, he saw the Lord looking him straight in the eyes.

"I have always been there for them. Just like I have been there for you even though you did not seem to want my fathering. Be comforted, for there lies a battle ahead and soon all things will be made right. All things!" The Lord's voice boomed out this final decree and He disappeared from Cathaoir's sight.

Rising slowly to his feet, Cathaoir felt a great weight falling from his shoulders. He was free from the past… He could love! There was still time. He mused how when he was in his guilt he felt that there was nothing now that could be done on his part. Now that the guilt had been removed, he felt suddenly full of anticipation of all he could do.

Shaking his head in amusement and relief, he walked back to the road and fell in line with the dusty pilgrims on their way to the Source.

~

Caedmon swung his pack over his shoulder. He was hot and tired, but his heart was light. His father had said little, as he walked beside him, on their journey. They could see the dust of the pilgrims rising from the road in front of them. So Caedmon knew they must be only a few furlongs behind. Caedmon took a sip from his canteen and offered it to his father. His father took a long drink. Wiping his mouth, he handed it back. "Thanks, I needed that."

"We will be catching up to the others soon. I will have to go and meet with some of them. Do you want to go with me? Or would you like to be left alone in the crowd?" Caedmon asked hesitantly.

"I would like to meet your friends, Caedmon. I truly would. Will your grandmother be there?" Vaughan asked.

"No, Da. She has passed over the veil. I am glad though, for she struggled with the whole fortress thing so much. Now that she is gone, she won't have to do battle and be torn," Caedmon spoke and as he did reassurance rose up in his own heart.

The tired pair picked up speed and soon caught up to the others. Caedmon introduced his father to the different pilgrims he knew. It felt good to Caedmon to realize that his true family were these people, even the ones he did not know. He had been longing all his life for a relationship with a father ~ or so he'd thought ~ when deep down inside it had been given to him. The unseen Lord had fathered him through many men. Gilroy, was a grandfather type. Then there was Cathaoir, though a little distant, had taught him to be practical hard worker, and now Driscoll, who was always watching out for him. He looked at Vaughan, and reaching out for his arm, he pulled the man close in a side hug as they walked.

"What is that for?" Vaughan nervously asked.

"For nothing in particular," Caedmon replied. "I just felt like hugging you. Did you know I expect nothing from you? Nothing ~ only what you want to give!"

With that Caedmon began to laugh, and others around them joined him. Soon everyone was chuckling or laughing out. Caedmon's infectious laugh turned to a victorious marching song. Others joined him in singing and the song was joined by still others farther ahead, until soon the land resounded with the sound.

Vaughan joined in, relief and wonder filling his soul. He had been afraid that his son would want something from him that he could not give. He suddenly felt shame flood his face, realizing that it was himself that always wanted something in return. Vaughan felt tears washing down his face, and he refused to hide them. Looking over at him, Caedmon smiled and stopped singing, but only long enough to give his father another clasp.

"You're all right! You are going to make it yet," Caedmon encouraged and then picked up the song again.

Teague, a league up ahead, had heard the song coming from far behind him. He, too, started to sing, adding his own rendition to the marching song. Pulling his lyre from his satchel, he played and sang, keeping up rhythm with his long strides. Seanna looked up adoringly at her husband. Her stomach was large with their second child. Little Arienh was riding with her grandparents in the wagon. Keelin, who was walking even further up the road with Barris, pulled her flute from her pocket and began to join in the song. The melody of the flute rose and fell over the boisterous voices.

Tired pilgrims began to feel renewed hope and energy surge through their bodies. Pualani's voice rose and joined the melody of the flute. Little children began to dance and skip along. Some of the neighbouring people of the land began to gather along the road and watch the happy pilgrims on their journey.

"What are you people doing? Going crazy in this heat?" A man by the road jeered at them. Kikeona stopped and went over to the man.

"No. It is time! Come with us, because the unseen Lord of your land is calling to all to come," Kikeona spoke. His serious gaze caught the man off guard.

"Time? Well, yes... Maybe tomorrow, for I have plenty of farming to do yet today. You people have a good time," the man sneered back.

A woman in the back of the crowd, holding the hand of two very dirty, little children, made her way through the throng towards Kikeona.

"Please sir, we want to come. I heard the unseen Lord years ago, but did not join Him then. Do you think He would still have me?"

Kikeona, tears streaming down his face, stooped down and picked up the children one in each arm and nodded his head. "Yes, little lamb, He always will take us in."

"Woman! You come back here now!" A man's angry voice rose above the crowd.

"No, not again!" she screamed back. "I am going with the unseen Lord. You may come if you like, but I will be your slave no longer."

"Slave? You are my servant! I pay you well." The man came storming through the crowd towards Kikeona.

Kikeona stood tall and straight, and looking the man in the eyes, he said, "Sir, she is leaving. She has a new master now. One who will be good to her and not use her."

- 364 -

Kikeona rose to his full height as he spoke, one child resting on each of his hips. The glint of Kikeona's armour reflected in the angry man's eyes. He quickly bowed and strode back through the crowd.

Others, after seeing the courage of the servant woman, began to join the pilgrims and together they marched up the road to the Source.

The ancients say… "Wherefore I say unto thee, her sins, which are many, are forgiven."

Artur ~ strong as a bear
Birgitta ~ resolute, strength
Cailyn ~ rejoicer

A long wisp of hair blew by her delicate face. Her head was resting against her arm as her slender form leaned against the old oak tree. She gazed out over the valley below. How she longed for just one of the old days! However she knew it would never be the same again.

Sighing, she tried to gain her composure to go back and join the others around the bonfires at the river's Source. Just as she was turning to return down the long path through the forest, a taloned hand clasped over her mouth. Fighting and struggling with all her might, she tried to reach for her sword.

"I wouldn't do that, my pretty. If you want me to let the others know how false you are, then go ahead…" the rasping whisper of the Dragon was hot in Keelin's ear. She quit struggling immediately. The Dragon let go of its grip on her.

"What do you mean? I am not false," Keelin said. Her eyes were wide with fear, which did not go unnoticed by her enemy.

"*I mean?* You know very well what I am talking about," the Dragon hissed. "You have pretended that all is well between you and the unseen Lord, but I know that you do not talk to Him very often about the things that really matter. Because of your weak relationship with the Lord, your past condemnation hangs on you and has separated you from the others. It is like a wall that your screams will not penetrate." The Dragon gurgled a chuckle and puffs of green vapour came out its nostrils.

- 366 -

Keelin could feel the old iciness creeping over her heart. It was true ~ she had not been real with anyone, not even her beloved Barris. She wanted to have an intimate relationship with the unseen Lord, but she was not strong enough to admit her mistakes. She could have done things differently ~ she knew she could have ~ but it was done now. It was easy just to pretend with everyone that things were back to normal with her.

The Dragon smiled and drool began to pool down its chest and on the ground, making its way towards Keelin's feet. Keelin looked at the Dragon ~ what a pathetic creature it was! The ugliest thing she had ever seen! She recoiled as she saw the slime oozing its way towards her feet.

"Lord…?" Keelin's plea was barely audible, but it was enough to bring the unseen Lord to her immediately.

The Dragon screeched and tried to disappear, but not before a blinding light seared it in the eyes. The unseen Lord strode past Keelin and grasped the Dragon by the throat and began to shake it.

"It's not time!" the beast squeaked out.

"You are correct, but we both know your time is short. Get out of here and leave her alone!" His strong voice echoed through the trees.

~

Barris, sitting by the fire and feeling somewhat uncomfortable still with these pilgrims, was waiting impatiently for Keelin to return. Hearing a low rumble of thunder, he decided to go find her and took the path she had left on.

~

"Keelin why can't you believe that I forgive you?" the gentle voice of the unseen Lord undid all of Keelin's pent-up reserve. Great sobs shook her frame as she held her abdomen where a small life was beginning to grow.

"Oh, I want to. I really do, but it has been so long and I have erred so much. I had despised You and Your will for my life. I thought I knew better than you. I know you said before I was forgiven, but the feeling that I am not, will not leave me," Keelin sobbed out.

"Oh, my little lamb!"

The next minute Keelin felt herself being picked up off the ground and swung around and around. She felt like a small child again, innocent and happy. The unseen Lord sat her feet gently on the ground and as she straightened she saw Him for the first time. Falling at the Lord's feet, she began washing His feet with her tears. He gently took her by the shoulders and lifted her to her feet.

"The flute I gave you will heal many of the wounds your fellow pilgrims will receive in the great battle. Play it strongly, even when you feel too weak. I will come immediately when I hear it and give aid. Now, my dear heart there is someone coming down the path to you and I think it is time you were honest with him. He is a good man, but he too needs to know that I want to meet with him." The Lord slowly faded from Keelin's sight as He spoke.

"Keelin! Where are you?" Barris' voice called from down the forest path.

"I'm here! Out by the cliffs! Come and watch the sun set with me," Keelin called back. She would tell him all the secrets of her heart and, she would tell him of her great love for the unseen Lord.

~

Shylah leaned close to Treasa and whispered in her ear, "Let's go mediate. I want to go to *The Glade of the Forest Pools*. The children are settled for the night. Cathaoir and Briant have gone to feed the horses."

"Shylah. I don't think we need to. I think we are supposed to encourage the bewildered pilgrims and the new followers tonight. I think it is time for us to put into practice what we have learned and teach it to others. Come, let's go to that tired woman with her two children over there," Treasa said encouragingly.

"You're right. She is new to the pilgrimage. I have heard that she left a terrible master. She had worked for him to help feed her children, but he was a cruel man who abused her physically. Let's go at once."

The two women walked over to the young mother, who was holding her children close by the fire.

"Hello there. What is your name?" Treasa asked as she knelt down by the little girl.

"Hello," the woman answered shyly. "Her name is Birgitta. She is my little strength and helper." The little girl snuggled down closer into her mother's cloak, hiding her little face from the strange woman.

"My name is Treasa, and this is my friend Shylah. We want to help you get settled. We don't know how long we will be here before the unseen Lord comes for us. Come, there is a place over beside our camp. We have blankets and plenty of food. When did you eat last?" Treasa asked.

Tears of gratitude began to course down her tired cheeks, but bright sparkling eyes looked up at them.

"My name is Cailyn. This little boy is my son, Artur." Rising to her feet, she picked up her son and giving Birgitta's hand to Shylah, they made their way across the camp. Cailyn began to laugh and quickly covered her mouth.

"Don't be embarrassed. We all feel that kind of joy when the unseen Lord comes to our aid. Only this time, He used us, and it makes me want to laugh too," Shylah, who found it easy to laugh, giggled out.

~

Teague, Edan, and their wives and children sat close around their fire. Teague was strumming gently on his lyre to quiet the children for sleep. Edan was singing a soft lullaby while Tully and Seanna spoke in hushed whispers. It was so exciting ~ the waiting had become like a big camping trip. Life had been very taxing ~ with the drought and the darkness ~ and suddenly everything was simple and uncomplicated. Caedmon and Vaughan walked up and joined the men on their side of the fire.

Soon their voice joined in the lullaby, harmonizing with Edan. Pilgrims at the other fires quieted down and listened, their hearts settling down into a wonderful feeling of peace.

"The Dragon and its cohorts are about," Caedmon said as their song had finished. Their little girls were sound asleep, nestled in their blankets by the fire.

"You're not serious," Edan spoke sarcastically, but quickly became conscience of his cynicism and added, "How do you know?"

"Well, I felt its presence, but not only that," Caedmon responded, leaning closer finished, "We were just over at Barris and Keelin's fire. Keelin said it had attacked her, but the unseen Lord came when she called to Him. I think it is waiting for someone to leave to devour them or attack them with their slimy lies and doubts."

"Come on. Let's go to it. Why should we wait here for it to pounce on someone?" Teague said as he rose and drew his sword. The sword began to gleam in the waning light of the evening.

"Well, I am staying put right here. I am sorry I sounded rude. I guess I need to change some more," Edan sheepishly added.

"No, Teague. The unseen Lord told me to wait for Him before we battle again. I am waiting here," Caedmon spoke and reaching up pulled Teague back down beside him. "It won't be long now. I think the Dragon is aware that something is about to happen."

"You're right, but that creature causes my blood to boil. All the lies and deceit it has spread among us, and the poor fortress dwellers it has in its grip!" Teague rubbed his sword with the edge of his tunic as he spoke, and then lovingly put it back in its scabbard.

Vaughan sat there, lost in his own thoughts, thinking of the wonderful joy he had lost by not spending time with his son. However, he shook the despairing feelings off, they would do no good now and he decided to enjoy the comradeship of Caedmon and his friends.

Gallagher and Aine joined the small group.

"Can we join you? I was feeling restless, so Aine suggested we come and see what you people are up to," Gallagher said.

"Yes, of course," Seanna spoke. "Come, Aine. Join Tully and I as we watch over our little girls. We can let the men talk of the Dragon and its work while we get caught up on our woman talk." The men and women talked in hushed tones into the dark of the night and then left to go to their own blankets to sleep.

The settlement pilgrims had made their way back to their homes. Treva snuggled into her bed and wondered if Gilroy knew of what was happening here or if life after death was quite separate from them. She smiled to herself, it did not hurt near so bad to think of her beloved husband now. The anticipation of the upcoming battle seemed to have made all other things fade for the moment.

~

As the stars came out overhead, Abelio made his way silently through the camp. The campfires were burning low and the glowing embers looked like sparkling diamonds scattered throughout the large clearing. Setting his fingers to his lips, Abelio let out a low whistle. It sounded like a musical note that blended with the wind. The trees began to stir and their leaves rustled and joined the lone note.

"You called," a voice spoke into Abelio's ear.

Whirling around, Abelio looked into Eammon's face.

"Yes, and you almost startled me. Of course I am used to your just appearing suddenly."

"I did not appear suddenly, my friend. You walked right past me. I was leaning against that tree over there," Eammon said with a low chuckle as he pointed to a tree across the camp.

Abelio gave a playful slap to Eammon's shoulder and the two walked among the sleeping pilgrims.

"Tomorrow?" Abelio asked.

"Yes, the Prince has sent us here to guard the camp tonight. The Dragon is about and so is its horde, though they have not been able to lure a single pilgrim away. Look." Eammon pointed to where the Source, the artesian well had at one time gushed out in a stream of water. Sitting on a rock in the middle of the now-dry basin was Carden. Aithne was standing, with her head slightly tilted, listening intently to whatever Carden was sharing. Soon many others from beyond the mist joined them. Sophronia walked gently among the pilgrims and placed her hands tenderly first on one brow and then on another.

- 371 -

The Dragon hissed out its insults at the Lord's servants, but they ignored its presence. Gathering the horde of hideous creatures, the Dragon left the camp and headed quickly to the valley and the large fortress. The head guard needed to be awakened and alerted to the impending doom the Dragon felt coming.

"'Till tomorrow," Abelio whispered to the departing Dragon.

"Do you think it knows?" Eammon asked.

"No, but I think it suspects that something big is up," Abelio answered.

The night lingered on and each pilgrim slept more soundly than they had in days. Their dreams that night were full of joy and expectation.

If one looked closely, they would have seen many a smile upon a sleeping face that night...

The Ancients say... "These are they which have washed their robes, and made them white in the blood of the Lamb."

Chapter 17

Cathaoir awoke before dawn and went to the water barrel in the wagon. There was enough water for one more day, but only if they all drank very sparingly. Walking out of the camp toward the settlement, he met Driscoll.

"Good morning, friend," Driscoll greeted him.

"Good morning! Even though I think it is still night!" Cathaoir laughed. "Driscoll, we only have enough water for today. How are the wells here?"

"I was able to get a small bucket of muddy water up out of our well this morning. I am letting it settle so we can put it in our canteens. I am afraid that is it. The Lord must be coming today! He would not leave us now when we need Him so much."

"Yes, you are right. Let us go and check the other wells and talk to the other men before we alarm any of the women," Cathaoir said.

Both men headed back into the settlement, but they knew it was useless. Other men had already gathered by the wells and it was apparent that there was barely enough water for the day. Some suggested digging more wells, but then they all realized the time for well digging was over.

Returning to the camp, Cathaoir settled down on the blanket beside Treasa.

"Hmmm... Did you find any water?" she murmured in her sleep.

"How did you know I was looking for water?" he asked startled.

"I went to get some last night and saw we were just about out. It is all right, though, I had this most beautiful dream last night. I was riding on a magnificent horse in front of the unseen Lord. He leaned down and spoke into my ear that everything would now be made right. And then I awoke," Treasa snuggled close to Cathaoir and went on, "Sophronia was here and she told me to go back to sleep as the servants were guarding the camp last night."

Soon Cathaoir heard Treasa's heavy breathing and knew that she had gone back to sleep. He too would rest until dawn.

The sound of rolling thunder shattered the stillness of the early morning. Cathaoir sat up, startled, for he had fallen back asleep. The sky lit up with lightening, and thunder followed quickly. The storm was right over their heads. The pilgrims scrambled to get their fires going before the rain came. Another flash of lightening followed another crash of thunder.

Caedmon ran into their camp. "Treasa, Cathaoir, it's the Lord. Listen…"

Another thunder clap came, only this time they heard distinctly, "I am coming! Prepare yourselves!"

One by one the pilgrims knelt to the ground, old and young alike. With swords drawn and lying upon their laps, they waited. Another thunder clap came, only this time it was as if someone was laughing in the thunder.

The Prince, their unseen Lord, rode into the camp upon a majestic, white steed. The Lord's countenance was radiant. His royal robes draped over the horse, and the crimson and purple garments shone in the morning sunlight. He smiled to the waiting pilgrims and dismounted from His horse. Aithne appeared and took the reins. Abelio and Eammon, appeared in the centre of the camp, carrying armfuls of white tunics. They walked slowly to the Lord and knelt before Him, holding up the tunics for Him to examine.

"They are exquisite! We are ready. Come forward, my lambs, come and receive your battle clothes," His eyes filled with love as He spoke to the pilgrims. They filed forward and, taking the simple white tunics, wonder filled their hearts. *How could such simple white tunics in actuality be battle clothes?* They wondered, but soon put the thought out of their heads, for they trusted the unseen Lord completely.

"They have been woven with every good choice and every good word that you've ever done or spoken. Then, they were washed in the eternal blood that I shed when I walked among you in this land.

Finally, rinsed in the pool beyond the mist of the Source till they glistened. They may look simple, but their price is invaluable. These will keep you from falling from the enemies lies. My Father will be sure to watch over you. He will send aid to you in the battle if you have need, but remember you must keep your tunics on. The only way we will know one another in the battle is to keep our tunics on." As the Prince spoke He took off his cloak and beneath the purple robe He, too, had on a white tunic.

The army fell into rank behind Him as He mounted his horse and led them down the mountain. His own servants, from beyond the mist, walked among the pilgrims, encouraging them to not fear. Caedmon strode beside his father, and in front of them Pualani and Kikeona walked with the people of their island. Gallagher and Aine had joined them, feeling more at home with them than even their own families. Smiling, Gallagher took Aine's hand and pressed a gentle kiss into her palm.

Behind Caedmon and his father came the Source's pilgrims. The pilgrims who had left the fortresses and the farmers came next, with Cathaoir and Treasa, Shylah and Briant in the front of the group. Then came the beautiful people of the Lord's own land, where He had lived when He dwelt among them. Their faces shone with such humility and devotion that the other pilgrims honoured them highly. Though, they chose to take up the rear in the march to protect from attacks on the flank.

A soft rain began to fall, and the dusty pilgrims lifted their faces to the refreshing rain. The Lord halted beside the dry river bed. Looking up into the gathering grey clouds, He lifted back his head and shouted. The shout was like the roar of a lion, echoing off the high mountains above. The clouds were split apart by a flash of lightening, and a loud clap of thunder joined the Prince's call.

"Rain!"

The rain began to pour down in great sheets, but was warm as the noonday sun. The pilgrims laughed and danced all around the Lord. The rain washed off the dust of the drought and the remnants of the despair that still clung to each one of their hearts. The stream began to bubble and gurgle beside them as the water began to form a small stream and then a larger one. More water began to join the small stream, until soon a small river was roaring down the mountain side. Laughter filled the air, and soon singing was heard.

Caedmon, Teague, and Edan were marching shoulder to shoulder, heads held high, voices raised in song. The other pilgrims immediately sobered and fell into rank behind them. The Lord turned His horse and galloped ahead, down the final descent into the valley. Leaving the rain behind them, the sun shone brightly on the road ahead, with dust rolling across the dry plain. Behind them they could hear the rolling thunder and the rain, which was so heavy behind them that it made the mountains disappear from their sight.

Stopping, the Lord dismounted from His horse and it immediately disappeared from the sight of Teague and his companions.

"I want you to be strong and courageous," He said as He fell into stride with them.

"You make it sound like you are leaving us," Caedmon spoke with a tremor in his voice.

"No, I promised I would never leave you. In the midst of the battle if it appears that I have disappeared, remember that I am always with you. Do not rely on your senses. Rely on faith."

"The greatest battle that lies ahead has to do with your working together. Everything you have learned from Me, you now have an opportunity to put into practice. It is easy to fight the Dragon when you see it. However, the beast is not visible very often. Its most effective weapon is what it whispers in your ear ~ especially just after I talk to you."

The Lord sighed and then went on, "Don't forget what you have learned. Don't forget your weapons. Don't forget each other! Your strength is in your numbers together. When you are tempted to withdraw, flee from that temptation. Cling to those around you even more. I am with you ~ I am always with you. Now, you will see the enemy for what it really is and don't forget what you see."

Caedmon ran and embraced Him. Edan and Teague followed and the four huddled together, holding each other. Strength surged through the young men like liquid fire. They felt themselves growing strong and their minds becoming sharp. Laughing, Teague slapped

- 376 -

Edan on the shoulder and looked at Caedmon. The three of them seemed to be alone; the Lord was unseen again.

"Come," Teague spoke, "we must encourage the others. Let us go. The battle has begun…" As he spoke he pointed past them out onto the wide grassland of the valley. As far as they could see, pilgrims were in hand to hand combat with the Dragon's host. A thick, stale-smelling fog lay over the land, mixed with the foul smell of refuse.

Caedmon drew his sword and, with a battle cry, leapt at the first creature that stood in his path. The vile lizard-dog, snapped and snarled at the sword, evading each sweep of the blade like an expert swordsman. Caedmon darted back and forth, ever moving forward, pressing the beast backward. Dashing under the blade, the creature's huge carnivorous mouth grabbed at his leg. Caedmon leapt straight in the air, his legging tearing in the beast's mouth. Whirling in mid-air, Caedmon came down with the hilt of the blade against the hard skull of his enemy. The creature writhed in pain, squealing out, "You want me… I am loneliness!"

Caedmon did not answer the creature as he thrust his sword right through the beast and it disappeared from his sight.

Teague and Edan were fighting back to back as hideous beasts, identical in appearance, had them cornered in a drainage ditch. The creatures' slumped backs were covered in bristles like a porcupine and their small heads were swallowed by the mammoth bodies that resembled apes. They were throwing their spines at the two warriors, who in turn were shielding the assault with their raised shields. Caedmon rushing forward, sliced the one beast through. The other beast whirled and pounced before Caedmon had time to catch his balance. The large beast threw him to the ground, knocking the wind out of his lungs.

Trying to gasp for air, the creature squeezed Caedmon's throat, shutting in an iron clasp. "My brother and I are not easily dismissed, little man. Fear and Doubt will always rule your heart!"

With a long groan, the creature suddenly fell off of Caedmon and disappeared. An arrow had stuck between its shoulders. Caedmon looked up into Shylah's laughing face.

"I came just in time, I see!" She reached out her hand and helped him up. Teague and Edan were still fighting the other creatures that travelled with Doubt and Fear. Despair and Bitterness, identical to the other two, writhed in pain as pilgrims struck them through with their swords. Teague leapt onto the large rock beside them and began to do battle with a small raven creature. Teague smote Procrastination in short order.

"Are there any casualties?" Caedmon asked.

"No. The unseen Lord is giving us great victory this day. As we push forward into the battle, have you noticed the rain is just behind us?" Shylah waved in the direction of the mountain. Sure enough, the rain was just beyond the outside of the war zone, creeping forward as the pilgrims pushed ahead.

"Oh, look!" Edan exclaimed as he joined them. Carefully wiping his sword off on the grass, Teague also walked up. They all looked to where Edan was pointing. All along the river, the trees were in full bloom. The valley was turning lush and green where the rain was falling. The air was literally glittering with the large droplets of water, like millions of pearls falling to the earth.

Teague said, "I am going to find Seanna."

"I will join you," Edan and Caedmon spoke at the same time.

"Tully is with Seanna," Shylah said. "They are looking after the weak and wounded. They are with Treasa and Keelin, also. You will find them all at the crossroads that leads to the large fortress. The battle has been heaviest there. Nobody has abandoned the fight ~ the pilgrims remain strong. Some have fallen, but there was always someone there to get them to help. Keelin has been playing her flute to bring them relief, and Barris was bringing in any of the wounded he could find. We have not seen Briant and Cathaoir, since this morning when we first marched into the valley. We got separated in the first skirmish, but I am confident that they are where they are supposed to be."

The Ancients say… "But this is a people robbed and spoiled; they are all of them snared in holes, and they are hid in prison houses. But now thus saith the Lord that created thee, fear not: for I have redeemed thee, I have called thee by thy name; thou art mine."

Chapter 18

The Dragon had disappeared the minute the battle began and roamed around through the battlefield, looking for someone to devour with the slimy lies that gurgled deep within its throat. Coming upon Briant and Cathaoir, the Dragon stole through the forest that surrounded Evergreen, watching them closely. They seemed to be dodging the battle.

"Cathaoir wait up for me," Briant gasped out.

"We must make it to the back of the fortress and see if anyone is trying to escape and escort them to the other pilgrims…" he stopped speaking suddenly, holding his finger to his lips.

"Did you hear that?" he whispered.

"Yes! Sounds like someone is crying."

All became quiet except for the sound of the distant battle and the wind rustling through the dry leaves on the trees overhead. Stepping out onto the wide grass that surrounded the fortress, the two men walked slowly towards the back door of the fortress. The slime that covered the path, unbeknownst to them, slowly crept up their legs. This time the pitiful sobs of a child could be heard distinctly on the other side of the door.

Overcome by compassion, the two men, not realizing the danger that was surrounding them, opened the door. The Dragon felt elated ~ those stupid men were thinking they could do good with their own meagre power, and had never stopped to consider that the crying was the Dragon's counterfeit slowly pulling them into a deadly trancelike sleep with its slime. The beast knew that good intentions for self-motivated quests, that would cause one to leave the other pilgrims, would always put someone to sleep with just a little of its encouraging slime.

As the men entered the fortress, everything began to swirl before their eyes…

~

Suddenly, Cathaoir awoke, wiping his brow, and wondering where he was. He tried to shake off the slumber, but his mind would not focus. A dim candle lit the room he was in, and he made out Briant, lying on a cot opposite him, his loud snoring filling the air. Cathaoir struggled to his feet and tried to stretch out his aching body.

Briant groaned and rolled over.

"Where are we?" Briant rasped out.

"I don't know. I don't even know how we got here," Cathaoir said in half-awake voice. Yawning, he sat down on the edge of his cot. He kept rubbing his head, hoping the fog would lift and he would be able to think clearly.

"I remember someone crying," Briant said suddenly. "Then we came into the fortress to help them. I think it was a child."

Cathaoir began to remember and dropped his face into his hands. He mumbled between his fingers. "The s-s-slime."

"Slime?" Briant asked, puzzled.

Raising his face, he looked at Briant for a long time before speaking. "Just before we entered the fortress, I felt slime on my legs, but I thought that I was too strong for it to affect me. We did not even stop to ask the unseen Lord if we should come in here. When we did come in, all we saw was that… That *thing* crying like a baby."

Briant sat up quickly. Then, standing, he began to pace the small cell. Yes, he remembered now… It had turned its menacing eyes at them and began to cackle like a lunatic. It had been one of the Dragon's creatures of darkness, that was for certain. *False Duty.* Then Briant recalled how he had become so sleepy that he could not raise his sword to fight, even if he had wanted to. The recollection hit him like a pile of stones. *I had not wanted to!*

- 380 -

"It brought us down here and we just walked in, laid down, and went to sleep like good, obedient little idiots," Briant said disgustingly.

"And do you know what? I still feel half asleep, like I don't want to wake up. But I must!"

Briant pulled his sword from the sheath. Raising it above his head, he slowly walked back and forth until he felt himself begin to awaken. Cathaoir also pulled his sword and, kneeling down, he held it high over his head.

"Forgive us, Lord!" he shouted out with all the strength he could muster. Like a blanket that was heavy upon his shoulders, a feeling of despair slipped off of him. Briant began to pace faster, like a caged animal ready to spring upon its foe. Cathaoir rose to his feet and walked to the door. Raising the sword high with both hands, he struck the door full force with the hilt.

Shattering wood flew like a shower of splinters into the room as the door split in two and fell to the floor. Both men stood for several minutes, too stunned by their success to move. Then, with a shout of triumph, they ran out into the dungeon's passage and found the stairs leading upwards.

Stopping, Cathaoir turned back down the dimly lit passage. Briant made it to the top before he realized that Cathaoir was not with him. Slowly he descended and watched Cathaoir from the base of the stairs, knocking on each cell door. He could hear low moans and cries coming from within each one.

"Water…"

"Get us out…"

"Please help me…"

The hoarse whispers pleaded with Cathaoir. Raising his sword, he smashed the first door with the hilt. Dust flew into the air as the shattered door hit the stone floor with a thud. A man, thin and pale, held his wife and children around himself in the corner. As the light streamed in the door, they shielded their eyes with their grimy hands. Their clothes were filthy and ragged.

"Don't be afraid! Come with us. The unseen Lord will deliver us from this place," Cathaoir spoke tenderly and, walking forward, picked up one of the small children. "Come. It is time to leave."

Briant strode down the corridor and began to knock other doors down. Some fell, while others did not budge. From within one of those doors, the distinct sound of snoring could be heard and the putrid smell of death crept from under the door.

"They have given up," the man whispered to Cathaoir. "They used to cry for help, but they became bitter that no one came, though the guard had repeatedly told them that if they wanted to leave the fortress they could. We were all told that, but none of us did...."

He continued, dropping his head in shame and fear. "Even now I am afraid to leave the protection of these walls, but I have come to realize the truth. I am not protected here ~ I am a prisoner. If I don't leave, my family will die here."

Cathaoir put his free arm around the man's shoulders and gave him a squeeze. "It is all right, my friend. You will see. I have been where you are in your thinking. Now, we must go! The unseen Lord is on the move, so we must hurry." As the prisoner pilgrims gathered at the base of the stairs in the dimly lit corridor, Briant stepped up onto the steps and raised his hand to get their attention.

"Listen, friends," he spoke out confidently and without whispering. A realization coming to his heart that he was not afraid of being heard anymore. *Let the Dragon hear me! Let the guard and his company hear me! The unseen Lord is on my side.*

"There is a battle raging outside these walls. You will all be needed. Be alert at all times as we leave. The Dragon does not want you leaving. It will send Fear and Vulnerability against you. Shake off those lying creatures! It wants to keep you imprisoned so that you will do its kingdom no harm."

As Briant turned to go, the whole corridor filled with light. The Lord, Abelio, and Carden appeared and began to walk among the prisoners. Each one was given a white tunic. Tears streamed down their faces as they clung to the Lord as He passed by each one.

"My lambs…" Tears fell from the unseen Lord's face as He held each one in turn. "You don't know how much I have longed for this day, when you would choose Me for your protection."

As the prisoners slipped the white tunics over their soiled garments, a wonderful transformation took place. Their rags disappeared and their faces shone with a bright cleanliness that moments before had not been there. Carden began to sing the song of the shepherd over them and each one's armour appeared, including the children. Abelio lovingly wiped each sword with the lambskin and handed them out. The men, putting their women behind them with the children, began to ascend the stairs.

The light gradually left as the Lord faded from their sight. Abelio and Carden went before them with their swords held high. They passed through the fortress and reached the great assembly room. The guard and some of the other fortress dwellers were there in the midst of an emergency meeting to discuss the war waging nearby.

Looking up startled, the guard saw Briant and the others following, but he could not see Abelio or Carden.

"Where are you going?" he asked insolently.

Briant did not respond, but walked past the onlookers and straight out into the atrium where the pool was. The water in the bottom of the pool looked thick with slime. The prisoners shuddered as they saw the true condition of their once-beloved pool.

"I said ~ *where* are you going?" the guard repeated. "You son of rebellion, would you dare lead these poor people astray? Away from all common decency and protection? They were put into the dungeon to protect them from the Dragon's lies, because it was infiltrating them with discontentment. They wanted to stay there!" the guard's angry voice rose into a screech.

Abelio reached his hand over and squeezed Briant's shoulder, saying, "Do not listen, my friend. You know the truth. Draw your sword and do not look back."

Carden began to sing and the prisoners all drew their swords and took Briant's lead. Cathaoir, who was at the very back of the group, broke into song with Carden. They sang of the unseen Lord, His compassion for His people, and His deliverance from the

- 383 -

Dragon. The guard could not hear Carden only Cathaoir, and his anger became a full-blown rage as he charged towards him. Carden stepped between them and the guard fell to the ground as if he had run into an invisible wall.

The group that had been meeting with the guard rushed to his side and helped him to his feet.

"Let them go," they told their guard. "We don't need them! They have only been a burden to us and we have barely enough water and food for ourselves," they counselled.

"You are right, they are all children of the Dragon. All of you are!" The guard shouted to the retreating backs of the prisoners as they went out the great front doors of the fortress. At that moment the unseen Lord appeared in the middle of the atrium in all of His greatness and glory. The light that emanated from Him blinded them.

"You speak of things you do not know," the Lord's voice thundered.

"Go from us!" the guard spat, trying to sound like he was the one with the authority.

The Lord was not moved. "No one from this day forward will listen to you. You have led too many astray, falsely persuading them to believe in you instead of Me! I am their Lord, not you! Repent! I am giving you one more opportunity to repent." This time the voice of the unseen Lord seemed almost pleading as He entreated the guard and his council.

"Repent? You must not be real. If you were real, you would know that we have always maintained Your highest standards. You would know that we have dealt with all traitors to the fortress and its guardship like You wanted. If you truly were the Lord of this land, You would know our worth," the guard's voice still held the same insolence.

The Dragon stood behind the guard, sneering at the Lord. Drool was dripping down its chin and falling over the heads of the guard and his companions. The Lord strode forward and grabbed the Dragon by the throat. He began to shake the beast until it hung limp like a rag doll that had lost its stuffing.

The guard shouted, "Get back from us, You... You... Vile impostor! Let go of our guardian! He was sent to us from the unseen Lord, and he has protected this fortress for many years."

The great Prince hung His head in sorrow. Speaking quietly, He said, "You choose this beast over me?"

The guard looked at where the Dragon was hanging, but all he saw was the limp shape of a man. "It is not a beast! It is the servant of the unseen Lord to protect us! Look, you have nearly killed him." The guard strode towards the unseen Lord. "Drop him and leave us."

"Let me go...you heard the man, he wants me!"

The Lord dropped the Dragon and the beast immediately disappeared. Striding out of the fortress, he slammed the door. The whole building began to shake violently, as the mortar crumbled and then, in slow motion, one stone after another began to fall loose. The entire structure finally fell in a thunderous pile of dust and crumbled stone.

The Prince, wiping the tears from His eyes, mounted His majestic horse that Aithne was holding and galloped to the battle.

The Ancients say… "Wherefore take unto you the whole armour of God, that ye may be able to withstand in the evil day, and having done all, to stand."

Chapter 19

reasa wiped the perspiration from her brow as she looked at the clouds gathering in the west. The rain appeared to be past their farm now and was slowly coming towards them, like a sparkling white sheet coming down the valley. The women were working quietly, helping the tired warriors mend their tunics and clean their weapons. Abelio was sharpening swords and Aithne was guarding the camp from enemy infiltration. A flute melody could be heard like the soft threads of a silken garment wrapping itself around the camp. Keelin's flute was healing many that had believed some of the lies during battle. The music encouraged them all to keep up the battle, victory would come!

They had set up the camp in the middle of the valley not far from the village. Neighbouring fortress dwellers had been coming hesitantly into the camp, looking for refuge and food. Farmers and villagers were bringing them food and water from the now-running river. The people of the land did not really understand what was happening, but in their hearts they knew that these ones they had so hated were bringing good changes to their land.

Treasa carefully washed the Dragon's slime from Caedmon's shield, while the young knight ate ravenously at the food Shylah had prepared. Pualani was directing her people and looking after the aged. Her grandfather, Kikeona, was out with warriors doing battle against the Dragon's creature called Destitute. Sophronia was helping them by bringing wisdom and counsel to each one on how to annihilate the evil creatures completely from their lives.

- 386 -

Treasa smiled to herself; she had let the cows, chickens, and pigs out to fend for themselves at home. She knew they would be enjoying the rain. Her practicality amazed her at times. Here they were, deeply entrenched in a war, and she was thinking about her cows! Polishing the shield with the lambskin that Abelio had given her, she walked over to Caedmon. Wiping his mouth on his sleeve, Caedmon smiled up at her.

"Thank you, friend," Caedmon said. Taking the shield, he lovingly stroked the lion embossed on the front.

"Is the battle still in our favour?" Treasa asked, as she sat down beside him.

"It is hard to tell, but so far no one has left the battle to return home. At least I have not heard of any deserters," Caedmon said. "Sometimes in the heat of battle you forget that you are not alone. Several times I was helped by another pilgrim warrior who happened upon me. Without waiting to find out what the strategy was or if they even knew me, they would just jump into the fray and vanquish the enemy. It's really fantastic when you think about it! I love it out there, fighting and winning. The Lord is so present ~ "

Caedmon's response was cut short by the deafening sound of thunder, and the earth shook. Treasa fell to the ground. A cloud of dust and smoke flooded through the camp. Caedmon leapt to his feet and ran in the direction of the sound. As the dust settled, the pilgrims started to see people coming out of the cloud towards them. Their faces shone like the sun. Treasa laughed in delight as she saw Briant and Cathaoir leading the group into the camp.

Caedmon ran past the prisoner pilgrims toward Evergreen. Within minutes he was there, amazed at what lay before him ~ a huge pile of crumbled stone. Smoke and dust still hung thick in the air around the rubble. He ran up to the pile of stones, wondering if anyone was trapped within.

"No, my young knight. All those that could escape have left to battle for Me. You must join them," the Lord spoke tenderly. "The Dragon is regrouping the creatures of darkness. I am coming to join the fight, and reveal a truth to all the pilgrims."

Caedmon did not see the Lord, but somehow it did not matter anymore. Just to hear His voice was all he really needed. Walking slowly back to the camp, knowing the enemy had fled at least for the moment, Caedmon fell into rank with the other pilgrims that were ready for the next battle. The ones from out in the valley soon arrived and they all marched towards the fortress.

~

The Dragon slapped its general on the side of its ugly head. The beast snarled back, but did not dare strike in retaliation.

"Get all of our army now! They are advancing on Evergreen," the Dragon snarled.

"But master," the creature whined, "that is what I wanted to tell you."

"*Tell me?* You blubbering fool! Tell me what?"

The sloth-like creature shuddered as the breath of the Dragon spewed slime onto its face. Stammering and stepping back out of reach of the Dragon, it replied, "The fortresses are no more…"

"What? No more?! What do you mean by 'no more'?" the Dragon screamed.

The general turned and fled, but the Dragon lunged quickly and clenched its steel-like talons around the general's throat before it could escape. The creature writhed in pain, trying to loose itself.

"They all fell flat," he gasped out. "The Great Prince slammed the door as He left the large fortress. Then, one by one, the other fortresses of the land fell flat. Most of your guards and their company are trapped inside…"

"Gone? Flat? All of them?" it gasped out.

The Dragon released its grip and the creature fell gurgling to the ground. With a loud roar, the Dragon flew into the air and out over the land, seeing smoke rising from every village in the wide valley where its fortresses had once stood grand. Screaming in a murderous rage of pain, the Dragon called all the creatures of darkness to come.

A dark cloud passed over the heads of the marching pilgrims and descended on Evergreen's rubble. Hurling insults and abuse at the Lord, the Dragon taunted Him to come and battle.

"I struck you down once. Would you have Me do that again?" the Lord called.

"Do not hide behind that sick lot that You would call soldiers! We all know what they really are. They are nothing but cheaters, liars, drunkards, and wenches with bad reputations. They know I speak the truth that they are fatherless, cowards, thieves ~ "

"They are FORGIVEN!!!" The Lord's voice boomed out like thunder, drowning out the protests of the Dragon. Rising up on its hind legs, the Dragon dove straight at the Lord. The Lord's horse reared high in the air in protest, flashing its hooves to strike the enemy. Aithne flew straight at the Dragon, letting an arrow fly, hitting its eye. The Dragon did not falter, but flicked the small arrow aside. The Lord dismounted and strode towards the Dragon.

The beast faltered as it remembered their last encounter, but only momentarily. Rising up, it strode on its huge hind legs. Towering above the tall frame of the Lord, it spewed out slime mixed with fire and smoke. The Lord strode right through the onslaught, and none of it even clung to His garments. Drawing His sword, He turned His back on the Dragon. Lifting it high, He smiled at the pilgrims and spoke loudly. "See the enemy for what it truly is!"

With a backward throw, the sword flew, end over end, sinking deep into the belly of the Dragon. As if it was still within the hands of the unseen Lord, it sliced upward and came out again. Like a boomerang, the sword flew back into the hand of the Prince. The Dragon looked stunned at the gaping hole in its belly. Slowly the skin peeled off, starting from its head, and fell into a heap around its feet.

A small black viper slipped out of the hideous carcass and crawled through the grass towards the Lord. A small hissing voice that could barely be heard squeaked out.

"No more! P-p-please, no more..."

"Take the liar and tie it to the rubble it so loves and see if any of its host will dare rebuild that which I have torn down," the Prince said commandingly.

~

Driscoll and the Source pilgrims came forward one by one. The Lord embraced each one, stooping down and speaking quietly in their ear. Soon, they all marched towards the setting sun. They looked tired, but their faces shone with new courage and valour.

Dei walked slowly with Brina, and Treva walked quietly behind carrying the baby. Treva meditated on her parting words with the Lord. He had told her that only a little longer and they would all be going into the Source to be reunited with their loved ones who had gone before. Treva shook with excitement ~ Gilroy! The Lord also asked her to be strong, and diligently teach the younger women how to do battle in their homes.

Caedmon walked silently beside Treva, not knowing where else to go. His father had left to go back to his village with the pilgrims from there. He was going to seek the unseen Lord and ask his other children for forgiveness. Caedmon declined his invitation to go home to his village with him. Briant and Shylah had asked Caedmon to come back and live with them, but that too did not seem right. The valiant knight felt suddenly loose, like he didn't fit in anywhere.

Treva looked over at her silent young friend. Caedmon seemed so sober and intense since they had left the camp behind.

"Would you carry Caiomhe, for a while?" she asked him. "My arms are tired from the battle today. Look at poor Brina. Dei is practically carrying her."

Brina was leaning heavily upon Dei as he had his arm around her, supporting her. Caedmon took the tiny bundle and looked down at the sweet sleeping face of the child. His heart lifted. How he wanted his own child! The ache in his heart surfaced and a lone tear slipped down onto the sleeping babe.

"I am sorry for being so glum, Treva. It was such a wondrous day! Battles were won and the enemy exposed. Tomorrow will be a new day for sure! I just feel like I don't belong anywhere ~ like I am lost without a home."

"Oh, Caedmon, that is exactly how I have felt since Gilroy passed over. Sometimes, I feel utterly useless, like I don't fit in anywhere anymore," Treva said, then paused.

"Don't wait up," she called to Dei. "We will catch up. Just need to change the baby's swaddling and I need to sit for a moment."

Dei waved to them and then Treva taking Caedmon by the arm, led him to some rocks by the Unchanging River. While she changed the swaddling on the baby, Caedmon sat and skipped rocks on the river. It was a joy to have it back. Lying on his stomach, he drank deep of the refreshing water, his mind remembering back to his first sip from Gilroy's canteen all those years before.

As he drank, he remembered things he had learned from Gilroy and the other mediators ~ truths that would keep his heart and mind whole. As the water flowed down his throat, liquid energy coursed through his veins. He could hear every word that was ever spoken to him by the unseen Lord. His time beyond the mist and every time he had been to *The Glade of the Forest Pools* washed through his mind.

"Remember..."

The quiet whisper brought Caedmon's attention back to his surroundings. Treva was sitting, watching him, gently rocking Caiomhe back to sleep.

"Every memory you have of Him and His mediators was for your protection today," she said lovingly. "Come back home with me. Be refreshed and listen again for His leading. He is coming sooner than we think, you know. He does have someone for you, Caedmon, of that I am sure. Don't look surprised. I saw the tears in your eyes when you held Caiomhe. Of course you desire your own children. He knows that! Our Lord has everything worked out for you in His timing. Please come home with me. Dei and Brina are moving into their own cabin. I will be alone. We can mediate together, until you know what you are to do."

"Thank you, Treva. You are like a mother to me. I would be honoured to come home with you," Caedmon accepted happily. "I can help around the place with the wood splitting, and maybe even try helping Driscoll with the marketing," Caedmon smiled at her and took the baby back in his arms. Feeling refreshed, the pair walked quickly to catch up to Dei and Brina.

Caedmon looked back down the road towards where the camp had been. The valley's grass was green from the quiet rain that was still gently falling. Pilgrims were mingling around, trying to find places for the remaining fortress dwellers who hadn't yet found a place to stay. Looking them over slowly, Caedmon felt joy rising in his heart. He felt a newfound confidence that the unseen Lord was going to give them many victories in the days ahead.

His eyes fell upon a lone pilgrim making her way towards her group on the road. As he looked towards her, she lifted her face and their eyes met.

And he knew…

~

The majestic horse tosses his head and gently stomps his front foot to the ground, eager to be off. His white flowing mane blows in the wind as he snorts again and moves slightly to turn. The Lord strokes his neck and whispers a soft command. The horse immediately stills, relaxing his arched neck; a content look enters his eyes as he waits patiently for his rider's command. Aithne reaches up to gently stroke his face.

"Look, my friends," the Lord speaks to his warriors and points to the pile of fortress rubble far below them in the valley. They could see the serpent writhing out of its chain. The creatures of its kind are assembling around it, even though most of them now are towering over the small serpent.

"They will assemble again, but their attack will have no effect on my precious ones this time. Those who see now know the truth ~ that to see is fine, and to know is priceless, but to *be* is where My Spirit dwells with them. Now the people of the land where I had lived are also like these precious pilgrims. In the days to come, as persecution arises against them, My glory will be revealed in them. They will become strong!"

"And they will all mediate. You will be very busy!" Laughing, the Lord leans over and slaps Abelio on the shoulder. Abelio reaches up and grabs the outstretched hand, clasping it in unspoken acknowledgment.

"My Liege. We will always look after your pilgrims. For they give us such joy," Carden speaks up from behind them.

"Yes, my shepherd, you are a true warrior. They will need your songs in the future," the Prince's gaze looked down at the departing pilgrims. They are His obedient ones. He looks lovingly at Treasa and her family, just arriving at their farm. Shylah has her head resting on Briant's shoulder as they walk up the lane to their home. And Caedmon ~ there he is, more certain than he has ever been. This young man has made some hard choices, and now he shines with the glory of the unseen realm. He will be doing much in the near future, of that the Lord is certain.

Raising their swords high, the Lord and His company disappear from our sight.

...Or have they?

The Ancients say… "Finally, be ye all of one mind, having compassion one of another, love as brethren, be pitiful, be courteous."

About the Author

R Phillips grew up in northern British Columbia, Canada. Living on the farm, where life was simple and uncomplicated. Her and her husband, David, raised their three children on the family farm and remain there to this day.

Life, in the North, can be harsh, but the neighbours are good and fellowship is sweet on a winter day or on a hot summer afternoon. Her storytelling has been part of her entire life to entertain people of many ages.

Printed in Canada